MW00326010

THE
ABANDONED

JAKE CAVANAH

The Abandoned By Jake Cavanah
Published 2021 by Your Book Angel
Copyright © Jake Cavanah

All rights reserved. No part of this book may be reproduced, stored, or transmitted by any means—whether auditory, graphic, mechanical, or electronic—without written permission of both publisher and author, except in the case of brief excerpts used in critical articles and reviews. Unauthorized reproduction of any part of this work is illegal and is punishable by law.

The characters are all mine, any similarities with other fictional or real persons/ places are coincidental.

Printed in the United States
Edited by Keidi Keating
Layout by Rochelle Mensidor

ISBN: 978-1-7356648-9-7

CONTENTS

To my parents,
who I hope see the good in it.

AUTHOR'S NOTE

*T*he *Abandoned* was in large part inspired by harsh realities people face in the United States and all around the world on a daily basis. Living in an era with so much information available has made society more aware of these injustices, which has led to more people wanting to make a change.

How I hope to make a difference is by telling stories.

While I enjoyed writing *The Abandoned*, many parts were hard to get through. Some include people inflicting pain on others, both physical and emotional, and describing perspectives I disagree with but exist. Another uncomfortable aspect was including racial slurs. There was a lot of back and forth in my head regarding what to include versus what not to, but ultimately, I decided I needed to paint the entire picture.

Being offensive is not my intention; however, these examples do serve a purpose: to make readers recognize we live among people who deal with this kind of cruelty regularly.

The only way to leave the world a better place than it was when we got here is to help others, and that starts with being aware of their circumstances.

Thank you for reading. I hope you enjoy.

Sincerely,
Jake Cavanah

Nearly ten percent of children in the United States are sexually abused before they turn eighteen.

Thirty percent are abused by family members.

Sixty percent are abused by people their family trusts.

Ninety percent know their abusers.

Per Darkness To Light.

PROLOGUE

2032

Ronny Soren always woke up before his roommate Victor Poban. Before tackling the day's work, Ronny liked to have time in the morning to collect himself. Victor on the other hand was one of those who just shot up out of bed and headed to where he needed to be that day. Ronny, however, utilized the time to reflect on the past's better days, contemplate how he would cope with the day's trials and tribulations, and ponder about his family, hoping they were safe and healthy. Citing safety protocols, camp officials only allotted two hours a month for him to visit with his wife Marissa, son Eddie, and daughter Robin. Depending on what restrictions were in place, he sometimes didn't get to see them all at once. The other three Sorens were held in a different section of camp, one that served as a nursery of sorts. Wives of working men with young children, Eddie was four and Robin was barely two, resided there to care for their young, but able-bodied men like Ronny and Victor had too much work to do. There wasn't time to care for their families. There was a war to fight, and every capable person was needed if humanity was going to win. At least that's what the government told its people.

One of the few luxuries Ronny had was a coffee maker and a distant view of the Pacific Ocean. His 400 square-foot unit was on the tenth floor of the building housing him, Victor, and tens of thousands of other deportees. Before they arrived in Morple, the land was desolate, allowing the government to build horizontally. This was the reason their vantage point was the highest of all in Villa 6, the camp they were quarantining in. Every morning, Ronny brewed his coffee and sipped it as he stared off in the direction of his former home. Reminding himself how much simpler life was before sonoravirus spread in 2030, Ronny wondered if he'd ever enjoy life like he once did. Marissa and he were young when they married, both just twenty-four four long years ago, but they had been so enthralled with each other it seemed like the right move. Despite what they were currently up against, Ronny still believed it was. Having her and their two young children is what kept him from completely losing it in Villa 6. It enabled him to remain hopeful about getting out and resuming the life they once shared.

Prior to being thrown into a working camp at the hands of their own government, Ronny and Marissa rented a little apartment in Sherman Oaks, a section of Los Angeles that wasn't well known to outsiders but possessed a great sense of community and originality. The city prided itself on having countless small businesses, creating a culture in which everyone supported one another because they knew how important it was to their livelihoods. Once upon a time, Ronny and Marissa would wake up every Saturday morning and walk their little family to a coffee shop a couple of blocks from their two-bedroom apartment. Eddie and Robin weren't always the most behaved in public, but on these mornings, they were always little angels. Ronny and Marissa would bring novels they had been trying to dedicate just ten minutes to all week to their Saturday morning outing, where they were sometimes lucky enough to read for nearly an hour as long as the children were either entertained or napping. As Robin dozed off peacefully and Eddie played a game on his father's tablet, Ronny and Marissa would simultaneously peer up from their books to exchange smiles with one another, reveling in the simplicity of pleasures their family enjoyed.

These were the memories running through Ronny's head as he let his mind wander each morning. He was a true believer that his thoughts shaped his reality, so he did his best to will a brighter future to fruition each and every day, even though the government had torn his family apart.

Every time Ronny visited Marissa a thick piece of glass was there to prevent them from making contact, causing him to feel like a wrongfully convicted prisoner; this is what their quarantine in Morple was starting to feel like. He could tell his young wife was doing her best to present a strong front, trying to reinforce her and their babies were getting through this government-mandate okay. But Ronny knew better. The bags under her eyes deepened every month; Ronny could tell she hardly smiled, despite her wearing a mask the government required all inhabitants eight years old and older to have on around the camp. She didn't take the time to do her hair, something that was once part of her religion as a former hair stylist; her once slender figure was becoming frail. Two long days ago was their last visit, when Marissa seemed to be more dispirited than ever.

"Hi sweetheart," Ronny said, palming the glass so he could be as close to her as possible.

"Hi hon," Marissa said, hoping her mask hid her dejected look.

"I miss you. You look beautiful."

Marissa scoffed and looked away. "Stop it, no I don't. I look like a rag doll that was forgotten about in place of a new Barbie."

"No, no you don't, sweetheart. You look like a mother who works her ass off to continue taking care of her babies. A hot mother, I might add."

One of the things Marissa loved the most about her husband was his ability to inject comic relief into a situation, but on this day, she barely acknowledged the attempt.

"Sweetheart, please smile. I miss you so much, and I can't stand seeing you like this."

"What am I supposed to smile about, Ronny?" Marissa tilted her head back and wiped her bottom eyelids. "Eddie is maturing so fast, and he is beginning to ask questions. He doesn't know why his daddy isn't around. He needs a father figure in his life, and you aren't there. He's rebelling, saying nasty things. It's just, it's just so hard without you, darling."

Ronny pressed his forehead and looked down. He was overcome with an intense guilt, even though it wasn't his fault the government segregated him from his wife and kids.

Sensing it, Marissa apologized, "I'm sorry, honey. It isn't your fault, I'm sorry. I shouldn't make you feel any worse than you already do about it. I'm sorry." She laid her hand against the glass and used the other to gesture blowing him a kiss.

"We're going to get out of this, Marissa. This madness will be over soon, and we will be a family again. I promise."

Marissa's eyes welled up, unable to look at Ronny. Her upper cheeks quivered and body shook, the most rattled she had appeared since being exiled from their home.

Doing his best to maintain a strong front, Ronny said, "Right, sweetheart? We're going to get through this. Okay?"

She nodded and sniffled audibly.

"I love you, Marissa. I love you so much. Please send the kids my love and tell them their daddy is always thinking about them."

"Okay, Ronny. I will. I love you too. Please come for us soon."

"I'm doing my best."

Like I have a say in it.

Since their last encounter, Ronny sensed Marissa was beginning to pin it on him that their family was enduring what they were. Maybe she had to put the blame on somebody, but he was unsure as to why he was receiving the brunt of it. Marissa had the tendency to overreact in situations not going her way, making Ronny the voice of reason.

Ronny found himself in a trance, not even noticing the ocean he was staring at, replaying the last conversation he had with Marissa. Harping on it too much wouldn't do him any good, but he couldn't help it. Reuniting with his family is what kept him going day in and day out. His last encounter with Marissa cast doubt on how their lives would be once they were free to go home, but he couldn't allow negative thoughts to cloud his judgement. Pushing forward and remaining positive would be how he and his family persevered. He just prayed they'd be together again before reaching the point of no return.

As Ronny took deep breaths and tried to calm his nerves, Victor began stirring, earlier than usual.

"Oh, fuck. Is it time already?" Victor asked in between audible stretches.

"Nah, it is only six forty-five. You still have fifteen minutes until we have to go."

"Oh, hell yeah. Okay, cool. Can you let me know when it's time?"

"Yeah."

"Thanks, man," Victor said before resuming his deep snoring slumber.

Ronny brewed another cup of coffee and walked closer to the window, this time surveying all the government factories that were beginning to come to life.

Fourteen months had gone by since the government deported Victor, his girlfriend Leslie, and their daughter Stella from Los Angeles to

Morple's Villa 6 working camp. In the early stages, Victor didn't mind the government-funded accommodations. He hated his job as a cook at a breakfast diner in Downtown Los Angeles, plus it barely covered his "family's" expenses. He thought getting off at two o'clock in the afternoon would be a perk, but all it did was cause Leslie to nag at him even more to get another job since he had so much time on his hands.

"Fuck girl, I'm up at 4:15 and work 'til two. I ain't getting a second fuckin' job. Why don't you get a job?" was how Victor responded to Leslie trying to motivate him to earn more money for their baby.

Victor and Leslie, both just twenty-five, conceived Stella four hours after they met at a club in Hollywood on a random Friday night. Right off the bat, Victor determined Leslie was more into him than he'd ever be into her. The pro to this was he'd be able to take her home that night and hit, but the con was it would be difficult to get rid of her, especially when a child was thrown in the mix. Just twenty-two at the time, the last thing Victor had on his mind was committing himself to a serious relationship or fathering a child. He never even considered a child a possibility.

He advocated for Leslie to get an abortion. Even though her family disowned her after she revealed she was carrying a child out of wedlock, her Catholic upbringing prohibited her from considering what Victor was suggesting as a viable option. Victor moved her into his apartment after she couch surfed for a couple months. He feared moving her in would solidify them as a couple, but how his mother, if alive, would've ridiculed him for refusing the mother of his child to move in gnawed away at him. Victor eventually caved, and Leslie settled into his apartment in Downey, roughly fifteen miles south of Downtown.

During their two years living under the same roof, Victor lived in misery. His bachelor pad lifestyle was no longer acceptable; leaving his clothes wherever he pleased; allowing dishes to pile up for a month; getting too stoned to care about closing the dishwasher and cabinets. He soon learned Leslie was meticulous, needing order in her home to maintain sanity. They clashed on this, plus a plethora of other issues, on a daily basis, creating a chaotic, toxic environment, especially for a newborn.

Their fights about his untidiness, lack of work ethic, and general dismissiveness towards Leslie and Stella exhausted him. The refuge home once was no longer existed. Going there after work became something he dreaded, anticipating a shouting match with a young woman he didn't really like who birthed a baby he never wanted to be responsible for. So, when 2030 rolled around and another pandemic caused the government to act swiftly, including moving a portion of the population to an island off California's coast, Victor welcomed the change. He needed some variety in his life, something to get him the fuck away from Leslie. When he learned Villa 6 segregated the workers from the caretakers, he had to conceal his smile. As the army man gave Victor and Leslie a rundown of Morple's structure, rules, and restrictions, Victor felt elated while Leslie was on the verge of tears. After their meeting was over, the army man told him, "Hopefully this place makes you appreciate what you have so you aren't such a fuckin' deadbeat no more, spick."

The comment irked Victor, but at the end of the day, he didn't care what this white trash, buzzed hair army man had to say about him. He'd continue living his life however the hell he wanted. If he was being honest, the uproar soronavirus had the world in didn't really register with Victor. He wasn't the type to check on a go-to news app on his phone and staying current on headlines wasn't really his thing. When he learned the US government selected his apartment building's tenants to move to Morple to quarantine, he went with the flow and accepted it as the next phase of life.

Victor actually found himself adapting to Morple's structure. All of the work he had to do was clearly explained to him, requiring little to no actual thought. Busy work was what he preferred to do since he didn't enjoy applying himself to anything worthwhile. Since starting work at five in the morning back home was his norm, the 7:15 start time was a piece of cake. What made it easier was he had Ronny to wake him up at seven so he could sleep in as long as he wanted to. Fuck a morning routine, he'd rather get as much sleep as possible.

"Yo, Victor. It's time to go, man," Ronny said, shaking his roommate up.

"Oh fuck, man. Are you serious? You said I had fifteen minutes."

"And those fifteen minutes are up. Let's roll. The last thing we need today is Officer Lawrence chewing us out."

Victor grunted out of tiredness and at the thought of dealing with Officer Lawrence. "Oh, man. Don't bring up Lawrence this early. I don't want to deal with him."

"You're about to see him in fifteen minutes, so you might as well get used to it."

Victor audibly exhaled. Officer Lawrence was capable of making his life a living hell on any given day.

"Count off!" Officer Lawrence said to Ronny, Victor, and the rest of the workers, who were all garbed in their identical brown jumpsuits and masked up, lined up against the wall in the factory's common room. Ronny and Victor were both assigned to work in the factory manufacturing vial equipment for testing. It was constantly reiterated their work was the most important on the entire island because it was how agencies like the World Health Organization could quantify how many positive cases there were, deciphering the next step in their handling of the pandemic. Victor didn't put much thought into what the driving force behind their labor was, but Ronny was skeptical of the intentions of these esteemed organizations. He thought it was a fear-based strategy to keep the population in check, ultimately limiting the opportunity of working people like him and Victor.

"One."

"Two."

"Three."

"Four."

"Five."

"Six."

Victor fixated on the ground, still not fully awake enough to be in the present moment. Ronny gave him a light-hearted elbow to snap him out of it.

"Oh, shit. Seven," he finally said.

"Eig—" Ronny began to say before Officer Lawrence cut him off.

"For fuck's sake, Poban. Wake the fuck up!"

Officer Lawrence approached him, stepping just inches away from his face in an effort to appear intimidating. Victor stood straighter and squinted his eyes closer together to express his dissatisfaction with Officer Lawrence's disciplinary tactics.

"What's that look for, Poban?" he asked, rhetorically. "What, did your roomie not fuck you good this morning, and that's why you're a little out of it?"

Victor didn't take life too seriously, but gay jokes were something he didn't find any humor in. It probably stemmed from his father.

"Don't grow up to be a faggot now, hombre," his father would tell him when he'd do or say things that weren't "manly" enough.

Officer Lawrence welcomed Victor's hardened look, stepping so close to him their noses grazed.

"What? Did I hit a nerve there, infick?" the officer asked just over a whisper so only Victor could hear the racial jab. Infected combined with spick resulted in "infick," a recent term the island's military personnel began using to refer to the primarily Hispanic island inhabitants.

As much as Victor wanted to sock him in the face, the amount of army personnel there would make for an uneven brawl, especially because none of the other deportees knew him well enough to risk any involvement.

Sensing Victor didn't have it in him to retaliate, Officer Lawrence said, "Fuckin' right, bean. Learn how to fuckin' count."

The officer stepped back with his hands clasped behind his back and traps lifted forward, demonstrating physical superiority over Victor and the rest of the deportees.

"Finishing counting," Lawrence said.

Ronny resumed the count before noticing Victor was seething, indicated by his heavy breathing and reddened face.

"Relax, man. It isn't worth it," Ronny said.

Victor nodded, even though he didn't agree.

After an extra strenuous day of working the production line came to a close, all Victor wanted to do was head back to his and Ronny's room to knock out until they had to do it all over again tomorrow. It was just past five o-clock, but as exhausted as he was, sleeping for over twelve hours seemed quite feasible. His confrontation with Officer Lawrence caused him to realize how the six-day work week had been taking a toll on him. Out of nowhere, he found himself questioning his purpose in Morple, why it was only Blacks and Hispanics working the factories while White military men and women supervised them. The optics were suspect, and how they were treated was oppressive.

Victor dismissed his sudden thought-provoking questions he had for the government establishment he was slaving away in. He was just a cook with no expertise; he was in no position to question those occupying authoritative roles.

"Poban," a female officer called to him as he was leaving the building. Victor turned around and raised his eyebrows.

"Your wife and daughter want to see you," she said.

Visibly annoyed, Victor's shoulders sagged, and he sighed. The officer mistaking Leslie as his wife only made it more of a nuisance.

"Now?" he asked the officer.

"Yes, now," she said, "Did you have something else on the schedule?"

There was that demeaning tone the officers reserved for the deportees. If the officer was a man, Victor would have been more motivated to decline, but something about a woman telling him this surfaced some guilt. Plus, it was sometimes against protocol to see Leslie and Stella at the same time, so he might as well take advantage of it.

Victor followed her lead to the visiting room.

Leslie was bouncing Stella on her leg while she waited for Victor to appear on the opposite side of the glass.

The last month had been extra hard on both Leslie and Stella. Their portion of Villa 6 was becoming more crowded as new deportees from across the US started to move in. Since the camp didn't have access to the news cycle, Leslie got her dosage of the headlines sweeping the nation from the new mothers she now lived with. Most revealed similar sentiments slightly altered based on their own biases and interpretations. The gist of it was the government was labeling more Hispanic and Black communities susceptible to the virus than more affluent White communities. The President and his crooks conveyed deporting high-risk citizens to a remote island to quarantine was the best way to keep them healthy. What they failed to mention was they'd be nearly worked to death in order to produce the supplies the wealthy needed to continue their luxurious lifestyles. Opposing politicians couldn't get a strong enough backing to combat the government mandated deportations. Therefore, most of the country's population was at the mercy of the government and elite that funded their existence. Several recent arrivals believed there wouldn't be any jobs left once they returned home, worried the government prioritized enabling the prosperity of big corporations over their livelihoods.

This notion was scary, and it made Leslie wonder what kind of world they would live in once the pandemic was finally over. But as disturbing as these revelations were, Leslie's primary concern was Stella. Her three-year-old angel was what kept her going every day, providing her with more of a purpose now than she did as just a helpless infant. Most mothers would never have to navigate through a situation like the one Leslie was in, motivating her to be the best mother she could possibly be. But in a predominantly male-supervised environment, every day tested her.

Victor finally took a seat and let out a sigh, as if being there was such a burden on his day. Leslie didn't know why, but she loved him. As time went on, nothing convinced her she'd be able to make him realize he had to mature if they were going to come out of this as a family. At this point, her assumption that he didn't want to be a family seemed truer than ever. As badly as she wanted to ask him if what he wanted was his independence, she couldn't because she feared his answer.

Leslie mirrored his annoyed exhale and picked up the phone, "Hi Victor. Your daughter has been asking about her daddy all day."

Some life emerged from him. "Hi baby Stella. Look how beautiful you are, sweetheart. You're getting so big on that side of camp."

"Victor."

Leslie loathed when he talked about their living situation like that.

"What? I'm just telling her what I see."

Leslie widened her eyes and gave him a look that told him not to do that again.

"Da, da, daddy!" Stella managed to say, elated that she got it out in front of her father.

"Yes, I'm daddy, baby. I'm right here." Victor pressed his hand against the glass. Stella mimicked him, almost bringing tears of joy to his eye. This was the emotional side Leslie craved more of, but only Stella could extract.

Knowing Victor didn't have much interest in catching up with her, Leslie sat back while father and daughter interacted through the glass that kept their existences separate. She was cognizant Stella's episodes outside of visiting hours occurred because she was reacting to growing up without a present father figure. If Victor could comprehend this, maybe he would be more inclined to put forth more effort towards making their little family a happy one. Maybe the separation would do him some good, but they'd been quarantined in Morple for over a year now; if anything, his attitude towards Leslie had only gotten worse.

Witnessing Stella tear down Victor's tough-guy front made Leslie jealous because she spent the majority of their time together trying to get him to reciprocate her love but had continuously failed. Maybe what she was about to reveal would make him care.

"Victor, I need to tell you something."

Victor continued playing hide and seek with Stella, ignoring the mother of his child's declaration. Realizing he wasn't going to give her the time of day, she resorted to a more direct approach. "Victor, the guards have been raping me for the last eight months."

"What?"

Leslie's eyes watered as she nodded to confirm what she said was true. She'd been contemplating telling him for months, but she didn't feel like she needed to burden him with her troubles.

"Why haven't you said anything before? Are you going to report it?"

"Who am I going to report it too, Victor? The people in charge are the ones doing this to me. I don't know what to do. I'm scared. I'm so scared."

Leslie smeared the tears off her face before her mask absorbed them and bopped Stella up and down on her knee so she'd remain occupied. Victor's hand nearly seared into the phone, and he nervously tapped his foot against the ground. He couldn't lie to himself, Leslie was not the love of his life, but he did care for the woman. After all, she dedicated herself to raising their daughter. Most of the time she was a pain in his ass, but that didn't keep him from valuing her life.

"Don't be scared, Leslie. We're going to do something about this, you hear me? I'm not going to let this continue. I'm going to make sure the commander or whoever the hell is in charge knows this is happening."

Leslie cried harder and her body convulsed. Even though it was happening with multiple mothers in her part of camp, she had never verbalized what she'd been enduring. Hearing it aloud released emotions she'd been bottling up since the torture started. It had been going on nearly every night for almost a year, yet she was just gaining the courage to confide in Victor. She didn't know if this was a sign of how weak she was, how fractured her relationship was with Victor, or both. Either way, she was happy to have gotten it off her chest, but she was uncertain as to what he could do about it.

"Victor, they won't do shit, and that's why I'm so scared. The people who run this place are the ones doing this to me. To other women, too."

With military personnel in their vicinity and potentially listening in, Leslie spoke in a hushed tone.

Victor was fuming; the only thing preventing the temper he inherited from his abusive father from unleashing was Stella's presence. If she wasn't there, it was likely he would've gone over to the nearest officer and strangled him. Or her.

Victor lowered his mask so she could see how serious he took this. "I'm not letting this go on, Leslie. They can't fuckin' lock us up, and do this to you," he said, disregarding the volume of his voice. "This is all bullshit. We're caged in this place like fuckin' animals. I'm not letting this go on."

Leslie found herself admiring Victor's display of passion. He had never gone to bat for her like this. Not even the fact it took her revealing she was being raped could dampen her elation, evincing just how enthralled she was with him.

"Stay strong, Leslie. I know you can, and I know you will. I promise I won't let this happen any longer. We have a daughter to take care of once this is all over. Just remember that."

His conviction caught her off guard, but she welcomed it with open arms. She assured him she'd be okay. Their allotted time was coming to a close, so they said their goodbyes and were off to their respective sides of Villa 6.

If they knew Officer Lawrence had eyes and ears all over the camp, they would've been more discreet.

Victor fumed as he stomped back to his living quarters. Military personnel littered the premises, but it was clear their guard was down. Attacking them when they were the most vulnerable would've given Victor the upper hand, but he didn't know who it was raping Leslie. Men he had never seen before could be responsible, but it didn't matter who it was. He'd get his revenge by hitting them where it hurts. He just needed more time to formulate a plan, something his temper didn't always allow him to do. Victor observed this as a sign of his maturation and was a little proud of himself for practicing this kind of self-control. It was vital if he was going to make a statement.

In an effort to blow off more steam, Victor jogged up the twenty flights of stairs instead of riding the elevator to get to his tenth floor unit. Wearing a mask on the way up caused him shortness of breath, but he didn't slow his pace. He needed more time to absorb what Leslie just confided in him.

As he readied his key to unlock their front door, he noticed it was not all the way closed. This wouldn't have piqued any suspicion, but he heard someone from the inside struggling for his breath. At first, he hesitated, but when he realized it may be Ronny, he barged in. The light switch on the wall next to the doorway didn't turn the light on. Odd because the hall light was on and lights from other units seeped from under their doors. After playing with it a few times, Victor heard the hampered breathing evolve into a voice, one trying to say his name.

"Vi, Vi, Vic, Victor. Hel, help me, man," Ronny said.

His voice was coming from the window where he drank his coffee every morning. Victor hustled over to him, remaining cognizant to be careful since he sounded wounded. Due to the darkness, Victor could only make out Ronny's figure. Victor grabbed his roommate's shoulders and asked, "What happened? What's going on?"

Ronny's heavy breathing sped up as he tried to respond. His cries were not cries of pain but of fear; Victor sensed Ronny knew he was going to die.

"Ronny, what happened? Come on, we have to get you to the medical ward."

"There's no point, man. I'm going to die. Just please, take care of Marissa and the kids. Once they're allowed to leave this God-forsaken please, please just make sure they're taken care of. I won't be there for them."

Ronny knocked his head back on the wall behind him out of frustration, like being stabbed multiple times in the stomach was his own wrongdoing.

"Nah, fuck that, Ronny. You're going to be fine. I'm going to get help. You stay here and keep breathing, man. I'm going to get help."

Ronny let out a snicker only someone dying could do.

"No, man. Don't get help. They're the ones who did this to me. Don't trust them or anyone else. Just make it out alive with our families. Don't do anything to piss them off."

Victor barely had time to process Ronny's last words before heavily armed military personnel bombarded their unit.

"Get the fuck back! Get the fuck away from him!"

"Arms in the fuckin' air, Poban! Arms in the air!"

It all happened so fast; Victor didn't even notice the lights in the unit were back on. He felt the heavy weight of the soldiers and their equipment collapse on him, forcing him on his stomach and tying his arms behind his back. Within seconds, someone cuffed his hands behind his back and zip tied his feet. Unable to flip himself over, he squirmed around, pointlessly trying to turn himself over to counter his attackers. He felt a knee dig into the small of his back and the tip of a rifle press against the back of his neck.

"Poban, quit fuckin' moving!"

Who else but Officer Lawrence?

"What the fuck is going on? I didn't do shit. Let me fuckin' go," Victor said, attempting to fight a fight he had no chance in.

"Besides your dead roommate, you're the only one in here. You expect us to believe that son?" the officer asked.

"Fuck you, Lawrence. Fuck you, I didn't do this."

The knee into his back submerged into him harder, causing his legs to convulse. His teeth clenched as he tried to control his breathing to handle the discomfort and suppress his fury. Once the MP5 lifted from his head, he tilted his neck up and found himself staring into Ronny's lifeless eyes. They seared into his own, appearing disappointed. Even in death, Ronny looked despondent that Victor failed to take care of their families. It was as if Ronny already knew he didn't have a chance at evading guilt.

"Let's call the hospital and get this cleaned up," Officer Lawrence said.

Referring to Ronny the way he did infuriated Victor more than he already was. Ronny was the only friend he had made during quarantine in Morple, and the authorities were going to pin his death on him. As two soldiers brought Victor to his feet, Officer Lawrence stood in front of him with his hands on his hips; he had a sick smile on his face that confirmed he was gaining satisfaction from this. He leaned into Victor's ear and said, "I couldn't let you interfere with the fun we've been having with Leslie lately."

Victor tried to unleash his arms, using all the strength he had in an attempt to break free and kill the officer with his bare hands, but it was useless. No matter what he did, Victor had failed Leslie, Ronny, and their families.

"Cut that shit out, infick. You won't have to worry about any of them anymore. Take this piece of shit out of here," Officer Lawrence said.

The officer's men did as they were told, and neither Leslie nor Stella saw Victor again.

CHAPTER

2050

S tella Soren wished the constant commotion echoing through her family's apartment building didn't upset her so much anymore. Glass breaking, flesh hitting flesh, drunks' rages of fury, and shouting matches were heard on a daily basis. It disturbed her to think just how frightened other young, struggling mothers confronting domestic violence on a regular basis were. Stella couldn't imagine having to shield her daughters from that every day. Life was challenging enough with the minimal opportunity Morple granted people like the Sorens.

Luckily for her, Stella's husband Eddie had a gentle soul, and he was relentless in his pursuit of moving his family out of Morple and back to the mainland, where they hoped for a better shot at prosperity, where the government remembered every life was one worth living.

Husband and wife grew up alongside each other in unusual circumstances, having both been quarantined in Morple's infamous Villa 6 camp for nearly fifteen years. In a certain aspect, their story was romantic. In another, it highlighted the government's oppression. Allegedly, Stella's father killed Eddie's father, but both of their mothers told them not to believe that nonsense. When they were too young to understand what happened, other kids and parents in the camp shot them funny looks for spending the majority of their time together. Fellow Villa

6 residents ridiculed their mothers for developing a friendship after Ronny Soren's death, but both women maintained strong demeanors, refusing to let what others presume to be the truth dictate how they lived their lives. Their message to their children was to never concern themselves with what those who do not matter think. If they could do that, they could do anything. Their mothers formed an alliance in raising the three children: Stella, Eddie, and Eddie's sister Robin, who died at a young age due to sonoravirus complications; another fallacy their parents told them not to believe.

Shortly after being released from Villa 6 in 2045, Stella and Eddie told their mothers what the latter knew all along: they were madly in love and wanted to marry. Because the families were so intertwined, they didn't think this would be acceptable. Relief came over them when the news elated both Marissa and Leslie to officially become one family. After all their shared hardships, this was part of the light at the end of the tunnel. Since Eddie was a little older than Stella, they had to wait until Stella was of age, but right when she turned eighteen, they married. Immediately, they conceived Robin, named after his late sister, and were so obsessed with being parents they wanted another. Ariana came a short two years later. So here they were living in the US' fifty-first state as a young family with no money, no opportunity, and, based on the trends of modern-day life, a bleak future. Their apartment was deteriorating. The family frequently had to ration out their food because their grocer often didn't have enough supply for the countless families similar to them. Clothes were worn long after they began looking like rags. But that didn't matter to the Sorens. Eddie and Stella had already made it to hell and back; they were confident they could weather any storm that came their way as long as they had each other and their daughters. Their reward for doing so would be eventually making it to the mainland where in typical American fashion everyone had too much of everything.

Stella was rocking Ariana softly after she woke up fussy from a late afternoon nap. Robin, the most perfect child any parent could ask for, sensed Ariana's unclear demands overwhelmed their mother. Robin situated herself next to them and softly rubbed the top of Ariana's hand and hummed a peaceful melody that calmed her little sister. Most of the time Stella knew how to fulfill her youngest daughter's needs, but at times, Robin was the only person who could give Ariana what she wanted. Something about her sister's touch put Ariana at ease, warming their mother's heart. Robin's maturity at such a young age was incredibly impressive and indicative of the woman she'd grow up to be.

Ariana, now in a blissful state, was giggling at the dorky faces her sister was making at her. Witnessing their sisterly bond develop at such a young age was rewarding to see. In that moment, Stella reminded herself to never let them forget how they must always stick together, no matter the circumstances.

Although Eddie's job as a car mechanic was in less than ideal work conditions and susceptible to falling victim to advancements in artificial intelligence (A.I.), he always came home happy to see his girls and energetic enough to help Stella with parental chores. Whether it was changing Ariana's diaper, teaching Robin a new word, or preparing their dinner, Eddie always gave it his all. This is why the dejected look he walked in with worried Stella.

"Hi honey," she said. "How was your day?"

"Hi my love," he said before coming over to kiss Ariana and Robin on the cheek and his wife's forehead.

"Hi Daddy!" Robin said. She grabbed her feet and was giddy for him being present. Eddie thought of this as his reward for surviving another day in The District, Morple's inner-city.

"Hi, pumpkin."

Stella could tell his smile and enthusiasm weren't authentic. Her stomach turned upside down, and horrible thoughts started racing through her head, knowing their lives could change forever any given day. But she had to give all the credit in the world to her husband. He knew how to make their daughters happy no matter what dire reality they were up against.

"How was your day?" Eddie asked.

"I've been taking care of Ariana with Mommy."

"Yes, you have. Can you tell Daddy what you did to make Ariana happy?" Stella asked.

The couple exchanged smiles, as they had seen this countless times before, but they never tired of their eldest showing off how she cared for her younger sister.

3

"I went like this, and then she got happy."

It pleased Robin that her demonstration garnered more giggles from her little sister, proving her efforts were viable in front of her biggest supporters.

"Oh, wow! Do you think I can do that?" Eddie asked.

"Try, Daddy!"

"Okay!"

Eddie lifted his hands up and playfully roared before tickling Ariana's feet, causing the infant to kick and squirm uncontrollably. Her precious laughter was too much for her little body to handle, evinced by her gargling saliva all over her apron and consequently Stella.

"Get her, Daddy!" Robin said. She was jumping up and down on the couch, endlessly amused by how quickly he could transform himself into the tickle monster.

"Okay, honey. Stop," Stella said after Ariana drenched her arm in saliva. As usual, he abided and proceeded to kiss all three again.

"I need to talk to you," Eddie said in Stella's ear.

She nodded and asked Robin to entertain herself for a bit while her mommy and daddy talked. Eddie took Ariana in his arms so Stella could wash her arm off before meeting him in their room.

"What's wrong?" she asked.

"The shop is shutting down."

Now that Robin wasn't in the room, his melancholy expression was back. Finding a new job was always a challenge, but in their class, it was nearly impossible. The government had special payment programs for anyone indefinitely unemployed, but its recently implemented Morple Youth Movement, or the MYM, added unfavorable provisions to them. If one listened to the politicians boast, MYM was a government-funded program that educated and taught life lessons to Morple's disadvantageous youth. For the ones who could read between the lines, they knew it was a way for the state to occupy its young population and avoid compensating parents whose jobs no longer existed because of favorable legislation for A.I. initiatives. Against most of its citizens' desires, Morple passed MYM, which stated officials could assume care for children if they determined what their parents were providing wasn't sufficient enough. This was the main reason for Eddie's distress.

"Oh, Eddie. I know what you're thinking, and do not, do not let that thought cross your mind. You did nothing wrong. You work too hard to blame yourself. Okay?"

He buried his face in his palms and wept.

"Eddie, do not pin this on yourself."

"I am failing my family," he said between cries.

"Hey, look at me."

When he didn't listen, Stella commanded him to do so again. Sterner this time.

"Look at me."

Eddie wiped the tears from under his eyes and, despite feeling too ashamed to, looked his wife in her eyes.

"You are the most dedicated and loving father and husband any child or woman could ask for. Okay? You and I, together, are going to get through this. Just like we always have. We've been through it all, Eddie, and we have always, always come out on the other side stronger. This time will be no different. Do you hear me?"

Stella mentioning their past troubles combined with the severity of their current situation intensified Eddie's emotions, but also reinforced how much he loved this woman. He couldn't say a word without bursting into tears, so he just submerged himself into his wife, nearly smushing Ariana.

After Stella consoled her husband, she heard the faint sound of an unknown man's voice. Their apartment's walls were thin, but the normal tone he was speaking in wouldn't have been audible enough to carry through. Plus, she heard Robin responding.

"Who is that?" Stella asked, but more was thinking aloud.

She jolted herself off Richard and ran into their family room to find Reginald Lawrence asking Robin about her favorite toys.

"This one is my favorite because of her hair. She's the prettiest, and I li—"

"Excuse me, who are you, and what are you doing in our home?" Stella asked the intruder.

"Ah, excuse me for barging in unannounced. Robin here opened the door and welcomed me in. I hope that isn't a problem," Reginald said.

5

"Do you think a two-year-old's permission is sufficient enough for you to enter a stranger's home?" Eddie asked.

Reginald put his hands up in surrender, as if he was just now realizing he made a lapse in judgement.

"My apologies. I did not mean to upset either of you. Robin here was just showing me her toys. My intentions were not to get off on the wrong foot."

After an awkward silence, he introduced himself, "I'm sorry. I'm Reginald Lawrence. I'm with the state."

He flashed his government identification card to validate his claim, an immediate red flag.

"What can we do for you, Mr. Lawrence?" Eddie asked.

"Do you mind if we sit?" he asked.

Eddie gestured his permission. Stella ordered Robin to come sit on their side of the living room; this man positioning himself so close to their daughter frightened her more than his undetected intrusion.

"Mr. Soren, I am here today to—"

"Eddie's fine," Eddie said.

"Eddie, I am here today to discuss with you and Stella about the news that came down today regarding your place of work. Hearing another local business close because of uncontrollable circumstances pains me, but fortunately for you and your family, there are government-funded programs in place to combat this occurrence. As you already know, your family will be eligible to receive bi-monthly payments for your troubles. That way, you and your wife shouldn't have any problems with your expenses from one month to the next. You can submit a monthly budget to the state for approval and be paid accordingly. So please, do not worry about covering your rent, groceries, and other necessities. Morple will gladly front the costs."

Eddie rocked back and forth with his elbows perched on his knees, anticipating where this conversation was heading. Ariana must've sensed Stella's nervousness because she suddenly became finicky in her mother's arms. Stella did her best to rock Ariana back and forth to sooth the angst she felt from Reginald's presence.

Assigning full responsibility to himself for bringing this situation upon his family, Eddie felt obligated to step in and do the talking, "Mr.

Lawrence, thank you for reminding us of the resources at our disposal, but I have already begun to think about where I can work next so our family doesn't have to be supported by the state. I really don't think we will need it as I have already begun thinking of where I can go next. There are options out there, it's just a matter of finding and taking advantage of them. But again, we appreciate your concern."

Proud of her husband for voicing their independence, Stella laid her hand on his back in a sign of support for him, and to demonstrate to Reginald they were much stronger than the state deemed them to be.

"I understand you wanting to take care of your family, and it is quite admirable I might add, but there are important factors to consider," Reginald continued, "You and Mrs. Soren have two young children to look after. In these times, they cannot be put at risk living in a household that cannot properly provide for them. This is why the state has put these types of programs in place, like MYM."

Stella gasped at the mention on MYM.

Ignoring her, Reginald carried on, "It really is a beneficial organization that ensures children are taken care of while their families handle some adversity back home. Its intentions are in the right place, and it would free you both of the burden."

"Our children are not burdens Mr. Lawrence," Stella said.

"And I understand that but obtaining the means to support them during these times might be. Your husband's soon-to-be unemployment is quite unfortunate, but Morple wants you both to know you two are not in this fight alone. We have the capabilities to groom your children into fine contributors to society, including living accommodations where they will be around other children and have access to educational resources that will shape who they grow up to be."

"How can children become fine members of society under the care of someone else besides their parents?" Stella asked.

"How can children become fine members of society under the care of parents unable to provide for their basic needs?" Reginald asked, rather hastily.

At this, Robin began crying. She sensed their conversation was escalating as it abandoned diplomacy.

"Mr. Lawrence, I am going to find a job and take care of my family. We appreciate your concern, but we are going to be fine. Luckily, we budget enough to withstand difficult times like the ones up ahead, so we'll be okay."

A sardonic smile enveloped Reginald's face. Apparently, being nice didn't get the message across.

"Mr. and Mrs. Soren, I did not come here today to give you an option. You, Eddie, have no means of income. With a wife and two young children to feed and house, this is a problem. The state has parameters in place to help people like you and your family, and denying these external resources is prohibited. Morple prides itself on helping its citizens and enabling all of them to reach their full potential. You and your wife will receive monthly payments to continue living here, and your daughters will be taken under the care of the state at week's end and begin living in the organization's facility. You both will be allotted a certain amount of hours a month to visit them, but they will be raised in MYM's care. Most are thankful for this safety net, and I think after the initial shock of your unemployment wears off, you will be, too.

"Representatives from the state will be in touch about the logistics of everything. Good day to both of you."

Reginald smiled at Robin and Ariana, stood up, and left the apartment without another word.

Eddie stared ahead with his hands over his mouth, unable to process the state was going to legally take his children from him and their mother.

"Daddy, what's wrong?" Robin asked, her voice shaking with trepidation.

Unable to answer, Stella tried to appear confident when she said, "Nothing for you to worry about, Robin. We'll all be okay."

CHAPTER

PRESENT-DAY, 2089

Robin was cleaning up the remnants of the meal she helped prepare and serve when a wailing baby boy caught her attention. His mother couldn't have been older than twenty, and he was rather big for his age; not in a concerning way, but in an adorably chubby kind of way. He reminded her of Jonathan.

She threw the trays in the bin and sanitized the tables thoroughly, a practice the state took seriously. Morple threatened to cut funding if officials observed they weren't doing this correctly; Robin and the fellow volunteers at Free Morple she worked with knew the state made this a big deal because it needed a reason to shut the operation down. The state didn't really give a shit about the people Free Morple cared for, including providing meals for, caring for children, distributing vaccines, and providing education. In many ways, Morple's dynamic hadn't changed much from the time the government broke up Robin's family to now. Anyone not born in the top of the state's hierarchy still didn't have a legitimate shot at making it.

Every month was a struggle just to stay afloat, even though the community revered Robin and the rest of the organization, especially the less fortunate stuck in The District's cycle of poverty. Most were families of diswors, or displaced workers. A.I. had been replacing them for decades, and these people had nowhere to turn to; a struggle Robin was all too familiar with. Until Morvo, Morple's social revolution that occurred from 2066 to 2070, diswors and their families didn't have resources to lean on, but ever since their hardships became more visible to the rest of the nation, external pressures guilted the government into establishing a more sustainable safety net for them. One less detrimental than Morple Youth Movement.

Catching herself half-assing it, Robin slowed down as she sanitized the table to ensure it appeared good as new before taking the dishes to the kitchen. If the state came down on the organization because of her careless mistake, she would never forgive herself. When Robin came out of the kitchen, she approached the young, masked mother holding the baby that reminded her of her eldest son.

"Excuse me miss," she said.

Startled at first, the woman jolted her head towards Robin, looking fearful that a person with presumed authority had approached her. Robin assumed there was a good reason those in charge frightened her. Now that she was closer, Robin noticed how old the young mother looked for her age. She had crow's feet surrounding both eyes, and worry lines ingrained on her forehead. Her blue eyes lacked life, reflective of the toll an impoverished life was taking on her. Having a baby didn't make it any easier.

"Hi, I'm sorry to alarm you," Robin said, noticing she tightened her hold on her baby, "I just wanted to tell you how precious your baby boy is, and I wanted to introduce myself. I'm Robin. Robin Karros."

Sensing her paranoia, Robin didn't offer her a hand to shake. She had already unintentionally alarmed the young woman and wanted to change her initial impression.

"Oh, hi, Robin. Uh, thank you so much. I'm Taylor. Taylor Jennings," she said.

Sensing Robin's motherlike presence, Taylor unstiffened.

"So nice to meet you. Was everything okay with today's meal?" Robin asked.

"Oh, yeah. Of course, it was. It was excellent. Why, did you think I didn't like it?"

"No, no. Not at all. I just like to make sure everyone is satisfied."

Robin began to regret introducing herself, as it seemed to distress Taylor. To save face, she told Taylor the real reason she went out of her way to meet her, "Honestly, your son reminded me of my oldest when he was this age. Those chubby cheeks get me every single time, and I just had to get a closer look. I'm sorry for being intrusive, but I just can't resist a baby boy like yours."

"Oh, well thank you. This is Jimmy. He'll be one tomorrow."

"Well, he is absolutely adorable. Happy birthday to you, Jimmy. Anyways, I have some work to do, so I'll let you be. Thank you for allowing me to get a closer look."

"Would you like to hold him?" Taylor asked.

Taken aback by the question, Robin didn't answer right away. It was uncommon mothers let others hold their babies, especially strangers.

"Yes, of course. I'd, I'd love to," she said.

Robin wiped her hands on her apron before reaching out to hold Jimmy. As she situated him in her arms, his eyes widened as far as they could and gazed up at the beautiful mystery woman. When they locked eyes, Robin became nostalgic. Memories of Jonathan around this age were some of her fondest. Robin had just been released from the state's custody and was on her way towards winning her fortune that served as her escape from a bleak future Morple designated to certain members of society. Bobby Karros had just entered her life and embraced her and all the baggage she warned him about, the first sign of his admirable character she fell so hard for.

"He is such a good baby, but I feel like his daddy's absence is already affecting him," Taylor said.

Despite their current differences in class, Robin and Taylor seemed very alike.

"Well Taylor, you're doing a great job," Robin said, unsure if she should pry on what happened to Jimmy's father, "The fact you're here shows you are seeking the necessary help for the benefit of not only him, but for you, as well. Be proud of yourself."

"His daddy was so excited when he was born, just ecstatic. Then when Jimmy was about six months he was just gone. I haven't seen him since, and that was six months ago. Life wasn't always kind to us, but I thought Jimmy and our relationship outweighed the bad. I guess I was wrong."

Taylor's tears fled down her face, drying up on her mask. It was clear she needed someone to talk to, and Robin made herself available to her. She didn't expect to come across someone who on the surface appeared to live in a different reality than Robin, but really, their paths seemed to be quite similar.

"Jonathan, my son who Jimmy reminds me of, was four when his stepfather went missing. Sixteen years ago. One day I came home, and he was just gone. Nowhere to be found. Jonathan and my youngest son Moe were both crying in their rooms, petrified, but the authorities and I couldn't get any information out of them. Moe was just a baby, and Jonathan's brain development is behind for his age, so they couldn't help us out, but it was obvious something horrific happened. It's hard for him to process things, but by looking in his eyes I could tell he saw what happened. Whatever occurred that day was clearly a traumatic experience for them.

"But unfortunately, we'll never know what happened. All I could do was to keep being the best possible mother I could be. That's what my boys needed, so that's what I did."

Robin gathered from Taylor's facial expression she was not expecting them to have much in common. Ever since getting her life together, Robin was regularly met with skepticism and surprise by those she shared her life experiences with. She didn't boast or even acknowledge it, but she knew her impressive physique and natural beauty were the reasons others assumed her life had always been a breeze. One of Robin's primary goals was to serve as a symbol of hope for women like Taylor, which is one of the reasons Robin dedicated so much of her time to helping the likes of Taylor out. If a little girl who suffered unimaginable amounts of trauma could grow up to be what Robin was, then anyone could.

Including Taylor.

"Doesn't it anger you why he left?" Taylor asked.

"It angers me he isn't here, yes, but I'm not sure if he left. Coming home to find my boys crying the way they were tells me something worse happened, but I will probably never know for certain. All I can do is focus on the now and keep pushing forward. If there's one thing Morple has taught me, it's persistence prevails."

Encouragement from a kind-hearted volunteer was much more than Taylor seemed to expect from Free Morple.

Sensing her own story resonated with Taylor, Robin said, "Just keep pushing, sweetheart. You'll be alright."

With a mother's touch, Robin handed Jimmy back over to his mother and continued finishing what remained of her chores.

Since Moe was now a senior in high school and Jonathan was more self-sufficient, with the help of his American Staffordshire Terrier Wallace, Robin spent most of her spare time at Free Morple's main facility. Once she got her bearings after her husband's disappearance, Robin had made it a priority to give back to a community that had torn apart multiple generations of her family. One of the core reasons Robin prioritized charity work was because she realized most people in her situation didn't have a light at the end of the tunnel like she did.

She was fortunate enough to have been found by a top-notch social justice lawyer, one who won her $75 million in a lawsuit against the state. After hearing her story and studying the family's roots in Morple, he put it upon himself to change her life. Robin liked to tell herself even if she didn't have that fortune to fall back on, she would still be passionate about helping others, but really, she didn't know. She had enough inner demons to deal with to concern herself with a hypothetical question.

Robin battled with the ability to open up to her family. She fully trusted her sons but didn't want her burdens from the past to contaminate their thoughts. Jonathan never questioned the irregular parts of their lives, like who his biological father was or their nonexistent extended family. In a way, Robin envied this. Jonathan's condition allowed him to find joy in life's simplicities, a trait she'd forever admire about her eldest; Jonathan's perspective shaped their values as a family.

Robin didn't have it as easy with Moe, as his curiosity clashed with how reserved she was about her personal life. Moe was charismatic, humorous, and nurturing, but these qualities weren't outwardly expressed. Strangers tended to assume he was dark, angry, and the product of a broken, dysfunctional family unable to get its footing after Morvo. His Hispanic features combined with this demeanor fueled the stereotype. Robin's youngest son wasn't one to walk down the street with a fixed smile on his face but would put whatever he was doing on hold to help an elderly woman load groceries in her car.

Understanding him became a challenge when he began asking questions Robin couldn't answer:

What happened to Jonathan?
Why don't you ever talk about your parents?
Why don't you ever talk about your childhood?
Where is my dad?

It wasn't until Moe became a teenager when Robin realized he needed closure to continue maturing, something she was failing at providing. This barrier in their relationship convoluted his teenage years. Despite doing everything in her power to shield her sons from her past life, Robin had started to come around to the idea she would have to come clean, to at least Moe, for them to have a healthy mother-son bond in his adulthood.

Volunteering at Free Morple also acted as a method to offset the guilt that ate away at her for not coming clean to her sons about their roots. By helping those who had similar deprivations as her, Robin rationalized avoidance behavior towards being transparent with them. It enabled her to believe she was doing everything in her power to address her first twenty years of life, but it didn't help her configure how to confront the gaps in her life that affected her on a daily basis; something Moe liked to remind her of when they engaged in their spats.

All of those who played significant roles in Robin's past were out of her life, leading her to believe she evaded all of its turmoil. Little did she know, one would soon resurface and reveal how Robin never really had escaped what she was hiding from.

Ariana Jackson poured herself a glass of her finest wodin before heading out to spend the rest of the afternoon under her cabana. Normally, she waited until closer to dinnertime for her first drink, but today she had an urge to start her self-care prematurely. How the brown liquor warmed her insides revitalized her. This combined with its dense, oaky flavor and potency is what constituted wodin as Ariana's drink of choice. Since her husband didn't indulge in alcohol, the entire at-home bar was at her disposal. By no means a drunk, Ariana recognized she was an alcoholic. She rationalized her consumption by persuading herself she deserved it.

The plantation had been in turmoil all day. Fights between two of the rival gangs erupted during the first shift in the fields, and even though her husband's men broke it up relatively quickly, the gangs' beef carried over into the afternoon. The morning skirmish started when two Hispanics jumped a new White diswor after breakfast. The latter retaliated by killing one of the original perpetrators by repeatedly beating him with a shovel. Her husband wanted the White diswor's head chopped off in front of his entire gang, but Ariana advised against it.

"What would you do if you were him?" she asked after the incident took place. Yes, the killer was on track to getting himself eventually killed, but in the meantime, Ariana had saved his life.

Ariana didn't want to be just an accessory to her billionaire husband; she preferred to be in the loop and about his business dealings, and not so long ago would represent his interests at meetings. Despite their different cultural backgrounds, they discovered their pasts were quite similar: Morple was responsible for the demise of both their families, and that shared source of resentment is what brought them closer. Their oppressive, abusive, and traumatic upbringings fueled both husband and wife. To feel avenged, they had no limits, proven by their rise and dominance at the top of the human and drug trafficking world.

Ariana brought her glass to her lips and embraced the heat the liquor ignited in her body. After ensuring the coast was clear, she downed the rest and poured herself a fresh glass. Her husband didn't mind her drinking, but Ariana knew witnessing her binge alcohol firsthand triggered unpleasant memories for him.

Ariana grabbed her now full glass and headed out to her cabana to await her husband's company. Earlier she pleaded to him to wrap up the workday early and enjoy the rest of the afternoon with her. To entice him, she wore a strapless bikini top that pushed her breasts together and cheeky bottoms that didn't hide anything. The transparent shawl draped over her curves left nothing to the imagination.

Ariana's security detail, two heavily Barrett REC7-strapped bald guards paid handsomely to take a bullet for her, followed her outside. She considered the constant surveillance of her pointless since the fortress she called home was on a plantation with around the clock armed guards paid to kill and die for them, but her husband wouldn't have it any other way.

"You ain't gonna be left alone with how many mother fuckers out there want us fuckin' dead, Ariana. End of fuckin' story," he said the last time she mustered up the energy to argue with him about it. Sometimes Ariana felt the suffocating security was to keep her in rather than keep others out.

"That'll be all gentlemen," she said to her personal guards, referring to how close they could stand to the cabana. One win she had was establishing boundaries when she wanted to enjoy their outdoor amenities. She got this approved by asking her husband, "How am I supposed to fuck you out here with them watching?"

Ariana slid her shawl off and sunk into the cushions. She took another healthy gulp of wodin while admiring the empire her husband had created. In the distance, she could see the late afternoon diswors examining which crops were good for processing and which weren't. On another end of the property, she could see the facilities where the drugs underwent modifications, such as adding the necessary additives to get their consumers hooked and chemicals that improved their aesthetics. Even if an orgacal leaf appeared weathered, its potentness didn't suffer, but consumers didn't believe that, which is why her husband designated factions of his diswors to polish every leaf leaving the facility. LaVonte did not become the most notorious and richest kingpin the world had ever seen by taking shortcuts. He was never satisfied with his accomplishments; a mindset Ariana was attracted to. A powerful man had once ruined her life, but the one she married injected life into her, providing Ariana with an appreciation for what it was like to control others, what it was like to instill fear. After living the first part of her life under someone else's rule, Ariana vowed to herself she would now be the one others bowed down to.

This vantage point never got old to Ariana. A still infinity pool sat between her and her husband's realm, which expanded through hundreds of acres in wide valleys that were once filled with California's extinct wildlife and a river. Its beauty is not what intrigued Ariana the most, but rather the power it symbolized. She helped LaVonte expand his empire, and while she was not proud of all her contributions, she couldn't help but gloat at her own rise to the top.

"Man, I don't give a fuck. That was part of the fuckin' deal, and this mother fucker ain't living up to it. I want him out," LaVonte could be heard saying from afar. Clearly his last dealing of the day had not ended up in his favor.

To diffuse the attention, Ariana made her presence known. She peered over the top of the cabana and said, "Baby, come join me. I've been waiting for you."

His men sent their gazes down. Getting caught checking out their boss' wife was a death sentence.

"I'm coming, baby," LaVonte said, "Get this shit fuckin' handled. You hear?"

Ariana sat on her heels and clasped her hands on her lap so her breasts pressed forward, hoping it would distract LaVonte from whatever he was up in arms about.

His raised eyebrows proved his appeasement. He kissed his wife and shed his shirt as he sat beside her to survey his empire. The couple cozied up next to each other and let their hands rest on their favorite part of their significant other: Ariana's on LaVonte's abs and LaVonte's on Ariana's ass.

After a comfortable silence passed, Ariana asked, "What's wrong baby? Who upset you today?"

LaVonte breathed audibly before responding. "These mother fuckers in business don't follow the rules anymore, baby. We had an agreement, and now he doesn't want to do his part. Mother fucker."

Seeing what had unfolded was obviously still agitating him, Ariana thought it was best to move on to another subject, but her curiosity got the best of her. "Tell me, baby. What happened? I'm listening."

"Peru got confiscated."

Ariana lifted her head off his chest at this news. LaVonte recently forged a new relationship in South America, and their first endeavor was distributing to various organizations in Peru. Apparently, they weren't off to a great start.

"How much?" she asked.

"All of it."

That meant *tons.*

Ariana tilted her head back and let out an exhale.

"Oh, baby. Just another headache for you to deal with, I'm sorry," she said. "But this is why you have those people on your payroll."

"That's the main issue. He isn't living up to our agreement. I'm going to have to use politicians, which will not make me or them happy. I gave them my word they wouldn't have to deal with international issues, and now I look like a fuckin' idiot. I want him gone."

LaVonte didn't have to say his name for Ariana to know who he was talking about. Even though the individual wasn't directly responsible for her trauma, his kin was. This is why it was best for his name to go unmentioned.

"As much as I despise him for simply existing, I can't advise you to do that. That will attract too much heat. His reach is big, baby."

LaVonte seethed, not at his wife but at the fact he knew was right. His soon-to-be former business partner had fucked him, but LaVonte couldn't retaliate how he would've liked. Luckily for him, his wife had an urge to get back in the game.

"What if I helped? I've been out for a while now, and I can see this is upsetting you. I'd love nothing more than to help my man out," she said.

"Oh baby, come on. You know you can't help me with this."

"Why not? I did some great things for you in my day, no?"

"Of course you did, but you know why. Don't make me point out the obvious here, come on."

"A lot of time has passed since then. I'm a big girl; I can handle it. Come on, I miss helping you rule the world."

LaVonte cracked a smile at this. It aroused him when his wife talked about his accomplishments and wanted to contribute to his kingdom.

"What about your sister?" he asked.

"What about her?" she said while stroking his abs.

"Are you going to see her?"

"Not intentionally."

"Ariana."

"If it happens, it happens, and I wouldn't be mad at it. But no, I'm not going to go out of my way to contact her."

As much as she wanted to rekindle her relationship with Robin, Ariana didn't know if she could stomach it.

LaVonte was patient in formulating a response, testing Ariana to see if the silence made her realize she had jumped the gun committing to this. As expected, the killer look in his wife's eyes told him she was all business.

"Your business savvy does things to me, baby," he said.

"I can feel that," she said, gripping his cock through his trunks. "Let me take care of you, and we'll talk details later. Okay?"

LaVonte bit his lower lip and nodded slowly. Ariana unstrapped her top, grabbed the back of his head and buried it in her chest. He rolled down his trunks and slid into her with no trouble at all, immediately moaning at her softness.

Ariana felt her wetness increase each time he throbbed inside her, unsure if it was because of their physical connection or because she was back in the game.

CHAPTER

2089

With families in different classes that opposed one another dating back to Morple's inception, Dillon Lawrence's and Moe Karros' friendship was unusual.

Before Morvo, a kid with the type of wealth and family stature Dillon had would have received his education from a private teacher or in a pod, a group of three to five students with one private teacher, instead of attending a public high school. A kid cut from Moe's cloth would have been fighting an uphill battle just to make it to the next day.

Morvo successfully integrated education programs in order to level the playing field for Morple's youth. The wealthy argued its youth's quality of schooling would diminish due to being exposed to students with backgrounds like Moe. Elites protested a majority of these students' mental capacities were too limited to maximize the opportunity a high-caliber curriculum provided them. To add salt to the wound, enraged parents pointed out these impoverished students had the potential to inflict another pandemic because, after all, people of their class were the ones who spread sonoravirus. Morple's one percenters felt it was an injustice for their offspring to suffer consequences their state's government was responsible for incurring. What they failed to recognize was how the working class suffered from being a scapegoat for decades. The division that used to exist between Morple's two classes brought the well-to-dos comfort.

The oppressed were hesitant to agree with integrating schools, but for different reasons. Parents of the working-class worried children from wealthier families would ostracize their children for things like going to school with lesser quality clothes, the color of their skin, and symbolizing the false stereotypes the government created over the span of decades. They couldn't trust their children would remain unharmed under the supervision of their old masters' progeny.

With family trees coming from opposite sides of the revolution, there weren't many Dillon and Moe duos at their high school. In fact, each of the boys had unintentionally become distant from their other friends over the years because of their hesitation to diversify their groups.

Blind to it all, neither knew how far back their roots went.

Dillon and his family lived in one of the most exclusive mansions in all of Costa Mor, Morple's coastal city where the one percent resided. The monstrosities in this part of Morple were all spread apart from each other for the purpose of privacy, but the Lawrences' was the most secluded of them all. Set back on the corner of the island, the nearest neighbor was nearly a mile away.

When the US' upper class began to realize how prosperous a new state could be, Morple's rich population increased. To avoid living too close to previously quarantined citizens who found themselves stuck on the island, military officials who elected to stay after receiving promotions to either a higher ranking or to a role in government and wealthy Americans decided to make their new homes along the coast. It was more desirable because of the oceanfront views, the land would prove to be a profitable investment, and, most importantly, it put them further away from the Hispanics and Blacks who lived inland.

Morple was infamous for its ominous clouds that hovered over the outer edges of the island. This was no different where the Lawrence mansion was, but a few beams of sunlight always managed to break through behind the house, providing a dramatic backdrop when approaching.

Because their home sat on a jagged cliff remote from the rest of the neighborhood an access road had to be built. Since their house was the only one on the road, Costa Mor okayed for its name to be Lawrence Drive. The perfectly paved path winded towards the palace uncomfortably close to the edge of the cliff so when people drove in, they had an upfront view of the Pacific Ocean. It ran so close to the perimeter of the island the waves could be seen crashing down into the rocks one hundred fifty feet below. The rocks resembled black oversized upside-down icicles.

If crashing down into the cold ocean water after falling one hundred fifty feet didn't do the trick, the rocks were there for backup. Morple's cliffs were undefeated.

Despite the countless number of times Moe had been there, he remained enamored with the entrance to his best friend's home. Dillon noticed his infatuation.

"Man, get over it. It is the same ocean that surrounds the rest of the island," Dillon said with a smirk on his face.

Moe tittered. "Yeah, but that doesn't mean everyone can see it from their fuckin' *private* streets."

Dillon rolled his eyes after hearing him emphasize "private."

Dillon's Tesla finally approached the driveway. Even though Moe considered it his home away from home, the Lawrences' stately manor was still intimidating upon arrival. When you knew it was for three people and two dogs, it appeared ridiculous.

The front door was in the middle of the house and had two vertical windows on both sides. The second and third story windows were perfectly aligned with the ones on the first, highlighting the home's symmetry.

Between the bottom floor windows and driveway were immaculate gardens with green, no matter the season, plants and seasonal flowers in front of windowpanes with flowers and little baby angels carved in the stone. The windows on the second and third stories had identical architecture. How lush the gardens were didn't make sense given the minimal amount of direct sunlight the Lawrence mansion received. Morple was under the blanket of California's offshore clouds that shielded the state and surrounding waters from the sun. One of the few constants of the climate throughout the years.

From the outside it appeared the exterior door led directly inside, but it actually opened up to a capacious hallway that ushered the way to the actual front door on the other end. In this unnecessary space were two statues Moe considered eyesores. One was a life-sized leopard sitting like an obedient dog waiting for a treat, and the other was a life-sized jaguar mimicking its counterpart.

Always waiting near the sculptures eager for the boys to get there were Frank and Finn, the Lawrences' Basset Hound and Goldendoodle, respectively.

"Frank," Moe said, rubbing the hound's belly. "What up big man!"

Finn scurried over to get some affection from Moe, too.

"Yeah, yeah I didn't forget about you Finny," Moe said.

He simultaneously scratched Finn's ears and accepted some licks.

"My pups like you more than me," Dillon said.

"I like your pups more than I like you."

"I don't blame you. Let's go throw the ball in the back."

The entryway's round table substituted centerpieces all the time. They were abstract pieces of art that raised eyebrows. On this day it was a blue-marbled, two-foot statue of a man pondering with a tree trunk as his lower half.

Behind the entryway, there was a living room so exquisite it was uninviting. The couches, chaises, and coffee table were all metallic gold with black trimmings. The rug underneath it all was predominantly black but had matching gold curvature designs on it that seemed to run aimlessly. All the light fixtures illuminating the room were black with, of course, gold shades. The lights were never brighter than what one would consider dimmed. Moe always found it odd there wasn't a single family photo of them in the living room, as his family had several. All that were on the end tables next to the furniture were additional black and gold lamps that remained on at all times for the sake of the family's and visitors' visibility. When Moe and Dillon walked through it to get to the backyard, Moe tiptoed, fearful that putting his entire weight on the ground would somehow break something or diminish the posh gold beneath and around him. The back door opened up to a concrete walkway bordered by more luxuriant gardens with a waterfall on each side and statues of Greek gods and goddesses in deep thought scattered around leading to the pool where Heather and a friend were laying out.

Heather had brown hair slightly longer than shoulder length. Unlike most women in her echelon, Heather was all natural. In her mid-forties, her face showed no signs of age, and her figure was as fit as it was before she birthed her one and only son. Her dark blue eyes, defined jawline, and proportional feminine features caught any man's attention, no matter his age. Her body was evidence of how much time she had in her day to work out. She still had defined abs, complementing her small breasts' perkiness, and toned legs that served as the foundation of her lifted ass, the most impressive part of her figure.

When Heather heard the dogs rumble into the backyard, she and her friend stood up to greet her son and Moe.

"Who is that?" Moe quickly asked Dillon before they were in earshot of Heather and her friend.

"I don't know," Dillon said, captivated by the mystery woman's beauty.

Moe couldn't pinpoint it, but he knew he recognized her.

She was about an inch taller than Heather, so five and-a-half feet. Her thick, dark brown hair fell down to her ass. This woman's boobs barely fit in the confines of her brown bikini, one so close to the color of her skin she could've been mistaken as being naked from afar. To top it off, she wore a floppy sun hat, not too big, and aviators perfectly suited for her complexion.

"Hopefully your mom's friend doesn't notice I'm hard as a rock right now," Moe said.

Dillon and Moe watched her strut towards them with her fingers playing with the strings of her bikini bottoms on both hips, teasing them by flooding their thoughts of what she'd look like with it off.

"I have my own boner to worry about," Dillon responded under his breath, annoyed he thought his mother's friend was just as hot as Moe did.

"Dillon, hi sweetheart," Heather said. Her hand guided her friend from the back up next to her before issuing out pleasantries and hugging Moe. "Moe, hey honey, how are you? I didn't know you were coming over tonight."

"Hey Heather," Moe said, hugging her back. "Yeah, Dillon said you were making dinner, so I couldn't not come over."

"You're the sweetest. This is Ariana, she's a friend of mine."

"It's nice to meet you boys," Ariana said. Slowly, she removed her glasses, revealing mesmerizing round, brown eyes under long eyelashes that caused Dillon and Moe to question what they should concentrate on: her voluptuous body or on her gorgeous face.

"Heather raves about you both all the time!" Ariana said, squeezing her arms together as if meeting them was the most exciting thing to ever happen to her. What she also squeezed together caused the most excitement both Dillon and Moe had ever experienced.

"I'm sure," Dillon said, smiling shyly. "It's nice to meet you."

"Yeah, very nice to meet you too, ma'am."

"Wow Heather, he really does have manners," Ariana said, putting her hand on her right breast to show how impressed she was. "If all eighteen-year-olds talked to women like you they'd be doing much better out there. But please, don't call me ma'am. Ariana is just fine."

Dillon and Moe both noticed she was a bit younger than Heather and most of her friends. They also concluded she was the sexiest woman they had ever seen. Dillon imagined how euphoric seeing her naked would be. Imagining going any further would have made his physical urges impossible to suppress. Moe, while trying to fathom her beauty, couldn't stop thinking about how familiar she was.

"I told you, they're the best. Anyways, Ariana loves to cook, too, so we are going to get food prepped and ready to go. We'll eat out here tonight but not for a few more hours so you boys do your thing," said Heather.

"See you in a bit," Ariana said. Heather and she walked into the house.

"Nice to meet you," the boys said in-sync, nervously. The dogs were panting excitedly at their feet waiting for the boys' attention to turn to them.

"Dude, how hot was she? Wow," Dillon said in a loud whisper as him and Moe started throwing a football on the lawn that overlooked the Pacific Ocean from one hundred-fifty feet up.

This was one of their favorite things to do together. They used it as time to shoot the shit, decompress from school, talk about girls, admire the ocean, and wear out the dogs by making them chase whatever ball they threw back and forth. Their four-legged friends always collapsed after, panting happily.

"That was wild," said Moe. He was trying to match Dillon's enthusiasm about her looks, but couldn't stop thinking where it was he would have seen her before. "Man, I swear. I recognize her. I have seen her before, but I don't know where."

"Where the hell would we go where someone like her would be? She makes Megan Rincon look less than mediocre."

Megan Rincon was the hottest girl at their high school. Dillon liked to bring her up "casually" because she drank enough one time to have sex with him. Moe had slept with her countless times, but only Moe and Megan knew that.

None of Moe's friends, including Dillon, knew because Moe was not the type to kiss and tell. Megan's friends didn't know because her reputation would take a hit if people knew she was hooking up with someone like Moe. His family's status in society came with some baggage, causing a high school girl of Costa Mor to keep it under wraps. Moe knew this but didn't mind. Getting laid with no one knowing was better than not getting laid.

"Fuck, you're right. You've never seen her before? Your mom's friends are usually siliconed-out with fake lips and shit."

"I know. This one is a nice change of pace. Where would you have seen her?"

Dillon and Moe were shameless when it came to discussing the differences between their families' social circles. Dillon knew Moe's family's social outings didn't consist of women who looked like Ariana, and Moe knew Dillon knew. Their ability to be so transparent with each other kept them close.

People are so scared to point out the obvious these days.

"Dude I honestly think I've seen her in the neighborhood," Moe said, trying to get the ball he dropped out of Frank's mouth.

"Really? Wow, well shit I might have to move to your neighborhood," Dillon said, unable to conceal his smart-ass smile.

"Fuckin' funny."

CHAPTER

2089

"Holy shit. Phil, come over here and check this out," Richard Lawrence said to his closest friend and colleague. Phil Gorge was sitting with his left ankle resting on his right knee on the opposite side of Richard's mahogany desk. His lackluster posture looked more improper than it was because of how pristine Richard's eight hundred-square foot office was.

"You know me, I'm a one-woman man, but Heather, sweetheart, you can't bring this around," Richard said as they took a closer look at the camera feed on his holographic computer screen.

Because of his wife's culinary skills, Richard liked to tap into his home's security system at around four every afternoon to peek at what was on the menu. Watching his trophy wife cook was a pleasant sight, too. This particular time, he saw something not on the menu, but something he really wanted.

"Mother fuck, who is that?" Phil asked, putting his face inches from the screen in an effort to get closer to Ariana.

"I have no idea," Richard said.

"I need a woman like that. How the fuck do I find this?"

"With as much money as you have and as single as you are, you shouldn't be having trouble finding this."

"Can I come over for dinner tonight?"

"So you can gawk at my wife and her friend? No."

"Friend? No way, she isn't her friend."

"They're both in bikinis, and Heather wouldn't hang out with someone who isn't her friend by the pool. At our house. God, look at that ass."

"I mean, she's most likely just Heather's newest help and just happens to be super, super hot. Maybe she's actually pleasant to be around so Heather wanted to go swim with her, I don't know. I know I'd hit it though."

"If Heather isn't using the automated system that cost me a fortune because she's paying the new help to go swimming with her, hang out in bikinis and cook, threesomes better be on her list of duties, too. Fuck, I'd take advantage of a hall pass if I ever did get one for her. Even if I knew it was a test and I'd get in trouble for it after, it'd be so worth it."

"Wouldn't that be something! I wouldn't hear you bitch about Heather's spending if that were the case."

Richard silently laughed as he gestured with his head for Phil to go back to where he was sitting. He had yet to exit the camera feed, becoming perplexed seeing his wife's head lean on Ariana's right shoulder.

"Why do you have that look on your face?" Phil asked inquisitively, ready to jump out of his chair to ensure he wouldn't miss anything notable.

"Nothing. I'm just trying to shut this thing off," Richard deflected.

"Ok, so yeah. We were actually talking about something before your latest fantasy came up."

"That we were." Richard's tone indicated he didn't want to continue the conversation.

"Dude, you can't leave this guy hanging. You know the consequences."

"Phil, there is nothing I can do about it. Operating internationally right now could be a fuckin' death sentence for Rapture. Investors would put my fuckin' head on a stake if I was out there campaigning for him."

"Oh please, you can always cover that shit up with minutia no one will care to look into that hard. You and this guy have a very specific arrangement in place, and I think you'd be fuckin' up by failing to live up to it."

Richard leaned back in his chair and grunted, more in frustration with being in this predicament than with Phil because at the end of the day, he knew his best friend was right, but he'd put himself in an impossible situation.

"Listen, I told him I just need some time before reaching out to them. Anyone with a pulse and a decent IQ knows him and South America are in cahoots, so even if I go down there on the premise of representing his legal business ventures it won't look good. For fuck's sake, we are in public relations. We are the ones who are supposed to fix the fuck ups of our clients, not create them."

"I hear you, but I'm just going to be honest with you right now—"

"Aren't you helpful," Richard said, clearly becoming more agitated the longer they discussed this. Phil paused to let him calm down some.

"All I know is, for as loaded as this guy is and for how many proper connections he has, he hasn't lost any of his ruthlessness. You need to make it clear what your intentions are and communicate that you are at least formulating a plan that will free him of any burden. Even if you're not, which it appears you aren't, Jackson ne—"

"Don't say his name here."

"Okay, sorry. He," Phil said with extra emphasis, "needs to be under the impression you are going to bat for him. I don't want to see your fuckin' head on a stake for Christ's sake."

That reality was more likely than Richard would've liked it to be, but he couldn't help but smirk at this.

"Okay. You're right. I need to reevaluate how I'm proceeding with him. If being decapitated wasn't a possibility I'd just terminate our agreement. You should've heard how this fuckin' guy came at me the other day. I thought his hologram was going to beat the shit out of me."

"That's probably what it wanted to do, Mr. Lawrence."

Richard scoffed. "I don't know if that name means anything anymore."

"You're still alive, so it must."

Richard and Phil earned billions as Executive Vice Presidents of Strategic Solutions for Rapture, the most successful PR company in all of Morple and one of the most prestigious in the country. Its mission was to dissipate all the problems, mainly, ones Morple's most prominent politicians and biggest businessmen accrued with their shady practices and lack of morals. Polarizing figures employed the firm, putting it in the crosshairs of politicians hopelessly fighting for the dwindling working class. It endured enormous amounts of scrutiny from activists in Morple and humanitarian organizations from the mainland. Accusations ranged from being responsible for enabling big businesses' mistreatment of their workers to lobbying for pre-Morvo laws preventing certain citizens from having access to the same opportunities as wealthier citizens. Despite all the turmoil, Rapture not only stayed afloat but continued to thrive. One of its strengths was the ability to not deflect negative attention but benefit from it. After all, it was a world-renowned PR company.

"Is the pitch finalized?" Richard asked, shifting gears to inquire about one of the firm's legit clients.

"Yes. I saw it after lunch," Phil said, silently interpreting the paperwork on his lap. "That fuckin' intern from the pod, Marvin, showed it to me. He did all the work. This one should be easy. Kid's good."

"Perfect. That means, I'm out of here."

"Mr. Lawrence is leaving just after four in who knows how fuckin' long on the same day his hot wife has her hot ass friend over. Whoa, whoa, whoa, is there something going on at home I should know about? Maybe get in on? If you're up for trying new things maybe I can get Heather while you take her friend. Just an idea."

Richard couldn't help but chuckle at himself for lacking subtlety. Even though Phil would probably fuck Heather if given the chance, Richard appreciated the reassurance she was hot enough that his friend consistently thought about sleeping with her.

"Whatever, I'm out of here. I'll see you bright and early," Richard said as he walked out of his office with Phil following his lead.

"Hey, if you change your mind, I'm still open to the idea of coming over for dinner."

Phil grew up in the Pacific Palisades, an uber wealthy part of Los Angeles, before enrolling in college in the early fifties. His upbringing consisted of private schools, first-class trips around the globe, single-digit golf at Riviera Country Club, alcohol, cocaine, fuckin' his mother's coked out friends, and witnessing his parents' physical altercations.

Thanks to the Gorges' parties, Los Angeles received plenty of snow during the holidays. During Phil's senior year in high school, the Gorges' holiday party spiraled out of control more than it usually did. At first, everything was status quo. Mr. Gorge and his friends, mainly business partners, were downing dirty martinis and doing blow from the at-home bartop. Mrs. Gorge and her friends guzzled chardonnay, sauvignon blanc and pinot grigio and did key bumps to balance their drunks out. Phil and a couple close buddies crushed beers in the backyard, waiting for a trio of milfs to drink enough to rationalize fuckin' them.

When the party winded down at around one in the morning, Mr. and Mrs. Gorge were arguing about how much blow the other one does in the presence of company because, apparently, there was an acceptable amount. When Phil overheard this from the backyard, relief came over him because he knew by their tones they weren't mad enough to strike each other. Deciphering when it would versus when it wouldn't became second nature to him. Their fights usually classified under the former.

Not paying it much mind, Phil and his buddies were walking to the movie room to sulk in their sexual failures when they heard rumblings in the guest room. Phil carefully nudged the door open and saw one of his father's partners chopping up cocaine on the nightstand while one of Mrs. Gorge's friends had her ass in the air with her heels on looking all types of fucked up. Terry Stone, his father's business partner, noticed the boys and suggested they come in to join them.

"Yeah, come on in. Come on, come on, come on. Do this shit with me. Do this shit with me," he blabbered. Terry gave her a nice smack on the ass, followed by a pleasurable moan.

"Uh, it's ok Mr. Stone, we're just going to watch a movie," Phil said.

"A movie? Are you kidding? You're kidding. Come on, come do this shit with me. Come on."

Caving to the pressure, Phil and his buddies looked at each other and shrugged as if there was no other choice. Chronically sniffling, Terry vigorously lined them up cocaine. During this teaching moment, the high schoolers snorted blow off her ass, downed the beers they originally planned to polish off while watching a movie, and took turns having sex with the woman. She moaned louder and talked dirtier as everyone became more fucked up. Phil didn't think she was coherent enough to know men were alternating being inside of her.

Induced by the cocaine, alcohol, and sexual instincts, no one in the room possessed enough sense to mind the noise they were making.

Unfortunately for them, Mr. and Mrs. Gorge actually ended their argument amicably and heard skin hitting skin and the vocals of sex.

With Mr. Gorge leading the way, Phil's parents barged in the room and immediately halted with widened eyes when they saw what was happening.

"What the fuck are you doing, Terry?" a fuming Mr. Gorge said.

"Oh come on, we're just having a little fun with the boys. They'll be doing this shit in college next year, so they might as well learn how to do it the right way."

"Are you fuckin' kidding me?" Mrs. Gorge said through her teeth, barely managing to speak over her disbelief. In a trembling voice, she continued, "If you don't get out of my house, I'll strangle you myself. You disgusting mother fucker."

"Jesus fuck, get her under control, Gorge. I'll get out of here, but I'm bringing her friend with me," Terry said to Phil's father.

Then all hell broke loose.

Phil's father leaped across the bed, knocking over the woman on his way to spearing Terry against the wall. Too coked out to properly react, Terry found himself pinned on the ground, unable to establish a better position. Mr. Gorge grabbed an empty beer bottle from the nightstand and whacked it across his partner's left cheek, tearing his face open. Mr. Gorge stood up to stomp on Terry's chest while he was still subdued.

Enraged, Mr. Gorge took a second beer bottle and whacked it across the other side of Terry's face. The houseguest was now unrecognizable.

While the beatdown was escalating to the point of it being fatal, Mrs. Gorge shifted her attention to the bed to see one of Phil's friends, the most incoherent one of the bunch, interlocked with her friend. Both grown woman and high schooler were too much in their own world to be aware of the ongoing brawl in the same room. Mrs. Gorge's self-control left her as she hammered her son's friend with a lamp, sending him off the bed. Mrs. Gorge was incessantly slapping her friend in the face, verbally demeaning her as she did it.

Phil, realizing someone had to act like an adult, sobered up and ripped his parents off their respective victims to stop the pandemonium.

When the cops and paramedics arrived, the Gorges and Phil's friends reported Terry was raping the woman, beat her up and that was why Mr. Gorge beat up Terry. To the cops, Phil's friend was an unlucky casualty in the midst of the chaos.

Besides the participants in the afterparty's scuffle, no one else knew what exactly transpired. That no longer rang true when Phil, drunk and emotional one night after a party, told Richard.

Richard and Phil met as freshmen at Rumbus Poly College, or RPC, a niche private university in Los Angeles. Its specialties included how to coexist with A.I. in politics and business. Eighteen, handsome, privileged, and driven, they were eager to join their fathers in their bubble of consolidated wealth.

For the first time in his life, Phil developed an organic friendship with someone who didn't have an existing perception of his life. Someone who would actually listen and hear things from his perspective, rather than brushing off Phil's tough times by sayings things like "Who gives a fuck? You're loaded and getting more pussy than all of us." In high school, Phil was the envy of his peers. In reality, Phil was a troubled soul in need of a comforting presence in his life.

Richard was someone Phil could open up to. Someone who genuinely listened to the emotional toll Phil's life experiences caused him. Phil found comfort in that.

Richard was born and raised in Morple. He never knew his mother, who died giving birth to him. Multiple doctors attributed it to sonoravirus complications from when she had it earlier in life, but other health professionals were adamant the problems she experienced during birth did not point to the virus being the culprit.

He was an only child and his father's pride and joy. Richard was never a victim of domestic hardships rich parents put their privileged children through. After learning more and more about Phil's upbringing, Richard caught himself being happy he did not have two parents. During his childhood and adolescence, Richard longed for a woman's presence, but if it was going to be similar to what Phil underwent, he determined having one adult in his life was one of his life's fortunes. How Richard processed his emotions related to this topic became uncomfortable because it caused him to feel guilty for being grateful his mother was not around.

When Phil vented to Richard about his family's dysfunction, the conversations were one-sided because Richard's home life didn't have much in common with Phil's.

For as long as he could remember, Richard's father was always in his son's corner. He encouraged him to put his best foot forward and embrace the challenges he would encounter on his way to the top. A constant message his father would convey to him was he would always be there for his son, contrary to his work consuming a lot of his time, but when he was there, he was great to Richard.

Richard loved his father but always knew the safety net he provided, mainly financially, stunted his mental development. As he matured, he became aware he lacked confidence inserting himself in social settings. Talking to girls was not easy, making his peers laugh seemed impossible, and being the "cool guy" was never his forte.

Everyone who knew Richard acknowledged he was a looker but would note he hadn't grown into himself yet, or another similar notion.

To Richard, Phil was the person who took him out of his shell. He ignited the previously unknown adventurous side of Richard. Phil showed Richard if he was himself people would gravitate towards him, wanting to be in his circle.

The pair became inseparable. Throughout their four years at RPC, Richard and Phil lived together, were in all the same classes, and chased girls together. After graduation, they both moved to Morple to work for Andy Prescott, a friend of Richard's father who earned his billions as a high-profile publicist in Morple.

Prescott's resume earned him the reputation as one of the most admirable businessmen not only in Morple but in America. He turned political scandals into political opportunities, refrained CEOs from losing their nine-figure salaries, brought venture capitalists' latest projects to fruition, and sold the world on employing Morple's eco-friendly businesses.

Even though various large corporations and even governments employed Prescott, he only worked for one person: Andy Prescott. He was aware how sought out his services were. He knew he was a hot commodity and demanded the compensation he knew he deserved.

Richard and Phil hit the ground running with Prescott. They were, as he liked to call them, his right and left hands. Anything he needed, Richard and Phil handled it.

If there was a speech he forgot to review, a pros and cons list he didn't have a chance to create and evaluate, Richard and Phil would get it done.

After a few years of having the luxury of two tirelessly working proteges at his disposal, Prescott wanted more hungry youngsters at his command in order to expand his influence. He founded Rapture and named Richard and Phil his only VPs. His former hands took the company to new heights and expanded the company's reach to influence organizations Andy never imagined his company would service.

CHAPTER

2089

In his typical destructive fashion, Jonathan Karros barged in his house with Wallace at his side profusely panting, who stared up at him with a look that said, "I'm not taking my eyes off you until I know you're inside safely".

Wallace had cut ears and a six-inch scar on the left side of his neck, evidence of the abuse his former owners would inflict on him. An animal shelter took in Wallace, nursing the once malnourished dog back to health so a loving family, like the Karros's, could save him. The family adopted him thinking he would be everyone's dog, but it soon was apparent his loyalty was to Jonathan.

"Uh, hey Momma," Jonathan said, kissing her on the cheek.

"Hi sweetheart," Robin said, "Do you feel better?"

"Uh, no. I, I, I did a little before when we started but it didn't stay that way. It isn't badder than it was this morning though," Jonathan said. He crouched down to Wallace's height to scratch his right ear as the dog audibly lapped water from his bowl, creating a new mess on the floor Robin just cleaned.

"Oh baby, well you look a lot happier than you did this morning. I have some good news."

Jonathan lit up like a kid who is told he is getting ice cream. The simplicities life had to offer excited Jonathan; a trait Robin admired until she reminded herself it is due to his stunted brain development.

"I was going to take you out to dinner tonight, but public, social gatherings are restricted right now. But the Lawrences invited us over for dinner tonight, and I said yes since I know how much you love going over there."

"Uh, ok cool! Is Moe there? I, I, I want to go now if him and Dillon are there."

"Yeah, he went back with him after school. I'm ready when you are."

"Uh, yeah. I, I, I am going to change though. I, I, I want to put on something nicer. And I, I, I have to feed Wallace and make sure he goes to the bathroom before we go over there. I, I, I don't want him to go in their backyard."

"Ok baby. That's why everyone loves you. You're always so polite."

"Uh, thanks Momma."

Robin told Moe Jonathan was born with a birth defect that prevented his brain from fully developing, but she remained vague about it Moe's entire life. Despite continuous therapy and countless visits to various doctors, no treatment was capable of regulating his brain development. One of the consequences of his mysterious condition was a slight stutter.

Jonathan was very in tune with his surroundings and people in his life, but there was no end in sight for his dependence on being reminded to complete simple, day-to-day tasks. He struggled with straightforward chores most people treated like clockwork. Remembering if food belongs in the fridge or pantry and pulling down his pants before shitting were just two obstacles he regularly confronted.

After Bobby Karros, his stepfather and Moe's father, went missing in 2073, raising Jonathan became more time consuming and difficult. Even though Jonathan was not his biological son, Bobby treated him better than most fathers treat their own. His patience, admiration, and devotion he had for Jonathan was one of the many reasons Robin fell for him so hard.

"Uh ok, I-I-I'm ready Momma," Jonathan said. He came out from his room with Wallace trotting right behind him. The canine was now more at ease and could let his guard down since he could confirm his person wasn't in danger.

Robin looked at her eldest with a proud smile on her face and put her hands on her hips like she was seeing him off to his prom.

"As always you look so handsome," she said. She rubbed his arms down as a sign of affection, which was genuine, but doing so allowed her to smooth out the wrinkles the best she could. Jonathan most likely grabbed his shirt from the hamper as opposed to picking a clean one from his closet.

Under no circumstance did Robin or Moe make Jonathan aware of when he made mistakes like these because they didn't want him to think less of himself. How much pride he had when he accomplished chores on his own was evident by the glow on his face.

"Uh, thanks Momma. I, I, I want to look good for Heather since her house is so nice and she is so nice."

"I'm sure she'll appreciate it. Make sure Wallace goes out and let's head over."

It was hard for Robin to fathom why she thought her eldest son having a crush on her youngest son's friend's mother was so adorable, but his effort to be a gentleman to Heather was too cute to ignore.

CHAPTER

2089

Richard designated his short drive home to catching up with his father.

"Hey Dad, How're you today?" Richard asked his father's hologram on the dashboard of his car.

"Well, well," Reginald Lawrence bellowed in his deep, hoarse voice. "If it isn't my favorite son. How are you, young man?"

"Hopefully I'm your favorite kid and not just your favorite son. Since, you know, you only have one."

"Oh, take a joke, and don't get so sensitive on me now. Enough people have done that to me over the years. If it helps you can always remind me, you're much wealthier than your old man. How's work? How's life?"

Reginald, now with a healthy head of white hair, minimal wrinkles that assisted him in maintaining a youthful appearance for his age, intense brown eyes under thick, gray eyebrows, and always flirting with being fat but never quite becoming so, labeled himself as a lifelong politician. This would be a vague description of his profession since, even though he held office at times, he predominantly lobbied for various Morple companies' interests on a global stage. Reginald represented multiple medical research firms claiming they developed vaccinations for feared viruses. He held board positions and held the hands of generously funded corporations while guiding them to instantaneous profitability. Consulting the brass of several Morple businesses during negotiations for international transactions under the United Nations environmental initiatives earned him the bulk of his wealth. Reginald spent some time in law enforcement and worked with Morple's youth in various capacities.

Being eighty-one Reginald was more familiar with the pre-Morvo Morple than he was with it in 2089. His political philosophies were stubborn and too ingrained in him to progress, halting his perception of minorities to keep up with the times. One of the positive constants in his life was his affinity for his family. Reginald was genuinely proud of Richard's professional and personal accomplishments. Despite how much he poked fun at Richard for obtaining more wealth than himself, Reginald could honestly admit he harbored no resentment. Accumulating a mass fortune was what Reginald raised him to do.

"You know, shit is the same over at the office. It was more fun when we were making the rules, but you know, I guess it means the world is a healthier place. The good news is these businessmen pay well since their livelihoods depend on it, you know? Jobs continue to dwindle no matter who's in office so these mother fuckers know they have to hold on. The bummer is they don't have as much pull as our previous clientele. You know how it goes."

"Oh, that I do. How the fuck do you think your old man made his living?" Reginald chuckled. "Fuck work, you're good at that and are still making a shit ton of money. Even if you are bored. How is Heather? How's Dillon? Mother fuck, I never get to see my grandson or lovely daughter-in-law."

Profanity was a staple in his diction. Business partners constantly fretted he would let one slip at the most paramount of times, especially in a world with eyes on every move. To his credit, he never slipped up and allowed an opportunist to capture a video or audio clip of him being vulgar.

"Well fuck," Richard mocked, "Dillon is doing really well at school and the college discussion has begun. But to be honest, he hasn't decided what he wants to do yet. He recognizes this, and it's fine by me. I'm happy he isn't saying shit just to make me happy."

"He wants to go, right?"

"Yeah, he does. I haven't told him this, but the online two-year route might be a good option. That way he finds his footing and narrows down his options."

"He has to eventually go."

"Yes Dad, I know. Don't worry. He knows that and, when it comes down to it, he doesn't have a choice."

"Okay, good. How's Heather? She doesn't come by anymore to say hello or bring me her cooking. It's the only healthy shit I like for fucks sake!"

"Heather is doing really good."

"Fuck, that's convincing. Is everything okay?"

"Yes Dad, everything is fine. Her and I have just been super busy. We have been meaning to do some catching up, which I need to get on the books sooner rather than later. What would I do without you reminding me?"

"Probably working on not getting completely fucked in a divorce."

"Thanks for your vote of confidence."

"Hey, why don't I come over tonight? I bet Heather is making something good, and I miss seeing you all. Plus, your place is nicer than mine."

Six acres and five thousand square-feet for a single eighty-one-year-old isn't so bad.

"We have company tonight, but what about Monday night? Three nights from now."

"Fuck, I know what day it is. I'm eighty-one, not ninety-one."

Richard couldn't help but smirk at that.

"Just a friendly reminder. I'll let Heather and Dillon know we are on for Monday night. You're bringing Wilford, right?"

Richard knew his father would bring his old Airedale Terrier with him but liked hearing how worked up he got whenever he questioned it.

"Oh fuck! Of course, I am! You think I'm just going to leave him home alo—"

"Dad, Dad I know! Okay, Wilford and you are coming over on Monday for dinner. I'll make sure Frank and Finn are worn out, so they don't bombard the old man."

"Good. He can't play how he used to for fuck's sake."

"Okay, Dad. I'm happy you picked up. I'll see you Monday. Be good, I love you."

"I love you too, Richard. Tell the family I love them and can't wait to see them."

"I will."

Richard turned off his father's hologram as he cruised further down Lawrence Drive.

CHAPTER

2089

Richard enthusiastically greeted Robin and Jonathan as he jumped out of the back of his self-automated car once it rolled to a stop in his driveway. How excited he was every time he saw them used to irritate Robin because she didn't believe it was genuine. She couldn't quite identify what exactly, but something about him initially rubbed her the wrong way. But as their sons grew closer Robin developed a particular fondness for him. Richard became someone she ended up admiring.

"Richard, hello. How are you?" Robin smiled back at him while Wallace and her guided Jonathan safely out of their car. His clumsiness frequently resulted in falls.

"Doing great, how are you?" Richard asked. He kissed Robin's cheek and hugged her. "Hi Jonathan, how are you bud?"

"Uh, hi Mr. Law— Richard!" Jonathan stuttered, "How ar-ar-are you?"

"I'm doing good, doing good, thanks for asking. How is Wallace?" he asked. He crouched down to scratch the top of Wallace's head.

"Uh, uh, we're good. We had class today and are hungry now."

"Well, you've come to the right place. Let's get inside."

Robin exchanged a close-mouthed smile with Richard. She adored him for the soft spot he had for her boys, particularly Jonathan. She worried bringing Wallace was imposing, but Richard insisted he was always welcome.

As the three of them, plus Wallace, walked to the exterior door that led them inside, Robin caught a glimpse of someone familiar. Out of the corner of her eye, she saw a face she hadn't seen in nearly twenty years through the window laughing with Heather. Shock paralyzed the rest of her thoughts.

When they finally entered the Lawrence residence, Frank and Finn galloped to the door, their nails slapping against the tile. Wallace released his deep bark to announce his arrival. Rough housing between the three of them quickly ensued, as it usually does with three young males, humans or dogs.

"Oh, hi sweetheart," Heather said before giving her husband a kiss. She greeted their guests, "Hey Karros clan." She gave Robin a peck on the cheek and Jonathan a big hug around his neck.

"This is my friend, Ariana. Her and I have been working out together a lot lately but thought we'd relax together on our off day."

Robin didn't hear anything Heather said after making eye contact with her sister.

"Hi Ariana, Richard Lawrence. It's super nice to meet you."

Richard couldn't have been any less subtle checking out Ariana's breasts.

After exchanging pleasantries with Richard, Ariana said, "Hi, so nice to meet both of you," nonchalantly, as if she wasn't seeing her older sister for the first time in nearly two decades.

Jonathan shyly told her he had to go keep an eye on Wallace.

Ariana's hand lingered in Robin's. Both sisters suppressed their urges to reveal the emotions that were beginning to resurface.

"He's very shy. It's very nice to meet you, Ariana," Robin said.

"Oh, he's adorable. Moe is, too. You are very blessed to have them both."

"Well, thank you."

"Ladies, excuse me. I'm going to get into something more comfortable and will be back shortly. Heather darling, there are a couple more bottles of that merlot we like. Open that up and I'll see you soon," Richard said.

"Robin, you know where the wine is. I'm running to the bathroom but open it and feel free to pour yourselves a couple glasses. I'll be back shortly," Heather said, shuffling away.

"Shall we then?" Ariana said with raised eyebrows and arms crossed.

After what felt like another lifetime, Robin accepted she would never see Ariana again, let alone encounter her at the Lawrences. Her little sister radiated confidence, a sense of purpose. The Ariana Robin grew up with lived in fear every waking moment, constantly distraught, and with good reason.

As they walked in the bar area, numerous scenarios went through Robin's head: *Did Richard and Heather set this up? Is Ariana here to break bad news? Has she been living in Morple this entire time? Has Moe met her before?*

Like it was a sixth sense, Ariana peered her head back and said just above a whisper, "Can you please calm down? It's good to see you too, by the way."

Ariana took a seat at the bar as Robin took out some merlot, only taking out three glasses since she herself wasn't much of a drinker.

"How about you tell me what is going on? I haven't seen you in twenty years and you just appear here. I've been worried about you Ariana. You ca—"

"I've been living my life, Robin. Working on myself to find my place in this God forsaken world. Sorry you haven't been around to con—"

"Hi Mom," Moe said slowly. He treaded lightly, immediately gathering the conversation he intruded on was not warm and fuzzy. "How are you doing?"

"Oh, hi hon," Robin said, walking out from behind the bar to hug her son. "I'm good, how are you? I'm just happy it's Friday. I was just getting to know Heather's friend, Ariana."

"Now I know where you get your charm from," Ariana said to Moe, ingesting a much needed gulp of wine.

"Yeah," Moe blushed. "Okay, I just wanted to say hi. We're outside throwing the football around. We'll see you out there for dinner."

"Okay darling."

As Moe ran back outside, Robin turned to Ariana, "Now isn't the time, but you will eventually tell me what's going on here. You know I at least deserve that."

Ariana took another nervous sip of wine, pushing her hair back behind her ears. She didn't know if she'd ever be able to tell her sister the truth.

CHAPTER

2089

"Uh, I, I, I really like their house. It's really big and nice, but our house is better, Momma," Jonathan said.

After every visit to the Lawrences, he told his mother how much he liked their home better. Jonathan was in the backseat so Wallace could situate himself in his preferred place: body across the seat with his bulky head on his best friend's lap getting scratched.

"Sweetheart, that means a lot to me," Robin said. She smiled at him through her rearview mirror like it was the first time he told her this. Whether or not he realized he regularly expressed this, she didn't know, but hearing him say it never got old.

"I want our house to always be a special place for us and to always be a place we enjoy being," she added.

Their modest home in The District was nothing compared to the Lawrence mansion. Its worth and aesthetics weren't comparable, but what it did have was sentimental value. It was under two thousand square feet with three bedrooms, two bathrooms, and a tight-knit family.

"What are you thinking about?" Robin asked Moe. Her youngest was gazing out of the front passenger window.

"Ariana."

Robin smirked. She wasn't very surprised a young man with raging hormones had Ariana on his mind. Too bad for him they came from the same bloodline.

"Yes, she was nice. Have you ever met her before?" she asked.

"Uh, yeah. I, I, I liked her too," Jonathan chimed in.

"Have I? No," Moe said, "I could tell Richard liked her, too."

"Okay, stop. It was funny at first, but stop with that," his mother responded.

"You've met her before, right?" Moe said softly.

"Excuse me?" she said.

"I asked if you've met her before," Moe said, speaking up and turning to face her.

"And what's that supposed to mean?"

"I'm just asking if you've met her before."

"You're insinuating I know her, but I don't. I've never seen her there before. Have you?"

Jonathan was so engrossed in soothing Wallace he didn't observe his mother and brother were having an argument disguised by small talk.

"No, I haven't. It was just a vibe I got, I guess. You don't have to get angry. Sorry," Moe said.

The rest of the ride home was silent.

Coddling his third wodin since dinner, Richard caught himself enthralled with Ariana, whose right hand rested on her breast, laughing at some story Heather was having trouble finishing telling because of how funny she found it. From his chair adjacent to the couch they were on, Richard smiled when they looked his way to feign his level of engagement. He had no idea what his wife was saying, nor did he care. Unless it involved high-paying clients, settings that required him to be loquacious didn't appeal to Richard. He preferred his personal time to be spent on the golf course or home with a glass of wodin, and, at this very moment, Heather's hot friend.

Luckily for him and Heather, Dillon's idea of a good night was similar to his father's. He stayed home most weekend nights and tolerated them until they finished their first post-dinner drink. As he took a sip that pleasantly burned his chest, Richard thought to himself Dillon could be out and about while Heather and him would drink into oblivion every weekend.

Heather, whose smile was second to none, was shamelessly exposing her purple teeth as she laughed so hard, she had to hold her stomach intact. Her inability to control her laughter was one of the main reasons Richard fell so hard for her.

"No, no, no, stop!" Heather managed to yell out in between her laughter.

"I swear! That's how it was, oh my gosh. Oh, that's too good," Ariana said as they got their laughter under control and caught their breaths.

"Richard, I'm so sorry. Here I am in your house, and I'm just off on a tangent with your wife practically ignoring you. Excuse my manners, but she's just too fun!" Ariana said, squeezing Heather's shoulder.

"Oh no, please. You're a great guest. Anyone who makes my beautiful wife laugh is always welcome in our home."

"Well thank you, I appreciate that. I'm sorry, I don't even think I mentioned how gorgeous your home is. It's just so easy to tell how much care has been put into it. A lot of the homes in this area are so big and have so much potential, but they don't have a cozy feel to them, you know? This one has that element a lot of the others lack. It just shows it all depends on who lives there."

"Ah, well that's a credit to Heather," Richard said as he gestured to cheers his wife. "She set her mind to it and made this a home for us three. Five if you include the dogs."

Heather smiled tightly and sipped her wine.

"Ariana, you say 'a lot of the homes I'm in in this area' so do you sell real estate?" Richard asked.

"No," she said more abruptly than she meant to, "Well, not anymore."

The first awkward silence of the night took place because Richard expected Ariana to elaborate, but she was a little too buzzed to think clearly and play her part. Knowing alcohol prohibited her from being the best possible version of herself would disappoint LaVonte.

Richard ended it. "Oh wow, that's great. I'm sorry, I didn't catch what you do now." He didn't really know what was so great about not doing it anymore, but it filled the void.

"Oh, now I spend a lot of time traveling with my husband."

"Is that what brought you to Morple?" he asked.

These small talk questions caught Ariana off guard. She had rehearsed it with LaVonte, but apparently, she still needed time to shake the rust off.

"Oh, uh, no. I'm here staying at our house just to get away. He, uh, has some friends visiting him back home, so I let the boys have some time to themselves."

"I see. Where's your place here? And sorry, where's home?"

"It's in The District, and California."

Ariana's vagueness didn't go unnoticed by Richard, but he thought asking her more questions would come off as rude, especially as a host. Ariana claiming her house was in The District confounded him, too. For someone who appeared as wealthy as Ariana, Richard would've thought she'd have property in Costa Mor, but then again, if someone felt the need to flaunt it, she was probably full of shit.

"Wow, that's great," was all Richard could muster up.

Heather exchanged a look with her husband that said he had asked enough questions already.

"I'm going to excuse myself and smoke my Friday joint with Frank and Finn. Ariana, I don't know your plan, but you're more than welcome to stay here. I know we've had a lot so if you don't feel up to heading all the way back to The District, please, feel free to stay."

The subtle shot didn't get by Ariana.

"You're so thoughtful hon, I thought she could sleep in the upstairs guest room," Heather chimed in.

"Perfect," Richard said as he bent over to kiss Heather. "Great meeting you Ariana."

"So great to meet you too, Richard."

Ariana told herself she was going to have to be much sharper if she wanted to accomplish what she came back to Morple for, and Robin being so close to the Lawrences didn't make matters any easier.

She's apparently a rich guy's wife, Richard texted Phil while puffing a joint overlooking the dark ocean.

Who is? Phil immediately replied. This told Richard his best friend wasn't able to reel anything in that night.

Heather's hot friend. Her name's Ariana.

Who cares? Was he around?

No. She didn't go into much detail about him. It was kind of weird come to think of it.

Well thanks for putting in the good word and the invite.

I'm holding out hope for a threesome before I throw her your way.

Oh Jesus, if I'm waiting on that I'll never get a shot.

Funny. See you bright and early on the tee box.

See you then, winner gets to bang Heather.

Phil's golf game was much more refined than Richard's, which is what was supposed to make his jest so funny.

CHAPTER

2089

Ariana considered herself extremely fortunate her evening with Richard and Heather Lawrence wasn't a complete debacle. How unprepared she was really irked her, causing her to feel worthless to her husband. If LaVonte had been a fly on the wall during their post-dinner gathering, she would've received an earful, and deservingly so. Because of the alcohol and because Richard couldn't stop staring at her tits, she had gotten away with a sloppy showing. She'd be sure to let a decent amount of time pass before she encountered Richard again. That way she would get a clean slate. Besides, now she had plenty to keep her occupied.

The smoothest Ariana was the entire night was when she maintained her cool as she was "introduced" to Robin and Jonathan. Seeing them in the Lawrences' entryway shell shocked her to the point she thought she would faint. Ariana knew avoiding contacting Robin would be difficult, but now it was going to be impossible. It took everything Ariana had to refrain from breaking down and embracing Robin when it was just the two of them in the Lawrences' bar.

Leaving Morple after Morvo was the wise decision, but what unraveled shortly after constantly ate away at Ariana. This is partly why LaVonte wanted her to remain separated from the only family she had left; the other part was because he preferred his wife to remain under his control.

Ariana's life with LaVonte had its limitations, yes, but it also had its perks. The truth was he truly cared about her. He allowed her to make decisions, experience what power feels like, and of course showered her with an exuberant lifestyle only billions could buy. Being Mrs. Jackson got her further in life than struggling as Miss Soren ever would, but now that she was back in Morple, she questioned for the first time whether or not it was worth it.

Ariana thought about Robin and her boys quite frequently, but unexpectedly encountering them stirred up emotions she had been burying for quite some time. The other night provided her with a glimpse of what her life would have been like if she had stayed in Morple, exposing her to the family she would have had to lean on. Ariana wouldn't have been as rich or as powerful, but she would've been surrounded by people she cared about and who cared about her.

Ariana had always longed for her life to involve Robin again, but the flurry of emotions she felt after seeing her nephews as young men blindsided her. Being a nonexistent sister polluted her thoughts more than being an absent aunt, but now that she had encountered both Jonathan and Moe, she felt obligated to play a role in their lives.

Thinking back to the afternoon Heather introduced her to Moe, something about him intrigued Ariana. Now it was obvious: his resemblance to Robin was undeniable. Those striking hazel eyes that were so distinctive for his dark, Latin skin tone should've been enough to indicate he was her sister's son.

No matter what distractions presented themselves, Ariana had a job to do, and she wouldn't let anything deter her from accomplishing it.

LaVonte purchased the condo Ariana was staying in because he needed a place to stay when he would be in Morple on business. If she had it her way, he would have purchased a property in Costa Mor, but LaVonte argued it would draw too much attention. Ariana couldn't argue against that. A fully tattooed Black man and his Latina wife would have turned heads in a neighborhood full of White families residing in mansions peering over the ocean from 150 feet up. Their Black security detail carrying Barrett REC7 rifles and Desert Eagles would distress the neighbors, too. Costa Mor residents relied on A.I. security systems, but LaVonte didn't trust computers to protect him and his wife. Persuading him to let her go to

Morple without security was a chore, but he eventually caved. Ariana insisted it would make fitting in more difficult, something she was already having trouble with. A concession she had to make in order to get LaVonte to agree to send her to Morple without any of his men was she was required to check in with him more often than she usually would.

Although Ariana's preferred Morple home would've been in Costa Mor, there wasn't much about the flat she could complain about. With five bedrooms and six bathrooms, it was bigger than most houses on the island. One of the ways Morple gentrified The District was by tearing down rundown apartments that were once homes to diswors who could no longer afford their rent-controlled rates. To replace those obsolete buildings, real estate developers built luxurious condos under the premise they would serve as second homes to executives who frequented Morple for business. The initiative worked, attracting billionaires from all over the country and world to invest in The District's real estate. Since the state's capital was now hosting the world's one-percent community, it had to ensure it could provide entertainment so their stays were enjoyable. This led to the city's uptick in fine dining establishments, legislators allocating more funding for infrastructure, the implementation of modern architecture, and creating a more attractive destination.

The Jackson's condo was on the top floor of the city's most expensive building, providing Ariana with a bird's eye view of the city that raised her. All of the best restaurants to eat in The District were right below her, a quick jaunt from her building. The surrounding area demonstrated affluence, but as she lifted her gaze, she could see the neighborhoods where the people whose families had lived in Morple since its inception lived. Swiftly, development pushed them to the undesirable, underdeveloped outskirts of the city. After the next cycle of expansion, Ariana didn't think they'd have anywhere to go. This contributed to her reason for moving out of Morple so quickly.

If Ariana couldn't have a spot in Costa Mor, it would be this specific condo. She was so gung-ho about it because the vantage point gave her a view of Robin's home, one within the boundaries of where The District's wealthy residents called home. Until now, Ariana never expected to spend any time staying here, but knowing they owned property that could see her sister comforted her.

The last time Ariana checked in with LaVonte she informed him her past had already collided with her present. Usually one to boast about being right, LaVonte surprised her by demonstrating empathy towards how this affected his wife. Yes, he assured Ariana her original purpose was to remain her primary focus, but he was less concerned about it than she anticipated he would be.

"Take advantage of the time to see her and her kids. You may never have the opportunity again, so make the most out of it," he told her. Her husband didn't say the last part in a threatening way, but she understood it was his way of telling her he would never allow her to go to Morple again. Which was probably best for her conscience, anyways.

"Thanks, baby. I still want to make you proud," she said.

"And you will. You've been a good soldier, and that won't stop now. When you come back home, we will have some new ass to play with. I showed you to my favorites, and they can't wait."

A pillar of LaVonte's operation was keeping his men happy by allowing them to supply themselves with women. His men kidnapped them in the same cities they captured diswors and returned them to the plantation to live in houses scattered among the property. His crew essentially brainwashed them into believing life on the plantation was better than anything they'd get in the real world. With jobs decimating, industries collapsing, and the gap between the rich and poor widening, convincing the girls the plantation life was their best chance to escape uncertainty and poverty wasn't too difficult. With all these extra women at their disposal, LaVonte and Ariana often engaged in menages a trois.

"That makes me want to come home to you sooner," she said.

Having new girls available aroused Ariana, as she found pleasure in her and her husband's untraditional way of lusting. Discovering her infatuation with women added another element to her sex life but exercising the control over them was what really stimulated Ariana. Mentioning this to her was a calculated move by LaVonte, since he knew his wife revered the power dynamic they shared over the plantation's women.

After touching base with her husband, Ariana dedicated the night to self-care. She had a bottle of wodin delivered to the condo and immediately began sedating herself with its contents. Sitting on her balcony, absorbing the expansive view of the city that was responsible for killing the livelihoods of millions of innocent people, a sense of reassurance regarding her purpose came over her. For as long as she could remember, Ariana had constantly worked towards pleasing others, both voluntary and involuntary. Nothing in her life revolved around what was best for her. In that moment, with a dense glass of wodin encouraging her inner monologue, she decided Ariana was going to do what was best for Ariana. The self-empowering thoughts combined with the buzz that was starting to kick in excited her, leading her to handle her titillation by herself.

CHAPTER

10

2089

Marty Perlman's features subjected him to onlookers' judgements and assumptions. He was five-foot-seven with white Jew curls that told his adversaries interpreting the law in their favor versus his would be arduous.

Marty grew up as an only child in Agoura Hills, California, a suburb with a prevalent Jewish community about thirty-five miles north of Los Angeles.

The Perlman family was part of the one-percent community but lived modestly. Sally Perlman, his mother, took care of the house in their affluent gated neighborhood and dedicated herself to raising Marty. His father, David Perlman, was the head honcho at a wealth management firm. Retired athletes, celebrities, commercial realtors, and big-time board members with limitless bank accounts accounted for his clientele. David was particular about whose money he grew and wasn't bashful to turn away business generated by someone who made him feel uncomfortable.

"I don't care what the upside is. Don't ever get involved with people you don't feel comfortable with, and your gut tells you otherwise. It will lead to trouble and make you remorseful in the end because all of the headaches it caused could've been avoided," David once told a ten-year-old Marty.

David's principles made a long-lasting impression on his son.

Marty's love of the law developed while attending the University of California Los Angeles in the early 2020s. Being in a liberal city during a tumultuous time in America, Marty was conscientious of the world's injustice. Coming off the recent killings of Ahmaud Arbery and George Floyd in 2020, Marty immersed himself in a proactive, progressive, and disruptive student body.

Iconic demonstrations and riots occurred the weekend after Floyd's death. By that time, the country was a few months into its quarantine because of the novel coronavirus, adding to the frustration of injustice. President Donald Trump's lack of initiative, inciteful comments, and loyalty to his base, a substantial amount consisting of proud racists, during this hardship amplified the tension.

Especially since law enforcement killing members of the African American community was a common occurrence.

In July 2020, a journalist asked President Trump why African Americans were still dying at the hands of law enforcement in the US. He immediately answered, "So are White people, so are White people. What a terrible question to ask. So are White people. More White people, by the way. More White people."

Arbery and Floyd were not the only notable Black people senselessly killed in that era.

Breonna Taylor, shot in her sleep.

Steven Taylor, shot in a Walmart.

Philando Castile, killed during a traffic stop.

Walter Scott, shot on the run.

Tamir Rice, a twelve-year-old killed at a park.

Michael Brown, shot six times.

Eric Garner, wrestled to the ground before dying from a chokehold.

The roots of the justice system's fatal flaws did not start in 2020. In fact, police brutality may have been less frequent, but smart phones and the Internet exposed when they did occur. Progress was not moving fast enough.

Hearing stories from Americans across the country suffering from unlawfulness resonated with Marty. As a proud member of the Jewish community, he took the time to educate himself on his own ancestors' experiences in concentration camps during World War II. He took it upon himself to be well versed on the consequences of mass incarceration.

Learning how harmful the Thirteenth Amendment and organizations like the American Legislative Exchange Council were for minorities, particularly Blacks, made Marty's blood boil. As he delved deeper into its damaging effects and discovered how prevalent they still were in society, Marty familiarized himself with the works of those like Bryan Stevenson, a lawyer whose life's work revolved around exonerating wrongfully convicted prisoners and removing them from death row before it was too late. Despite the sad realities he became privy to, Marty found inspiration in this. It was then he identified his calling was to fight for those in need. Marty dedicated his life to fixing a broken system most were too afraid to stand up to.

Coronavirus allowed Marty's whereabouts to be flexible when it came to his undergraduate and law school classes. His professors allowed him and his peers to attend lectures and take tests virtually, and as traveling by car became more common, Marty found himself on the road more often than he ever imagined, heading from one Airbnb to the next with a group of social justice warriors he met at a time classes still met in-person. He spent the next twenty years driving around the country further educating himself on the pitfalls of America's history, becoming an activist in parts of the country needing it the most, demonstrating in front of the White House, raising hell on Wall Street, exposing Silicon Valley's finest intrusive practices in their own backyard, and attending political rallies of candidates he supported all while finishing up school on the go.

By the end of his journey, Marty's resume consisted of endless accolades and an impressive education.

It wasn't until after his country-wide social justice tour when Marty began to turn his attention to Morple's corruption and systemic racism. He had discovered his niche.

"Knock, knock," Robin said, tip toeing into Marty's office, forgoing actually knocking.

Marty's left index finger leaned alongside the left side of his face as he read what Robin assumed was an important document in his other hand. He had a pronounced wrinkle in between his eyes and was hesitant to acknowledge her, a telltale he was hyper focused.

"Oh, well hello my dear," Marty said. "Jeez, is it already one o'clock? I'm sorry, I was going to have Carrie bring in lunch for us."

"Please, please. Don't worry about that. I didn't come to mooch off your firm's expenses."

"Always so witty Robin. Please, sit," Marty said. Like the gentleman he was, he pulled out the chair opposite of his.

Marty's office stood a couple blocks from the governor's building in The District, a building flooded with his foes. Perlman Law occupied the nineteenth floor in a modern building with numerous corporations, mainly ones in the public sector that were in cahoots with the state and federal government. His firm had one hundred twenty-five employees, almost an unimaginable amount in 2089, consisting of legal secretaries, legal assistants, paralegals, court-runners, lawyers, and more. All of them adored Marty. Employees received fair treatment, earned promotions they rightfully earned, and were told when it was time to move on to bigger and better things when there wasn't room for growth at Perlman Law. Marty was a man of character and committed to his principles. These qualities attributed to his financial success and enabled him to create real change in a world that saddened him more often than not.

His employees also felt safe working at Perlman Law not only because it was the biggest disruptor working against Morple's corruption, but also because everyone's health was prioritized. An abundant amount of hand sanitizer was readily available, and the office had a machine taking everyone's temperatures upon entering and exiting the building. If his employees weren't comfortable with doing so, Marty didn't require them to be physically present at the most important of meetings. If they felt safer as holograms, that sufficed.

After living through two pandemics and approaching ninety, health was extremely important to Marty and everyone under the Perlman Law umbrella.

"So, what's going on? I didn't see any notes next to your name on the schedule. I don't know why you called Carrie to schedule an appointment when you know you can always let me know you want to come in. Or you could just pop in unannounced. You know this."

Marty truly loved Robin. She was the daughter he never had. Marty's wife of fifty-four years died in a two-car, both unmanned, accident in

2084. They never had kids, and he was too heartbroken to entertain the idea of dating again. Especially at his age.

"I know, I know. But you're busy, and I didn't want to bug you. Plus, I was thinking about cancelling, and booking it through Carrie makes it easier to do that than if I directly told you I was coming."

He exchanged a close-mouthed smile with Robin.

"Well is everything okay?" he asked.

"Yeah, yeah. Everything's fine. It's just, something odd happened the other night. Someone resurfaced."

"Someone who legally isn't allowed to?" Marty inched forward when he heard this; his interest piqued.

"No, but someone you wouldn't have thought would."

"Robin, you've known me for years and know I don't like beating around the bush. Get it out alre–."

"Ariana."

The lawyer's blank expression told Robin this news caught him off guard.

"Really? Did she find you? Did you just run into her?"

"We were at the Lawrences' last Friday for dinner. Me and the boys," Robin said, seeking composure from within.

"It's okay. Take as much time as you need to here," Marty said in the comforting tone Robin needed to hear at that very moment.

She snagged tissues off Marty's desk and wiped her eyes and nose before continuing.

"She was just there with Heather."

"Heather is Mrs. Lawrence, correct?"

"Yes, and they were acting like they've known each other for years. And all of these crazy thoughts started going through my head. I didn't know how to feel. It just brought back so many dark memories."

It took everything Robin had to get out the last part before sobbing. Ariana and she suffered inexplicable amounts of physical and emotional pain together. And when Ariana moved out of Morple, she had purposely lost touch with her older sister, leaving Robin wondering what had become of her after all these years.

"Robin, dear. Let's take some deep breaths here and think about this. Maybe Ariana found her footing and is getting her life back on track."

Marty's optimism is what kept Robin afloat during her legal battle against the Morple Youth Movement. He fought for her well-deserved settlement all while playing the role of a therapist. Marty had become a father figure to Robin, but she was having difficulty aligning with his thought process right now.

"I don't know, Marty. You know how screwed up she was. She didn't even want your help. She couldn't come out of that dark place. And then she just reappears like this. For her to come out of the woodwork like this is just too much. I always thought the worst ended up happening to her."

Robin's sniffles and suppressed cries were the only things audible in Marty's office. He knew he couldn't say anything reassuring Robin would believe. He regularly went against the most conniving individuals in the court of law and saw right through them, but this particular situation was a curveball he didn't see coming.

"I love her, Marty."

"Robin, you are sisters. That's an unbreakable bond, no matter the circumstances. You fought for her as passionately as you fought for yourself all those years. If you're thinking you could've done more, you need to take a deep breath and remember how hard you worked to change her mind so she could better herself. Sometimes people just need to figure out things on their own terms. How did she seem?"

"That was the weirdest part about the whole thing." Robin's eyes were wider and focused on something obscure. "She just acted as if she was running into a casual friend she hadn't seen in years. Like how you run into someone at the grocery store you know but don't know well enough to actually want to talk to, you know?"

Marty stared at her, unsure if she expected him to answer her rhetorical question.

"She goes, 'I've been living my life, Robin. Working on myself to find my place in this God forsaken world.' Her tone made it feel like she blames me for her life."

"I don't have to remind you of this, but I'm going to anyway. This all goes back to her being in that dark, dark place she was in. Getting her out of it was impossible. Maybe she has finally found a way to deal with it and move on. It might not be the healthiest way or one you approve of. But if it's working for her then who are we to intervene?"

Robin digested his perspective as she stared out of the window at a city that caused her and her family so much turmoil. Yet, for reasons she couldn't explain, it enamored her. Her life wouldn't be what it was if it weren't for tragedies, torture, and tribulations. She wouldn't appreciate the blessings as much as she did if it weren't for her misfortunes. Maybe this was another hurdle for her to overcome, and reinsert her long, lost sister back in her life.

"What's going through that brain of yours?" Marty asked.

"Nothing in particular."

"Oh, I doubt that."

Robin finally made eye contact with her long-time confidant.

"Look Robin," Marty said. "Let me talk to you as your lawyer for a second."

"Get it over with."

"If anything else happened you're not telling me about, like certain people violating the terms of our agreement or you feeling threatened, please let me know."

Robin's perturbed stare told him she wasn't omitting any details.

"Okay, great. Back to being your friend," Marty said, gesturing his hands in surrender.

"Please."

"Let's try to get her to meet with you. Maybe if we can get you all in the same room you can express yourself to her. She can to you, and that will help both of you through this. Maybe you two will be part of each other's lives again. Wouldn't that be something?"

Tears streamed down Robin's face as mixed emotions ran through her. Morphing her two lives into one would be a step in the right direction for her mental state and for her boys, especially Moe.

"I didn't even get her phone number," Robin said, defeated.

"You have to come up with a better excuse than that."

"Okay, let me think about it. Thanks for being you, Marty. It means a lot, you know," Robin said.

"And I always will be. You have about seventy-five million reasons to thank me, and I'll happily hear them anytime."

Marty finally got a chuckle out of Robin.

"You're too much. Come by and see us soon, yeah?"

"Absolutely. Just call me and let me know when. Don't call Carrie either because then you might uninvite me over, and that would just be awkward."

Robin always knew paying a visit to Marty would cheer her up.

"Okay, thanks Marty."

"Goodbye dear, we'll talk soon."

Two old friends hugged goodbye and thought to themselves how lucky each one was to have the other.

CHAPTER

2089

"Hello, hello. Is anyone there?" Reginald bellowed as he let himself in his son's mansion. Frank and Finn bolted to the front door to smell the intruder, barking to acknowledge their presence.

"Oh fuck, Richard. I thought you said these dogs would be tired. They're going to stress out Wilford."

"Hi Reginald!" Heather yelled over the barking.

"Ah, always a grand entrance for the great Mr. Reginald Lawrence," Richard said.

Richard trotted down the stairs while rolling up the sleeves of his button-down so they gripped his arms just below the crease of his elbows. "They express their excitement to see their grandpa a little differently than we do, that's all."

"If the old man has a heart attack, it's their fault," Reginald said.

"When you say 'old man' you have to be more specific."

Reginald laughed off his son's smart-ass remark.

"It's good to see you. It feels like it has been too long," Reginald said as father and son embraced each other.

"Great to see you too, Dad. Want a drink?"

"No, at eighty-one I've decided to live a life of sobriety. Yes, I want a fuckin' drink."

"Hi Grandpa," Dillon said. His trot down the stairs mimicked his father's. "How are you?"

"Dillon, my boy. You're getting more mature looking every time I see you. How are you?"

"I'm good, what about you?"

Avoiding eye contact, Dillon halfheartedly hugged his grandpa before expressing more genuine affection to Wilford.

"I'm happy to be here. Where's your mother? Heather!"

"Heading to the back with your drink already in hand, come join me!"

The three Lawrence men and three wound up canines headed out to meet her. Richard and Dillon moved fast so walking at Reginald's pace felt awkward to them. Even Frank and Finn seemed dumbfounded as to why it took so long to get outside.

Heather had glasses of wodin poured for her father-in-law and husband and beer for Dillon. A glass of merlot accompanied her.

"Hi sweetheart. It is so good to see you," Reginald said, his hug pressing his daughter-in-law into him tight.

"Hi handsome. Great to see you, too. I'm so glad you came over. Please, sit."

Reginald eased himself down into a patio chair and accepted his drink from Heather, one with contents equivalent to three pours.

"Ah, thank you Heather. Dillon, fuck you're already drinking!"

His grandson's face reddened, "Only on special occasions, but you know, it is legal now."

"Oh fuck, that's right. I can't keep up. How's school? Where are you headed after this year?"

"I don't know yet. I've been thinking about it and doing courses online at first could be a good move since I don't know exactly what I want to do yet. We'll see. I'm thinking about it though."

He didn't elaborate much in an effort to deflect the topic.

"As long as you're thinking about it, that's good. You know you can always come to me for advice, right? But fuck, your dad is more successful than your grandfather so just go to him. He's smarter than me, too," Reginald said.

"I had to learn it from someone," Richard said.

"Enough of money and school," Heather said. "How are you, Reginald? How are you keeping that brilliant mind of yours entertained?"

"Well, this helps," he said, raising his glass. "But you know Heather. Once you've lived the type of life I have lived, you know, one that has allowed me to live as comfortably as I do you spend a lot of time reflecting. You think about where the time has gone, but at the same time, how much work was put in during all those years. It went by so quickly yet so slowly all at the same time. But I have nothing to complain about.

"I'm excited for you, for my son, and grandson to keep thriving, keep pushing forward all while prioritizing this." Reginald opened his arms at the three of them to emphasize their importance. He sipped wodin to clear his throat.

"Words from the wise, Dillon. Take note of it," Richard said in his best father-teaching-son-moment voice.

"I'm happy you're able to reflect proudly on what you've accomplished, Reginald," Heather said. "You've accomplished a lot personally and professionally. You should be happy. Make sure every day counts."

Her father-in-law couldn't help but laugh at that one.

"I'm sorry. That's not what I meant," she said in a failed attempt to retract her implying death was in the near future.

"No need to apologize, sweetheart. The time comes for everyone. Right now, I have all of you, Wilford, and for the time being, my health. My biggest concern is what type of world Dillon here will be working in one day. Back when I was a true, working man, there was much more structure. Not everyone could just do whatever the fuck they wanted. You had to adhere to laws, and I am proud to say our family contributed towards establishing order here in Morple.

"Dillon, your great-grandfather put his life on the line to keep the rest of the world safe by committing himself to quarantine with high-risk citizens in the thirties and forties. Once they were allowed out, I dedicated the early part of my career to helping their offspring not turn this beautiful place into a complete shit show. Back then, there were rules. Now, everything seems to be fair game; everything is acceptable. For the last, I don't know, twenty years, as long as you are neither White or successful you get a free pass. Meanwhile, it was us who got this place off the ground. Believe me, these beggars out there wanting everything to be handed to them didn't do shit."

"Alright, alright, Dad. We don't need to discuss any of that tonight," Richard said, doing his best to avert a monologue no one wanted to hear.

Ignoring his son's plea, Reginald continued, "I don't want any opportunity taken from this family because we were guilted into trying to make amends for how criminals and irresponsible citizens were treated. Us Whites worked our fuckin' asses off to establish a place for them to be safe in, and now we have to sacrifice *our* success so they can get a piece. *We* advanced sustainable industries; *we* established this country's fifty-first state; *we* deserve what's rightfully ours.

"I worked my ass off to try and educate their youth, make them contributing members of society, and all they did was complain and attempted to overthrow the government. All I'm saying is, look out for yourselves out there because if you don't, no one else will. That is unless your skin is brown or bl—."

"Dad, that is enough. We are not going to talk about this tonight, okay?"

Heather sipped her wine more frequently. Dillon mimicked her nervous behavior with his beer.

"They have played victim for so long. All that will cause is trouble for you and undeserved success for them. Especially you, Dillon. It worries me for what your future holds."

Dillon glared at his grandfather, "Grandpa, it is widely known that Morple's camps back in the day was a way for big business to become less dependent on workers and move towards using artificial intelligence, hence why there aren't any jobs anymore. The whole pandemic was a hoax; it was just an excuse for the government to pull that bullshit."

"A hoax? Boy, your own family helped save the world from it. How dare you call it a hoax," Reginald said.

"Yeah, a hoax. The evidence spells it out. In those fifteen years working jobs for Black and Brown people had disappeared. It is easy to take something away from people if they're trapped on a remote island and aren't able to do anything about it."

Richard and Heather exchanged dumbfounded expressions with one another. Dillon had never thrust himself into a debate pertaining to politics, nor had he ever revealed his opinions on Morple's history. His passion, position, and boldness baffled his parents, especially since he challenged Reginald so directly.

"Oh, don't listen to that crap the media feeds us, Dillon. All of it is nonsense. If Mexicans and Blacks wanted a fair shot, they should've kept themselves and others healthy. Do not let any of that bullshit convince you this had anything to do with us wanting to leave them jobless. It's all bullshit. We get blamed because we are capable of creating opportunity for ourselves, and they aren't. They're worthless, Dillon. Completely, utterly worthless. Once you begin making your own money and see how they want a piece of it to feed themselves and their young, you'll make sense of it.

"Please, this is America. They had all the same chances we did. Unfortunately for them, they just weren't smart enough to earn their success. So now, they're trying to take it, and to my dismay, we're letting them."

"Fuck, you are just such a racist, bitter old man," Dillon said. The declaration paralyzed his parents and drew a cold stare from his grandpa. "You're always bitchin' about what Black and Hispanic people are doing to take what is ours, but all you're fighting for is making sure anyone not White has a shitty life. They've been oppressed for years, Grandpa. We literally shipped them off to the island we are currently living on so we could replace their jobs with computers. They've been in a rut ever since. Do a little bit of research then you'll see what I mean. It's 2089 for fuck's sake. What I'm saying is no secret. There's a reason they fought so hard for change in the sixties.

"I'm sick of hearing you bitch about it. If that is all you're going to talk about get the fuck out of our hou—"

"That is enough, young man. Do you hear me?" Richard said. His roar caught the entire Lawrence family off guard, including himself.

An awkward silence ensued, as everyone was dumbstruck by Dillon's unexpected demonstration. Heather cradled her glass with both hands. Richard got his breath under control and nervously scratched his forearm. Reginald's scowl fixated on his grandson. He had been having his doubts about Dillon's propensity to succeed, hesitant to believe he was capable of continuing the prominent work all the Lawrence men had dedicated themselves to. Now that he was aware of his modern, brain-washed perspective of race relations in their country, Reginald concluded he didn't have the wherewithal to continue the Lawrence's legacy.

Dillon, taken aback by his own actions but proud of himself for shutting his grandfather up, kept his gaze down and did his best to suppress angry tears; failing to do so would indicate weakness.

After Richard regained his composure he said, "Do not talk to him that way. And Dad, do not talk like that in front of your grandson, okay?"

The lack of support put Dillon over the edge. He picked up his beer and spiked it on the ground. Glass shattered in every direction, nearly causing his grandfather and mother to drop their drinks.

"Fuck this. I'm not going to sit around and hear this shit anymore. I'm tired of it. If he's going to be here, he needs to be respectful," Dillon said.

"One beer and you think you have a right to talk to us like that?" Reginald asked, mockingly. "Boy, if I was your father, you wouldn't even be standing. I would've slapped you five minutes ago. Th—"

Dillon reached over the patio table and slapped his grandfather across the face so violently Reginald finally did end up dropping his glass. Heather shot up from her seat and jolted backwards to avoid any physical harm. She immediately regretted not interfering because it prevented her from blocking her husband from shoving their son. It all happened too quickly for Dillon to react, leaving him no time to break his fall with his arms. With unstoppable momentum, the back of Dillon's head slammed against the patio's concrete, resulting in a deafening sound that resembled a bowling bowl crashing into the ground.

Immediately regretting his impulsive act, Richard rushed over to his son's motionless body praying he wasn't seriously injured.

"Dillon, Dillon. Oh my God. Dillon, Are you okay? Dillon, talk to me," Richard said.

Blood circled the concrete around Dillon's head as he mumbled something inaudible. When he was finally able to formulate words he said, "I'm okay. My head hurts. My head really, really hurts. Is it broken?"

"Oh my God, Richard. He needs to go to the hospital," said a wailing Heather. "Oh my God, Richard, I'm calling an ambulance."

Dillon possessing the balls to stand up to his grandfather shocked Reginald, almost to the point of being impressive enough to reverse the notion his grandson would never amount to anything. At his age, Reginald was lucky to feel more shock than agony, yet his face still stung so hard it felt like thousands of needles were constantly poking him.

"Heather baby, can you please get a towel and ice while I get him up," Richard asked, all of the sudden very nurturing. "Dad, you can stay here. Heather and I will follow the ambulance."

"Oh, no. I'm coming with you. He's on my shit list right now, but he's still my grandson."

"Just please cooperate."

"I've learned my lesson for the time being. Where the fuck is Wilford?"

All of the commotion caused the dogs to retreat to the other side of the yard and cower under overarching bushes.

"I'll make sure they're inside before we go. Get inside before the paramedics get here," Richard said, directing his frustration at his displeasure with what his father was primarily concerned about. He reminded himself his own actions are what escalated the situation.

What felt like seconds later, they heard the ambulance coming down Lawrence Drive. Its sirens were roaring even though there were no other cars that would obstruct their drive. Heather ran to the front door to let the team of four paramedics into their house. They stormed in without much of a greeting and headed to the backyard to begin treating Dillon.

Because of how much blood he was losing, they hardly acknowledged Richard and ignored Heather after she led them to Dillon. They were efficient in minimizing his blood loss and cleaning his wound to minimize the risk of infection between now and when they arrived at the hospital.

Reginald was inside sneaking another beverage before he had to do the grandfatherly thing and join his family at the hospital.

By the time the paramedics loaded Dillon into the back of the ambulance his wits were coming back to him, but he was asking who everyone was and why they all appeared so worried.

"You will be fine, Dillon. I promise, baby. We'll see you there," Heather said as she followed the stretcher until it slid in the back. She wiped her eyes and wailed some more before Richard barked at her to get in the car.

CHAPTER

2089

T he ride home from the ER was uncomfortable. Dillon and his grandfather were in the backseat, but the former avoided eye contact with his elder. Dillon's body faced his window, and he scooched himself as far away from Reginald as possible. Richard was responsible for his concussion and eight stitches, but right now the fire inside Dillon burned because of Reginald.

As the Lawrence's were leaving the hospital Dillon explicitly said he wasn't in the mood to talk. His family, relieved to be outside the confines of a heavily sanitized environment, abided by the silence Dillon demanded.

Dillon was infuriated with his parents for being bystanders to his grandfather's antics. Reginald found his grandson to be an ungrateful piece of shit who possessed no drive. Heather fretted over the state of her family. Richard felt anxious about what the repercussions would be if members of the medical staff leaked out who they treated tonight.

Dillon, keeping his hand covering his mouth, mumbled, "I didn't say anything about what happened, so at least you don't have to worry about that."

Heather whimpered at the sound of his voice. What he muttered broke her heart. Materialism disguised it, but their turmoil was no longer the family's worst-kept secret.

Richard could no longer bear the silence. Once they turned onto Lawrence Drive, he said, "Dillon, I'm so sorry, son. I made a mistake. It was in the moment, and I didn't want things to get worse. Even though they obviously did. You know I have never hurt you before and did not intend to this time. I'm so sorry."

With the car in full auto-pilot mode, a watery eyed Richard turned around in hopes of catching any sign of forgiveness from Dillon. What exactly that looked like he didn't know, but he hoped he would if he saw it.

"Yeah," Dillon said just above a whisper.

Reginald rolled his eyes.

Knowing he wouldn't get through to him by pressing too hard, Richard patiently waited for Dillon to elaborate. Dillon's gaze remained out the window, pretending to peer down at the rocks poking out of the ocean even though the sun set hours before, and he had yet to remove his hand from his mouth. It was symbolic of holding back what he really felt. Avoiding confrontation was an easier route than addressing the quandary his family was in. This type of learned behavior was why dysfunction existed in the first place.

"Yeah, you forgive me?" Richard asked.

"Let's talk about this at home," Heather suggested. She continued, "Reginald, do you want us to pick up Wilford and take you back, or do you feel okay getting yourself back? It's getting late."

"I can press the right buttons. I'll get the old man and be on my way once we get back."

Reginald rounded up Wilford and left as swiftly as he could. When Richard's and Heather's awkward good-byes to Reginald were over with, Richard, Heather, and Dillon took their seats on separate pieces of black and gold furniture in their living room.

Dillon was the smuggest he had ever been with his parents, and the energy rubbed off on Frank and Finn. They appeared uneasy, constantly licking their lips and scratching themselves.

Dillon took it upon himself to break the ice.

"How can you let him be the way he is? Constantly racist. All the time. I'm sick and tired of his bullshit, and you never say anything, Dad. You don't say anything to him. What if Moe was here and he heard that?

Would you do anything then? What if he called him an infick to his face?"

Richard looked down at the ground, embarrassed with himself for his son's priviness to his weakness: lacking the courage to stick up to his father. Richard didn't set an admirable example for Dillon by failing to speak up for his beliefs.

"What about your new friend, Mom? What if Ariana was here and heard that? What if Ariana was an infick? But no, no one says anything. Everything's always okay as long as it isn't us getting shit on. It's fuckin' bullshit."

Dillon had never spoken so vulgar to his parents before.

After the densest silence yet, Dillon's voice cracked when he said, "Maybe no one does because then they get their fuckin' head cracked open."

Richard slapped his hands over his face and wept. Crying masked his inability to muster up an acceptable response. He was disgusted with himself and overwhelmed by the confrontation.

"When I go to my room at night it seems to be the best part of the night for you guys, so that's where I'm going. You guys can drink and talk about whatever you two talk about to make it seem like you're both happy. Infick free. Fuckin' bullshit."

Dillon stormed out with Frank and Finn not far behind.

After Richard regained control of his emotions, he straightened his posture and blankly stared straight ahead. He rubbed his eyes to dry them, but all that did was balloon their puffiness and further redden them.

"Where do we go from here, Richard?" his wife asked.

"I don't know. I'm sorry. I just don't know what happened. I don't know what happened tonight, and I don't know what's happening to our family. It's so easy for us to just go about our lives, stay in our own worlds, go through the motions, and not check in with one another. I'm the guiltiest one of that and will work on it. I promise. How it's come to me knocking over Dillon is incomprehensible. I don't know. Maybe family therapy is a good option for us. What do you think?"

"I want to try," Heather said, lacking enthusiasm.

Richard waited for his wife to continue but finally spoke up when he realized she wasn't going to. "Heather, look. I'm so sorry. I know that doesn't cut it. I have not been perfect and never was. I definitely don't have all the answers. Out of all of us, I'm the most in the wrong. Out of all of us, I could be the only one who is wrong. I have unintentionally been tearing this family apart, but I want to fix it. I want you, Dillon, and me to always live under the same roof and be happy."

"There's the issue right there, Richard."

He pressed his eyes together. "What do you mean?"

"You said you want us to always live under the same roof happily, but he is eighteen. He's going to move out soon and start his own life."

Richard understood Heather's message. It just occurred to him his family needed fixing, but it was far too late. So many what were supposed to be valuable years were forever gone.

"How long have you been unhappy?" he asked.

"I didn't say I was unhappy."

"You didn't have to."

Heather pulled her legs into her chest and wrapped her arms around them. "We haven't felt united in so long. We just go through the motions, like you said. We carry on about our own lives and treat each other as a person who just fills a role. It is like you have a wife and son so you can say you have a wife and son. I have a handsome and successful husband and son because that's what I'm supposed to do. I'm just so exhausted from doing this, Richard. What's our endgame? It isn't what I envisioned; I know that.

"I'm guilty, too. I go out and mingle with all these women in the neighborhood, wives of the guys you work with. I let myself fill that role while just standing by and letting our son raise himself. Do we even know him that well? Does he ever seem fully comfortable around us? We talk about how great he is for sitting through dinner, but right after, he is gone. We treat it as if a weight has been lifted off our shoulders, and our duties are done. I want us to want to be together. To have fun but for it to be real. I just don't know when we lost it. I don't know if we ever had it."

Richard crossed his arms and exhaled audibly as he digested his wife's outlook on their family.

"We've lost ourselves a little bit, and it seems to have taken tonight's event for us to try and fix it. Let's be better, Heather," Richard said.

He squeezed in next to his wife on the chaise she was in a ball on. Richard had an uncontrollable urge to touch Heather to prevent her from dissipating from him.

"I promise I'll be better. I'll work less. I'll be involved more. I'll address issues. I'll listen. I'll sign us up for therapy. We don't have the solution right now, but we will work on it and find it. I know us. I know we can do it."

Richard gently caressed his wife's face, causing her to slightly shudder, and wiped away her tears with his thumbs. He kissed her on the forehead and hugged her head against his chest. "I love you and always will. Whatever you do, please never doubt that."

Heather nodded against his body and hugged him back but failed to summon up the courage to tell her husband who she really was.

Eventually Heather would be forced to come clean on what had been eating away at her most of her life. As a child, she once tried to, but she received a punishment in return. This traumatic memory made her hesitant to confront the truth, but now living a lie seemed to be more painful than a second attempt at honesty. It registered with Heather she couldn't continue to live this way if she ever wanted to be happy.

CHAPTER

2089

To improve his literacy skills, Jonathan read aloud and wrote for at least thirty minutes nearly every day. While he educated himself, Robin completed chores in his vicinity because she knew he enjoyed an audience. Plus, observing her son's progress felt rewarding.

Wallace was the only one who loved it more than Robin because Jonathan would rub his belly with his bare feet while he read and wrote. Jonathan and Wallace both had their struggles finding their place in the world. The hardships they endured strengthened their bond. This is what Robin once thought would keep Ariana and her close their entire lives.

"After....all, the gov...er...nor enac...ted the law without hes...i...ta...tion."

"Honey, that was great. You're getting so much smoother. See, your work is paying off."

"Uh, thanks Momma. I, I, I am getting good with more hard articles. The words are getting more easy for me to say."

"I'm so proud of you," Robin said. She hugged Jonathan and bent down to accept some licks from Wallace.

"Uh, thanks Momma. When are we going to Heather's house again?"

"I'm not sure honey, why? I actually haven't spoken to her since the last time we went over there," Robin said. She went back to folding linens on the coffee table. She refused to invest in A.I. that handled these tasks for her, partly because she considered it lazy but mainly because contributing to an industry that tore apart her family wouldn't sit right with her.

"Uh, just wondering. Her new friend is nice. I, I, I like her."

"Ariana. Yeah, she was nice."

"Uh, do they like each other?"

"What do you mean?"

"Uh, it seems like they are more than friends. By the way they acted and stuff."

Robin stopped folding pillow covers when she realized what Jonathan was implying. "No, no, honey. They're just friends. Sometimes girls who are friends can be more affectionate to each other than guys are. That's all."

Jonathan exhaled a sigh that indicated to Robin he didn't agree.

Why her sister was back in a city she vowed she would never return to had been on Robin's mind since that night. "What makes you think that?" She couldn't help but ask.

"Uh, it's easy. When people like each other they look at them more different. I, I, I saw them do that at the dinner table."

"What's the look you're talking about?"

"Uh, I, I, I don't know they just look more different at each other than friends do. I, I, I can't really explain it."

As tempting as it was to continue pressing him on what he noticed, Robin knew it embarrassed Jonathan when he couldn't properly articulate his thoughts.

"I see honey. I know what you mean. That's just how girls can be. I didn't notice any of that happening."

"Uh, okay. And, you know what else?"

"Yes?"

"Uh, Richard kept staring at Ariana's butt when she stood up," Jonathan said, unable to conceal his smile.

"That I noticed," Robin smiled back.

For the remainder of the afternoon, Robin finished up chores around the house. Folding linens, washing Jonathan's clothes, cleaning the kitchen, washing the floors, dusting, and other tasks she had been neglecting. What most women of her financial stature dreaded Robin looked forward to. Robin allotted this time to lose herself in her thoughts. Now that Jonathan was more self-sufficient and Moe was growing up, she could designate more time to herself. Oftentimes, memories from her childhood surfaced, good and bad, but mainly the latter. Not understanding why the world was so harsh incensed her, but at this point in her life, she just wanted to brush those destitutions under the rug and move on. Internalizing all her anger, confusion, sadness, and insecurities seemed to be the best solution. The flaw of her self-diagnosed mental health solution was that the same problems always came back to clutter her mind.

Encountering Ariana after so many years apart ignited discombobulated thoughts. Robin didn't know if she felt relieved to know she was alive and well, if her presence was a bad sign, or if it would do herself some good to have Ariana back in her life. Maybe her little sister would encourage her to grow into the person and, most importantly, mother she needed to be for her sons. Since Ariana had been absent from her life for so long, Robin now associated her sister with a chapter of her life she would prefer to stay in the past.

Robin was so immersed in her own thoughts, she didn't hear Moe come home.

"Hey Wallace. How are ya bud?" Moe gave the stocky dog an aggressive stomach rub only a dog with Wallace's physique could handle.

It took Robin a moment to break out of the trance she was in.

"Hi Moe. You're home early," said Robin, "No Dillon's today?"

"Hi Mom. No, Dillon hasn't been at school since Monday."

"Really? Is everything fine?"

"Yeah. Everything's cool. Sup Jonathan."

"Uh, hi Moe. I, I, I have been reading good today."

"Oh yeah? Good stuff. Are the hard articles getting easier to read?"

"Uh, Yeah. I, I, I am able to get through them now."

"Nice. That's good to hear."

Robin smiled at Moe for encouraging his older brother.

"Well, I hope Dillon's okay. I haven't heard from Heather all week."

"People have things to do, Mom." Moe rolled his eyes.

"I know that. I'm just saying."

"Jonathan, can I take Wallace to the pier?" Moe asked, ignoring his mother.

"Uh, I, I, I already walked him today."

"I know, but he likes it there. He can run around and see other dogs."

"Uh, okay. He'll have fun."

"And who are you going to the pier with?" his mother asked.

"Megan."

"The one with the boyfriend?" she asked with a raised eyebrow.

"It depends how you define boyfriend. I'm putting my stuff away, and then I'm out of here."

Robin and Jonathan exchanged smiles once Moe was back in his room.

"It's just you and me tonight, sweetheart."

"Uh, that's okay with me, Momma."

Until recently Robin believed she would spend the rest of her life with her two boys; now, it appeared her past wasn't going to let that happen.

CHAPTER

2089

"So, what the hell happened?" Moe asked after puffing a joint Dillon had rolled. The two friends, plus Wallace, were sitting on a bench admiring the ocean from the Pacific Pier, one of Morple's original tourist attractions. Because of how trendy it had become throughout the years, locals from their parents' generation were sick of it, but Dillon and Moe cherished it.

"So, we're fuckin' outside, and my grandpa is over. He's talking all sorts of shit about how our family did their best to help quarantined people eventually be successful in Morple, but they were just too stupid to figure it out. He said something along the lines of 'All they did was complain and tried to overthrow the government. Their success is undeserved.' Blah, blah, blah."

Moe shook his head and let out a disgusted laugh.

"I finally fuckin' snapped, man. I told him how the government used sonoravirus as a tactic to displace minorities so big businesses could up their A.I. usage, and ultimately make more money. Pretty fuckin' common knowledge in this day and age. I reminded him how Black people and Hispanic people had no jobs to go back to, but no, they are the ones in the wrong, according to him.

"He goes off on a tangent about how what the media feeds us is bullshit, and how if Black and Hispanic people really wanted jobs, they should've been more aware of their health. He told me that they are, and I quote, 'utterly worthless.'" After he kept stooping down, I called him a racist, bitter old man. That's when my dad finally chimed in, and of course he was angrier with me than with him."

Dillon inhaled a few more hits before wrapping up the story. "Then, I don't know, I just lost it. I threw down my beer an—"

"I hope you didn't hit the dogs."

"Don't worry, they weren't near it. After I did that, my grandpa told me he would've slapped me if I was his son. So, that's when I reached across from where I was sitting and slapped him in the fuckin' face."

Moe, his high settling in, gasped and covered his mouth with his hands in astonishment.

"No fuckin' way. You slapped your grandpa in the face?"

"Yeah. Then he dropped his drink. More glass got everywhere. And then my dad intervened and pushed me back, which is how I cracked my head open. Hence the stitches and concussion."

Moe's amusement evaporated after Dillon told him how the story ended. There was a long pause. Dillon took that time to steal a few extra hits of their joint.

"Are you fuckin' with me?"

Dillon shook his head.

Moe noticed Dillon was doing his best to prevent himself from crying. This conversation marked the first time Dillon verbalized what had unraveled that night. His parents didn't check in with him as their attention was on themselves, consumed with their pathetic attempt to save their marriage, something Dillon considered a lost cause years ago.

"Damn dude. I'm sorry to hear you had to go through that. I didn't think the story was going to go there."

"Yeah. So, I got stitched up, and they told me I had a concussion."

"Does it hurt? What did you tell the ER about what happened?"

"Not as much as you'd think. I think the shock of it all made me forget about the pain. I just said I didn't remember. My parents told them I just fell outside playing with the dogs."

"Huh, real clever. At least you didn't have to go to school this week. That History test bent me over and fucked me real good. Obamacare vs.

Paul Riley or Ryan's, whatever his name is, healthcare bill took up a fat section. Of course, I know nothing about both."

"True. That's a positive. Fuck, I thought his name was Ryan Paul."

"No, but seriously, I'm sorry man. I never thought your dad would be capable of doing that shit. Why do you think he snapped?"

"Yeah, it's okay. I just don't think he can take someone talking to his own dad like that. He looks up to him a lot, I guess, but I don't understand how he can accept that kind of behavior. I think he knows how expired his way of thinking is, but then again, who really knows. He's probably just used to my grandpa talking like that. Shit, he has probably been saying that shit his whole life."

Moe and Dillon never engaged in a deep conversation like this before. For as close as they were, it was borderline uncomfortable for Moe, but he sensed Dillon needed someone to talk to. He imagined his discomfort was nothing compared to what Dillon felt reliving the night.

Moe stopped thinking about himself and formulated something positive to contribute. "Listen man. Your parents love you. They're just people. Your dad's a rich kid, and your mom's a good-looking, wealthy woman. But that doesn't mean they have this whole life thing figured out. I of course mean that in the most loving way possible."

Dillon's smile acknowledged he didn't hold the statement against Moe, especially since it was true.

"My point is they have flaws just like the rest of us. We view parents as these people who are supposed to be these like perfect beings, but they're not. They can be just as fucked up as the rest of us. Shit, look at my mom. She never talks about what she's actually thinking, or what her life before us was like. I really don't know anything about her. Then there's my dad. He's just gone."

"He went missing," Dillon said more confidently than he felt, given he didn't know the intricacies of the situation.

"No one knows what happened. Look, this isn't about my shit. All I'm saying is your parents are far from perfect. What your dad did is fucked up, and your grandpa is an asshole. But you gotta talk it out with them, at least your dad."

"That's the issue. He doesn't talk about things. I swear I'm more of an adult than him or my mom. When we got home that night, they just looked clueless and could barely say anything to me. There's no getting through to them. They think money makes real-life problems just go away. They don't have a sense of reality.

"But, fuck. I don't know man. Maybe they'll get divorced and give me enough money so I can live on my own. Then I'll never have to see them again."

"Ah, now I remembered why I don't feel bad for you."

Dillon and Moe exchanged grins, noticing the other's red, glassy eyes.

"But seriously, sometimes I just think going rogue would be so much easier. It is better than how other people lash out," Dillon said.

"What do you mean?"

"You know, like the Daniel Wilmingtons of the world."

"Oh come on, don't even say that shit. Jesus."

Daniel Wilmington was infamous for bullying children online and convincing them to commit suicide in 2052. Renown psychologists, investigators, and other professionals concluded his tumultuous childhood was at the root of his malevolent practices.

"I'm not saying I'm like that, but I'm just saying this is the type of shit that causes that type of behavior. Come on now, I'm not that evil."

Moe allowed for a prolonged silence to show he didn't appreciate Dillon referencing a psychopath. He changed the subject. "Shit, remember in elementary school we would talk about how we were always right when we had arguments with our parents? Our motto was 'kids are always right,' and we truly believed it."

"Fuck yeah I do. That shit's still true to this day."

"More true than it's ever been."

Dillon and Moe admired the breathtaking view of the Pacific Ocean Morple's residents took for granted. As they took it in, Moe felt a heightened appreciation for his home life. After hearing what Dillon was up against, he realized he didn't have it so bad.

"Thanks man," Dillon said.

"No problem."

CHAPTER

2089

Richard attended Rapture's bi-monthly executive meeting, but his mind was elsewhere. Since concussing his son, Richard had been beating himself up for how absent he was throughout Dillon's childhood and adolescence. It took Dillon's head cracking open for him to realize he should've prioritized raising his son more.

Richard succeeded in his duties as a provider, but he had never put forth much effort to know him under the surface. Now, Dillon was a young man with his own perspective on life, no longer a little kid who just went with the flow.

How did I miss that happening?

"Hey. You there? Snap out of it," Phil said.

Richard shook his head and rapidly blinked his eyes. He looked at where the holograms were and realized he zoned out for a significant amount of time. He didn't even remember them signing off.

"What the fuck? Are you alright?" Phil asked.

"Yeah, yeah. I'm good. I'm just, uh, thinking about the meeting," a flustered Richard said.

"Right. Hey, so what's up? You've been in the clouds all week. Luckily Prescott didn't ask you to chime in there. Did you even notice he was there?"

"Yes. I noticed he was there. Just a lot of this going on, but I'm good. How are we doing with the Sampson project? It feels like he's the first senator we've had in a while." Senator Cory Sampson was a well-known politician who needed to save face from a hate crime threatening to resurface.

"Shit. You really weren't listening. His ass didn't get too far from the plantation as a kid. His political foes are threatening to release a surveillance video with him and some buddies beating up a Black kid they saw at a grocery store when they were in college. Apparently, they hospitalized him and called him a nigger before telling him he was a virus. All while beating the shit out of him, but the big man is going to talk to his favorite adversaries himself to see if he can suppress it. Fuckin' America, right?"

"It's what we're paid to do," Richard said, rationalizing their unethical line of work.

"Yeah. We're super admirable. What's funny is if they actually wore their masks the video wouldn't prove it was him. Anyways, are we going golfing soon? It feels like we haven't played in forever."

"We played less than a week ago, but I can't anytime soon. I've got some shit I gotta do the next couple of weekends."

"What do you have to do? Come on. Let's go play and have dinner with Heather and her friend after. It'll be great."

"Not this weekend, Phil. I can't make it happen."

"Hey," Phil said, lightly hitting his best friend's shoulder to get his full attention. "Everything good with you?"

"Just because I can't play golf and try to get you laid doesn't mean I'm not good."

"Well, it should, but you being mopey and not yourself might mean you're not."

Richard gave his friend a regretful look for his snappy response.

"Sorry. Yeah. We're all good. Just family stuff, you know?"

"I had so much of it I decided not to create another. So yeah, I know. Let me know if you want to talk."

"Thanks man. If I can squeeze in a round, I'll let you know."

"There he is, see you there!"

Phil left the room fist pumping the air, thinking he turned his friend's frown upside down.

Richard remained in the conference room for a few more minutes deep in his thoughts. His time would've been well spent familiarizing himself with Senator Sampson's situation, but when Prescott assumed the lead on a project the best way to help was by staying the hell out of the way.

Richard had accumulated the resources to retire at year's end and still be swimming in billions the rest of his life. He earned a healthy stake in Rapture, and his wealth management team coded his investments to latch onto the most profitable companies in the market. The properties he owned around the world were desirable, overpriced, and continuously increasing in value. The most durable safety net he had was he shared financial interests with politicians. This meant he would always have the puppets protecting their shared prosperity. If that all shit the bed, which it wouldn't, his inheritance from his father would take care of the Lawrence's for generations. Plus, Dillon most likely smacked his way out of a portion of his grandfather's fortune, leaving more for Richard.

On top of being unsure if his son liked him, Heather confessed she was unhappy. Richard assumed all the amenities he afforded brought her satisfaction. After all, the lifestyle he gifted her was exponentially more luxurious than the one her father had built for her, her sister, and her mother. Their marriage ushered Heather into a whole other realm, one with endless possibilities accredited to exorbitant opulence, where all of her desires could be reality. She may not have realized it, but Richard let Heather dictate most of their expenditures. Yes, Richard loved earning billions and relishing in the power it came with, but he could have done without all the extravagant possessions. Their mansion, automated cars that wheeled them around, yacht that carried them around the island, private jets took them to lavish vacation destinations, and ornate decor were all over the top. All extracurriculars Richard deemed pointless but purchased for her sake.

Now that he knew none of this made his wife happy, squandering that much money really irritated him. But it was a lost cause. He'd get over it and focus on fixing his marriage because, apparently, all the work he had put in to elevate Heather to the echelon she dissipated all his money in wasn't enough.

Ariana swirled her wodin in her glass to entertain herself while she waited for Heather to come back outside. If she wasn't doing something fidgety, she would have gulped her drink too fast, and today she wanted to keep her wits intact. So, she committed to sipping it slow, which was an uphill battle. When Ariana was in situations requiring her to monitor her drinking, she realized how dependent she was on alcohol. The aroma, burn, and sensation proved to be a viable, albeit short-term, solution to her general uneasiness. For having parents whose livelihoods alcohol destroyed, LaVonte didn't ride her too hard on her habit. After all, pulling the strings for the world's most prosperous trafficking organization didn't give him much leverage to mandate her substance intake.

The Lawrences' view of the Pacific Ocean was mesmerizing. Even though California still had spectacular views, further inland than they used to be, Morple's were noticeably clearer and breathtaking. Having only been populated for fifty-nine years and being the capital of clean-energy industries, pollution was nearly nonexistent. How one of the most oppressive states in the country's history was also the most beautiful was quite ironic. Ariana even found it laughable.

Frank snapped Ariana out of her trance by lathering her bare feet with his slobber. His tongue tickled her toes, causing her to unintentionally flinch and kick him in the face. "Oh Finn, I mean Frank, I'm sorry. I didn't mean to do that."

She scratched him in between the eyes hoping he'd understand that meant she was sorry. The night the Karroses reentered her life she saw Jonathan doing that with his dog, so she assumed Frank would like it, too.

"Awe, I see you've made a new friend out here," Heather said. She came out holding an empty glass of wine, an unopened bottle of merlot, and a half empty bottle of Richard's wodin. Ariana made a mental note to be extra cautious now that an endless amount was at her disposal.

"Yeah, well, after accidentally kicking him in the face he has taken a liking to me."

Heather chuckled and said, "Oh, they forget about something right after it happens, who cares. They really aren't as intelligent as people make them out to be."

Ariana assumed Heather, someone who spent the majority of her time with two dogs following her around all day, adored them, but her diction proved otherwise.

"So, you're not the dog person in the family then?" Ariana asked.

Another chuckle. "Oh God no. They were all Richard's idea, but of course I'm the one who gets stuck with them every day."

Ariana, not the biggest animal lover herself, surprised herself by feeling disappointed Heather was talking like this. From what she observed Frank and Finn stared at Heather with great admiration, but clearly, Ariana had misjudged their relationship.

"Oh wow. To be honest I immediately assumed you were a big dog person."

Heather scrunched her face and shook her head. "No, but whatever, I just go with the flow."

Because she was playing a part, Ariana couldn't tell Heather she thought Heather came off as a spoiled trophy wife who did nothing but bask in the riches her billionaire husband had amassed.

Ariana stuck out her bottom lip and nodded before taking a sip. Allowing an elongated gap in their conversation would indicate her displeasure; she had to keep the conversation flowing.

"So how long have you known Robin?"

"Oh goodness, over ten years now, yeah. Dillon and Moe became friends in elementary school, so yeah, over ten years. She's just the sweetest woman, and how she cares for that Jonathan is so admirable. He must be such a handful, but she does such a great job."

Ariana didn't know if she would have been able to control her temper if Heather didn't acknowledge how great of a mother Robin was to "that Jonathan." It was evident Heather viewed his stunted brain development as a nuisance. Ariana wondered what she would have thought if she knew her father-in-law was responsible for it.

"He's such a sweet young man. You can tell he puts a lot of effort into fitting in. I found him adorable," Ariana said.

"Oh, yes. We love him and Moe." Heather sipped her wine before continuing. "I find that Moe to be just absolutely gorgeous, which isn't all that shocking because Robin is still absolutely stunning."

Ariana concurred.

"Leaving two young boys is horrible as is, but why do it when your wife is that hot? I just don't understand," Heather said.

"I'm sorry. What are you referring to?"

"Well, her husband," Heather used air quotes, "vanished well over fifteen years ago now. We didn't know them, but the story goes she came home one day and found Jonathan and Moe alone, and Bobby, who *was* her husband, was nowhere to be found. The whole thing is fuzzy. Investigators didn't suspect foul play, and they said they didn't stumble upon any notable leads on his whereabouts. But who knows how hard they really looked, you know?"

Ariana was losing her internal battle to control her wodin intake. Heather's inaccurate, presumptuous take on Robin's hardships fazed her.

"What do you mean?" Ariana asked. She knew Heather was looking for a cue to elaborate.

"Well, please know I absolutely love her to death, but she lives in The District. They just aren't as prioritized over there. As much as it pains me to say, it's true."

Ariana thought to herself, *some things just never change.*

Heather continued to say her piece. "Now, again, I wasn't in her life back then, but we are nearing the twenty-second century. How can you not find a missing person in this day and age?"

"It does sound fishy. Do you know if she has dated since?" Prying information about Robin from Heather was a great way to stay engaged in the conversation.

"Not that I know of. I have approached her multiple times about setting her up with some of Richard's single friends, but she hasn't expressed any interest."

Yeah, I wonder fuckin' why, Ariana thought.

"Maybe she has decided to go the other way," Heather said.

"You mean you think she's into women?"

Heather shrugged, as if to deflect the baseless claim she just insinuated. The assumption drove Ariana nuts.

"No, I didn't get that vibe. That's a traumatic event. She probably has just been busy taking care of her boys." Even though Ariana couldn't outwardly stick up for her sister, she couldn't let Heather's bullshit slide.

"Eh, maybe. Who really knows?"

As much as Ariana wanted to learn about what her sister had been up to, she couldn't endure Heather's speculative answers anymore. "So, remind me, how did you and Richard meet?"

"Oh, you know, we both grew up in the area. He actually grew up not far from here, and I was raised in the outskirts of Costa Mor."

Costa Mor's outskirts were closer to The District than Heather wanted to admit. The area was still affluent, but it wasn't the type of fuck you money the families residing in the coastal homes had. Ariana noted this because it was probably why Heather was attracted to Richard in the first place. She recognized her marriage to LaVonte was similar to Heather's and Richard's, but marrying a powerful man was the only thing Ariana had found they had in common. So far.

Heather carried on with the anticlimactic love story. "When I was in my early twenties and Richard was around thirty a mutual friend introduced us out and about, and the rest is history. Obviously, that was a crazy time in history, but we made it out alright."

Expecting some more detail, Ariana caught herself staring at Heather with a blank expression, one that didn't go unnoticed by the latter.

"I know. It's nothing special really, but hey, we both found love, right?"

"Do you think you'll stay in Costa Mor forever?" Ariana asked.

"I'm not sure. I wouldn't mind leaving one day, seeing what else is out there. I mean, I've been here my entire life. I've seen many places in the world, yes, but living in a new place would be an exciting experience. It would give me something to look forward to, who knows."

Ariana replied with an agreeable remark and indulged in her drink. Heather's tone and vagueness indicated she wasn't happy here or with Richard. Maybe getting her out of Morple would be easier than Ariana originally thought.

Sufficiently intoxicated, especially for it still being the afternoon, Heather walked Ariana out and watched her car peel out of the driveway and proceed on Lawrence Drive.

Growing up in Morple's elitist culture complicated Heather's ability to be expressive, no matter how the rest of the world was trending. After so many years of pretending to be just like every other rich girl wanting to stumble upon a man to take care of her, she brainwashed herself into believing marrying that type of man was the right thing to do in order to satisfy the narrative society wrote for her. Maybe starting somewhere new where no one knew her name would provide the clarity she needed.

But before she knew it, she was pregnant with Dillon. Heather wanted him to grow up with two parents committed to each other and him.

A marriage based on this premise was bound to fail because it lacked authenticity. Despite how dysfunctional it was, it was her norm, and she didn't know of any other way to live.

"Hi, sweetheart," Richard said.

His voice startled her. She glanced in a mirror to ensure she didn't look too drunk.

"Hey hon. You're home early," she said.

"Hi," he said an inch from her face, preparing to land a kiss. Lately she'd been getting more than the usual, abrupt peck. Heather reciprocated enough to assure Richard he nailed it. His enthusiasm told her he didn't mind the alcohol.

"I wanted to get out of the office. Everything's handled so I thought I could come hang out at home. And see you."

"Well, I love that decision, Mr. Lawrence." She was trying to sound enthralled.

"I love coming home to this. Look at you, baby."

Heather's skimpy outfit revealed a lot of skin, including the bottom of her ass cheeks. Richard caressed her hips and lightly pushed her towards the couch. He kissed her neck and squeezed her breasts. His hands hovered over her nipples, trying to arouse her. As Richard's warm mouth suffocated her neck, Heather gripped the back of his head to keep him there. He interpreted it as her excitement, but her intention was to prevent him from seeing her facial expression, one demonstrating disappointment and disinterest.

"Can I take you to the bedroom and continue this somewhere else on your body?"

"So promiscuous. What's gotten into you?"

"I don't know, but I hope I am in you sooner than later."

Heather picked his head back up so they were looking at each other.

"Maybe you can put me on my stomach how you used to, and lick it from the back before putting it in. I'd like that right now." That position was her favorite because she didn't have to see him.

"What are we waiting for then?" He flipped his wife over on one of their living room couches so she was on her stomach and squeezed her ass. His hormones kicked in; he attempted to pull down her bottoms and get down to it in their living room.

"No, babe. Dillon could walk in any second. Let me go shower, and I'll meet you in bed."

"Just don't take too long in there."

She gave him a quick peck and scurried off to their shower. Heather aimed to prolong this as long as she could, hoping Richard would get sidetracked and forget all about trying to make love to his wife.

CHAPTER

16

2089

Robin noticed Taylor Jennings sulking in the corner of Free Morple's cafeteria. She hadn't seen her since the first time they met, so she made it a point to go say hello.

"Hi Taylor. How are you?"

Taylor stiffened, practically recoiling.

"I'm sorry. I just wanted to come over and say hello," Robin said.

"H-hi. Robin, right?"

"Yes, Robin."

The struggles of the citizens Free Morple sought to help were evident by their hollow faces, malnourished bodies, deteriorated clothes, and trepid expressions, so seeing someone who looked like life had beat her up was commonplace. But Taylor's glum stood out to Robin. Maybe it was her motherly instincts. She found it odd her one-year-old son Jimmy wasn't with her.

"Do you want to come get in on the fun?" Robin asked. Aside from providing the basics for people technology left behind, Free Morple sprinkled in some fun here and there. Tonight was game night, and everyone had voted on Charades. Implementing joyous group activities boosted everyone's morale, but Taylor didn't seem to be in any mood to participate.

"No. Thank you, but no," she said.

"Okay. Well, if you change your mind, please come join us. Sound good?"

"Sure."

"Okay." Robin attempted to cheer her up with a smile, but that didn't work. She cleared the dishes on Taylor's table, taking the initiative to get a head start on the night's chores. Just as she was about to carry the dishes back to the kitchen, Taylor revealed why she was so dreary.

"Jimmy is gone."

Robin stopped in her tracks, wondering if she heard her correctly. "What do you mean, hon?" she asked.

"His dad came back to surprise," she said using air quotes, "us on the night of his birthday. He acted like there was nothing wrong with him being gone for the last six months, like I should just be happy he was back. He was always so good at making everything appear okay on the surface, and I can't lie, I fell for it. I was happy he was back, happy we could all be together again. For a few hours, it felt like we had a family again. You know?"

Robin nodded. She understood more than Taylor would ever realize.

Taylor continued the story. "We had a little celebration for Jimmy's birthday. Obviously, I couldn't afford anything too elaborate, but it didn't matter. He was only one and didn't know any better. I cooked, and we all shared a slice of cake. I let myself think we could all be happy together. I was willing to let the past six months stay in the past. Just let bygones be bygones. Like the angel he was, Jimmy fell asleep between his dad and me at the end of the night, but when I woke up, neither of them were there.

"At first, I assumed they had woken up before me and would be in the kitchen, but when I went in there it was empty. I searched our entire place and found no sign of them. After being frantic for the next couple of hours I filed a police report. While they were questioning me, they were notified they found a dead baby and approximately thirty-year-old man near the pier."

Robin put her hands over her mouth as Taylor confirmed her worst fears.

"He drowned my baby in the ocean and blew his own head off after."

Taylor barely finished telling the story before succumbing to her horrific reality. Her bawling turned the heads of the Charades participants, even though she buried her face in her hands. Mortified, Robin failed to maintain a strong exterior. The innocent child she met just days before, who reminded her so much of her Jonathan, was now dead at the hands of his own father. Several questions crossed through her mind, but this wasn't the time to get all the details. Taylor needed someone to grieve with her, someone to listen, and Robin was going to do all she could to fill that role. For as much agony as she had suffered, from being legally kidnapped from her parents to being raped on a regular basis as a child to losing her husband, Robin couldn't fathom going through the type of anguish Taylor was. Jimmy was the one bright spot in her life, yet fate stripped him from her. By the hands of his own father.

"Oh, Taylor honey. Words can't undo any of the heartache you're going through right now, but—"

Taylor's sobs bellowed through the cafeteria.

"But I want you to know sweetheart, me and everyone else here will be here for you. Whatever you need, we are here for you. I am here for you. Okay?"

Taylor tried to thank Robin but couldn't formulate a response. The wound was still so raw. Robin didn't think she'd ever show herself again if that happened to her; even considering that as a possibility was too daunting for Robin to think about.

After a few more minutes of consoling Taylor, Robin proceeded to finish her tasks. Several times, Robin offered Taylor a room at her house that night and for as long as she needed before getting back on her feet, but Taylor respectfully declined, claiming the best way for her to cope with her loss was by confronting it head on and alone. Based on her own experience, Robin didn't agree with this plan, but she was in no position to suggest anything to this heartbroken mother.

Robin had originally planned to partake in Charades that evening, but the distressing news from Taylor dampened her mood. She just wanted to get home and surround herself with who she loved the most. After letting one of her closest co-volunteers know she was going to leave for the night after wrapping up the tasks she still had to do, Robin headed to the empty kitchen and broke down the hardest she ever had since losing Bobby.

After collecting herself and completing her chores, Robin stormed out of Free Morple without paying anyone else any mind. She liked to believe the days of this state causing so much heartbreak were over, but countless others battled hardships every single day. Nothing could excuse what Jimmy's father had done, but Robin couldn't help but wonder if they had been in a different environment how that little family would've ended up. But there was nothing she could do about it, so there was no point in harping on the hypotheticals. A tragedy is why Ariana left. *How could I blame her,* Robin thought?

"Hi there."

Robin gasped and dropped her purse. She was so hyper focused she was oblivious of her surroundings. When she gathered herself, she found Ariana leaned against her car with her arms crossed. She wore skin-tight, all black clothes. The brim of her retro Los Angeles Dodgers hat hung low over her masked face, adding to the dramatic flair. But Robin knew those brown eyes when she saw them.

"Jesus. You scared the shit out of me," Robin said.

"Sorry. Just saying hello."

Robin stared at her sister in disbelief that they were in each other's presence again. Before the other night, they hadn't seen each other for so long, yet the days they spent nearly every waking moment together seemed like just yesterday. As much as Robin would have liked to forget a good chunk of them, they were forever ingrained in her.

Tongue-tied, Robin couldn't think of anything with substance to say. "So, what's up? You get better looking as the years go, and I fall off."

Grinning, Ariana exhaled a chagrin sound from her throat and rolled her eyes; partly because Robin was still beautiful, and partly because she expected a more authentic response. "Oh, shut the hell up. For having two kids, you don't look so bad."

"Thanks for the consolation." Robin scrambled to answer. Even if she didn't just learn of Jimmy's heart-rending demise, she probably still would have been at a loss for words, but at least now she had an excuse.

"So, are you disappointed to see me? It's been years, and I'm feeling some hostility. Or is that just me being sensitive?"

Robin shamefully gazed down and awkwardly scratched the back of her head. Without muttering another word, Robin gave herself up and embraced her younger sister. Her cries shook her whole body, causing her to convulse in Ariana's arms.

"I'm sorry, I'm sorry," Robin said.

"Oh, hon. I'm the one who is sorry. I've missed you like you can't even imagine. I can't believe you're finally back in my arms."

Ariana stroked the back of Robin's head and kissed her on the cheek, seizing the moment of her being there for when her older sister needed her the most. Despite her lavish life, the empty void Robin once occupied in Ariana's life was deeply missed, but even she didn't know how much she had missed her until this very moment. She clutched Robin as hard as she could, afraid that if she let go, she might not see her ever again.

After their official reuniting moment was over, both sisters dried their eyes and chuckled at themselves for letting their emotions get the best of them.

"Let's get dinner tonight, please. My treat," Ariana said.

Still wiping her eyes and sniffling, Robin said, "Oh, as lovely as that sounds I have to get back to the boys."

"Oh, come on. They'll be fine."

Robin knew this, but after what she just learned about inside, she felt like she had to keep them near. But then again, she didn't know how long her sister would be in town for.

"Okay. Can I at least go check on them, drop some things off, and change?"

Elated, Ariana was practically jumping up and down. "Yes, yes. Of course. I'll follow you home and we can take my car."

The compromise almost sufficed. "Can you please wait down the street? I don't want to have to explain this to the boys just yet."

Ariana's joy slightly diminished. "They don't know about me, do they?"

Robin shook her head.

Ariana understood, but it still hurt. "Okay. Yeah, that's fine. I'll follow you."

"Okay, thanks."

Robin kissed her on the cheek and got in her car. Ariana pretended she needed to follow her to know where they were going.

CHAPTER

2089

The Corridor was one of The District's swankiest spots, one of the first high-end establishments that was built when the city was gentrified. Italian-inspired, The Corridor poured the finest wines from around the world and prided itself on delicacies like Chilean sea bass and Bolognese pasta with sauce that had simmered for six hours before being served. In other words, properly prepared.

Even though The Corridor was dark and narrow, how it got its name, it was considered "the place to be seen". The likes of big-time Morple businessmen, politicians, celebrities with second homes in Costa Mor, and other affluent folks would dine there frequently. With countless regulars and big-named patrons, it was a staple in the city. Women as stunning as Ariana and Robin didn't often dine without prominent men, unless they strategically placed themselves at the bar to meet someone.

The pianist playing in the corner right of the entrance caught Ariana's and Robin's attention. He played at the perfect volume, loud enough to set the mood but quiet enough to conversate in indoor voices. Despite the live music and constant conversation, Ariana's and Robin's entry did not go unnoticed. At the bar, the men's focus was shifting from their current prospects to them, to the latter's displeasure.

The hostess, dressed as risqué as the bar goers, welcomed Ariana and Robin in after the automotor took their temperatures. Rather than require customers to wear masks, white-cloth restaurants invested in automotors and concealed them in a nearby wall or ceiling. Customers appreciated this nuance because it enhanced their experience, and restaurants determined it was worth the cost because maskless customers made the dining experience more inviting. The quality, functionality, and subtleness of automotor cost a quarter of a million dollars. Morple was America's number one manufacturer of these devices.

"Hi. How are you ladies tonight? Are you expecting two more?" the hostess asked.

"No. It's just us," Ariana said.

"Oh. Okay," the hostess said, surprised by their independence. "Um, great. We have a table open now. If you just follow me this way."

"We're a little underdressed, no?" Robin said.

"You feel good, you look good." Ariana failed in mimicking Robin's discretionary tone.

After being seated, the hostess said, "Your server will be right with you." She flashed a generic smile and let them be.

"If the men at the bar strike out at least they can try the hostess," Ariana said, still lacking subtlety.

"She is cute, isn't she?"

Robin's eyes widened as she examined the prices on the menu. Despite her fortune, she wasn't prone to spending lavishly.

"Absolutely is," Ariana said, who was still watching the hostess walk back to her podium.

"These prices are outrageous. We don't have to eat here," Robin said. She hoped Ariana didn't feel pressure to wine and dine her at a place of this caliber.

"My treat. Don't worry about that. I'd like a drink too. You?"

Needing something to loosen up, Robin agreed. Ariana didn't think twice about ordering an overpriced glass of wodin, and Robin decided on a vodka over ice.

"Sorry for acting the way I did when I saw you in the parking lot earlier."

"It's okay. You aren't used to seeing me in Free Morple's parking lot. Really, it's fine."

"A girl in her early twenties lost her one-year-old recently."

Ariana's expression changed. "What? How?"

Robin exhaled deeply. "His father killed him before taking his own life."

Ariana's eyes widened, and she covered her mouth with her hand.

"He drowned his own child before shooting himself in the head."

Robin's sister digested this and said, "It looks like Morple is still ruining people's lives, isn't it?"

"Yeah, seemingly so."

Luckily the drinks arrived soon after Robin dropped that bombshell, improving the mood of their first dinner together in nearly two decades.

"To my beautiful sister, who I have missed and love so much," Ariana said, hoisting up her glass to cheers her sister.

Robin shyly grinned and gulped a healthy sip of her beverage. The grin quickly vanished as the drink's burn radiated through her entire body. Between being a single mother and volunteering at Free Morple, Robin didn't indulge in alcohol often.

Ariana fixated her big brown eyes on her big sister. As elated as she was to finally be with her, she felt a deep sense of regret for delaying this moment all these years.

"You have no idea how good it is to see you. I've missed you like crazy," Ariana said.

"I'm sorry. I should've tried harder to reach out and find you. I just, I don't know. Life just got ahead of me. I somehow got to a place of acceptance of our situation, and for that, I'm sorry. I can't believe I failed you like that."

"We are both guilty, Robin. But screw it, we are here now. Let's just enjoy the now, right?"

"Agreed." Robin smiled and sipped her drink.

"My nephews are adorable. I should've known who Moe was when I first met him. His eyes are yours and seeing Jonathan all grown up nearly brought a tear to my eye. You've done such a great job. I'm sorry for not being here all these years to help you. I'm obviously a shitty aunt, and sister, but I would love to be part of their lives now."

Even though this wouldn't be likely, it was what Ariana wanted. She'd worry about what was possible and what wasn't later.

"I'd love for my sons to get to know their aunt. Moe might be a little disappointed when he finds out you're related."

Ariana opened her mouth, but nothing came out. She didn't expect Robin to take a shot at her. Robin rolled her eyes. "He thought you were hot, Ariana."

Embarrassed, Ariana grinned and smacked her forehead with her palm. "Oh, that's a relief. I thought he already had something against me."

The sisters laughed off their brief misunderstanding. After they settled down, the real catching up began.

"Tell me about my nephews, Robin. I want to know everything there is to know about them."

"Well, they're the best boys I could have asked for. In fact, I don't deserve them. Even with my husband out of the picture, they have really grown up to be such admirable young men. Jonathan of course has his struggles with comprehending exactly what happened, and naturally Moe is the one who wants answers and actively misses him. But overall, they have handled it so maturely and have helped me to cope with it."

Robin referring to Bobby as "her husband" revealed she was still holding out hope he would be back in her life one day. She continued, "And the way they look out for each other reminds me of two siblings I once knew. Two sisters who were up against an impossible situation but were there for each other no matter what. Funny how even though we weren't there to lead by example they followed suit, right?"

Ariana slowly nodded. "You may not know it, but you exert a strong energy, Robin. Losing your husband couldn't have been easy but look at the fine job you did. You raised those boys just right all along. You did lead by example."

"I've tried. I've really done my best," Robin said, hesitant to accredit herself too much. "I often think if finding someone else to be a father figure in their lives would have been beneficial for them since they only had a male presence around for a short period of time. I just could never get myself to date again. Partly because I wasn't interested, but also because I think there is something inside of me that still thinks Bobby is going to come back. Even though it has been sixteen years since he vanished.

"When you love someone like that, it is hard to accept he is just gone, gone. You know?"

"I can only imagine. What happened to him?"

Including Jonathan and Moe, Robin didn't let herself get close enough to anyone to have this type of candid conversation. All these emotions and memories had been bottled up for sixteen years now, and verbalizing them proved to be an intense, yet liberating, task.

"Once we married in late 2070, we decided there was no reason for Bobby to work. With what I had, we could be more than fine as long as we were frugal and continued to grow it, which Marty made easy because he connected us to all of the right people. So anyways, financially we were good and could both stay home to raise the boys. But there was a time one of the advisors I was working with informed me about some new venture he was working on that could end up being super profitable. The details of it don't matter, but I went for it.

"I authorized her to allocate $5 million for the investment, and I did so without speaking to Bobby. Once I informed him about it, he asked to be included in those types of decisions, and for some reason, I just snapped. I was on my high horse and flexed my self-perceived power. Oh, I said awful things to him that I don't want to repeat."

The rawness of these emotions was evident in Robin's inability to stop fidgeting and failure to look Ariana in the eye. She gathered herself and wrapped up the story, "And after that fight I stormed out of the house while he was there with the two boys. I came back a couple hours later after mindlessly strolling around the pier to clear my head, contemplating how I should apologize to him. But when I came back, he wasn't there, and Jonathan and Moe were both bawling their heads off. Moe was too young to remember any of it, and Jonathan was not nearly developed enough to provide us with any useful information.

"So that was the last time I saw Bobby. It was me telling him off, and ever since then I have been wondering what happened to him. It has been eating away at me for sixteen years now. I've been holding onto hope he will one day just appear back home, but who knows if that will ever happen."

Ariana wiped the bottom of her eyes. Hearing the pain this had caused her sister killed her a little bit on the inside. They had both endured too much as children. Neither of them deserved an event as traumatic as losing a loved one, especially Robin.

"Oh, Robin honey." Ariana laid her hand over Robin's in a show of support.

"I'm sorry, I'm sorry." Robin incessantly dabbed her eyes with her napkin. "I haven't expressed to anyone how hard this has been for me all these years. Raising two boys al—"

Shameful, Ariana broke eye contact and focused on her drink. Sensing she unintentionally hurt her feelings, Robin consoled her. "Oh no, Ariana, please don't take it like that. That isn't what I meant at all. I mean, yes, of course I would've loved having you around, but do not blame yourself. You weren't supposed to know this would happen."

"I wish I could've done something more to help. You have been here raising two boys on your own while I have been looking out for myself. I could have been stronger for you."

Robin gripped her sister's bicep. "Hey, do not ever, even for a second, think you were not strong for me. Not a day goes by when I don't think about how you were the driving force that got me through those hard times without Mom and Dad. When we were told they died you were the one that kept me above ground. For that and many other reasons, don't ever feel like you did wrong by me."

They wrapped their arms around one another and buried their heads in the other's shoulder. After a long embrace, they recollected themselves. They noticed fellow patrons were staring, but the reunited sisters let them know all was good despite the steady stream of tears.

"Okay," Robin said, laughing at herself for how vulnerable she had let herself be, "We were talking about something happy before that."

Ariana chuckled. "Yes, yes. Please, tell me about my nephews."

Robin boasted about how much progress Jonathan had made, and how dedicated he was to beating the odds and paving his own way in the world. She praised Moe for how great of a younger brother he was, how supportive and patient he was of Jonathan's shortcomings. Robin said without him she does not know if Jonathan would be where he is today. Now that someone who she considered trustworthy was back in her life, Robin vented about her struggles with Moe. As close as they were, there was a wall between them she couldn't knock down. She admitted she built it, and she could be the only one to tear it down. He had always wondered why his mother's life before having children remained so mysterious, and that disconnect was tangible in their relationship. It was a mountain she couldn't figure out how to climb.

"If it helps and you're comfortable with it, I would be more than happy to be there with you when you open up to him. You have done so much alone; you deserve some help, Robin."

Robin nodded. So accustomed to raising two boys on her own, being offered help was unusual, and she didn't know how to accept it.

"Thank you. I may take you up on that." After she swallowed a healthy bite of risotto and washed it down with another sip of vodka, she asked, "So what about you? Why am I the only one talking here? You have been out and about exploring new places for the last twenty years, yet I have been the only one babbling away."

Ariana gave her sister a sheepish grin. "That's because you're the one with the kids. The one with the kids is always more interesting than the one without."

"Kids or not, I would love to know what my baby sister has been doing to keep herself occupied all these years."

After polishing off her third glass of wodin Ariana said, "Oh, believe me. My life has not been nearly as exciting as you are making it out to be."

Eventually Ariana would find the appropriate time to come clean about who she had turned into, but she didn't feel like ruining this dinner with the truth.

Having been distracted at work lately, Richard was catching himself up in his home office with the help of a bottle of wodin before his phone's vibration broke his concentration. Along with a picture of Ariana and Robin from what looked like The Corridor, Phil texted, Dude, isn't the woman with the hat Heather's friend? She's hotter in person and her friend's hot too.

Yeah, that's her. You should've made your move.

Richard stared at the picture for an extended amount of time.

If I came here solo I would've but with a blonde tonight. Fake tits, juiced up lips, and even a fake ass, should be fun.

She sounds like a winner, was all Richard could muster up. He really didn't care about Phil's sex life tonight.

I'd be the winner if I left with both those women, Phil responded.

In a perfect world they'd be on their way to my house right now. Have fun out there.

Ha! Now you're talking.

How two women who barely acknowledged each other at his house just the other night could now be out to dinner appearing to be longtime friends puzzled Richard.

A blonde with fake tits, juiced up lips, and a fake ass was who Phil would have liked to be at the bar with. He was there on business with a man who was much more intimidating.

When Phil's company for the night sat back down after using the little boy's room he asked, "Who was that?"

"Who was what?" Phil asked.

"Who the fuck are you texting?" he said, attempting to snatch Phil's phone.

"Whoa man. Calm down. I'm allowed to fuckin' talk to people. Don't worry, I'm not out here gossiping about you. Look, I just sent my buddy a picture of two hot women he knows."

Phil put his phone in front of his contact's face to prove he wasn't up to any funny business. Phil immediately noticed a change in his demeanor after seeing the picture, a reaction he didn't expect a straight man to have after looking at a picture of women this hot.

"What's that look for?" Phil asked.

His contact continued staring blankly, seemingly unable to articulate what he was thinking.

"Hey, what the hell's going on with you?" Phil asked, pressing him a little harder with his tone this time.

"Uh, nothing. Sorry, sorry. One of them looks familiar, that's all. Threw me off for a second."

Phil slipped his phone back in his pocket and eyed him skeptically. He was new to the trafficking world, and his main point of contact had him on edge. But then again, he thought maybe all human traffickers were naturally anxious. That wouldn't be the craziest thing, especially because that's how Phil found himself feeling all the time as of late.

CHAPTER

18

2058

Reginald's slap burned half of Robin's face. It was so powerful she lost her balance. She couldn't break her fall in time to prevent her head from smacking the tile.

"You can't do anything right, you stupid bitch," Mr. Reginald said.

He dropped down to his knees, forced her to look up at him, and slapped the other cheek just as mercilessly. Reginald clawed her cheeks and lifted her face mere inches from his. She knew if she failed to look him directly in the eye her punishment would be more severe than it already was.

"Fuck, I've done so much for you, and you can't even be polite to my guests. What the hell is the matter with you? I try to save you and all you do is make me look bad. But you make yourself and your disgusting people look worse."

Robin detected an unpleasant odor on his breath, one that gave her more reason to be fearful. When his breath reeked like this, Reginald was more aggressive with her.

"I'm sorry, Mr. Reginald. I'll try harder next time," Robin said. Her tone was timid, but she didn't break eye contact.

Tonight's mistake was holding a dinner guest's water glass too close to the rim at a dinner for MYM donors held at the organization's headquarters in The District, where Robin and Ariana also lived. The guest, a White woman in her late sixties, told her, "You're lucky that was water you wasted with your germs and not wine, or else I'd have your cherry popped by something that isn't supposed to be there."

Robin was oblivious to what she meant, but hearing "you're lucky" was a breath of fresh air. Until now.

"You say that every time. It'd be nice if you could just get it right," Mr. Reginald said. He was huffing and puffing over her, exasperated by his rage and the exorbitant amount of wodin he consumed during dinner.

He finally hoisted himself off Robin. The enraged look in his eye transformed into something predatory. She knew the inevitable was coming, and Mr. Reginald confirmed it when he said, "Get on the table and take them off."

She listened to instructions and didn't attempt to fight tears from pouring down her face. Envisioning herself in a happier place back with her parents and Ariana was her defense mechanism towards her pedophilic legal guardian, but it didn't matter how hard she concentrated on placing herself in an imaginary reality. She failed to escape her actuality every time; Mr. Reginald's intrusiveness was too overbearing to escape from.

"Fuck, at least you're good for something," Mr. Reginald said. He was now aroused, evinced by his tone and his mouth hanging slightly open. "This is what makes having you all worth it."

On her stomach, Robin clasped her hands over her mouth and sobbed vigorously, causing her entire body to convulse. Robin clamped her teeth down into her hand forcibly in an attempt to manipulate her brain to focus on that pain rather than what Mr. Reginald was inflicting on her. Most of the time her hand bled, but even then, her brain wouldn't block out what she wanted it to. Because of centralized focus and Mr. Reginald's moans and grunts, Robin didn't hear the door behind them creak open.

Mr. Reginald's thrusting came to a halt, but Robin remained frozen with her mouth locked down on her hand, too terrified to turn herself over and find out why she got off easy tonight. Usually when he finished having her, he sighed heavily; his silence made her fearful.

"It's over. You can turn around. It's okay now."

Robin warily rolled herself over. Realizing her lower half was on full display, she hastily grabbed cloth napkins from a pile next to her to cover herself. Mr. Reginald lay unconscious and uncovered on the kitchen's floor. There were shards of broken glass scattered around his bleeding head.

"It's okay, Robin. He can't hurt you anymore tonight," Ariana said, "Come to bed with me, and I'll tell you a happy story so you can forget."

Robin didn't notice or feel her hand profusely bleeding until Ariana gently grabbed it and led her to the sink to rinse it off. As she did this, Robin continued swiveling her head back at Mr. Reginald, dreading him waking up.

"He won't wake up. When he has a lot of that brown stuff that smells bad, he never wakes up, and that glass hurt him a lot. It's okay, Robin." Ariana proceeded to clean Robin's bloodied hand. Even though her sister neutralized her threat, Robin still shook with fear.

"Don't bite your hand anymore, Robin. Your cuts will never go away if you keep doing that."

"Okay."

"Promise me you won't."

"Okay. I promise."

Ariana smiled as wide as she possibly could in such a dreary moment.

"Don't worry, Robin. He has a bad memory when he has that brown stuff. Let's just go finish our chores and go to bed."

Ariana pulled her mask back over her nose and mouth and resumed sanitizing the dining room. Robin kept her hand wrapped with paper towels to decelerate the bleeding. Once Ariana completed the last chore, the girls walked back up to their dorm-like accommodations a few floors above the dining room, where they shared a tiny room with two twin beds. On this night, Robin chose to sleep in her little sister's bed, who welcomed her with open arms.

"I love you," Robin said, shaking against Ariana.

"I love you too, Robin. I'll always try and save you."

As traumatic as that night was, Robin reflected on it with great admiration for her sister. She replayed Ariana saying "I'll always try and save you" in her head over and over again. Maybe that's exactly why her little sister was back in her life.

CHAPTER

2089

Robin woke up more cheerful the morning after her first meal with Ariana in close to twenty years. They promised to do it again soon; Ariana joked she would pray they would still look as good at sixty. Obviously catching up with her sister after spending such significant portions of their lives apart was lovely, but what Robin immediately noticed in herself when she got home, still enjoying the effects of the alcohol, was how Ariana's aura told her it was okay to be vulnerable, okay to free herself of the self-imposed burden she put on herself. Robin didn't have to force herself to pretend she was this almighty, perfect single mother who overcame any sign of struggle before it had a chance to manifest itself. She had forgotten how liberating it was to be true to herself. It wasn't until last night she had comprehended how much weight she had been carrying on her shoulders all these years, all because she wasn't secure enough to embrace herself for who she was and what she had endured. All the misfortunes that had worked against her all those years played irreplaceable roles in developing who she was today, which was someone she was proud of. Robin had just been too stubborn to come to terms with this, until Ariana waltzed back into her life.

As if on cue, her phone's vibration rattled on top of her dresser. Ariana's text read, I just wanted to let u know again how great last night was. It means a lot to me and I'm going to hold u to me being able to get to know the boys. They both sound wonderful. If u can, let's chat later. Love u

Just like when they were kids Ariana was up and going early. It was just past six in the morning, but Ariana's day appeared well underway.

Robin considered making coffee before responding, but since she already opened the text message, Robin knew she'd forget to respond if she didn't immediately. Good morning. I had a ton of fun and am so happy you're here. Let's get together soon. I want to talk to you before hanging with the boys. All good things, just want to talk. Have a great day, I love you too.

It pained Robin she couldn't let the process unravel without interfering, but her imperfections wouldn't resolve themselves after just one dinner.

CHAPTER

20

2089

Cooking and distributing orgacal had a higher upside than most attainable legal professions for the former working class. The drug was first discovered after the sonoravirus ended and has grown exponentially since. With marijuana federally legal and cocaine recreationally acceptable, there was a void to fill for a new, illegal drug to contaminate the market.

Its exact origins were fuzzy, but the common rumor was leftover chemically infused supplies on an organic farm in California created the first batch in the early fifties. This is how it got its name, even though it was the furthest thing from organic. Nosey politicians had a field day investigating organic farms convicted of growing the drug, questioning their abilities to feed Americans organic produce while drugging them simultaneously.

Orgacal resembled a basil leaf. The only way to tell the difference was by closely examining it and noticing the thin, bright red vein down the middle of the leaf. The brighter the vein, the more potent it was. Concealing, growing, and consuming it were discrete processes that contributed to its unprecedented growth.

Users smoked it, ate it, chewed it, sucked it, or even stuck it up their asses. As long as the vein of the leaf entered the body, an intense high ensued. It immediately made users lethargic; their eyes drooped; words slurred; pleasant sensations, some sexual, overtook their body. The high lasted for close to an hour, and most users came out of it their normal selves. There was no clouded or hungover feeling; days could resume from where they left off, but science eventually revealed its long-term effects stunted brain development.

Since A.I. equipment was heavily monitored by the government and transparency laws made the government's findings available to the public, orgacal trafficking organizations resorted to using manual labor. Orgacal's farming process was relatively straightforward, so the work in the fields didn't require much intellect, but there was an abundant amount of demand for it. The head honchos in the orgacal industry followed the trend executives in legal business were employing; do everything in their power to rid themselves of employees. This birthed a new practice in the orgacal industry: traffic diswors. The brains that operated the distributors discovered human trafficking was a practical method to continuously increase production. With all the diswors the decimated job market was producing, there were plenty to traffic.

Foot growers were the men orgacal kingpins deployed on the ground to infiltrate neighborhoods and kidnap diswors: preferably young, able-bodied young men, and, if you worked for LaVonte Jackson, young, desirable women were subject to capture, too.

Ariana found herself enamored with her husband's line of work and wanted to play a role.

If it weren't for her mouth feeling as dry as the Sahara Desert, Ariana would have woken up elated. Even by her standards, she overindulged in her wodin collection when she arrived back to her condo after The Corridor. Simply getting back in touch with Robin was a sufficient enough reason to feel gleeful but establishing they would remain in each other's lives provided so much to look forward to. Even though Ariana was unsure of how realistic that could be. Feeling like a young child the night before Christmas, she was too wound up to sleep. This is why she downed that half bottle of wodin.

Ariana had built up quite the tolerance and typically avoided excruciating hangovers. A little slower the next morning, sure, but nothing close to what she was suffering through now. It felt like someone stabbed an ice pick through the back of her head and it came out her forehead. She didn't have an appetite, but she still brewed coffee, only to throw up once its scent drifted through her nostrils. Walking like a wounded soldier coming off the battlefield, Ariana hobbled over to the sink and guzzled water.

For close to an hour, she remained in the fetal position on the kitchen floor. Thank God for the voice-controlled vacuum, or else her throw up would have remained there for a while. She was proud of herself for sending a text to Robin upon waking up because right now she couldn't stare at a screen or concentrate enough to articulate her thoughts.

Unfortunately for her, LaVonte wanted to speak with her soon. This meant she had to get her shit together before his hologram appeared on the island. If she was on the floor sprawled out on account of too much wodin, Ariana would never hear the end of it. Somehow, some way, she mustered up the energy and forced herself to concentrate enough to text him and ask when he could talk. He replied saying it would have to wait until early afternoon because he was in the process of damage control. Usually, Ariana would have been curious for more details, but her brain didn't possess the wherewithal to formulate the question.

She allocated herself ten more minutes to lay on the ground and embrace how pathetic she was before readying herself for her husband. To dissipate her hangover and cheer herself up, she shifted her thoughts from the wodin-induced torture to how fortunate she was Robin was back in her life, even if it would be short-lived. Learning her nephews had grown up to be such admirable young men had unexpectedly warmed her heart, and the concept of being involved in their lives excited her. Aside from her one big break, life worked tirelessly to ensure Robin failed, but she fought harder and persevered, raising two impressive young men on her own in the process. Sure, she oftentimes complicated the process by criticizing herself too harshly and falsely believing she should be perfect, but after the emotional trauma Reginald Lawrence inflicted on them, neither of the sisters could have grown up unscathed. Ariana was grateful their conversation predominantly revolved around Robin and her sons because she didn't know if she could convincingly lie to her sister about who she really was and what she had done.

After using up her time to be a useless alcoholic, Ariana commanded herself to her feet and embarked on what she needed to carry out that day. As counterproductive as it was, Ariana rinsed off before exerting herself in the condo's gym. The purpose wasn't to get clean, but to rather hit the refresh button. On an empty stomach, since she still couldn't bear eating or drinking anything aside from water, Ariana hit the gym hard. She warmed herself up by sprinting a six-minute mile. A rapid cycle of bicycle crunches, tuck and crunches, modified v-sits, and seated Russian Twists followed. She required twelve reps of each workout, and she flew through the cycle three times. Her abs were on fire, pulsing against her skin; a heavy layer of sweat drenched her entire body. Ariana allowed herself a water break before completing three sets of push-ups. As much pain as her body was in, it was thankful its mind coerced it into a beneficial activity.

In spandex shorts and a sports bra, Ariana rested her hands on her hips and let her heart rate slow. She stood in front of the floor to ceiling window and peered down at The District's busy bodies. The majority of them were White men strolling around like they owned the place. As much as Ariana despised their shameless air of arrogance, she couldn't deny it: they did own the place. Morvo hadn't brought Morple up to speed with the times as much as the media depicted it did. The disproportionate rate of wealthy White people to down in the dumps minorities was still appalling, but welfare initiatives like Free Morple masked the statistics telling the real story. More power to Robin and her fellow volunteers, but Ariana recognized all they were doing was enabling big government and business to rationalize mistreating most people. Ariana lost hope for an inclusive society a long time ago; she couldn't honestly claim she ever had it. Minorities' education rates in some parts of the country had increased, but Ariana perceived Morple as a metaphor for elitists remaining in charge. Enough uproar forced other parts of the country to adopt progressive policies, but the powerful figures who didn't want to concede any of their power found a solution: fabricate a totalitarian state. It was the ultimate fuck you move.

As she peered down on The District's epicenter, she chuckled to herself. Here she was, once a little Latina girl born in Morple who the government legally kidnapped as a baby to raise in an abusive environment that attempted to rape and beat any pride she had out of her. That little girl grew up to be a bombshell those same men would have killed for back then and married the most powerful kingpin the world had ever seen, who was Blacker, wealthier, and more influential than all of the nobodies she was currently glaring down at.

Ariana's view was symbolic of her accomplishments thus far. Proving she could overcome the impossible situation the world imposed on her fueled Ariana's fire. If she could defy those odds, anything was possible.

CHAPTER

2089

Prior to Ariana arriving in Morple, LaVonte had his people stock up her closet with brand new clothes from various high-end designers. Her expansive selection contradicted her husband's request she make the trip as short as possible. The finest cloth on the market filled all the racks in her walk-in closet, one of the perks of being Mrs. Jackson.

Ariana elected to wear a strapless bright red long sleeve shirt that hugged her bosom and exposed a sliver of skin above her pant line. As far as her bottoms went, she opted for comfort and chose a pair of slim fitting sweatpants that gripped all the right areas; of course, this is how they were meant to fit. Ariana studied herself in her bathroom mirror one final time before holograming her husband. After doing a few twirls, thoughts of insecurity began to creep in her mind. She began convincing herself this was the beginning of the end, that her superior physical assets were maturing, which was a nice way of saying they were beginning to sag. Clothing like this was meant to flaunt her features, not expose them deteriorating. She lifted her curves up herself, trying to figure out if they used to be that high. After some nutty, irrational back and forth in her own head, she snapped out of it and told herself, *you're being fuckin' ridiculous.*

The hangover was long gone, but sometimes the day after a night of drowning herself in wodin Ariana had illogical thoughts about herself.

They derived from her insecurities, and it was up to her to get her act together. She inhaled deeply, harmlessly slapped her cheek, and smiled at her reflection, judging her appearance before presenting herself to LaVonte.

He was bound to pop up on the island any minute, so Ariana hustled to the liquor cabinet to pour herself the day's first glass of wodin. Even though he would see her sipping it, she preferred he didn't have a visual of how much damage she had already done to the recently full bottle.

Ariana stowed away the bottle just in time.

"Hey baby," LaVonte's hologram said. He was sitting in his office puffing on a cigar. The smoke encircled his face and it elevated gracefully.

"Hello my love, how are you?"

"Better now. Let me see you."

Ariana gently set her glass down and spun around for him, conscious of puffing her chest out when he had the frontal view and sticking out her ass when he examined her from behind.

"That's what I'm talking about," he said as smoke exited his mouth.

"Thank you, baby."

LaVonte ashed his cigar before asking, "How was The Corridor last night?"

Ariana originally planned on telling him today, but him being the first to bring it up caught her off guard and made it appear she was hiding something from him. She was so concerned with how angry he would be she didn't even consider how he found out.

Her eyes wandered nervously before responding. "I promise I was going to tell you. I, I ran—"

"I have no doubt about that. I would just like to know how it went."

His tone wasn't harsh, but his diction indicated he wasn't pleased.

"Believe it or not, she is friends with Heather Lawrence. I ran into Robin at her house, and then found her in the city."

"Found her in the city?"

Ariana exhaled audibly. "I mean, I knew where she was and waited for her outside. I couldn't help myself. I'm sorry, baby."

LaVonte smirked. "Don't apologize to me. I am more concerned about you. The fact you are entertaining the thought of being back in her life when you know it is not possible is worrisome. I do not want this situation to hurt you more than it already has, and right now, you are not making this any easier on yourself."

"I know, I—"

"Let me finish."

Ariana resisted the urge to pick up her glass and down its remaining contents.

"Sending you back to Morple after all this time was a significant risk in itself, but I trusted you with this task. You have done nothing to fuck it up yet, but you are not on a good path right now. Do you recognize my concern?"

Spineless, Ariana concurred.

"The quicker you're out of there, the better it is for all of us. You get to come home, I get my woman back, and our issue with Mr. Lawrence is resolved. When you first got there, you sought out his wife and befriended her immediately, putting you on a fast track to get this done. Do not let this deter your progress."

"I understand."

The conundrum Ariana was in was she truly valued keeping her word, but she also loved and missed Robin more than even she had realized.

"Do not let this be a hiccup, or else I'm going to have to send in some reinforcements to get both of you out." This was definitely a threat.

Ariana nodded. "Okay."

"Okay, good. What did you tell Robin anyways?"

"About what?"

"About you being in Morple."

"Oh, right. Luckily, we mainly talked about my neph—, I mean her sons, but I told her I was here looking at properties to invest in for my husband Lucas. He is a bit older than me and has found success in politics."

Ariana was banking on her fib that wasn't necessarily a lie would lighten up her husband's mood, but he displayed no sign of feeling the need to commend her. Instead, he simply said, "Smart."

The resistance beat her; Ariana snatched her glass and indulged herself.

"Don't drink too much of that shit too early, baby. I have an ask for you."

Ariana would have rolled her eyes if he wasn't already peeved with her. "Yes?"

"Since you've been there, I have been working on landing a new contact in Morple. No matter what happens with the current situation, I do not want to deal with another Lawrence for the rest of my life. Can you meet with a new connect and see what he is about?"

LaVonte asked her, but it wasn't a question.

"Of course. When and where?"

"Tomorrow night at eight at your favorite place."

It took her a second, but Ariana picked up what he was laying down. "Funny. Does it have to be somewhere that is such a scene?"

"What difference does it make?" he asked.

"I was spotted there last night. Don't you think it could happen again?" LaVonte said no.

"Okay, fine. Corridor tomorrow. When will I have his information?"

"I'll be sure to keep you updated with all of that. Let me know if anything notable happens between now and then, yeah?"

"Of course, baby," Ariana said.

"And Ariana."

"Yes."

"Be careful over there. I miss and love you."

"I love you too, baby. Thanks for worrying."

After saying their goodbyes, LaVonte's hologram vanished, and Ariana chugged the remnants of her drink before bolting to the cabinet for more. The sun was still shining bright, but her mind was too conflicted to spend the rest of the day sober.

With a fresh glass in hand, Ariana headed out to her balcony to gather her thoughts. Her husband adopted that demeanor to instill some fear in her; it was his way of keeping her in check and remind her who she reported to. Since marrying LaVonte Ariana had been loyal and a good wife. Plus, she was well aware of what she was getting herself into before saying yes to this life. Part of the intrigue was the lavish wedding overlooking the Pacific Ocean from Lompoc, California's coast, the mansion, and the unlimited access to life's luxuries, but they did possess an authentic bond based on their pasts' commonalities. For that, they truly loved each other. Ariana knew his authoritarian approach was his way of expressing those feelings, but she had realized it was getting to a point where his gripe with the world carried more weight than hers. It had probably been that way for a while and returning to Morple had just exposed this. LaVonte was far too powerful of a man to concede his desires, even if it diminished the chances of Ariana achieving hers.

The realization that Robin and LaVonte couldn't simultaneously play active roles in her life fully set in after Ariana's last conversation with her husband. Why she ever thought they could was just her optimistic side coming out. Hell, she wasn't very confident Robin would even accept her back in her family's life if she learned the hard truth.

Either way, deep in her wodin-inspired thoughts, Ariana had to commit to a side before it was too late.

CHAPTER

2089

Marcelo's was the busiest Mexican restaurant in The District. A rambunctious crowd, mostly single thirty-somethings, populated the bar trying to get lucky. The restaurant was in demand because of its ambiance rather than its food, as it lacked authenticity. Other desirables, dim lightning, dense margaritas, salty chips, lively background music, busty employees, and aesthetically pleasing patrons was why people chose Marcelo's. All of these reasons are why Moe's mother being so gung-ho about treating him to dinner there confused him.

Marcelo's rowdy crowd was shameless in expressing interest in Robin. Heads turned and eyes followed her as mother and son found their table. Based on the looks of jealousy shot his way, Moe gathered some of them were under the impression he was her significantly younger boyfriend. As if that wasn't enough to warrant his wanting to get this dinner over with as soon as possible, Moe spotted Megan Rincon with a group of friends gathered around a table in the back corner of the restaurant. Her friends were uncontrollably laughing, but Megan fixated on Moe, who played it cool by acknowledging her with a slight head nod. Her cleavage and seductive stare diverted his attention from the eyes on his mother.

Once seated, Robin asked, "So sweetheart, how are things lately?" She pulled her mask off and stuffed it in her purse.

"Good. I mean, nothing new is really going on in life," Moe said, not really inclined to elaborate.

"No? Nothing you want to talk about?"

Moe scoffed. "No, Mom."

"Okay, fine. Are you and Megan not on good terms or something?"

"What? No, I mean, everything is fine. Why do you think that?"

"Because she is sitting over there, and you didn't go over there to say hello."

"That doesn't mean we aren't on good terms."

"Well then what does it mean?"

Moe tossed his hands in the air, fed up with her inquiries.

"Jeez Moe, it is just a question."

"No, it has been like a million questions."

"Oh, so dramatic."

Moe let his head fall forward and took a deep breath in. He was close to blatantly asking her why the hell they were there if all she was going to do was annoy him.

"How is Dillon?" she asked. At least this wasn't about him.

"He's okay."

"Back at school?"

"Mom, please."

"What, Moe?"

"Stop being so damn nosey. Why are we here?"

Robin widened her eyes and grunted, but she couldn't suppress the truth from him much longer. It was eating away at her, and she was finally in a place where she realized revealing who she really was would unchain her from the persona she worked so hard to maintain.

"Okay, fine. I need to talk to you about something. It's eaten away at me for a long time, and I think it's time to fill you in."

Learning she contracted a terminal virus or murderous disease is what initially popped into Moe's head. He always assumed the worst because, on the rare occasion his mother discussed a serious topic with Moe, her delivery made it seem like the apocalypse was approaching.

"Holy shit, Mom. Are you sick?"

"What? No. Everything is fine. Why would you guess that?"

"Because of the way you say things, and how you look like the world is ending."

Robin ignored the jab. "No, honey. Sorry. Everything is just fine. It is about my past and about someone in my life I want you to know about."

"Have you been seeing someone since Dad we don't know about?"

"No. Can you just listen?" Robin said.

"Can you just get to the point?" Moe fired back.

"If you'd stop interrupting me I will." It was her turn to expression frustration.

Moe slouched back in his seat, folded his arms, exhaled audibly, and waited for his mother to reveal the purpose of their dinner.

"I want to talk to you about Ariana," Robin said.

"Heather's friend?"

Robin laughed at him referring to her as that, "Yes, Heather's friend."

"You do know her, don't you?"

"I know her very well. In fact, she's my sister."

Visibly stunned, Moe was at a loss for words. All he could get out was a compilation of stutters before constructing a response. "What? You said you were an only child. What do you mean she is your sister?"

Robin collected herself before diving into the details. "Ariana and I were taken away from your grandparents when I was very young, and she was just a baby. Before Morvo, believe it or not, things were even worse for Morple's working class. I am not sure you have ever heard of it, but there was something called the Morple Youth Movement." Robin paused and examined Moe's face for any sign of recognition.

As a whole, Morple's modern-day youth were unaware of the hardships their predecessors either inflicted or suffered through. The government, media, and education systems did a sufficient job at highlighting what Morvo had done to improve the state's overall welfare and bypassed why those countless revisions were necessary in the first place. Moe's blank expression indicated he was clueless.

"Have you heard of that?" she asked to confirm her suspicions.

"Uh, no." He wasn't really sure if he wanted to.

"So, my father was a working man, and in that time, maintaining a job as a working man was incredibly difficult. Companies were laying employees off every day to fend for themselves in a, we'll call it, uninspiring job market. A good amount of these people, like your grandfather, had families to support, but were struggling to do so. They were eligible to receive payments from the government, but since the government was forced to issue out so many, they created the Morple Youth Movement. Long story short, the government was able to lawfully take children from their families to put them directly under their care and pay those families less than they would have to if they had children to care for."

Moe's blank expression had transformed into one of trepidation, fearing where this story was going.

"So, Ariana and I were part of that, and, to put it lightly, it was, uh, a troubling experience for the both of us."

"What happened?"

Robin stuttered before answering. "There was a lot, honey. We weren't treated how children should be. It was, uh, an abusive environment."

"Like emotional abuse?" Moe asked, hoping she would say the extent of it ended there. His hope was short lived.

"That was part of it."

"What were the other parts?" Moe's voice shook.

"Honey, it was a really, really sad childhood that you do not need to know the details of."

"You brought me here to tell me this, so tell the entire story and don't just half-ass it." More so than wanting to know the details, Moe said this because he had longed for his mother to be this candid with him. He was now realizing why she hadn't been. He didn't blame her.

Robin peered at her son, contemplating if she should break down this barrier and reveal the extent of her childhood and adolescent experiences. There was so much Moe didn't know because she hadn't wanted him to bear her burden, but if they were going to sustain a healthy mother-son relationship, Robin had to be forthcoming.

"Ariana and I were sexually and physically abused by the same man as young children until we were young adults."

Robin observed her son's body tense after disclosing this part of her past. Moe stuck his palm on his forehead and digested what he had just learned. In his gut, he knew his mother didn't have it easy growing up because if she did, she wouldn't have been so secretive, but Moe never imagined it was this severe. To no avail, he fought hard to fight back the waterworks. He squeezed his eyes shut tight and pressed a thumb and index finger into them, hoping to push the tears inwards.

Robin placed her hand on his free one and said, "It's okay, sweetheart. Everything is okay now."

Tears ran down both sides of his nose, and he freed the hand his mother had reached out for to wipe them off. Knowing how big of a bomb she had dropped on Moe, Robin let her son collect himself before continuing. Moe was hesitant to ask his mother to elaborate on her experience. Naturally inquisitive, he wanted to know the entire story, but the reality could be too gruesome for him to handle. Plus, he didn't want to pressure her to relive it just to satisfy his curiosity, but he did need one question answered.

"Is that who Jonathan's dad is?"

Her expression didn't change, but the question blindsided Robin.

"Yes. Yes, that is who his father is."

"Does he know that?"

"No."

"Has he ever asked who his dad is?"

"No. Your father was amazing to Jonathan. Amazing enough to fill that void. Also, I haven't had the courage to talk to Jonathan about that part of his life. Quite frankly, I've been relieved all these years he hasn't asked."

As recently as thirty minutes ago, Moe would've been bothered by this truth, as he was deeply affected by how closed off his mother had been his entire life. Now, he understood it; he even felt guilty for building up that resentment towards her.

"Wha—what happened to your parents?"

Robin's eyes glistened as she unloaded another grim family event. "Ariana and I were able to see them on occasion. During one of those visits when I was either nine or ten, I can't remember for sure, I told them—"

This dark memory was one she had not anticipated surfacing tonight. Robin tilted her head back and smiled in an attempt to vanquish the tears forming at the bottom of her eyes. Moe considered interrupting her, feeling culpable for the agonizing thoughts his mother was reliving, but he didn't know if she would ever be this transparent again.

"Sorry, hon."

"It's okay."

"I told them what had been happening to Ariana and me, but I didn't say specifics because I didn't know what it was at the time. So, um, but I knew they understood what I was telling them. I could tell by the looks on their faces. By how I was describing it there was no way they didn't know what was happening. They both looked so defeated, and so helpless. They said a few things to try to make me feel better, but nothing could be said to make a little girl going through that feel better.

"They promised they would try to get us back home with them, wherever that was, but a few days later Ariana and I were told they both committed suicide in their apartment. And that was that. We never heard about or from them again. The saddest part is I was so bummed because I knew what that meant for Ariana and me. I didn't have much hope of getting out anyways, but them being alive allowed me to be a little optimistic."

Reliving this chapter of her life was no easy endeavor, but Robin's exterior remained strong for Moe's benefit. "Now sweetheart, I don't want you to worry. That was a long time ago. There is nothing we can do about it now. I was one of the lucky ones who made it out. I came out stronger. Focus on that and focus on the now. We are who we are because of it."

"I just, I just can't believe you had to go through all that." Moe was hardly audible.

Robin scrunched her face, indecisive if unloading all of this was the correct decision. As if he sensed her questioning herself, Moe affirmed it was.

"Thank you for being so honest with me. I'm sorry I have been such a pain in the ass all these years. I understand why you wouldn't want to tell me any of this. It must have been really hard to do that. I'm really proud of you, Mom."

Robin leaned over and hugged her son, pressing his head into her shoulder because, credit to her motherly instincts, she knew he needed a safe space to cry. Once his body stopped shaking and she no longer heard his muffled sobs, she released him so they could return to sitting as they were.

"Hey, don't worry. Megan's gone," Robin said.

Moe managed a slight chuckle. "God, shut up."

He said this in jest, and his mother smiled at him.

"I love you," she said.

"I love you, too."

"So back to what we were discussing, yes, Ariana is your aunt."

Moe snickered at this. "Yeah, well that's kind of a bummer."

"And why's that?"

"Because I thought she was hot."

This deflated all the heavy emotion that only moments ago clouded their outing. Robin covered her mouth and laughed harder than Moe expected her to. Once she got it out of her system, she asked him if he would want her to become part of their family. He enthusiastically said he would love to get to know his mother's sister.

"I have another question, though," he said.

"Go ahead."

"Where did all of our money come from?"

"I won it."

"How?"

"In a lawsuit after Morvo."

"How much?"

"Moe, come on."

"What? Come on, tell me."

At this point, Robin thought she might as well reveal all facets of her life.

"Fine. Seventy-five."

"Seventy-five what? Fuckin' million?"

"Moe."

"Sorry, but are you serious?"

Robin raised her eyebrows and nodded.

"Holy mother fuck."

"That's a secret, Moe."

"I know, I know."

Mother and son enjoyed the rest of their dinner conversing about more positive topics, like how much progress Jonathan has made, the funny things he does and says, how integral of a role Wallace plays in their family. At the end of the night, Robin and Moe both walked out of Marcelo's grateful for one another, with a stronger bond than they had when they walked in.

Robin kept to herself she felt relieved Moe didn't ask about his father because that was a question she truly did not have an answer to.

The same hostess from the night she treated Robin to dinner at The Corridor greeted Ariana.

"Hi again! How are you?" she said once the automotor verified Ariana's temperature. The hostess' chipperness bugged Ariana.

"Hi. How are you?" Ariana asked, failing to match her enthusiasm. "I'm meeting a Phil Gorge here tonight. He told me he rented a private room, but I'm not sure which one."

Between the time they spoke yesterday and meeting Phil tonight, one of LaVonte's men provided her with more details pertaining to the topic of discussion. Apparently, Phil was proving himself to be a valuable source of information for newly available diswors. Ariana's task was to learn how advantageous his insight could be to her husband's organization.

"Oh, perfect. He came in about five minutes ago. We love Phil. Follow me right this way," the hostess said.

Phil tensed when Ariana entered their private room, immediately recognizing her as the woman from Richard's holographic feed in his office and the one he spotted at The Corridor just the other night.

Ariana noticed Phil's flabbergast upon her arrival. Immediately a red flag, but apparently, he wasn't nervous enough to miss out on the opportunity of checking her out while he had a view of her entire self. Ariana had anticipated this, since that was the purpose donning a tantalizing dress. LaVonte and her learned it increased the chances of a more favorable negotiation.

She took the liberty to introduce herself first and extended her hand for him to shake.

"Phil Gorge. Real pleasure to meet you. Please sit."

Their server poured wine for Ariana only to be told she wouldn't be drinking anything unless it was wodin or water. He swiftly swapped her untouched glass of wine with the finest wodin available.

Phil observed Ariana shifting in her seat, trying to find a comfortable position. To the pleasure of his hormones, Phil was fantasizing about what it would be like if she were moving on top of him like that. The image his mind fabricated had him on the verge of an erection under the table. He had to shift his concentration from her riding him to their business matters.

"So, how are you liking Morple?" he asked.

"I'm from here, and quite frankly, I'm not too fond of it, hence why I left. But I get why you're here. It has always worked out for people like you, right?"

Phil flashed a brief, embarrassed smile.

"Yeah, I've done okay for myself." Phil took a swig of wine out of nervousness. He felt beads of sweat forming along his forehead. Worst comes to worst, he could flatter Ariana by blaming his edginess on her rack. "Let's get to it then."

Ariana raised her eyebrow at him and patiently waited until he addressed the purpose of their meeting. The message from LaVonte was very clear: they didn't need him, but he could prove to be a value add. That meant if Ariana didn't like what he had to say, she had the green light to end the evening early.

Phil straightened his posture and cleared his throat before providing Ariana the rundown of what he was capable of contributing to her husband's organization. He explained that his role with Rapture enabled him to be privy of any massive layoffs before they actually happened. The firm's reach was international, and it consistently repped companies that were committing all its resources to A.I., which resulted in thousands of diswors with no place to go. If LaVonte and his organization had this level of insight, foot growers could deploy in these areas before opposing organizations had an opportunity to snatch them up. To validate his prowess, he conceded two companies in Oklahoma that would lay off their entire workforce in the next month. Phil claimed, for a self-described modest fee, his information would provide LaVonte with an endless supply of diswors to work on his plantation, and promised he knew of enough companies going fully automated that his information alone would keep LaVonte's plantation running for the next decade. Ariana began to buy Phil's credibility when he alluded to how frequently plantations cycled through diswors because either health problems ended their enslavement early or the gangs that formed on the plantations ended up killing each other. The workforce increased the profit margin, but maintaining it was no walk in the park.

Ariana didn't show it, but she considered his conviction and knowledge of the industry impressive. It was evident he wanted in, but possessing a mole with so much status, like Phil, was risky for an organization like her husband's. If it were to go south, LaVonte would have to shell an infuriating amount of hush money because prosecutors would rather see him go down than ruin the career of a White wealthy corporate executive. On a personal level, Ariana felt like a hypocrite because she wasn't fond of his drinking. Yes, she indulged quite often, but neither LaVonte nor her would be comfortable with someone on the payroll in Phil's type of circles drinking as much as he was. Before ordering their entrees he already downed two glasses, but that wasn't what ultimately deemed him as untrustworthy.

Once his spiel had concluded, Ariana straightened her spine and crossed her arms, purposely pressing her breasts further up her chest. She felt like toying with him until she decided to play her hand. "I like you Phil. You're confident, intelligent, and, might I say, attractive."

Ariana didn't break eye contact with him as she blatantly swallowed an abnormal amount of wodin. She set down the now empty glass and stood up to situate herself on his lap. Phil scooted his chair back to make enough room for her. She pushed her face to the side of his head to confirm her suspicions.

"Let's continue the night. My spot's in Costa Mor. We can have drinks, look at the ocean, and continue our conversation, maybe do some other things," he said.

Ariana shoved her chest closer to his face and simultaneously felt him harden under the back of her thigh, "I don't think tonight will work."

"Oh, come on. One drink at my place."

"One drink and then what?" she asked.

"Then we'll see where the night takes us." He placed his hand on her stomach and guided it up until it grazed the bottom of her breasts. "In honor of our first of many deals together."

Ariana grabbed his hand and placed them on her breasts. "It's what you want, right?"

Phil nodded, too transfixed on them to prevent her next move. Swiftly, Ariana dug her nails into his left ear and yanked out a square shaped earpiece the color of his skin and roughly half the size of a small pinky fingernail. LaVonte had trained her to pay attention to the smallest of details.

Even with Ariana's curves in his grasp, the consequences of what just happened hit Phil like a ton of bricks. Ariana's seductive stare had reshaped itself into a stern expression that dismayed Phil.

"I, I was put up to it. I swear, I swear I was."

Without taking her eyes off him, Ariana stood up and brought the earpiece to her mouth and said, "Careful who you are dealing with, now."

Ariana tossed it on the table and said, "It doesn't appear our goals align. I'll be sure to let LaVonte know. Thank you for your time." And with that, she was gone.

Wide-eyed and breathing heavily, Phil frantically picked up the earpiece and inserted it back in.

"Marty, are you there?"

"How the fuck did you blow that, Phil?" Marty Perlman asked. He was with a team of federal investigators at his office, and before the catastrophe that unraveled in a private dining room the government had paid for, the idea of obtaining sufficient enough evidence to nail one of, if not the, biggest trafficker in the world nearly made them hard. It was too bad their informer was too horny and incompetent to be of any use, and Ariana was too seasoned to say anything incriminating before confirming she was in the clear.

"God fuckin' dammit!" Marty said, causing an uproar in Phil's ear.

"Fuck Marty. She's just good. I don't know what happened."

"You couldn't have hid the fuckin' piece better? What the hell is the matter with you? Maybe don't drink so fuckin' much next time. You think a woman married to the world's most ruthless trafficker is going to want to go home with you, you fuckin' idiot?"

"Fuck you."

"No, fuck you Gorge! This is a huge shit show now."

"Like it wasn't before?"

"Now that I know who's in charge, it's nothing like it was before. Watch your fuckin' back, Gorge."

Marty clicked off before chucking his case files across his office and screaming at the top of his lungs. Even the coarsened federal investigators, who were at least forty years younger than Marty, were frightened by his outburst.

Phil rested his elbows on the table and pressed his hands into the sides of his head. When the food finally arrived, Phil tossed both entrees off the table, told the server to fuck off, and stormed out of The Corridor.

When Ariana arrived back at her condo, she hologrammed LaVonte immediately and briefed him on the meeting, minus the part about allowing Phil to feel her up. What her husband didn't know wouldn't hurt him. Besides, it was probably the last set of boobs he would ever feel. Fortunately for him they were hers.

After receiving assurance LaVonte would handle Phil, the power couple said their love yous and committed to touching base in the morning. Ariana then slipped into something more comfortable and cracked open another bottle of wodin. Tonight's events triggered some stressors, so rather than just bringing out her glass to the balcony she brought the entire bottle because she knew she'd need a refill soon enough.

Before returning to Morple, Ariana looked forward to inserting herself back in the game, thrilled to have another opportunity to assist her husband in the pursuit of prosperity, but now that she was in the midst of it, she had a difficult time remembering why she had ever enjoyed it so much. After all, because of her meeting summary, someone was going to lose his life. Granted, this Phil Gorge was no one of any significance to her, so she wouldn't lose much sleep over it, but fighting someone else's battle was getting old. There was someone else out there whose head she would much rather have on a stake than Phil's.

As she poured herself the second drink since being back, Ariana considered what Robin would think if she ever learned her younger sister had thrust herself into this life. One of spectacular wealth, drugs, sex, slaves, and killing. It once enamored Ariana because she didn't have anything else going on for her, but now with Robin slowly but surely becoming part of her life again, maybe it was time to reconsider her purpose. The desire to become part of their family was trumping the yearning to add to the billions her husband already had. That is if they could ever forgive her for what she did all those years ago.

Ariana prided herself on loyalty, so leaving her husband and the life they had built together was a drastic step she didn't know if she could ever take or wanted to take. Plus, if she followed through on leaving him, she would be looking over her shoulder the rest of her life, unless she made the first move.

CHAPTER

2056-2072

Lavonte stood about six and-a-half feet tall with eye-popping muscle definition. His body fat percentage was less than ten even in his mid-forties. If dictionaries included pictures, his face would be under 'chisel'. LaVonte's strong features intimidated and simultaneously demonstrated intellect, emphasized by his small rectangular glasses. Aside from his eyebrows and eyelashes, his face and head both underwent laser hair removal surgery. He claimed remaining bald was a sufficient way to keep eyes drawn on him, as if his presence and status wasn't terrorizing enough. Although his skin was very dark, his tattoos were visible. They suffocated his skin but couldn't conceal his bulging muscular system. Tattoos were once a painful and lengthy process but now could essentially sticker themselves on. Artists cultivated tattoos on a template and laminated them on people to sear them in the skin. This was painless, efficient, and produced higher quality work. LaVonte demanded all his tattoos be put on his body the old school way. He liked people knowing he did not only defeat pain, he welcomed it.

LaVonte's parents were former social justice warriors who the government moved to Morple in 2035 until the end of the sonoravirus pandemic in 2045. Originally from Los Angeles, his parents were heavily involved in their community. They regularly attended peaceful protests, volunteered for homegrown politicians' campaigns, donated their hard-earned money to fund Black-owned businesses, and traveled across the country to show their support for progressive initiatives. Out of all the causes they were enthusiastic about, they were the most dedicated to fighting for an adequate education system for poor Black communities.

LaVonte's parents never imagined their living situation, a five hundred square-foot apartment in a building with four hundred other units, would qualify as being an at-risk residence during the sonoravirus. As the situation worsened, the government broadened the qualifications of which housing situations were more detrimental to society as a whole. Shortly after officials confiscated their building, they shipped his parents to Morple, who were lucky enough to work in the same factory and remain close in proximity. A rarity during that time.

When they returned to Los Angeles in 2045, they found a demolished building where their old apartment once was and couldn't find work if their lives depended on it. Expecting a baby amplified these issues and mutilated their once admirable relationship.

LaVonte's father bounced around from dead-end job to dead-end job, unable to secure a sustainable gig because of the new A.I.-based economy. They coped with their misfortunes by drinking heavily. LaVonte's parents inebriated themselves into oblivion and would pour him drinks when he was as young as eight. The first time they did this LaVonte, not knowing what to expect, tossed back a sip like he would from a glass of water. He threw up immediately, putting his body in shock. His sloshed parents found it hilarious their son couldn't yet handle his liquor. They rolled on the ground laughing like it was a family memory from his childhood they'd forever reminisce on. LaVonte ran to his room crying and vowed to himself he would never ingest alcohol again; a vow he had stayed true to. Despite his evident distaste for alcohol, his parents continued pouring him drinks when they'd drink themselves into a stupor. His parents didn't comprehend his disdain for the poison, so rather than asking them not to do it he left the drinks untouched. He could have eventually overcome the bad memory the taste and smell of alcohol triggered but witnessing the melees his parents had drunk is what solidified his loathing of it.

At eleven years old LaVonte's home life imploded. The factory his father worked at for a little over a month shut down, putting him out of a job for the upteenth time. Lavonte's mother's initial reaction was to console him. She reminded her husband how proud she was of his persistence and how commendable his work ethic was towards continuing to fight for his family to make ends meet. After a heartfelt family discussion, his parents' nightly ritual commenced: tall and very full glasses of gin. Their financial struggles, unrewarding fight for social justice, and general unhappiness with their place in the world were too much to remain bottled up. They soon learned even the alcohol couldn't mask their issues any longer.

From LaVonte's perspective, it all happened so suddenly. One second, they were a loving couple, and in the blink of an eye, they were at each other's throats, literally.

"All you is is a stupid Black man who can't provide. Making us all look bad and keeping us at the bottom of the pole. I married a bum," his mother said to his father.

She continued berating him. "How is you supposed to set an example for little LaVonte if you can't hold a damn job? You're going to end up raising another worthless nigga. Just like you." As she babbled on her words slurred more and more. His father's cool could only last so long.

"I could've had myself someone worth somethin', but no, I picked you," she said before indulging herself with another big sip.

LaVonte's father one upped her by downing the contents of his glass and slamming it on the coffee table. He scoured the mess, disregarding the potential of severely cutting himself on his quest to find the biggest piece of glass. Once he had one to his liking, he charged at LaVonte's mother, yanked her head back by grabbing a fistful of hair, and angled the shard of glass against her cheek. There was such an excessive amount of gin in her she was laughing.

"Who the fuck are you, bitch? Huh? You'd be another fuckin' hoe on the street if you didn't have me. I'm the only reason you're not high selling your pussy." He pulled her head back again and slammed it into the wall, drawing blood and creating a large impression. LaVonte witnessed the debacle escalate out of the corner of his eye, too scared to intervene. Too scared to turn his head in their direction.

"I still might. That way we have some money coming in," she said.

He rammed her head into the wall three consecutive times. LaVonte didn't know if she was conscious, but he deduced his father had lost control. While barking obscenities in her ear, he ripped her pants and undergarments off before taking his dick out. Still grasping her bloodied head against the wall, he raped her with the shard of glass at her face, as if she was capable of protecting herself. He shouted vile and derogatory things in her ear the entire time.

"You still wanna sell this gross ass pussy?"

"No one's buying this fuckin' cunt."

"Your cunt is worthless, bitch."

Once he determined he got his point across, he let her limp body collapse to the ground, causing a thundering sound that caused LaVonte to jolt in his chair. Not paying her any mind, his father buttoned up his pants and b-lined it to the kitchen to retrieve the bottle of gin. Nonchalantly, he situated himself back in his seat and poured another drink. He told LaVonte, "Don't ever let a bitch talk to you like that, LaVonte. Show them you're in control, you hear me? All they is is bitches."

LaVonte mustered up the courage to look up and found his father's glassy, red eyes fixed on him. Eleven-year-old LaVonte reluctantly nodded, stole a brief glance at his unconscious mother, and sat there petrified, still too frightened to move his entire body.

His father noticed his singular, subtle movement. "She'll be fine."

With his father passed out sitting upright and his mother still unconscious, LaVonte packed everything meaningful to him, stole some money he scavenged around the apartment, kissed his mother's forehead, prayed she'd live and run away, and left. After that night LaVonte never saw his parents again and promised himself he would never depend on anyone else to provide for him.

An oppressive government determining his family's unfortunate fate was the fuel that burned his fire. It designated the Jacksons to live lives of hardship and uncertainty, eventually spiraling out of control into addictions that led to their demise. Once he matured, LaVonte understood what ruined his parents was society intentionally limiting their opportunities, not who they were as individuals. LaVonte's idea of getting even was to inflict suffering on others at the hands of an unjust system he would fabricate.

As a teenager, he swiftly became one of the most vicious foot growers in the orgacal industry. His ruthlessness, anger, physicality, and motivation proved to be a deadly combination. When LaVonte was one of the youngest members in the crews he ran with he still commanded the most respect based on his performance in the field. He led his team, hunting diswors for an orgacal plantation east of Oakland, on dozens of raids that multiplied the plantation's workforce. Any diswors who retaliated were eventually captured and were forced to witness LaVonte rape their daughters or wives before decapitating them. For LaVonte, there was no such thing as going too far.

The kingpins who ran the plantation he made a name for himself at treated their best employee to their luxuries. He earned the privilege to partake in eating gourmet meals with them; there was always a bag of gasey blow designated for him; above all else, the most beautiful women he had ever seen were at his disposal whenever he pleased.

Watching rape in his own childhood home groomed him into being violent with women during intercourse. Unlike his father, LaVonte did not intentionally seek nearly beating them to death, but his strength combined with his aggressiveness inflicted harm. The women on site dreaded when LaVonte called for them. Administering pain wasn't what he got off to, but he did relish in asserting dominance. Still developing himself, LaVonte didn't comprehend the severe damage he was causing. His experience demonstrated to him intercourse included violence and assertion.

While enabling his bosses to amass generational type wealth, LaVonte discerned how much more minted and powerful he could be if he held a stake in an orgacal operation. His experience up near Oakland taught him the business and how to preside over others.

LaVonte moved back down to the greater Los Angeles area and, as fate had it, got back in contact with six guys who lived in his building growing up. They already operated a small-time plantation but lacked the expertise LaVonte gained from working under real kingpins. Their product was potent, and they had made strides in being well-connected with politicians; their production, or lack thereof, was what was holding them back. LaVonte knew they needed more experienced, hungrier foot growers. He sold them on him heading that side of the business. He guaranteed they would expand and be printing money in no time. Without hesitation, they handed him the reins of everything related to that side of their operation, and, as advertised, he delivered. In a year's time, they tripled production and increased their margins, credit to dilating their diswor workforce. LaVonte hired the right men, eliminated the existing ones who didn't think like him, and had facilities built for his employees and future captives. His immediate impact impressed his partners, and as a result, they awarded him more power. Their fatal mistake.

Similar to his previous position, LaVonte became bored. His appetite for more came back as he sought to be the one and only boss. The don. At a certain point, his partners didn't see the need in expanding operations. They weren't enthusiastic about negotiating new deals with politicians to keep them off their backs as they continued their exponential growth. LaVonte contested that remaining stagnant was identical to regressing. No matter how hard he pressed them on his beliefs, he couldn't get them to budge. Shortly thereafter, he deemed killing them was the only way to acquire the results he was chasing.

On a night following a day spent finalizing the terms of a new distribution channel in Chicago, LaVonte and his six partners felt they deserved to celebrate. His partners indulged themselves in the fine wines imported from Spain and brought in fourteen escorts. Naturally, each partner honed in on two and went their separate ways to have some fun. What LaVonte's partners weren't aware of was what he promised to the escorts outweighed their payments for the night's services. LaVonte instructed the women to stab their respective customers once they were in a private room with them. Concealing knives in purses wasn't difficult, especially around intoxicated, horny men. Shooting them would've been more efficient and less of a mess but stabbing sent a message. LaVonte was well on his way to becoming the richest and most powerful trafficker there ever was.

Shortly after LaVonte had the escorts, who he didn't pay and turned into sex slaves, kill his old partners, his organization became more lucrative than his newly deceased colleagues ever had the balls to make it. Under his leadership, it reeled in hundreds of billions annually. Because of the relationships he forged with politicians, he didn't have to worry about facing legal consequences. He handsomely paid elected cronies at all levels of the government a total of billions a year and allowed them access to his women, who lived in homes on his plantation. By the time he met Ariana Soren, a total of five hundred women had called his plantation home over the years.

Allowing someone to grow as close to him as Ariana had was unfathomable to LaVonte at one point in time, but their shared struggle created a safe place for him to evolve as a person. People who he developed strong feelings for, whether they were family, friends, professional relationships, or romantic, never lasted because of his determination to constantly become an amplified version of himself. From when they first fell in love, he prayed it would forever work but couldn't promise himself he would change enough for them to die together.

No matter what happened, LaVonte knew in his heart he would always love her, even if it didn't always seem like it.

2089

Since running away from his parents over thirty years ago, LaVonte regularly rose before the sun did. Having more hours to work than his competitors did was one of his several advantages. It wasn't even five in the morning and LaVonte laid in bed with his eyes wide open and thoughts racing.

Ever since Richard Lawrence made it clear he wasn't going to honor their arrangement, life on the plantation had been a whirlwind. Part of the reason LaVonte paid politicians and well-connected businessmen was because he didn't like to travel, but with Richard failing to live up to his end of the bargain, LaVonte was preparing himself to head down to Peru to exercise damage control with his new partners in South America.

On top of that, factions of his diswors had been acting out, ultimately halting production and risking not meeting expectations. The diswors divided themselves up amongst where they were from and race, essentially forming gangs like they do in prisons. They were smart enough not to stage a coup against LaVonte's men, whose guns were always at the ready, but they could do some real damage to each other and disrupt Lavonte's intricate system. Just the other day, a group of ten Whites ganged up on three Mexicans and sodomized them with their farming equipment in the middle of an orgacal field during the sun's peak hours. One of the Mexicans ended up dying, and the other two were currently laid up in the plantation's medical wing. The doctor LaVonte paid to treat his employees and diswors and not say shit about it reported both would recover, but neither of them would be capable of working again. When the good doctor left, LaVonte would have them killed. He didn't order foot growers to capture diswors just to inherit more mouths to feed. The expectation was they worked long and hard every single day, and if they couldn't, bullet to the brain.

The ten White diswors, skinny and toothless pieces of shit from buttfuck nowhere in flyover America, were in a crammed cell tied up since the stunt they pulled. They received water twice a day, food once a day, and it was up to them to figure out where to piss and shit. As of now their fate was uncertain. LaVonte wanted them dead, but he needed the manpower. Killing ten would noticeably affect the plantation's workflow, even though at this stage in his organization's life it shouldn't. If LaVonte had the intel as to where he could deploy his men to capture and return with fresh diswors, it wouldn't be as big of a burden, but inventory had been scarce lately. He had to preserve the current diswors until he was able to obtain a new stockpile. This is why Phil Gorge fuckin' him over hurt him more than he let those around him think, including his wife. Secretly, he was banking on Phil providing the solution to this problem, but Ariana's report from their meeting squashed that possibility. Instead, Phil had created another headache for LaVonte to handle.

On top of all the dilemmas his business was currently facing, LaVonte constantly fretted over his wife being in Morple. Ariana caught him in a moment of weakness when she mentioned the idea of her going there. LaVonte sensed remaining stagnant on the plantation was boring her, so he caved and allowed her to go. He could have ordered his men to go and kidnap Heather Lawrence, but as much as LaVonte hated to admit it, Richard's prominence was something he had to respect. Kidnapping the wife of someone with his level of clout would have created too many headlines across the country, drawing much too much attention to his organization. He agreed for Ariana, as conniving as they come, to go because she had the finesse to manipulate Heather into leaving and making it appear voluntary. He knew it would take time, and in that time, resuming her relationship with Robin was a possibility. Apparently one already in the works.

Even from another state LaVonte kept a close eye on Ariana, observing she continued to spend a significant amount of time with Robin and her sons. He surprised himself by allowing it to continue because he knew taking away the family time she had been craving all these years would hurt Ariana. LaVonte decided he would wait to handle that.

LaVonte was struggling spending this much time away from his wife. It was the longest amount of time they spent apart since marrying seventeen years ago. During that time, he had often reflected on when he first spotted her. He was in Los Angeles on business, and she was the hostess at a restaurant where he was meeting a corrupt politician. LaVonte vividly remembered what she looked like that night. Her long-sleeved black dress hugged every part of her body up to her neck, revealing no cleavage while exemplifying her features. It matched her luscious, wavy hair sitting so perfectly over her breasts. She put him in a trance by simply standing behind her podium. He longed to know more about her and see more of her. He ordered one of his men to approach her during his dinner and make her aware the one and only LaVonte Jackson would like to treat her to a night out after his meeting. His tactics were usually assertive, but this time, LaVonte made it clear he did not want her to feel pressured. He wanted it to be authentic, for her to desire him as much as he did her. Luckily for LaVonte, Ariana accepted the invitation, and they immediately found each other compatible.

Their bond strengthened quickly, as their conversations had substance, and they discovered commonalities in the early stages of their companionship. LaVonte had never felt comfortable enough to be so transparent with anyone about his childhood as he was with Ariana, and after learning about what she had endured, he realized he was not the only one who had suffered. It wasn't until later on in their relationship he discovered one of his business partners was responsible for her trauma. Even though he didn't express it, his inability to sever that relationship for the sake of his wife ate away at his conscience.

Their main common ground was the role Morple played in ruining their families, which brought them closer together and led to them falling in love, an occurrence both of them later revealed they never thought would be possible. Until now, there were no glaring deficiencies in their relationship, but that wasn't to say they had never disagreed on matters. Ariana did not support all of the restrictions LaVonte had put on her, like the overbearing security and limiting her travel, but at the end of the day, she understood them. Over the years, there had been some episodes about her missing her sister, but she was more upset at the reality than at him. Now that her proximity to Robin had significantly increased, LaVonte was wary of her commitment to him and their life together. If it came down to it, he could blackmail his own wife in order to coerce her back home, but even the cold-hearted LaVonte didn't know if he had the balls to do that.

Staring up at the ceiling in his nearly pitch-black room, LaVonte was so consumed with his ongoing concerns he forgot Gabriela and Rachel were both lying to his left until the former stirred. Neither were over twenty-five years-old and both carried around asses unproportionable to their frames. Gabriela's was currently pointed in his direction, erecting him. Gabriela reminded LaVonte of Ariana, which is why he chose to have her stay at the main house while his wife was away, while Rachel was milder chested and wore her blonde hair shoulder length. Their contrasting skin tones and hair colors increased his arousal.

Because husband and wife were together ninety-nine percent of the time, when he had sex with other women, Ariana was there. They had never discussed their sexual arrangement, but LaVonte assumed his wife understood his masculinity had needs to be met. Rather than feeling the slightest bit of guilt, LaVonte rationalized sleeping with Gabriela and Rachel kept him sane because the former resembled his wife, someone he relentlessly craved.

LaVonte threw the blankets off the three of them with force and commanded the girls to wake up. Disheveled, both sat up and gathered themselves for their master's next instruction. He gestured to Gabriela to lean her back against the bed's headboard and Rachel to lie on her stomach between Gabriela and him. Rachel adhered to what LaVonte expected of her without him having to explicitly say it. The early morning sun was starting to creep into his room, and it made what LaVonte wanted to see visible.

He positioned himself behind Rachel and entered her somewhat forcefully because her body was not ready to accept him. As he inserted himself deeper her wetness lathered him. LaVonte began thrusting his entire self, nearly taking the tip out every time he pulled back. Rachel's muffled moans were still audible, but LaVonte was too hyper focused on Gabriela's body shuddering from what was happening between her legs.

He studied her curves sway as sensations enraptured her entire self. When Gabriela's moans indicated her climax was near, his gaze lifted to her face, but instead of seeing Gabriela, he saw Ariana. His wife was experiencing so much pleasure she couldn't control her facial expressions; touching herself in ways to increase her own arousal and sliding her hips up and down to ensure Rachel hit the sweet spot.

As Gabriela moaned an "Oh fuck, baby" LaVonte locked himself against Rachel's hips, squeezing her ass cheeks so hard they pinched her, and allowed himself to release.

Panting heavily, he rolled over on his back and worked to catch his breath. Gabriela said something she assumed he wanted to hear, but instead ignored. Her speaking ended his fantasy of having his wife back. For as long as he could remember, LaVonte always told himself he didn't need anyone by his side to be the person he was. He credited his success to himself and himself only, but now that Ariana had been away from him for an extended amount of time, LaVonte was realizing he needed his wife more than he even realized.

To make certain she felt the same, he had to eliminate the one person standing in between them.

CHAPTER

2073

A riana paced in front of LaVonte's desk. She was incredulous at her husband for disregarding her life's worst nightmare in favor of his business interests.

"I just don't understand how you think this is okay, LaVonte," Ariana said.

"It's called fuckin' business, alright? It isn't like I fuckin' like the guy. In fact, I actually hate him for what he has done to you, but I'm in a tough fuckin' spot here. As of now, he is the only way I can get into Morple without getting completely bent over and fucked in the ass. What part of that don't you understand?" LaVonte puffed his cigar for the final time and twisted it into his ashtray.

Ariana tossed her arms up and landed them on her hips. She couldn't determine if he truly didn't understand where she was coming from or if he simply didn't care. Whichever it was, he was still being a fuckin' asshole. She had been under the impression she was marrying someone who sincerely cared and wanted to create a happier life for her; after all, their pasts' similarities are what formed their bond in the first place. But apparently not even that was more powerful than the almighty dollar.

"Baby, look. I'm sorry. I really, really am, but this is the harsh reality of the business I'm in. He isn't going to be welcomed in with open arms, and it isn't like he will be visiting for pleasure any other time. There have been some problems with distribution in Morple, and I have been working on handling them. He told me he needs something done, and in return, I receive lifetime access to that channel without any trouble."

When Ariana voiced her desire to play a role in LaVonte's organization, this is not what she had envisioned. The other side of her conscious asked the obvious: what the hell *was* she expecting entering this dark world of trafficking with the most ruthless to ever do it? Cruelties weren't a surprise, but the possibility of her past and present colliding like this never even crossed her mind.

"And you're requiring me to be there?" she asked.

"It presents a strong front. Plus, you said you wanted in, baby. This is what it's about."

"What does he want in return?"

LaVonte cracked a smile, pleased his new wife was coming around. "That's what we're going to find out shortly."

"Let's just keep it as fuckin' short of a meeting as possible, alright?"

"I'll do my best, baby," LaVonte said.

"One condition."

LaVonte nearly rolled his eyes. "I'm listening."

"He doesn't get access to any of the girls."

LaVonte nodded. Ariana stormed out of his office to go ready herself to confront her demons.

Reginald Lawrence strolled out of an acquaintance's private plane on a private airstrip outside of Los Angeles and spotted two bulky Black men standing as still as statues outside of an SUV. Reginald observed their tailored suits weren't cheap. Buzzed from the three glasses of wodin he threw back on the forty-five-minute flight from Morple to Los Angeles, he took in his surroundings, pleased to be back in business.

"Mr. Lawrence. Pleasure to be at your service sir," one of them said as he relieved Reginald of his bag.

The other opened the car door for him and said, "Welcome, sir. Is there anywhere you'd like to stop before your meeting with Mr. Jackson?"

"You got a whore house on the way?"

"Mr. Jackson has you covered there, sir."

"Ah, no wonder why I have always loved doing business with LaVonte so much. What about any wodin for the ride over?"

"A bottle, glass, and ice bucket are waiting for you in the backseat, sir."

"Then let's get going. How long will this take?"

"Under an hour, sir," the second man said.

"Oh fuck me. Why doesn't your boss have an airstrip yet at that fuckin' plantation?"

"It would draw too much attention, sir."

Like a plantation with thousands of kidnapped diswors, hundreds of whores, and hundreds of niggers with guns don't, Reginald thought to himself. "I see. Well, off we go then."

It had been at least five years since the last time Reginald paid a visit to his favorite kingpin's plantation. When Blacks began populating the trafficking business, Reginald was initially hesitant to work with them, as his preconceived notions indicated they were irrational, motivated by the wrong things, and possessed no intellect towards running a profitable business.

LaVonte quickly squashed that prejudice. Reginald found his prowess in running the Organization incredibly impressive. Most traffickers Reginald had dealt with typically had a shelf life of only a few years because their egos got too big, created sloppy habits, or they were too timid to press their luck in attempting to grow their operations. But LaVonte Jackson was a different breed. He had a knack for sensing which way the industry was going, and what was required in order for him to remain on top. Rather than taking his foot off the gas when the competition pumped the brakes, LaVonte saw it as an opportunity to stomp their faces in and eliminate them from the race. Privately, Reginald considered him the best businessman he had ever known.

As the SUV trekked up the driveway to the plantation's mansion, Reginald tossed back the remnants of his drink and mentally prepared himself for what he planned to ask LaVonte. It did not directly affect their business but was rather a personal vendetta he needed help in executing. Failing to present it in an amicable fashion could jeopardize their professional relationship, but Reginald was no dummy. He knew how desperately LaVonte needed a secure dock to unload his shipments. The Morple local had the upper hand in this negotiation.

Before the SUV came to a complete stop, the man in the passenger seat hopped out and opened Reginald's door. "You can leave your glass in the back, sir."

"I was planning on it."

Both passenger and driver led him into the house, which was more immaculate and bigger than Reginald remembered it being. LaVonte must have added on and remodeled the place. He clearly had the resources for those types of projects.

"LaVonte and his missus are waiting for you in the study, sir," the passenger said as they led him down a hallway.

"Missus, huh? What's she like?" This caught Reginald off guard. Allowing a woman who wasn't sucking him off to be present during a meeting and settling down both seemed out of character for the almighty LaVonte Jackson.

"Mrs. Jackson is a fine lady, sir," the driver said.

"Oh, I bet she is."

The driver and passenger broke character for the first time since Reginald's landing, grinning back at him as if to say, "Yeah, she's fuckin' hot."

The driver knocked on the study door and received the okay to enter. He opened the door for Reginald and welcomed him in by extending his arm in the direction of where LaVonte and his missus were sitting. As Reginald sauntered in, he thought his mind was playing tricks on him. As he tip-toed closer, transfixed on her scowl, he knew she was her.

"Mr. Lawrence. Good to see you, old friend," LaVonte said, going to embrace his longtime business partner. Ariana rolled her eyes.

"Is this some type of fuckin' joke?" Reginald asked, hesitant to accept LaVonte's hug.

Playing dumb was not LaVonte's style, so he addressed the elephant in the room. "This is my wife, Ariana Jackson. As I have learned you two are already acquainted."

Constricted by the shock, Reginald stood frozen just inside the study's entrance. Not even all the wodin he had consumed over the last couple of hours could ease his nerves enough for a situation like this.

"Are you just going to stand there and stare, or are you going to sit and get down to business?" Ariana asked.

Her confident tone was unfamiliar to Reginald. It was something he thought he beat out of her all those years she was under his control. He looked to LaVonte in hopes he would be the one who offered him a seat, but LaVonte's stare had turned cold and seemed to be waiting on Reginald to situate himself where Ariana asked him to.

He plodded over to the couch opposite of Ariana and sat down. Her hardened stare was searing into him. Years of built-up animosity wanted to unleash on him. His former project now held a position of power, and Reginald would be lying to himself if he said this didn't intimidate him. As much as he tried resisting, he couldn't help but steal a look at her body. When he had her she had been a bombshell, yes, but now in her early twenties, Ariana was the most physically desirable woman he had ever laid eyes on. Her V-neck dress showcased her breasts squeezed together and embosomed their entire circumference. They were begging to be set free. Ariana's hour-glass body was firing on all cylinders, and it was clear why LaVonte had ultimately decided she was the one.

Evidently one of his habits rubbed off on her because she had a full glass of wodin next to a nearly full bottle. LaVonte wasn't a drinker, yet there was an empty glass next to Ariana's. Unsure of the best way to break the ice, Reginald asked, "Are you going to offer me a glass of that? You have developed a fine pallet."

"Have at it," she said.

Realizing she wasn't going to do him the favor of pouring his glass, Reginald reached over the table and began to do it himself.

"What number is this for you today?"

"Fifth since I hopped on the plane."

"Wow. Looks like the under won."

LaVonte wasn't a fan of this banter, but even he was cognizant of how Ariana needed to express her antipathy. Now that Reginald was in their presence, LaVonte felt his fury towards him build. Part of him even regretted continuing to use Reginald's connections for his own benefit, but it was too late to change his mind now. At least that's what the power-hungry part of his brain told him.

"Reginald, cigar?" LaVonte asked.

"Yes, please."

LaVonte snapped his fingers and one of his men in the room bolted out to fetch him one. He returned less than thirty seconds later with a perfectly firm cigar. Reginald lit it and immediately felt its effects.

"I am not going to allow your guys' past to interfere with our professional relationship, which I have already communicated to Ariana."

"Which I'm not happy about," she said.

"Which you don't have a say in, either," LaVonte said.

Reginald observed their dynamic. In a way, it reminded him of theirs when she was growing up.

"But Reginald, do not think us resuming steady business means we are back to having a relationship outside of making money. If I had known what you had been up to during those years, there would be no you and me."

Fuckin' hypocrite, Reginald thought.

LaVonte continued his opening. "Know this professional relationship is based on you providing me with what I need, and in return, I am going to get done what you need in return. Clear?"

Mid puff, Reginald said, "Clear."

Ariana nodded and finished her glass.

"Good. Before we address what you want done, I am going to need some questions answered about the dock you said can be used for my exports."

"Fire away, old friend," Reginald said.

Ariana sat in silence as her husband and old tormentor talked shop for the next hour. She took her role in the Organization seriously, but there were still numerous facets she had yet to educate herself on. When they weren't in meetings like this one, LaVonte answered her questions when he could, but he dedicated a majority of his time to running his highly profitable business, leaving Ariana to instruct herself on how to become a top dog. Her husband's questions to Reginald were well articulated, as he seemed to consider every possible scenario, such as when law enforcement patrolled the area every day of the week, if in certain seasons other businesses used it for imports or exports, had it ever been monitored by A.I., did Morple's state government have any plans for it that would disrupt their arrangement, and so on. Ariana hated to admit it, but Reginald boasted sufficient answers to all of his questions. It left her wondering how many traffickers he was in cahoots with while making Robin's and her life a living hell. Ariana knew he wasn't full of shit either because if he was, her husband would have killed him a long time ago. *That would've been nice*, she thought to herself.

Once Reginald eased all of LaVonte's potential qualms, it was his turn to inform Ariana's husband what he wanted in return.

"To be honest, LaV—"

"I hope that's all you are is honest, Reginald," LaVonte said.

Annoyed, Reginald feigned a chuckle.

"What I am asking of you is a personal favor, and it is one I would feel much more comfortable asking you and you only."

"Ariana is part of my business now, Reginald. She is equipped to hear what you propose."

"I understand that, but I think an exception should be made here. Trust m—"

"I will be the one who dictates when and if exceptions should be made. Ariana, do you want to step out or listen to what Mr. Lawrence has to say?"

"Listen." Even though it was far from what she wanted to do, choosing the other option was displaying a weakness.

"Okay, just don't say I didn't warn either of you."

"Get on with it, Reginald," LaVonte said.

"Well, okay then. As both of you already know, a wrongful lawsuit was filed against me, and unlike all of my legal dealings, I came out on the losing end."

Ariana's stomach turned upside down, but it did not surprise her that what he wanted stemmed from the money Robin had won from him after Morvo. Of course, he was evil enough to harbor this resentment towards an innocent victim even a few years removed from their legal battle.

"I lost tens of millions in assets, which hurt, yes. I cannot deny that. It's a large amount of money. Even you can recognize that, LaVonte."

He retorted Reginald's attempt to relate to him. "For me it ain't."

"Ah, well I should've learned your line of work much earlier in life then. Anyways, I'm close to earning the money back through other endeavors, so the money is what it is. That wasn't what hurt me the most. What hurts the most is someone I love and our son are off spending it with another man, another man who has no right to the $75 million dollar fortune and counting she won in her day in court."

Ariana's blood boiled and the enmity she felt towards Reginald heated up her face, nearly causing her hairline to start sweating. Involuntarily, Ariana held the tension building up in her limbs. Her heart was beating rapidly. She felt as if it was going to pounce out of her chest and land on the table between them. If that was what it took to get her out of hearing the rest of this, she would have been okay with it.

Hearing Reginald confess his love for Robin was sickening. No one in his right mind treats someone he loves the way he treated her. Most women in Robin's situation would've been ruined forever, but Ariana's older sister was too strong to let it destroy her.

Reginald allowed a moment of silence for what he just professed to sink in. "Now that that is off my chest, I'll get to what I need from you."

"Please hurry," LaVonte said.

"I want Bobby Karros eliminated."

"What? No. LaVonte, no, he didn't do anything. This gu—"

"Stop talking," LaVonte said. Ordering his wife to be silent satisfied Reginald. He knew how defiant the bitch could be. The punishments he issued were much more severe than a simple command, too.

Ariana shook her head and ran a hand alongside her temple. She felt her eyes flooding with tears and didn't bother trying to stop them.

"Define eliminated," LaVonte said.

"I do not need him wiped off the face of the earth, no, but I do not want him raising my son, spending my money, and most of all, fuckin' the woman I love."

Ariana scoffed.

Reginald continued describing what he required. "To put it simply, I want him eliminated from Robin's life." He shrugged his shoulders as if to say, "And that's it, simple."

LaVonte pondered the request. His expression didn't reveal it, but he found Reginald's ask maddening. Now that he knew how he was treating his then-future wife and her sister while they were making each other rich, LaVonte was pissed at himself for involving himself with someone like Reginald. But at the end of the day, he needed what his man in Morple had.

"If I do this, what we discussed earlier is a full go, and it is up to us what becomes of Bobby Karros," LaVonte said. This wasn't him confirming the terms with Reginald, but rather him dictating them.

Ariana sat there with her palm pressed against her forehead and tears dripping off her cheeks.

"Sounds fair to me."

"Good, because that's what it is."

Reginald concurred and humbly relished in getting LaVonte to do his dirty work for him and piss off his wife.

"Our business here is through. My men are waiting to take you back to the airport."

Disappointed by the abruptness, Reginald had the audacity to ask, "For old time's sake, you have anyone available for me ou—"

"Get the fuck out of my house, Lawrence," LaVonte said.

LaVonte's men inside the room inched closer towards Reginald in case he needed a hands-on escort. Knowing quitting while he was ahead was the wise choice, Reginald nodded and left without another word.

Once his business partner was gone, LaVonte ordered the other guard out of the study so he could be alone with his wife.

"I don't have a choice," LaVonte said once they were alone.

Ariana was now sobbing uncontrollably. Emotions she had been burying for so long surfaced after being forced to confront her long-time abuser. Leading up to the meeting, she felt confident she would be capable of holding it together, but the magnitude of the situation proved to be too severe for her to handle. That, on top of her husband committing to ruin her sister's life, as if she hadn't been through enough thus far, was already eating away at her. LaVonte deserved a tongue lashing, but her cries were preventing her from formulating a sentence. Besides, even if she could muster up something to say, LaVonte wouldn't take to it kindly.

"It's the way of this world, Ariana. This isn't the first time I've had to do something I didn't want to, but we have to in order to prosper. Do you understand this?"

She nodded more so to get him to stop talking than to follow his orders, even though she knew she'd remain loyal.

"Good because I want you to play a role in this."

If there was one positive that could come from this, it was that LaVonte had the power to permanently sever his wife's relationship with her sister, making her LaVonte's for the rest of their lives.

CHAPTER

2089

Richard suddenly becoming this super involved husband and father worked in Ariana's favor because it gave her a viable excuse to stall her plan, as Heather was too occupied with day trips to Mexico, yacht rides around the island, and nights at home dedicated to family.

Ariana took advantage of this time to integrate with Robin, Jonathan, and Moe. Of course, her older sister loved having her around, but Ariana worried if her nephews would accept her.

To her pleasure Robin explained to Moe their shared past and Ariana's significance in his mother's life. Ariana's instincts told her his relationship with his mother was stronger than ever because of how honest Robin became about her past, their family's roots, and her inner demons.

Moe genuinely enjoyed Ariana's company. He looked forward to when she came over, and appreciated having more family around, especially when she was a "cool aunt". The only bother he had was he couldn't shake the feeling that he recognized her from a previous encounter. Some days, he felt like he was on the verge of pinning it down, but he never quite could. On others he considered himself crazy for believing he had once seen her if his mother and her had no contact for nearly two decades. Moe's gut told him they'd previously crossed paths, and that it was just a matter of time before he would figure out when and where.

Despite this unanswered question constantly nagging at him, Moe's infatuation with Ariana grew quickly. He would never even think of admitting it, but he still thought she was incredibly hot. He rationalized it by telling himself it wasn't weird because she wasn't around while he was growing up. Besides, it wasn't his fault Ariana's outfits triggered hormonal thoughts. Ariana's physical attributes distracted him at times, but her real value to Moe was becoming a person he could confide in. Whether it was him venting about his girl troubles or what it was like growing up without a father, she was attentive and offered a useful perspective. Ariana had an aptitude for knowing what to say and how to ease his anxiety. Oftentimes, Moe felt guilty complaining about how difficult it was not to have a father when his aunt and mother didn't have either of their parents and were subject to rape and abuse at a very young age. His life was cake compared to what they endured.

Ariana relished in Moe feeling comfortable enough to discuss his life with her. It signaled he was at ease when she was around, and she was humbled she anointed her to this role. Ariana found his girl problems adorable and laughable. She joked with him that his romance with Megan Rincon was juicy, and she always looked forward to being briefed on the latest. It sort of evolved into a guilty pleasure for Ariana. To Robin's displeasure, the "cool aunt" treated her youngest nephew to an expensive bottle of wodin on a night Jonathan, Wallace, and her spent the evening at the pier. To both of their surprise, Moe fancied it, nearly enough to keep pace with his aunt. As they continued putting a dent in the bottle, Moe opened up about how his father not being around had put an enormous amount of pressure on his mother to raise two boys right. Similar to the rest of her life, the odds were against Robin, but she prevailed. Since the night Robin took him to Marcelo's, Moe confessed his guilt to Ariana for being a brat at times. He blamed it on immaturity and wished he had a better understanding of what she was going through. Rather than focusing his anger on his mother, Moe said it is better served being directed towards his father, who apparently found greener pastures.

The wodin nearly set the truth free.

Her time spent with Jonathan didn't entail as much girl talk or nights sitting at a table consuming wodin until they could no longer see straight, but Ariana was establishing a foundation with Jonathan, too. She dedicated hours to help him improve his literacy skills on top of talking about life. Ariana's favorite moments with Jonathan were accompanying him on adventures with Wallace because that's when he was at his happiest. They were simple outings, like walking around the neighborhood, having a picnic near the pier, and him and his canine tagging along while she did errands for herself. She often appeased him by treating them to boat rides around the island. Driving it herself was an option, but Ariana always elected to pay more to have the boat automated. He cried from laughter when they hit little waves at high speeds, leading her to uncontrollably laugh at his elation. The only one who didn't enjoy this was Wallace. He'd curl up in a ball next to Jonathan and didn't unravel until they docked.

Spending this much quality time with Ariana made Jonathan feel included in the new family dynamic. Although he detested wearing masks in some places, being out and about with her was always the highlight of his day.

After one of their exhilarating boat rides around all of Morple, Ariana, Jonathan, and Wallace headed to a cliff near the pier to allow their adrenaline to subside. The water was calm, the sky was clear, and they had no obligations to attend to. After mounting his nose up in the air for the first twenty minutes, Wallace positioned himself between Ariana and Jonathan, laying his beefy head on her thigh. It was the first time he expressed any affection towards her, the ultimate telltale she was forming a strong bond with her nephew.

Jonathan tepidly took her hand and said, "Uh, Ariana, can I, I, I tell you something?"

"Yes, of course, sweetheart. What's going on?"

She cupped his hand with both of hers.

"Uh, I, I, I just want to tell you I, I, I love you. You being around is awesome, and I, I, I am so happy you're in our family now. We love you. Wallace does too 'cause he is laying on you."

Ariana couldn't fend them off. Tears trickled down her face, falling onto Wallace's head.

"Uh, I-I-I'm sorry. Did I, I, I hurt you?" Jonathan asked.

"No, no, no," Ariana said. "I'm just so happy. That's why I'm crying, sweetheart. I'm not sad, I'm so happy. These are happy tears."

Ariana hugged him around his neck and brought him to her chest.

While being held against her, he said, "Uh, I, I, I feel like I, I, I have two parents again. You're the best, Ariana."

Ariana became hysterical, bawling because of the tragedy she beget. It was up to her to fix what she destroyed.

CHAPTER

2070

"He's so beautiful, Robin," Ariana said to her sister. Robin was sitting cross legged and cradling a one-year-old Jonathan in her arms on her twin bed.

"You're going to be an amazing mother. Don't worry about who his father is. Jonathan won't be like him. Good always beats evil."

Robin leaned over and kissed Ariana on the cheek. "Love you, sis."

"I love you, too. Can I hold him?"

"Of course."

"Hi baby Jonathan. You're such a handsome boy. You're going to be the perfect son for your mother. I just know it," Ariana said.

For close to twenty years, Reginald Lawrence shamelessly terrorized Robin and Ariana in their bedrooms at MYM's The District facility. Others knew of the abuse he inflicted on young innocent girls, but they were either involved or didn't consider his victims important enough to stand up for.

Robin and Ariana constantly feared the predator in him could reveal itself at any moment. Sadly, they became accustomed to this behavior and began anticipating when he was most likely to strike. But this didn't lessen the pain and trauma his rapings inflicted. Jonathan was the result of one of these nights, and despite the circumstances, both Robin and Ariana considered his life a blessing for both of them. He signified the light at the end of the tunnel and was a concrete reason to aspire for a better life. Since the day they found out Robin was pregnant, all they could do is dream about one day being on their own and taking charge of their lives. With Jonathan in the picture, it all became a real possibility.

"We're going to get out of here, Ariana. Get on our feet and do great things. I already met with a lawyer who will help us. His name's Marty. He's really smart. He has been doing this type of work his whole life. He cares about our situation and says he will win us enough money so we'll never have to work again."

Ariana looked up at her without saying a word and then resumed goggling down at Jonathan, rocking him peacefully.

"I don't know, Robin," Ariana said quietly so she wouldn't disturb her nephew's bliss. "I just want to get out of here. Morple has a lot of baggage. I can't be here anymore. I don't care about revenge. I just want to get out. We can figure out what we'll do together. Don't you think?"

Robin struggled to formulate a diplomatic response. She applauded her sister's confidence in them and understood why she didn't want to continue living in Morple, but Robin was responsible for more than just her own life. Financial security was atop her priority list, and Marty informed her not having an education in a world with a nearly nonexistent job market wasn't a good recipe for success. The battle Marty was fighting for her was the best solution in securing a prosperous future for her family. He guaranteed she would win upwards of $50 million plus ownership in profitable companies she would reap the benefits from in years to come. If she was being honest, Robin didn't comprehend what Marty was talking about when he detailed the specifics of the settlement, but it was a brighter future than any she could've built by herself. The offer was too good to turn down, no matter how desperately her sister longed to leave the island.

"Ariana," Robin said, waiting for Ariana to look up from Jonathan before continuing.

"Ariana, look at me please."

Reluctantly, Ariana slowly craned her neck up.

"We have to take what Marty can get us. We don't have a choice. We're going to be able to move out of here and then we're free. We can be rich. Can you imagine being rich?"

"What makes you think Marty isn't like the others?" Ariana asked.

"Because Ariana, these are different times. He told me the entire country knows about Morvo and is involved with what we have been going through. The e—"

"Don't act like you know what the fuck he is talking about," Ariana said.

Robin jolted back, surprised at how the usually pacific Ariana just snapped at her.

"Men are in charge out there. I'm not going to go from one man's control to another just because the new one says something different."

Disturbed with this sentiment, Robin's eyes watered. "Ariana, you can't think like that. You have to have faith in people. Look at who you're holding. He'll one day be a man. A man who will grow up with a kind heart because of the people in his life. His aunt included."

"Fuck this, Robin. Once we're free I'm getting the hell out of here. There's nothing anyone can do to keep me from leaving this place. I promise I'll make sure we make it, and you'll never have to worry about taking care of Jonathan. I know you want another one, too. Don't worry, I'll make sure we're taken care of. Just come with me when I leave."

"You don't know what it's like out there, Ariana. You think you can just go out there and fend for us? No, we don't know. There aren't any jobs. Those were all taken away before we were. All we have to do is listen to Marty, and we're set. Why are you being so difficult about this?"

For the first time in their lives, this was a topic they couldn't seem to agree on. Both sisters had a tendency to be defiant, but they were usually united in it.

"I'm not stopping you from doing what you want, Robin. I love you. I nearly sacrificed my life for you. I couldn't stand to see my sister suffering the way you were."

"Yeah, that clearly didn't work out too well because it kept happening."

Robin's dismissiveness left Ariana speechless. The morning after Ariana knocked Reginald out while he forced himself on Robin, he burst into their room with a vengeance they'd never seen before. One of his men tied Robin to the bedpost. He caressed her breasts and played with her ear using his tongue, ignoring her screams and tears. He ordered Robin to watch Reginald beat Ariana. He was whacking Robin's little sister's back so violently she bled and wailed uncontrollably. Reginald squeezed her neck from the back and slammed her head against the dresser.

Ariana's head and back were bleeding. Her youthful body had no strength in it to fight back as Reginald threw her on the bed and violently took her. Even the pillows pressed against her face couldn't muffle her screams. It sounded like a horror movie, and big sister couldn't do anything to save her.

All Robin could do was helplessly sit there and watch a grown man have his way with her little sister.

"I'm sorry," Robin said, unable to look Ariana in the eye. "I didn't mean that. I'm sorry."

Ariana glared at her with a possessed look and kissed Jonathan on his forehead before whispering in his ear, "I love you so much, Jonathan. I will always love you so, so much."

Ever so delicately, she set him in Robin's arms and said, "Enjoy your millions. I have only stayed this long to be here for you, but you no longer need me. I'll make a life for myself on my own. I only have myself who will help, just as I always have," Ariana said.

Neither knew it at the time, but this was the last encounter they would have for another nineteen years.

Visibly shaken, Robin sat there trying to quiet her cries so she didn't wake Jonathan. The original MYM declared the state had custody of a "child" until she was twenty-one years-old, so Robin was in her last year, but even though Morvo's progressive legislation wasn't official yet, Morple officials were allowing MYM children to leave early. Robin would have already left if it weren't for Jonathan, as MYM's medical plan covered his needs at no cost. Until moments ago, Ariana stayed back so her sister wouldn't be alone, but her patience for her sister's complacency had run its course. Until her settlement was final and she had the means to support Jonathan and herself, Robin would spend her final days in MYM without her sister.

A knock on the bedroom door brought Robin back to reality after losing herself in her thoughts. Robin said to come in, hoping it was Ariana returning to tell her she had a change of heart. Seeing Reginald and a nurse with a digital needle walk in instead surprised her.

Because of the lawsuit she was in against Reginald and the entire MYM program, he no longer posed a threat to her physical well-being, but his presence remained discomforting. Just as it had been for most of her life. Especially in this bedroom.

"Hello Robin," Reginald said.

Robin squeezed their baby closer to her. Reginald was very tranquil, especially for someone who was responsible for inflicting enough harm to constitute a settlement upwards of $50 million. She didn't know why, but Robin did expect him to exhibit some level of remorse. Remaining true to his character, Reginald was the same cold soul who had raised her up to this point.

"Well, since you are not going to allow me to see our beautiful boy ever again, I want to make sure I can provide him with the best medical care while I am still permitted to. You leaving here with him isn't a wise choice, since I would've given you the best possible life, one you cannot even fathom. Between you and me, your winnings from the settlement are nothing compared to what I have, love. I guess it was foolish of me to think you and I had a future as a family, but at least I can say I gave it my best effort when it came to trying to win you over. But that is me crying over spilled milk. No reason to continue doing so. Anyways, this is Catrina," he said, gesturing to the nurse. Catrina didn't acknowledge her introduction. Like a good soldier following orders, she continued fiddling around with the digital needle in her hands.

"Catrina will give our son the vaccines members who contribute to society receive."

With his hands clasped behind his back, Reginald stepped closer to Robin and bent over to more closely study their son.

"I've elected this to be the last time I see our baby Jonathan, so I want to get as close as I can before you take him away from me. My wits combined with your looks, oh my goodness. What a marvelous young man we could've raised. Even with your charity money you won't be able to provide the resources he'd need to succeed in this world. You don't know what it's like out there. Never forget, Robin, our world will never forget you are still an infick, no matter how much money is handed to you." Reginald arched over further and kissed his cheek, causing Robin to shudder.

"He's just as much mine as he is yours," he said, reminding Robin of a truth she'd like to forget.

He continued, "I'll leave you to it, Catrina. Make sure he gets all the necessary ones we discussed."

"Yes sir," she said.

"Bye, Robin. I'll see you around," he said.

Catrina walked over to Jonathan and began sanitizing his arm before administering the vaccines.

"Are, are you sure those are okay to give him?" Robin asked.

"Yes," Catrina said bluntly.

She began a series of injections that Jonathan didn't notice, easing Robin's concern. Robin wasn't well-versed on healthcare and didn't want to object to anything that would protect her son's health. As Catrina carried on, Robin foolishly convinced herself Reginald was too self-absorbed to wreak harm on his own kin, but deep down, she didn't believe that for a second. She was just too weak to speak up.

For the rest of her life, Robin beat herself up for not doing so, as she wondered what Jonathan could have been if his father didn't order an orgacal injection in his veins to irreversibly stunt his brain development.

CHAPTER

2089

In his heyday, Reginald possessed the power of persuasion, convincing politicians, businessmen, activists, and human and drug traffickers he was indispensable. But accumulating so many allies in that time came with many enemies, too. The latter perceived him with contempt because they felt he attained undeserved success. They classified Reginald as conniving, unethical, and corrupt. Whatever words they used to describe him didn't bother Reginald. Fervent enemies signified he had found success. Truthfully, learning about companies' goals to make the world a happier place and understanding politicians' policies crafted by the companies that funded their campaigns bored him, but being capable of manipulating his way to appear valuable resulted in a lucrative career. Companies and politicians found having ties to someone who dedicated so much of his life to raising Morple's disenfranchised youth benefited their image, too. They didn't need to know the specifics because that would place them in an ethical conundrum.

Now in his eighties, Reginald found himself feeling restless often. His mind wanted to work, but he no longer possessed enough energy to commit himself to learning how to adapt in the modern world, a drive he apparently used up in his youth. His portfolio dabbled in some low-risk, moderate-reward business ventures, but, as much as he loathed admitting it, he had lost his magic touch. Fortunately for Reginald, his ongoing investments and life's achievements were more than capable of supporting his life as a single elderly man spending the last chapters of his life in an oversized mansion in Costa Mor.

Reginald's days didn't have much on the schedule aside from admiring his view of the rising sea from the comfort of his own backyard alongside his Airedale Terrier Wilford and reading old John Grisham and Don Winslow novels, both released before he was born. His favorites were the former's *The Appeal* and the latter's *The Border*. He had read both at least twenty-five times. Reginald appreciated the lengths the billionaire CEO went to to appeal and win the lawsuit versus the lowly common folk in *The Appeal*, and the destruction the drug war caused in Mexico described in *The Border* reaffirmed his notion of the ineptitude of inficks.

When he wasn't indulging himself in a novel or soaking in his multimillion dollar vantage point, Reginald often reflected on his accomplishments and miscues. To the dismay of many, accolades riddled Reginald's resume. He negotiated the details of historical mergers with clean energy companies that heavily impacted Morple's economy, boosting the state's impact on the US' role in clean-energy initiatives across the globe. He bullied through legislation allowing the advancement of A.I. in The District to pass. He orchestrated deals involving Morple-based companies selling clean resources to states running out of them. Reginald's fingerprints were all over Morple's foundation. The good and the bad.

The years Reginald mentored Robin and Ariana were the most fulfilling of his life. Possessing that much power over two untouched girls was an incredible opportunity he felt extremely fortunate to experience. Regrettably, Reginald let it get away from him prematurely.

The night he let himself into the Sorens' shitty apartment and found Robin on the couch alone he knew he had stumbled upon someone special. During their first interaction, he could feel their connection begin to take its shape, as she showcased her toys to him and explained what made each one unique. A gesture he would always remember with great fondness is when he rubbed her soft cheeks with his thumb and she smiled up at him with those jaw-dropping eyes, even so early on in her life. Robin was too young to express her thoughts, but Reginald detected their bond right off the bat. From that point on, everything he did was in an effort to earn

Robin's genuine love. Reginald became more enamored with her as she continued to develop throughout the years. Her body and mind began to take shape at quite a young age, and he considered it a privilege he was the first and, what he thought at the time, the only man who will ever have her. As in love as he was with Robin, Reginald was regularly depressed at his inability to mold her into who he wanted her to be. Yes, he punished her periodically by way of sex, but he had the best of intentions. He thought if he demonstrated what followed unacceptable behavior she would no longer act in that manner. This proved to be counterproductive because her disobedience continued, and she associated them becoming one as a punishment, as opposed to immersing herself in their affliction. If it weren't for Richard, Reginald would have likely committed suicide well before Morvo, when he realized Robin would never truly love him. A few times standing at the ledge of his property, he almost found enough courage to do it, but he was too much of a coward to act on his true intentions. He told himself it was because he didn't want to leave Richard without any parents, but the truth was he was too craven. Reginald's disheartened love life took precedence over his only son's well-being.

He continued to lash out at Robin, taking her by force until Morvo split them apart, but Ariana faced the bulk of his frustration. Of course, the night she "saved" her older sister was the one that always stuck out to him. From that point on Robin looked up to Ariana with great admiration for coming to her rescue. Reginald had forever envied Ariana for this, and in turn, promised to make her life a living hell for as long as he could. The morning after Ariana knocked him out with a glass bottle to the head was the most infuriated he ever remembered being. After consuming that much wodin and suffering an injury like that, one would assume he'd be out of sorts, but the adrenaline his rage ignited diminished any pain or hangover he was up against. Reginald considered the level of pain he inflicted on her the next morning to be one of his finest moments. A close second was the look on her face when LaVonte Jackson agreed to fulfill his request of taking Bobby Karros away from Robin and their son, who he learned had a full-blooded infick brother.

Sixteen years had come and gone, but Reginald remembered his last encounter with Ariana like it was yesterday. Resentment shot out of her eyes from the moment he entered her husband's study to when he laid out his demands in return for granting LaVonte's organization access to a key Morple port. Learning she had gravitated towards another powerful male figure didn't surprise Reginald, but he still didn't expect to encounter her again. Now that he had gotten the last laugh, he hoped he never did have to see her again. Both her and Bobby could rot in hell for all he cared.

Impregnating Robin was both a blessing and a curse. A blessing because they created something concrete together, and it was a curse because the system didn't allow them to share the experience of raising their child in conjunction. During the case, Reginald begged Robin to permit him and his resources to have a role in raising their boy. His lawyers argued how phenomenal of a job he had done with Richard as a single father. Not having any emotions towards the cause, Reginald's lawyers knew this fight was not one worth fighting, but their client was adamant on contesting Robin's no custody component of their settlement. They had to remind him several times how their opposition had substantial evidence he raped young children, but Reginald still refused to go down without a fight.

Without a prominent male figure in his life, Reginald deemed Jonathan a waste of life. He arranged for a nurse to purposely stunt Jonathan's brain development with an orgacal injection in order to rationalize how pointless his existence was.

Reginald kept tabs on Robin and her modest little life. On multiple occasions, he had his car take him to her street, where he would spend up to four hours trying to muster up the courage to knock on her front door and reenter her life. The time he was daring enough to step foot outside of his car and pour out his regret and love for her, Dillon and Robin's infick son walked out of the house laughing about some nonsense. As swiftly as was possible at his age, he bolted back inside his car to escape from being seen. Explaining to his grandson what he was doing on a street in The District would have been messy. After dodging that bullet, Reginald continued to observe her from afar.

Eventually, Reginald accepted he could only control so much. He succeeded in creating a quality, enriched life for most of his family, and if the opportunity ever presented itself, he would work on earning back the rest of them.

CHAPTER

2089

As Richard's car rolled him closer to Phil's three-story fortress, he saw a busty brunette strut out with a big hollow smile planted on her face. She appeared to be high on something, but at least her lack of clothes provided some eye candy for Richard. Choosing not to engage with her, he entered the bachelor pad and found Phil draped in a robe pouring two wodins.

"What's up, dawg?" Phil's face looked weathered and drained, and his eyes had a layer of red glass over them. They sunk deep in their sockets, confirming how inebriated he was.

"What's up, yo." Richard mocked. "That girl who just left was smiling."

"I just banged her."

"Which is why I'm surprised she was smiling."

Phil let his head fall back and belched out a sarcastic laugh. He slid Richard's wodin to his side of the island and cheers'd him from across the way.

"So what's going on with you? You're shitfaced," Richard said.

Phil gulped wodin from his glass and gestured for Richard to follow him outside. They made themselves comfortable on his poolside furniture and admired the sea in a comfortable silence, until Phil divulged something quite momentous.

"I fucked up big time," Phil said.

"Alright. Do you want to be a little more specific?"

Phil took another sip and gargled the wodin in his mouth like a child does with milk.

"I made some really bad investments. They've put me in a hole."

"Phil, you're a billionaire. How much fuckin' money did you lose?"

"No, no, you idiot. Not a financial hole. A legal hole."

"Insider trading again?"

Phil grew up with a guy who became an influential A.I. executive and made a killing for himself but fucked over his friends with poor investment advice. In the early eighties Phil determined it was wise to take it and invest in a Las Vegas-based company. It ended up backfiring because the Securities and Exchange Commission caught wind of it and considered the tip insider trading. Since Phil was oblivious to this, as proven by his lawyers, all he had to do was forfeit his initial investment plus his profits, totaling almost $750 million. The bummer was he had spent nearly three quarters of it.

"Worse, man. Way worse."

"What could be worse?"

"I got in on the action with the Organization."

Knowing his current standing with LaVonte Jackson wasn't good, Richard considered Phil might have been pulling his leg just to irritate him.

"Are you fuckin' with me?"

Phil took another sip. "No. One of his guys reached out to me and informed me the Organization was in need of someone in the loop. To be honest, I had no fuckin' idea what the hell he was talking about, but I didn't have anything better to do one night so I met him on a yacht, probably LaVonte's, near the pier to hash it out. Apparently, diswors are becoming much more difficult to come by because it is all about proximity. Other parts of the country are laying off more workers than California, Morple, and I guess Hawaii, so other traffickers have the advantage over the Organization.

"Anyways, long fuckin' story short, I was told the Organization needed someone with an in with businesses on the verge of creating some more diswors. LaVonte is obviously privy to us representing big-time corporations that go full A.I. all the time, so that is why they reached out to me. At the first fuckin' meeting I gave them surface-level information just to prove I was valuable, and I didn't want them to have anything too concrete before we agreed on how I would be paid. So, remember that night I told you I was at The Corridor with a woman? Fuck, I don't even remember my exact lie, but it was when I saw Robin and Heather's hot friend. Remember?"

"Yes."

"I was meeting with a member of the Organization to discuss more details."

"In public?"

"Yeah. He insisted on it."

Richard's eyes rolled. "Okay."

"I thought the night went really well, but that is because that is how it was supposed to go."

"What do you mean by that?"

"It turns out the guy was a mole. He t—"

Richard exhaled a grunt from the back of his throat. The severity of the situation his friend found himself in was worsening by the second.

"Oh fuck is right. When I got home there were about ten feds waiting for me on my front porch. They arrested me on the spot and sat me down in my own fuckin' living room and briefed me on what would happen if I didn't cooperate."

"Does Prescott know about this?"

"No. Please help me keep it that way."

Richard didn't confirm or deny he would.

Phil continued his story. "Cooperating meant being bugged in my next meeting with another Organization representative. A lawyer who is currently working on a big human trafficking case would be listening in. We spent hours running through mock conversations, went over questions, and all that shit. Even after all that practice, I blew the real thing, man. Absolutely blew it. The girl I met with knew I was bugged, and basically told me to watch out for my life. So now, I have the government and a trafficking organization on my ass. I don't know what the fuck I'm going to do."

Phil's liquid courage evaporated. He buried his face in his hands and bawled.

Compartmentalizing his anger with Phil for being so careless, Richard put an arm around him in an effort to console his friend. He assured him they would pay for the best lawyers money could buy and beat both sides. To try to lighten up the mood, he joked persuading the government to cut a deal with the rich was always a feasible move. It didn't land how he hoped it would.

Whatever transpired, Richard vowed he'd help his friend persevere through this. Phil was unable to verbalize a response, but Richard knew he was grateful for his company as he submerged himself into Richard's shoulder.

After about five minutes, Phil regained control of his emotions. He nearly neglected telling Richard the part that affected him most. "I forgot to tell you who it was I met with."

Richard stared at him blankly, disappointed he wasn't through being the bearer of bad news.

"Fuckin' Heather's hot friend, Ariana. She is part of the Organization, man."

Richard's stomach dropped, and he darted off without another word.

CHAPTER

2089

If Richard knew what kind of bomb Phil was going to drop on him, he would not have drank as much wodin as he had. Holograming with LaVonte sober was a less arduous task, but Richard didn't have any time to waste.

Rapture had been alleviating the Organization of its troubles for roughly a decade. When foot growers kidnapping diswors went awry or a drug bust occurred, Richard would assert himself, and all the weight he carried, to redirect the attention to other orgacal farms. The scapegoats were usually in the Midwest since LaVonte wanted to avoid a turf war with the few competitors he had on his side of the country. Winning would come easy, but it wasn't in the kingpin's best interest to attract that kind of attention. Handling business problems in suits was preferable over doing it on the streets.

In the past, their dealings had proceeded seamlessly, but their most recent interaction didn't go so smoothly. The Organization was not off to a hot start in its alliance with an outfit in South America, evidenced by an orgacal delivery being subject to confiscation in Peru. If the international community decided to take the Organization to court for intending to distribute orgacal across international borders, LaVonte's pride and joy faced a plethora of legal complications that could cost hundreds of millions to handle. After recently agreeing to what he thought was a lucrative trade agreement, LaVonte didn't need this headache. He knew the combination of his legal team and political connections would get him out of facing any charges, but he didn't want to resort to that. LaVonte needed Rapture to brush this problem under the rug so all parties could move on. After all, this type of service is what he expected after shelling out the type of money he had to the younger Lawrence.

When Richard arrived at his office, he took out an unopened bottle of wodin and poured himself a drink with a heavy hand. If he didn't keep drinking, he'd become lethargic and lose focus, a mistake that could be fatal in dealing with LaVonte. Richard situated himself in his chair and sent LaVonte a hologram. He answered after a couple rings but didn't immediately greet Richard. He instead sat there without muttering so much as a "hello" and puffed a cigar. Composed as ever.

"I know what you're up to you son of a bitch," Richard said.

Lavonte's hologram sat up and leaned closer to Richard, cigar clenched between his teeth.

"Is this how to conduct business now, Lawrence? Your old man came through on his promises, but evidently, he didn't pass those values down to you. I don't pay you to pick and choose what you deal with. If I have a problem, I go to you to handle it. That was the mother fuckin' agreement."

"The issue in Peru will get handled like all the other issues do. I told you I needed more time so things could cool down."

"I'm in a results-oriented business, Lawrence. Aren't you too? Pieces to the puzzle move fast, and you're struggling to keep up. If your daddy knew about this, he would be disappointed in his oldest son."

The "oldest son" remark caught Richard by surprise since he didn't have any siblings, but there were too many other pressing matters to handle than to educate LaVonte on the Lawrence family tree.

"Fuck off, LaVonte. First you get Phil involved in this bullshit, but now you get my family involved by sending over one of your whores. I know all about what you're running now. You're not as discreet as you like to think."

LaVonte had a smile planted on his face until Richard referred to his wife as one of his whores.

"And you're not as smart as you like to think, Lawrence. Do you think finding out this late in the game puts you ahead of it? What, did your boy

Phil let you in on the little secret? His dumb ass didn't know what he was getting himself into. Apparently, you don't either. Just like we told him, you better watch yourself out there. You all think that wealth will shield you from real-life consequences. You ignorant pieces of shit. You're in the real world now, Lawrence."

Richard's head began to swirl. All he had in his system was wodin and rage, and he was beginning to experience how ineffective of a concoction this was during a business meeting. Especially one of this magnitude. Richard feared his tirade made the situation for Heather more dire. Begging on his hands and knees seemed to be the only thing left to try.

"Listen, just stay away from my family, and I'll do anything you need."

"Oh, now you want to live up to your agreement? You dug your grave a while ago, Lawrence. Now you'll have to live with the consequences. Something your people aren't used to."

"Please do not touch them."

"If you really wanted to do something about it, you'd be with them and not bitchin' to me right now. I'll be seeing you."

LaVonte's hologram disappeared, and Richard downed the rest of his drink. The best he could do was go home and be with his family.

CHAPTER

2089

Richard's head was spinning during the ride home from his impromptu hologram meeting with LaVonte when a message from Heather came in.

Hi hon, I'm staying at my sister's tonight. I'll see you in the morning. Dillon's home, I love you.

Is everything ok? He texted back quickly.

Everything's fine. I love you, good night.

Ok, tell her hello for me. I love you too.

Richard decided waiting to explain the severity of the situation they were in could wait. He didn't want to scare his wife while she spent quality time with her sister.

Just about every other night, Moe was having a recurring dream he had trouble interpreting. He was a baby and sleeping in his crib before an unrecognizable woman with thick dark hair covering any identifiable facial features peacefully woke him up. Even though he wasn't able to identify anything specific about her excluding her hair, he felt a deep-rooted emotional connection to her that was so strong it was tangible. What should have been frightening for a baby was the complete opposite.

As she delicately lifted him up, he felt protected from the danger he sensed coming from outside his room. There was some commotion, but in his current state, there was no reason for him to worry about any of it. Even though it was occurring in his own house. He thought the mystery woman could've been his mother, but he didn't recall her ever wearing her hair like this. Besides, he would've known if it was his mother who picked him up. A mother's touch is unmistakable.

The woman gracefully rubbed the side of his right cheek and exuded a calming, comfortable presence to offset the maelstrom in the hallway. As if she sensed he began observing it, she spoke softly in his ear. "I know it's tough to understand, but I love you so much. You're so beautiful, Moe. I love you so much."

After she said this an ominous feeling suddenly took shape. Moe felt the pit of his stomach turn. Even though he was a baby in the dream, his perspective was one of an eighteen-year-old. His panic heightened when he heard the rumblings from the hallway grow louder. Unfamiliar, threatening voices roared through their home. To whom they belonged, Moe couldn't be certain. Then he saw his father being dragged in by two burly men Moe was positive he did not recognize. On his knees and with his arms constrained, Bobby's tears spilled out of his eye sockets onto Moe's bedroom floor. He sensed his father wanted to snatch him from this woman's arms, but with these two men restraining him he had no chance to take back his son.

"Please, do not do this," Bobby said. This earned him a knee to the rib strong enough to puncture a lung. It caused refractory coughs. He sounded like he was fighting just to breathe.

"I have to fuckin' do this!" she said.

Her voice sounded more familiar each time Moe dreamt, but he couldn't pinpoint it. His focus sharpened as he tried to discern the mystery woman holding him, but just as he felt like he was about to piece it all together his mind wandered to what was happening to his father. It was as if he was never meant to know who was responsible for this.

"Okay, okay, please. Just put the knife down, put Moe back. I'll go with you guys. Fine," his father said.

To prove his surrendering was genuine, Bobby's body went limp. The woman ordered the two men to get him on his feet, which they did with minimal effort. Moe's captor lifted him up to her and whispered in his ear, "I'm sorry," and tenderly kissed his forehead, leaving her lips planted there long enough for Moe to feel the spirited love she had for him.

As she was laying him on his back where she found him, Moe stared directly at her and saw beautiful, big brown eyes that were not visible just moments ago. Their eye contact caused her eyes to blur with tears, but her cries were silent, like she was trying her hardest to keep it a secret from the others in the room.

"I'm sorry. I love you so much, Moe."

It was barely audible, but she was leaned down close enough for him to hear. She straightened herself and blew him another kiss before telling him she loved him again. Her tone and words contradicted her actions, yet Moe believed every word.

"Let's get the fuck out of here before she gets home," one of the men said.

Ariana ignored him for as long as possible in order to savor what she thought would be her final moments with Moe.

"Come on, let's go," the other man said, more impatient than the first one.

And with that, Ariana was gone.

Moe gasped when he woke up, vaulting himself up abruptly and throwing the sheets off himself. He barked at his lamp to turn on and surveyed the room expecting to see Ariana standing over him how she was seconds ago.

Once Moe was certain she wasn't hovering over him, he relaxed against the bed's headboard and worked on calming his breath. The dream had him so aghast he forgot Megan Rincon was lying next to him. By the time he was able to slow his breath, she stirred awake.

"Baby, what's wrong?" she said. Her eyes were barely open, but she did her best to attend to his obvious distress.

"I just had a weird dream, that's all," he said. Wide awake, Moe kept his stare straight ahead and didn't even look her way.

"You're okay. I'm here, you're okay," Megan said. She grabbed his soft dick and began fondling it. "Let me make you feel better."

Megan commanded the lights to turn off, pulled the sheets off herself to reveal her naked body, and inserted Moe in her mouth.

"I'll make you forget about it," she said after using her tongue to harden him, even with what was racing through his mind. She resumed going down on him passionately, bopping her head up and down faster, flicking her tongue around the tip of him, and moaning louder like it was her on the verge of an orgasm. She was enthusiastic, drenching him with her saliva and rubbing herself.

Megan's efforts weren't enough to distract Moe from the reality of Ariana having a hand in kidnapping his father. If his dream didn't feel so real and wasn't so repetitive, he would've dismissed it, but the longer he contemplated it, the more it became a memory rather than a dream. He didn't know how, but he'd have to tell his mother, even if it unraveled all the progress Ariana enabled her to make with herself.

Since meeting his aunt at Dillon's house that one afternoon, he had a relentless inkling telling him he had met her before. Ever since she had reentered his family's life his subconscious had been attempting to communicate this to him. Moe finally put it all together, and in the process, became a step closer to knowing what happened to his father.

Preoccupied with this realization, Moe didn't notice his body was on the verge of an enlightening sensation Megan was working on so hard to achieve until he exploded in her throat.

CHAPTER

2089

Heather passed out on Ariana's couch the night before. She guzzled enough wine to fall asleep fully clothed without any pillows or blankets. She exhaled a painful grunt. A headache radiated through the left side of her head, and opening her eyes only intensified it. Disheveled by waking up in an unfamiliar place, Heather patted herself down and looked around the condo.

Ariana offered a helping hand. "Stay here. I'll make some coffee and bring you some," She kept her voice low to cater to Heather's obvious discomfort.

Ariana tip-toed to the kitchen and changed into an outfit she laid out on the kitchen table when she woke up a couple hours earlier. Her bag of essentials was leaning against the front door ready for an abrupt exit: phone, computer, a few extra outfits, and a couple of financial documents representing Ariana's sliver of independence, undoubtly the most important items in her getaway bag. There weren't digital copies of them, and LaVonte didn't know this account existed, making the hard copies vital to determine the money's whereabouts and owner. Years ago, she began stowing away parts of her allowance and whatever other funds she could get her hands on in an account one of LaVonte's lesser financial guys assisted her in creating and concealing. If her husband found out about his role in it, he was a dead man, but apparently the risk was worth it because in turn he could claim the one and only LaVonte Jackson's wife once went down on him. At the time she didn't know what she needed it for. Now it was quite essential to her livelihood.

Ariana tied her hair back, confirmed Heather fell back asleep to let her hangover subside, and tiptoed to an office to hologram her husband.

"Good morning, baby," he said.

Ariana blew him a kiss and smiled. "I'm coming home today."

"Thank God. When will you be here?"

"Most likely this afternoon. One of the guys is picking me up at our dock, and then we'll be on our way."

"Who is getting you?" LaVonte appreciated details.

"Marvin."

"Okay. Your timing couldn't be better. I woke up thinking about telling you to say fuck it and come home."

"What do you mean? What happened?"

"Richard and I spoke last night, and Phil told him about the meeting at The Corridor. I'm afraid I put you in a bad situation, compromising your identity with them. Richard knows who you are and why you're there. He can't go anywhere with that information or else he's fucked, so don't worry about that, but it puts you in danger. Just remain on schedule and come home today. I'm proud of you, baby. You've done well over there."

Ariana grinned. "Happy to do it. I'll be home soon enough, and this will all finally be over."

"Okay. I'll be waiting for you."

LaVonte and Ariana said their goodbyes and love yous before hanging up. Her husband being okay with compromising his wife for his own selfish intentions reaffirmed to Ariana it was time she put her needs above his.

"Who, who was that?"

Ariana pivoted around and saw Heather in the doorway. She didn't hear it open, so she must've slipped up and forgot to close it.

"Oh, hi. I didn't know you were standing there. I thought you were still nursing your hangover," Ariana said, scrambling to formulate a response.

"Who was that? What's going on?"

Heather's trepidation canceled out her hangover. She detected a dark persona encompassing Ariana. She no longer looked like the woman Heather just spent the night gossiping with. Ariana's brown eyes transformed from gorgeous and welcoming to devilish and piercing. Her silence and close-mouthed smile only increased Heather's worry.

At this point, Ariana saw no point in continuing to play her part. She stomped towards Heather and pinned her against the wall. Ariana's facial expression remained tranquil as she pressed her hand into Heather's neck, stickering her on the wall. Tears impeded Heather's vision by wetting her eyelashes, amplifying Ariana's pleasure. Heather's father-in-law instilled this type of fear in Ariana more times than Heather would ever know. In her mind, it was only fair Reginald and his family experienced something similar to what Robin and her endured.

"Sorry, Mrs. Lawrence. Someone has to be punished for your family being the pieces of shit they are. Unfortunately, it's going to be you."

Heather struggled to articulate a response, limited by Ariana's hand clasped around her throat and confused as to where this anger originated from.

"Did you all think you'd really get away with all that shit?" Ariana continued searing Heather into the wall.

"I-I-I don't even know what you're talking about, Ariana. Please, please let me go. This is all a mistake. I promise."

Ariana squeezed her throat harder and slammed her to the ground before stomping on her stomach with all her might.

"That's a lie right there. Stupid bitch. You could've avoided this all along if you stayed true to yourself and didn't try so hard to make yourself available for someone like Richard Lawrence. So pathetic."

Coughing and crying, responding to Ariana was cumbersome. "Please, stop. Just please talk to me. I don't know what this is about. Do you want money? We can pay you."

Ariana stood over Heather and planted both feet next to Heather's hips. She plopped down on her stomach and clawed her cheeks, yelling at the top of her lungs, inches from Heather's face. Ariana's face reddened and shook with fury, putting Heather on the verge of wetting herself. "You fuckin' idiots think it is always about money. That's all you ever think about. What about doing what's right? Does no one do that anymore? What the fuck is wrong with all of you?"

As her cold stare singed through Heather's petrified eyes while she got her breath under control, Ariana realized she had lost control, something she never did on the job; however, no job had ever involved so much personal revenge.

Once Ariana regained her composure, a rationale that was missing for the last few minutes returned. Seeing the look in Heather's eyes caused her to question why she thought inflicting this type of distress to an innocent party would make her feel better. Even if she was a relative to the sick man who nearly killed her and her sister, Heather did not deserve to face the punishment. Ariana was familiar with the damage it could do to one's psyche and imposing that on a guiltless individual was not something she wanted to be responsible for. A deep sense of regret suddenly hit Ariana like a ton of bricks, leading her to release the hold she had on Heather's now blood-red cheeks and lightly set her head down. She wiped the tears from her own face, making herself vulnerable to Heather retaliating.

Ariana's shift in temperament blindsided Heather, making her unable to determine if the brisk change was indicative of Ariana being a clinical psychopath or her friend-turned-aggressor truly had repentance. Using her hands, Heather walked herself backwards until she bumped into a wall.

Ariana pulled her knees to her chest and sobbed. Between cries she said, "I'm sorry. I'm so sorry, Heather. I—I just don't have a choice."

Observing how mentally unstable Ariana was, Heather's goal was to talk her off the cliff.

"What don't you have a choice in? Please Ariana, talk to me," Heather asked. Something inside of her told her Ariana was genuinely remorseful for how the morning unraveled, but she still kept her distance so she had time to defend herself in case there was another attack.

"I was under your father-in-law's care in the MYM." Ariana admitted this barely above a whisper.

Heather hoped she was lying, looking for any sort of nervous gesture suggesting so, but there was none to be found. What exactly being under Reginald's care in the MYM meant wasn't entirely clear to Heather but based on what she felt in her gut and Reginald acting inappropriately to her on multiple occasions, she deduced it couldn't have been pleasant. How he used to brag about the children, especially young girls, he molded into contributing members of society always felt phony, and now, his daughter-in-law knew why.

Ariana elaborated on her past, "Robin and I are sisters. Before dinner at your house the other night we hadn't seen each other in years. Reginald took us from our parents when Robin was two, and I was just a baby. Him and the others in charge of us at MYM told us our parents committed suicide when I was seven years old, but I don't necessarily buy it. It isn't like I have proof of anything else, it is just a feeling I have. Anyways, Robin and I grew up being raped, humiliated, tortured, and all other types of abuse at the hands of your father-in-law.

"She stayed here and raised her two boys, but I had to leave. I couldn't be here any longer. She is much stronger than I am. Once the state let me go from MYM I was out of here. I needed a new life, which I found. I even found love and a, we'll call it, financially healthy life, but in the process have done some horrible, horrible things. I thought it would fulfill me. I thought it would make me feel like I got my revenge, but I obviously still have that void to fill."

Ariana spent the next portion of their conversation describing her husband and how he made his living. She tied it all together by telling Heather Richard was on LaVonte's payroll, a fact she would have never found out if it weren't for Ariana. Even when Heather was more enthusiastic about their marriage in its earlier years, she wasn't the type of wife to inquire about the inner workings of his job because, quite frankly, she had no interest. If she learned this about Richard sooner, maybe she would have been bold enough to leave him and live her life how she wanted. But that was easy to say in hindsight.

As Ariana continued opening up about her past and present, Heather's fear subsided. She had to remind herself not too long ago she thought this woman was on the brink of murdering her, but really, it was misguided pain and anger she was releasing. If Ariana was truly menacing, Heather didn't think she would still be alive. As their conversation deepened, Heather found their lives were more alike than either of them would have guessed.

It was Heather's turn to open up. "My dad and I were super close when I was young. I thought I could go to him about anything. When I was twelve and we were alone at home, I told him I liked girls and thought boys were gross. I told him I wanted to have a girlfriend instead of a boyfriend. He, he—"

Heather tilted her head back and fought her tears. "He violated me that night. Asking if I still liked girls while he did it."

Ariana lifted her gaze from between her own knees to look at Heather.

"Oh God, for fuckin' years I have kept that bottled up inside. Until now I planned on keeping it a secret for the rest of my life. For months after it happened, he would ask me if I told anyone, and threatened me by telling me if I did, he'd do it again. But then after that, he would go back to being the dad I originally loved. God, I was so young I just went along with it, but at a certain age, I knew I hated him. I regularly think about how much I despise him; how horrible of a man he was; how naive I was for thinking someone capable of doing what he did could ever love me. When he died, I pretended to mourn, but when I was separated from my family, I basked in my glory. Proud of myself for giving him what he deserved."

This raised Ariana's eyebrows.

Heather answered her question before she asked it. "He was prescribed some intense pain killers after getting his hip replaced. My mom, sister, and I would switch off helping him out even though my sister and I no longer lived at home. You know, helping him get around the house and making sure he took his medicine and had what he needed. One day, my mom and sister decided to take a day trip to California and asked me if I could watch him. I said sure, right, it wasn't a problem. And then when they left is when I got the idea. He was so out of it because of the pain and medicine he would sleep most of the day, so when he was in one of his slumbers, I disintegrated an excessive amount of pills into his water cup just to be sure he wouldn't have a chance at making it.

"My mom and sister got back before he woke up, so I took that opportunity to get out of there as soon as I could. I guess he woke up soon after because before I knew it, they called me to say doctors were at the home attempting to revive him. I pretended to be distressed about it, but really, it felt like the weight of the world was off my shoulders. I would no longer have to pretend to love a man who ruined a little girl's life."

Heather sighed before continuing. "Of course, being the last one with him, I was questioned by the police about what exactly happened. Lying to them about how he demanded the pills be next to him because he was in more pain than ever was easier than I thought it would be. Suicide rates are off the charts, so they didn't even look into it too thoroughly. After my first interrogation, I left without a worry in the world.

"And until now, I have never told anyone that for obvious reasons, but I wanted to tell you because I want you to know I understand your pain. But most of all, I understand your need to get back at the son of a bitch who tried to ruin you. And I want you to know I want to do everything in my power to help you make it right."

When Ariana woke up this morning, bonding with Heather was about the last thing she anticipated happening, but here they were, two women with similar demons and aligned methods to deal with them.

After a few more minutes of consoling each other, primarily Ariana apologizing to Heather for manipulating and putting her in harm's way, Heather received a detailed rundown of past events leading up to this point, including how Bobby's disappearance transpired, Ariana's plan to get him back to Robin, and even Heather's original fate. Ariana laid it all out there because the least she could do was be transparent to an innocent bystander. Minus her original unfortunate outcome and plus an added stop before heading back to California, Heather suggested they keep most of the initial plan intact.

To quell Ariana's concerns about her ability to tag along, Heather said, "I've convinced Richard I've enjoyed fuckin' him all these years. Don't worry about my acting skills."

Their situation received some well-needed comic relief.

CHAPTER

32

2089

R obin just got back in time from her impromptu shift at Free
Morple to answer Marty Perlman's hologram. Since losing her
son to the hands of his own father, Taylor Jennings had to forfeit
her apartment and now called Free Morple home. Housing was scarce, but
accommodations were made for those in the direst of situations, which
Taylor's certainly classified as. In a state of hysteria, Taylor requested Robin
after the overnight crew subdued her following a suicide attempt. Robin
was furious with them because she informed the entire staff how fragile
she was with the loss of her son, yet they were sloppy and failed to take
extra steps towards ensuring her safety. Spending her night listening to a
young woman in desperate need of a shoulder to cry on did not bug her in
the slightest, but the carelessness by her peers was infuriating.

"Hi Marty," Robin said. Stress and worry were both evident in her
voice.

"Good morning. Sounds like you've already had a day. Everything
okay?" Marty asked.

"Oh, well yes and no. I mean, we are all fine over here, but I had to
take an unexpected trip to Free Morple last night. Don't want to talk about
it now since it has consumed me for the last sixish hours or however long
it has been."

"I understand. If this wasn't important, I wouldn't pile it on, but can you meet soon?"

"What's wrong, Marty?"

"This conversation should happen in person, and as soon as possible. Despite your sleep deprivation," he said in all seriousness.

Robin signed. "Alright. Yeah, I can meet. When?"

"I can be at your place in less than five minutes."

"Ok. Moe is here, though."

"He's old enough to hear this."

"Okay. See you soon."

Right after Marty's hologram disappeared, Moe walked in the kitchen.

"Hi Mom," Moe said.

"Good morning, sweetheart."

"I need to talk to you."

"Okay, what's going on? Marty is coming over in five minutes. Can it wait?"

"Not really."

"Are you sure? He sounded very rattl—"

"I know what happened to Dad."

Robin's head jerked back. Moe was just a toddler when Robin lost Bobby to fate, causing her to deem it highly unlikely he could investigate something that happened sixteen years ago.

"How is that possible?"

"Ariana kidnapped him," he blurted. He was up all night contemplating the best way to deliver this news to his mother and decided being direct and concise was the most effective.

After spending the night listening to what Taylor was going through combined with the stress of wondering what Marty was coming over to tell her, Robin was on the verge of imploding. Ariana's insertion back in her life brought her a certain degree of happiness that had been missing since becoming a single parent. Because of this, Robin immediately assumed Moe was saying this out of jealousy. Jealous because his mother was paying attention to someone besides him and his brother.

"What? Moe, how is that even possible? How could you come up with something like that? After all she's done for us lately, you're going to lie about that?"

"I'm not lying, Mom. I knew I recognized her when I met her at Dillon's house. I kept having the same dream over and over again and I finally realized it was her in it. It's a memory, Mom. I was being held and Dad was being kidnapped. I promise you. It happened."

"I don't doubt the dream happened, honey, but tha—"

"The dream happened in real life. It's a memory that came back to me. I know she did it."

"Fuck you, no you don't!"

Moe jolted back, his eyes widening at her outburst.

Robin exhaled audibly and pressed her palm to her forehead. "You had a bad dream that seemed real, fine. That doesn't make what happened a reality, Moe. You can't just come in accusing people of things that serious. Jesus Christ."

After a tense stare down, Moe muttered a few obscenities and stormed out of the house, almost knocking Marty down on his way.

"What was that about?" Marty asked.

"You don't want to know. Please, come sit down," Robin said.

"Where's Jonathan?"

"He's at therapy. With Wallace."

"Come to think of it, privacy is probably best."

Over the last twenty years, Morple's human trafficking epidemic continuously worsened. The correlation was clear: the more diswors companies created after transitioning to A.I., the more product traffickers had to choose from. The government turned its head the other way when the issue became a topic of discussion because trafficking was solving the state's unemployment problem.

For a while, word of mouth was a sufficient method for traffickers to learn about available product. Foot growers in Morple and other states across the country would let their higher ups know diswors were on the streets desperate for opportunity. Through abduction, teams of foot growers transported them back to their bosses' orgacal farms or wherever else needed bodies. Police in The District didn't care enough to prevent these crimes or investigate them when citizens filed reports. But in most cases, they were simply paid too much by the traffickers to dishonor their arrangement.

As Morple became a more competitive source for product, traffickers needed to get a leg up on their competition. They achieved this by putting local politicians and businessmen on the payroll. These people, like what Phil was aspiring to be, had a primary contact in the trafficking organization they'd tip off. If legislation allowing more A.I. technology in a certain sector was on the brink of passing or a company was readying to lay off most of its employees, the Phil's of the world let their contacts know.

A Phil's compensation depended on the number of diswors foot growers were able to round up based on a particular tip. At the rate Morple businesses were depending on A.I., these moles established an additional healthy stream of income for themselves.

The practice disgusted Marty so much he became obsessed with stopping it.

Roger Ballard, a longtime friend Marty practiced law with once upon a time, was now one of Morple's sitting senators, one of the few in the Senate who maintained his ethics. At eighty, he was so wealthy the money offered to him to be a mouthpiece for corrupt corporations' favorable legislation was laughable. He might as well do the right thing.

Roger prioritized not only stopping human trafficking in Morple but also paying victims and their families reparations for their hardships. Getting the initiative off the ground was proving difficult, but he gained some traction by obtaining enough evidence to expose the involvement of fellow politicians and businessmen. To propel his cause, Roger brought Marty onboard. Roger asked if he'd want to handle the investigative side of things because he was the only person Roger could trust with a task of this magnitude.

From that point on, Marty dedicated himself to it. He did his homework on trafficking's history in Morple by reviewing unsolved abduction cases, common trends amongst people disappearing as jobs continued to diminish, who were the main players in the trafficking world, and even hired himself a mole he extracted valuable information from and placed in the field.

The foot grower he was able to flip revealed invaluable insight. He educated Marty on the industry's protocols, who mattered versus who didn't, the structures of the top organizations, when and where certain gatherings amongst leaders took place, but what he refused to detail was how to identify and track down LaVonte Jackson and his wife, whose involvement was a well-kept secret unless you worked hard enough to put it all together.

Based on the information Marty gathered about them primarily by his lonesome, he concluded their presence in Morple started fifteen to twenty years ago. He just needed concrete evidence to support this. Marty lucked out when his mole got Phil Gorge to incriminate himself. The lawyer's fortune really began to see the light of day when Phil's next meeting was with the kingpin's queen.

Marty identified her right off the bat, and now it was time to inform his former client and longtime friend who her sister was and what she had done.

"Look, Robin. There is no easy way to tell you what I'm about to tell you, but—"

"It's okay, Marty. You can tell me anything."

Marty gathered himself before divulging his findings.

"Robin, your sister is married to one of the most renown criminals in the world."

Agape, Robin looked for any indication Marty was pulling her leg. Unfortunately, his serious expression never wavered.

"What are you talking about?" she asked.

"After Ariana left Morple, she moved to California—"

"Yes, I know that. That doesn't mean she is a criminal."

Sensing Robin was becoming defensive, Marty paused before continuing to avoid coming off as combative. Robin apologized and blamed her insolence on her night with Taylor and morning with Moe.

"Somehow, Ariana got linked up with LaVonte Jackson, who I have assumed you have at least heard of, yes?"

"Yes, I've heard of him. I can't say I follow or admire his work, but I am familiar with the name."

Marty briefed Robin on everything he could since starting this project. Some of the confidential information he was privy to he kept tight to the vest, but he disclosed more than he would to just any other client. He described the elaborate foot grower missions she assisted LaVonte in orchestrating. He informed her what life was like for diswors after their men brought them back to the plantation; he revealed everything he knew about the lifestyle on the Organization's plantation, briefly mentioning the women enslaved there.

Robin's interest piqued once he mentioned them. Marty didn't want to elaborate on their lifestyles, but she wouldn't let up.

Marty cleared his throat, "There are various different houses, I'm not sure how many exactly, that in total hundreds of women reside in. Most of the houses are available to Jackson's men, so after a hard day's work they can round up whoever they want and do whatever they want with them. Th—"

"What do they do, Marty?"

"They have sex with them, Robin. From what I've learned, they basically condition the women to accept the lifestyle being forced upon them. They brainwash them into thinking that is what their lives are supposed to be, and that they have no other choice because at the end of the day, they really don't. Jackson's foot growers get them from cities decimated by A.I., so they do not have bright futures. So, after a certain amount of time, they accept their new reality because they are convinced what LaVonte provides is better than anything else they'd have at home."

Marty said the last part quietly, disturbed by the harsh truth.

Robin nodded to indicate she understood. "She finds it familiar."

"Excuse me?" Marty asked.

"Ariana. She finds the situation familiar to what we grew up with. Jackson is an authoritative male figure. From what you said, it sounds like he exercises his power over women by way of sex. They're all helpless, and they're easy targets to pick on because they don't have many other options, similar to how Ariana and I were as little girls. That was Reginald's intent, to convince us he could provide the best life for us."

Having been so focused on the criminal side of it all, Marty had never pondered Ariana could find a sense of belonging this way. It was cohesive, but it didn't change his outlook on her.

Robin continued. "What Jackson is doing to these girls, Reginald did to us. Except for this time, Ariana's not the victim. She feels powerful, she's brainwashed, Marty."

"I know you two have come close since you recon—"

"We were always close."

"I know you two have been spending substantial time together," Marty said, "but there is something I am nearly certain she did that you will find more disturbing than anything I just revealed."

Robin scoffed before sarcastically asking, "Oh what? Did she kill my husband, too?"

Marty's chin dropped to his chest and looked down, not wanting to see the look on Robin's face when she realized this may be a possibility.

"Marty—say something."

"I have strong, indicative evidence she had a hand in kidnapping him under Jackson's instruction. I'm so sorry, Robin, so sorry."

Robin squeezed her eyes shut, clenching the top of her nose with her thumb and index finger.

"I am doing everything I can to find out for certain what happened, but there is a strong likelihood she was involved," Marty said.

Marty allowed a significant amount of time to pass before continuing, respecting the time it took for Robin to process what he just disclosed.

"I'm sorry Robin. I hate it's come to this. But you tried to make things right with her a long time ago. And recently, too. We have to move in as soon as we can. Her next move is coming."

"Her next move?"

"We recently learned Jackson is involved with Richard Lawrence, but they've had their qualms lately. I should've put it together when you came to my office and told me she was at their house. She's here to hurt them. How specifically, I don't know, but something is off."

Now it all made sense why Ariana was going out of her way to befriend Heather. Robin knew she couldn't bear families like the Lawrence's, as she hated the traditional wealthy types.

"She's been spending so much time here and with the boys. Everything seemed to be going perfectly. They love her, Marty. They absolutely love her."

Robin broke down and planted her face in Marty's shoulder. His heart broke at the fact she continued to suffer from misery so often. Marty was compassionate enough to understand individuals with trying upbringings struggle to adapt in life even as they age. He believed in second chances, but Ariana's crimes were too severe. She wasn't worthy of exoneration.

"So, what are you going to do?" Robin asked, lifting her head up from his shoulder now that her tears were manageable.

"Well, Roger, you remember Roger ri—"

Robin nodded.

"Roger and I are trying to find Heather as we speak—she's officially missing. We paid Richard a visit this morning to let him know the situation. He already knew Ariana was getting closer because he figured out who Ariana is. Heather told him she was at her sister's, but we found out she hadn't been there. Richard stated he was skeptical right off the bat but didn't report it because he didn't have anything credible to go off. We found the condo Ariana has been staying at and concluded they'd both recently been there. There were also signs of a struggle."

Robin closed her eyes and breathed deeply.

"Will Richard be in legal trouble?" she asked.

"No. He and his legal team would make it too complicated for us to convict him of anything. Maybe we'll get lucky, and he'll help us out of the goodness of his heart."

He stared at Robin for a while before she noticed what was coming next.

"Marty, are you shittin' me?"

"I'm sorry. I'm required to ask."

"Ask away then." Robin waved her hand in the air, mocking the process.

"Are you helping Ariana escape and or hide?"

"No."

"Do you know where Ariana is?"

"No."

There was an awkward pause.

"I'm sorry," Marty said. "I was required to ask."

"It's okay. I understand."

Marty knew Robin wasn't going to like his next request, but he wouldn't be able to live with himself if he didn't try. "Robin, I want to set you up with protection around the house until we get this figured out."

Despite Robin defiantly shaking her head, Marty continued, "As close as we are to putting a stop to this thing, we can never be too sure of who is who and what they are planning to do. I know Ariana has been here recently and all has been good, but she is too unpredictable. LaVonte may know where you live, and that scares me."

"Absolutely not. I will not have my boys wondering why we suddenly need men with guns surrounding our house. That is not necessary and will never be necessary. She is not going to put us in danger, Marty."

"Robin, how can you be so sure? Look what she's—"

Robin wasn't having it. "No, Marty. I appreciate and love you for looking out for us, but please let me take care of my boys while you catch the bad guys. Please. I don't want them believing their lives are at risk."

Not liking the answer, Marty reluctantly agreed to leave Robin and her family be. He considered reminding her their lives were at risk, but then thought otherwise. Although he felt it was his responsibility to protect Robin and her sons, she had final say on how she ran her family.

Marty assured Robin he'd keep her updated on the search and notify her if anything significant unraveled. He also made her promise to reach out to him if she suspected she was in danger. He purposely didn't ask her to turn Ariana in if she happened to tell Robin her whereabouts, knowing it was too tall of an order.

Robin plopped on the couch and cried some more once Marty left.

That's when it hit Robin.

All the information Marty unloaded caused Robin to forget about Moe's dream. One that began to feel more like the truth than she thought just a short time ago.

CHAPTER

2073

All new arrivals started in the bottom of the barrel on the Organization's plantation. Despite his connection to the boss' wife, Bobby Karros was no exception. The plantation's diswors were either Hispanics CEOs of billion-dollar corporations left behind in favor of A.I., or White trash-folk who were too dumb to take advantage of their skin tone and progress with their people. Naturally the Organization's slaves segregated themselves up by the color of their skin.

Their harsh previous living situations hardened most of the plantation's inhabitants. They were either already part of a gang or familiar with the lifestyle. Bobby quickly gathered he was the only slave whose family was worth millions. Since his family was originally from Mexico and he lived in Morple up until this point, joining Hombres of Morple was the logical choice. Not being affiliated with any of them would be suicide.

As a Homer, what the group referred to themselves as, Bobby was immediately classified as an enemy to the Power of Whites. The Power of Whites, or POWs, consisted of lower-class White men from predominantly California and Oregon whose core, shared belief was Hispanics ruined their opportunities at holding any type of job, ignorant to the fact White billionaires were the ones stripping them of their livelihoods with the advancements of A.I.. So, when a group of POWs caught wind Ariana

Jackson personally handled the newest Homer's capture, they put a target on his back.

After spending one of his first of what would be thousands of days deciphering which orgacal leaves were potent and which weren't, Bobby retired to his bunk in an 80,000 square foot sleeping porch he now called home, forgoing dinner in favor of catching up on rest. When he arrived at his bunk, four POWs were waiting for him, ruining his chances at calling an early night.

"Hey guys," Bobby said nonchalantly.

The four POWs straightened up and exchanged smiles with each other before the apparent leader inserted himself in front of the group.

"Karros, yeah?" he asked.

Bobby confirmed his identity. "That's right."

The other three circled around him. Bobby noticed one of them was carrying a gunmetal rod. Fellow Homers warned Bobby about the gang rape tool used on the plantation. One of the things his new friends advised him on was to never head back to his bunk alone, as letting his guard down would cost him.

The POW holding the rod whacked Bobby's right kneecap with it, causing him to collapse and compound the sharp pain shooting through his entire leg.

"Where's your girl now, Karros?" the leader asked, "Think you get special treatment around here? I don't give a fuck who you are. You get fucked like every other infick Homer in this nigger-infested place."

He booted Bobby's ribcage. The two POWs without the rod each speared a knee into his kidneys, clasping his arms against the ground so he couldn't move. The rod-holding POW pulled his pants and boxers down and spread his legs using heavily weighted objects so Bobby had no chance of resisting it. Bracing for what was about to happen, Bobby bit his lip and did all he could to ready himself for the torture.

"Stick it in," the leader instructed.

Right when Bobby felt the tip of the rod make contact where it was to enter him, a gun fired. A skull slammed the concrete floor and split open. Blood drained and brains surrounded the dead sodomizer and Bobby. Some of its remnants landed on Bobby's bare legs.

"Unless you pieces of shit want a pole up your asses and out your mouths step the fuck back," Ariana said.

Two Black men with bowling ball-type bodies were on both sides of her, each with Desert Eagles drawn and AK-47s hanging on their backs. A trail of smoke was drifting out of the man on the right's pistol. He was grinning at his kill shot.

"What the fuck is this, Cody?" Ariana asked the assumed POW leader. "What did we say about this shit? If you get off to it so much, do it to your own friends."

The sodomizer's killer whacked Cody in the face with the butt of his pistol, breaking his nose and knocking out a handful of teeth.

"Faggot ass White boy," he said under his breath.

Ariana's muscle detained the other two men until Bobby put a stop to it.

"Don't touch them!" Bobby said.

Initially they expressed outrage a slave would raise his voice at them.

"They're right. I don't get special treatment in here. If I'm not going to have a pole shoved up my ass it's because I fought back and kicked their asses. Four on one is tough, but fuck these guys, I'll go two on one," Bobby said.

Ariana's company released their detainees, mocked surrendering with their hands raised up, and smiled in approval. Ariana's smirk demonstrated she approved, too.

"Fine. Your call. Don't say I didn't try," she said.

"Once dinner is over it'll go down fight-night style in here. I want everyone to see me kick these two sons of bitches' asses. And if I don't, they can fuck me all they want. Controlling the crowd will help plenty, but besides that, I'll handle 'em," Bobby said to Ariana's muscle.

"We don't take orders from you, infick," the guard who hadn't killed anyone yet said.

"You don't, but you do from me," Ariana said, "and I like the idea. Get everyone else and make sure LaVonte knows in case he wants some entertainment tonight."

"Yes ma'am," they said in unison.

"Be ready in an hour," Ariana said. She led her men out of the sleeping porch and left the POWs and Bobby alone.

Just under an hour later, all the bunks surrounded the center of the warehouse to create an arena-like atmosphere. A mixed crowd of Homers, POWs, and other interested parties encircled the area for the night's main ticket. LaVonte, Ariana, a couple high-level employees, and guards situated themselves in a booth that was the lone room on the second story of the warehouse.

The man who murdered the sodomizer "officiated" the fight and explained to onlookers the rod Bobby was guarding was what the "faggot White boys" tried raping him with. If he failed to protect it, they could do whatever they pleased with it and him in front of the entire audience. Once the makeshift official felt confident all parties involved understood the rules of the melee, it was time to roll.

Bobby's strategy initially appeared timid and counterproductive. He wasn't retaliating against the POWs advancements that were cornering him towards the rod they wanted to shove up his ass. Allowing themselves to assume he'd give up easy, the POWS excited as they neared entrapping him. Both of them were seething at the thought of taking down a Homer and asserting their dominance in front of a throng of spectators. The POW observers were becoming rowdier each step their compatriots took towards Bobby, while the Homers desperately yelled for him to make a move for the sake of their pride. Some of the latter were already expressing regret for permitting him to claim their gang. They feared Bobby didn't grasp he represented their brand. A pathetic showing would embarrass all Homers, resulting in his exile from the group, and most likely earning him a vile punishment from his own kind. Being cast out on an island on the Organization's plantation wasn't a place anyone wanted to be, especially one lacking the experience of fighting for survival.

His fan base's lack of confidence in him caused Bobby to second guess his approach, until he sensed his plan was unraveling exactly how he envisioned it would. He settled himself into a defensive position, crouching down with his arms extended out in front of him like he was intending to stiff arm the POWs off him once they got close. Physical strength wasn't how he was going to win this fight, but he made up for those deficiencies mentally.

"Just look at him. This infick knows he is going to get fucked," one of them said.

"Come on, fight back a little bit and make it interesting before we shove that shit up your ass, boy," the other said.

Bobby had them right where he wanted them, cocky and seeing the finish line before remembering to run to it. As their guard continued to go down, Bobby snatched the rod from behind him and in one motion swung it forward to whack the POW to his right on the left side of his head. The blood pouring out of his ear confirmed he struck him good. Bobby turned his attention to the other POW. He looked perplexed as to how the lone Homer managed to gain the momentum in the blink of an eye. Bobby took advantage of his hesitation and struck him atop the head. Bobby's vertical wallop came down with so much force the second POW crumbled to the ground. Not wasting any time, Bobby continued bashing his head until it was red mush. The first POW he hit was out cold but still breathing. Three sledgehammer-esk blows to his head and he joined his friend in eternity. Neither face was recognizable, and chunks of brain littered the arena.

The POWs in the crowd were shell aghast, unable to fathom how a newbie just pulled off what he did on the plantation's biggest stage. Two members dying in one night signaled a sign of weakness, especially in this fashion.

Homers were jumping up and down, hitting their own chests, pumping their fists, and chanting "Bee-Kay! Bee-Kay! Bee-Kay!" Embracing the crowd's energy, Bobby tossed the rod on the ground and lifted his arms up triumphantly as if he was a gladiator. Knowing the men's cheers were for him provided Bobby with a rush he had never experienced. He was proud of himself and proud to represent the Hombres of Morple.

After basking in all the glory, he shifted his gaze up to LaVonte and Ariana and said, "I do my own fuckin' work around here!"

The Hombres of Morple ate it up, celebrating thunderously at its new leader's boldness. This earned Bobby legendary status on the plantation, a reputation he maintained until his last day slaving away for LaVonte Jackson.

2089

Bobby thought about the life in Morple Ariana deprived him of on a regular basis. Even though he had now spent sixteen years away from Robin he remained madly in love with her. They met during a complicated time in her life. Robin was close to finalizing her settlement with the state, but they immediately developed a chemistry few people had the privilege of experiencing. Before she came into Bobby's life, the only information he knew about the MYM was surface level. That changed as their relationship deepened. Bobby accepted there would forever be things he wouldn't know about Robin's childhood simply because it was too traumatic, but she revealed enough for him to get the gist of it. One of the reasons she fell so hard for him was because of how understanding he was, and he never pressured her to profess more than she was comfortable with. Bobby respected Robin's fragility.

Even when he slept with women on the plantation he'd think about Robin, fantasizing he was making love to her and not the brainwashed prostitutes LaVonte housed. Bobby often times felt remorseful after sex with these women, but it was the only way he could pretend he was still intimate with Robin.

LaVonte wasn't shy about his respect for Bobby. He developed a fondness for his brother-in-law and granted him access to the same women his employees had at their disposal. But the only ones he chose resembled Robin. Bobby instructed them to confess their spurious love for him. The feigned passion was the only way he could climax. As much as he wished they would, these women didn't satisfy Bobby. They only made him miss Robin more. Their love was too genuine for LaVonte's prostitutes to impersonate.

Bobby was initially under the impression Jonathan was an accident from a sex escapade Robin had during her days under MYM's care until she fessed up later on in their relationship. Thinking this would upset him, Robin cried in his arms as he told her, "I love you for who you are and him because he's yours. He has a meaningful purpose. He's going to be one of the many joys in our lives."

Bobby immediately bonded with baby Jonathan. Even with severe brain damage evident at such a young age, Jonathan's kind heart began to reveal itself. He would look up at his mother and Bobby with so much admiration. Bobby could tell by the look in his eyes he inherited all his mother's traits and left his biological father's behind. He symbolized the positive changes happening in Robin's life.

Creating a beautiful baby boy was Bobby and Robin's biggest accomplishment during their short time together. The day they brought Moe home Bobby knew he would grow up looking just like his mother.

Bobby was a handsome man, but Robin's physical features were in an entirely different echelon. He often wondered if Moe's personality ended up more like him or Robin. Logic told Bobby he was more similar to Robin because she was the, what he hoped, only parental influence in his life. Even so, Bobby liked to fantasize about his own mini me living with his beloved in Morple. It was hard to believe he was eighteen now, especially because Bobby would never know him as a kid. He could only hope he would one day get to know him as an adult.

Family is what Bobby thought about while he slaved away in Lavonte's warehouses, involuntarily contributing to the international epidemic that was orgacal. For as often as he fantasized escaping Bobby never truly considered making an attempt. The plantation was under LaVonte's constant surveillance and littered with his men that would make him wish he were dead once they captured him. LaVonte manned it from his office's security feed. Quite frankly, any attempt would be pathetic. But something inside Bobby continued reminding him to keep his spirits up. If he was persistent enough, he would prevail.

"BK!" one of LaVonte's bodyguards shouted from the other side of the production line.

"Yes sir," Bobby said.

"Boss needs you. Let's go."

"Alright. I'm coming now."

Bobby jogged over and hopped in the car outside of the warehouse.

CHAPTER

2089

As usual LaVonte was working away in his office. It was rare for Bobby to meet him any other place besides there. Bobby was the most trusted slave on the plantation, but this didn't mean LaVonte's men skipped out on patting him down before he met with the boss. If Bobby met with him after the plantation recently received a new crop of diswors, they tested him for viruses. But since the headhunting side of the business was struggling as of late, Bobby didn't have to endure that nonsense.

Whatever his computer was projecting on his desk had LaVonte in a trance when Bobby walked in. Over the years he developed an understanding of when it was appropriate to announce his presence and when it wasn't. This was one of those times when it wasn't. LaVonte's computer projected various graphs revealing how profitable he could anticipate the Organization being for the rest of 2089. Bobby noticed enough margin that would make any other big-time business owner happy, but LaVonte was not like any other big-time business owner. For as long as Bobby knew him, LaVonte constantly emphasized how if the business is not growing it is failing, and that was unacceptable. The decreased profit margin was primarily due to the hiccup in South America, and Bobby expected heads would roll because of it. Whose exactly he didn't know, nor did he really care. If hundreds of billions of dollars wasn't enough to satisfy this man, nothing could. Bobby hated it when he remembered LaVonte and him were family.

To LaVonte's right was an all-in-one monitor showing the camera feeds from the women's housing on the plantation. There were multiple screens recording footage of women in the houses scattered around the property. He regularly kept tabs on them to ensure they were abiding by his rules, such as acting happy, eating clean, exercising, and listening to orders from his men. Failing to abide by his curriculum was a death sentence.

The entire process sickened Bobby. It was disgusting how someone already so powerful felt the need to take advantage of so many helpless women. His men brainwashed, raped, and allowed them to live in cages disguised as houses. Bobby was certain something went wrong during LaVonte's childhood for him to continue this, especially as a married man.

Being on good terms with someone as fucked up as LaVonte made Bobby feel shitty about himself from time to time. As much as he wished he was bold enough to stand up for himself and the diswors he slaved away with day in and day out, he knew he didn't have the balls. Bobby was aware whose rule he was under, and that wasn't going to change unless fate had anything to say about it.

"Smoke?" LaVonte finally asked after he finished studying a graph.

"No, sir. No, thank you. I still have work to do," Bobby answered. He didn't like reeking of cigars but often engaged to be polite.

"Nah, you have the rest of the day off, BK. Light one with me."

Bobby shrugged and thanked his brother-in-law for the cigar he rolled across his desk.

LaVonte then told his phone to dial one of his men. When someone picked up on the other end LaVonte asked him to go get Kalin.

"Fine as hell, Bobby. She'll be here any minute."

Bobby feigned a smile through a cloud of smoke.

"Ariana is coming back today."

"Okay. Where did she go?" Bobby asked.

"She's been in Morple."

Bobby stayed as stoic as possible. From their private conversations over the years, he knew how much Ariana wanted to be part of Robin's life again, but neither of them viewed it as a real possibility. It sometimes made Bobby laugh how Ariana and he wanted the same thing yet she dragged him here.

LaVonte puffed his cigar and stared at Bobby. "Come on, BK. I know you're curious."

"Curious about what?"

"Don't play dumb with me, infick."

Bobby's demeanor didn't falter, but LaVonte calling him that was infuriating. He knew LaVonte hated Whites and looked down on Hispanics, but he had never addressed Bobby like that before. At least not in front of him.

"She had been seeing Robin. And your boys, too. To be honest, I started to second guess her loyalty. She seemed to be getting sidetracked trying to be part of the family."

It took everything he had not to get up and punch LaVonte's nose in. He knew it wouldn't end well, but that didn't mean the urge wasn't there. One thing he couldn't suppress was his curiosity.

"How—how are they?" Bobby asked.

"From everything I've seen, they're doing good."

Saying he had "seen" them frightened Bobby.

"Your girl still looks good. Rich and fine as ever, shit. She would've been a helluva addition here."

Bobby's fists clenched and breathing became heavier.

"Relax, BK. I wouldn't do such a thing. You've been one of the best people I've ever brought in. Maybe the best. That's why you get rewarded."

LaVonte gestured for Bobby to turn around. A blonde woman with shoulder length hair strutted in his office wearing only white lingerie. She purposely exaggerated her hips swing, which was unnecessary because she was already curvy, but it was probably something LaVonte was conditioning her to do. The top she had on squeezed her breasts together and up towards her chin. She wasn't his type, but Bobby couldn't deny her blue eyes and everything else about her was gorgeous. Her facial expression was serious, which indicated she wasn't completely brainwashed by LaVonte. Yet.

Kalin stopped next to LaVonte but faced the opposite way so her ass was across from Bobby. LaVonte gave it a good smack. Besides what jiggled, she didn't budge.

"Nice, yeah? Kalin is a new addition to the crew. One of the few White girls we have on the plantation, but is fitting in quite nicely, as you can see, BK. Right, Kalin?"

"I am LaVonte," Kalin said. She was enthusiastic enough.

"All of this is yours if you want her. You want all of this, right?" LaVonte asked Bobby.

Bobby didn't want any of LaVonte's women, he just *needed* the ones who resembled Robin to stay sane. He could acknowledge Kalin was a desirable woman, but he felt no physical attraction to her. If he didn't accept LaVonte's direct offer, the Organization's head would feel insulted. Bobby not taking advantage of all the women he had at his disposal already didn't sit well with LaVonte. Bobby had to take Kalin, as she was the first one LaVonte personally offered.

"Of course," Bobby said. He sold his own interest by checking her out from head to toe and asking her to give him a twirl.

"Good. She's all yours then. It is good for you to mix it up every once in a while, you know? That's why I keep so many women around, BK. I want my best to have the best."

"For that I thank you," Bobby said. He was trying to make it a bro-type bonding moment between him and his brother-by-marriage.

"You're welcome. You deserve it. Go on off now. Have some fun with this one and let me know how it is. Besides myself, I've kept her untouched for you."

He shoved Kalin towards Bobby and nodded his head for the both of them to leave.

"Appreciate it, boss," Bobby said.

LaVonte didn't acknowledge them as they left, and he immediately resumed studying the graphs he had been before their meeting.

LaVonte didn't feel remorse often, but he did feel guilty for all the hardships he put Bobby through. Since his latest plan would continue to make his life a living hell, LaVonte was doing everything in his power to make things right with his lone brother-in-law.

CHAPTER

2089

Ariana got Reginald's address from Heather and plugged it into her car. Heather was handling the situation better than Ariana expected and was quite receptive towards the additional task Ariana recently implemented. What formed their newly found alliance was they both knew what it felt like to possess resentment towards an identical evil. Even though Heather already got her revenge, she fully supported Ariana's pursuit in obtaining hers, disregarding its effect on her family. The single time she expressed hesitation was the moment Ariana told her she couldn't promise she'd see Dillon again.

"I've come too far to go back now," Heather said.

Reginald considered Heather incredibly attractive and adored her for playing the role of his billionaire son's easy-on-the-eyes wife. To a certain extent she represented what Reginald wanted Robin to be: a jaw-dropping younger wife who catered to her husband's needs, dependent on him for her livelihood, and raised his son. Over the years, Heather accepted his praise even though she hated where it came from. His occasional suggestive behavior only made matters worse. On multiple occasions he made a pass on her. Grazing his hand over her ass in the kitchen. Gawking at her chest. Flirting with her when Richard wasn't nearby. When Heather told Richard his father made her uncomfortable at times her husband brushed it off, attributing it to him coming from an era when that type of behavior was acceptable. Richard appeared more flabbergasted by his wife's discomfort than his father's actions. This made pretending to love Richard more difficult than it already was. But she did, and she did it well.

"You're confident he'll go for this?" Ariana asked as they turned onto Reginald's street.

"Absolutely. He's been trying to come onto his daughter-in-law for years. He won't turn me down."

"Good. We'll make this fast."

The two rode in silence the rest of the way. Ariana grabbed Heather's hand and squeezed it tight until they were a few houses away from Reginald's.

Reginald's cameras' facial recognition capabilities focused on Heather when she rolled down the window of Ariana's car. She smiled and waved while Ariana ducked in the backseat.

As Heather and, unbeknownst to Reginald, Ariana rolled up his driveway, Reginald came out with Wilford at his side. He hadn't seen his daughter-in-law since the night they went to the emergency room, and a sense of relief came over him as he observed she seemed to have moved past the family skirmish.

Reginald's awareness was still keen at his age, but Heather's presence lowered his guard. He didn't care to ask where she got the car that drove her over. Partly because if your husband had billions, buying a new car out of the blue wasn't the most peculiar thing in the world.

"Hello beautiful," he said.

"Hi handsome man!"

She jumped out of the car and hurried over to give him a big hug.

"Awe, it is so good to see you. It's been too long, Mr. Lawrence."

"I want to apologize for everything that happened that night. I just feel so awful about what I said. I wish I could take it back. I wish none of it happened," he said.

"Please. Family forgives. Everyone is fine now, so please, don't worry about it."

They walked arm in arm into his mansion.

Once they were in Heather excused herself to use the bathroom. She requested Reginald pour them some morning cocktails while he waited. This excited him and bought her time. Heather's first responsibility was to disarm the home's security system. Ariana made it clear she'd only have five minutes to do this.

Heather went to the bathroom to check in with herself before their plan took shape. The calm external composure she saw in the mirror didn't reflect her discombobulated emotions. On one hand, helping Ariana get her revenge was empowering, as it permitted her to stop masking her real feelings, too. On the other hand, she wasn't sure if she was handling it the right way. Hurting a family member would not be something she'd be proud of, but this man was pure evil. Heather reminded herself what Ariana told her he did to Robin and her as kids. Taking advantage of children was an unforgivable offense, even if it was her father-in-law who committed it. She lightly slapped herself and refocused on the task at hand. Ariana assured Heather she'd be there to interrupt any of his advances if they exceeded what they had in the past. Heather was the decoy. There wasn't anything else for her to do besides play a part, what her life was up to this point. It wouldn't be difficult. She splashed water on her face, washed her hands, and braced herself.

Heather lathered her index finger with a sanitizer provided by Ariana that would prevent her leaving a fingerprint behind on the security system's monitor. After punching in her father-in-law's birthday, the system was disabled.

Heather planted a smile on her face and headed off to the kitchen to join Reginald, where she found him holding a big glass of wodin, and a steak knife in Ariana's hand. The tip of it was close to puncturing his neck. The old man had a scornful facial expression, but the wodin wobbling in his glass indicated his fear.

"Sorry, hon. I got too impatient. I've been waiting for this moment for far too long," Ariana said.

Heather surmised the knife was the first lethal weapon Ariana could get her hands on. She was too flabbergasted to remind Ariana Reginald's cameras most likely caught her entering the house.

"Ariana. Fuck, how long has it been? Nearly twenty years, right? You look better now than you did the last time I saw you with your husband," Reginald said.

Despite his age Reginald was the same pervert Ariana remembered him to be, and she didn't doubt he'd have her the same way now as he did when she was a girl if she let him. But that wasn't what was going to happen today. Standing in front of him, Ariana felt sick to her stomach as Reginald shamelessly took his sweet time eyeing her down top to bottom. When his gaze hit her breasts, he exhaled a smutty grunting sound as if he was about to get off to the sight of them. Reginald was so enthralled he smiled, as if a knife wasn't about to chop his head off the rest of his body.

Wilford was sniffing Ariana's leg when she kicked his ribs. He went down whimpering and cowered out of the room.

"Don't you dare touch him, you cunt!"

"Cunt. Huh, nicer than most things you've called me," Ariana said. She pressed the knife closer to his throat, beginning to draw blood.

"I knew you'd end up being fuckin' worthless. You didn't amount to shit when you left me. Just riding the coattails of that nigger. At least your sister proved she can provide for herself, but not you, you were always too pathetic to even try," he said.

Ariana's chest heaved up and down. Heather thought she was on the verge of losing control of her temper for the second time that morning.

"You fuckin' bastard. You raped and tortured me as a little girl, and you are here still acting like you were trying to do good by me. You sick fuck. You ruined my goddamn life!"

The more Ariana yelled the harder she squeezed the knife. Reginald had never known what it felt like for someone else to be in control of his fate. For the first time in his life, he was getting the shit end of the stick.

"Don't look at me like that, you pathetic bastard. Do you want to tell Heather how you used to bend me over at ten years-old and fuck me in the ass? Do you want to tell her how you did it to me when I was eight? What about the time you let your men pass me around on my thirteenth birthday? I must've fucked, oh, six of them. You let six grown men gangbang a thirteen-year-old girl. Oh no, what about all the times you brought me in your office and made me get on my knees for you? You loved blowing your load into a little girl's mouth, didn't you? Go ahead, tell her about yourself, Mr. R."

Heather clasped her hands over her mouth and started crying.

"You deserved it. I helped you almost make something of yourself, but you refused to acknowledge that."

"By raping me? Is that what would make my life worth something? If I was constantly raped as a little girl?"

Ariana wasn't trying to hold back her tears anymore. Emotions from her traumatic childhood poured out of her. Her yells were deafening. Heather feared the whole neighborhood would hear.

"Heather, sweetheart. Please, don't believe this infick cunt. She doesn't know what she's talking about."

She glared at him without saying a word.

"Heather, dammit. You answer me!"

"This is who your father-in-law is, hon. He's a pedophile. He loves raping little girls."

"No, No, Heather. No, that's not true. I respect people who deserve to be respected. You know this. This cunt didn't deserve to be. Just look at her, Heather. I could've given her everything, but this is what she chooses t—"

Reginald stopped blabbering when he observed who his daughter-in-law's loyalty lay with.

"You're such a fuckin' asshole, Reginald," Heather said.

Until Heather broke her silence, Ariana worried she wasn't going to stick it out. Relief came over her once Heather muttered those words.

Reginald was incredulous. "Excuse me? After all my son and I have done for you, you're going to side with her?"

He threw down his drink, sending glass everywhere.

"You fuckin' women are all the same. Worthless, fuckin' worthless!" He turned his head back and forth between Ariana and his son's wife. "Don't think for a second you would be anything without me and my son."

He directed himself to Ariana. "Fuck, and you. Don't think you are something now. You think you've accomplished something in your world. I fuckin' invented your world. You're no better than me. Just remember my cock up your ass each time you almost convince yourself LaVonte values you you pa—"

Ariana cocked the knife back before stabbing Reginald between his left eye and eyebrow. He shielded his wound with both hands and howled in pain. His legs gave out and he hit the floor hard. His body shook uncontrollably like a fish out of water. Blood seeped through his fingers and ran down his arms.

Heather couldn't bear the site of her father-in-law bleeding out from his eye socket, but Ariana grinned as she looked down on her long-time torturer finally getting a taste of what he deserved. The excruciating pain he was in satisfied Ariana more than she imagined it would. Just because he was now an older man didn't mean she planned to take it easy on him. If anything, his age made the moment more rewarding because he was unable to defend himself.

Just like Robin and her were unable to defend themselves as little girls.

His yells eventually turned to cries, and he rolled his body side to side like he was on fire, which he probably felt like he was.

Ariana stepped towards him and wiped the bloody knife on his robe. "What did you expect Mr. R? You knew I was the one who liked to fight back. Did you think I would let you live in peace until your dying day? You sick son of a bitch. You should consider yourself lucky. Oh, fuck it."

Ariana drilled the knife in his gut and moved it around like she was trying to fit a key into a lock in the dark, compounding his misery. Reginald instinctively tried to grab the knife's handle to pull it out of him, but he didn't have the wherewithal to come close. The blood from his initial wound blinded him in one eye, and his torso was red and gutted from Ariana carving him. His yells were now suppressed by the vomit trying to erupt from his throat. Displaying serenity, Ariana towered over Reginald and watched his facial expression accept death was near. Ending it early for Heather's sake crossed Ariana's mind, but her longing to witness him suffer overrode any compassion she felt for her new partner-in-crime. Blood continued to spew out of his face and torso and vomit came from his throat. After a few more audible gargles, Reginald Lawrence took his last breath. Blood filled his left eye, but his right eye remained open, staring up at his former victim.

Ariana fixated on Reginald's lone open eye. A day didn't go by when she didn't reflect on all the agony this man was responsible for causing her. He went out of his way to ruin her life and try to ruin Robin's for no other reason than being sick in the head and power hungry. Storming in their room in the middle of the night to force himself in Ariana was a regular occurrence a little girl could never become accustomed to, even if she knew the chances of it happening were more likely than not. Ariana got into bed shaking with fear every night for her entire childhood and adolescence because of this man. Even as a free woman living in another state, she was perpetually looking over her shoulder worried it was only a matter of time until Reginald tracked her down to pick up where he left off. Marrying LaVonte should have been enough to eliminate this angst from hindering Ariana to live happily, but all it did was position her back in Reginald's crosshairs. His partnership with her husband made her marriage one of the most regrettable decision of her life. If LaVonte truly loved and cared about her, he would have never allowed Reginald to continue hurting her. All Ariana accomplished marrying LaVonte was finding a new man to dictate her every move. Now that one was gone, it was time the other paid for his actions, too.

Ariana shifted her focus back to the present moment. She blinked her eyes to snap out of it and found Heather shivering against a wall with her forearms covering her face. Ariana tossed her knife aside to make it known she was no longer armed. She stepped towards Heather carefully to avoid alarming her.

"Heather, it's okay. It's over. He's gone."

It was hard to sound so reassuring shortly after brutally murdering someone. Especially when that someone was the father-in-law of the person in need of being consoled.

Heather managed to briefly look at Reginald's bloodied body on his kitchen floor. She shuddered at the sight of it.

"We need to go," Ariana said. She went back to being all business and guided Heather out of the house, but not before retrieving the knife.

Ariana finally executed a personal vendetta she fantasized about for most of her life. Now, it was time to reunite the Karros family.

CHAPTER

2089

Ariana ordered a foot grower to pick Heather and her up at the dock the late Reginald Lawrence made available to LaVonte all those years ago. It was ideal because one, a warehouse blocked any visibility passerbys might have to the Organization's foot growers trafficking people and drugs, and two, more importantly, authorities knew the terms of the agreement and to leave it alone.

As Heather's car pulled them into the empty warehouse's garage, Ariana asked, "Okay, you're good with everything?"

"Yeah."

"Okay. You're ready to do this?"

"As ready as I'll be. Let's go before I change my mind."

"You're too far in to change your mind, sweetheart."

Ariana exited the car and dragged Heather out. She was nearly certain Marvin was unable to see them, but she couldn't afford to risk being seen treating Heather like anything else but a captive. To ensure she sold it, Ariana shoved Heather in the direction of the dock. Ariana warned Heather how she would treat her, but it still caught the latter off guard.

As Heather was regaining her balance Ariana grabbed her getaway bag from the car, which contents now included a bloodied outfit and murder weapon stolen from the victim's kitchen.

After situating Heather in the car before leaving Reginald's house, Ariana ran back inside to change into clean clothes and get her tormentor's blood off her. She contemplated rinsing off in his shower, but she knew Heather and she didn't have that type of time. Plus, that seemed a little *too* serial killer-esque for Ariana's liking. She determined using his towels sufficed.

Both women rode the lift down Morple's one hundred fifty-foot-cliff in silence, partly because they were disguising themselves in their roles, and partly because they were each thinking about how many unfortunate souls had traveled down this exact lift on their way to live their remaining days in suffering.

If it wasn't for his round stomach inflating up and down, Marvin would've appeared dead laying on the deck of the boat they were set to ride back to California in. He fell asleep with his hands folded over his gut and a bucket hat resting on his face.

"Reassuring to see how alert you are," Ariana said.

Marvin jolted up abruptly and pretended he was paying attention the whole time. "Hey, whas up girl. You took a minute. I had to catch some zs."

Since joining the Organization in 2080, Marvin was one of Ariana's favorite foot growers. He was a short Black man in his early thirties. He had the legs of a track star, highlighted by out-of-this-world calves, but his torso was abnormally round. Fellow foot growers teased him by asking how far along he was in his pregnancy. He rocked a nappy, spotty beard and wore a bucket hat that hid his prematurely bald head. A scar split his forehead in two equal pieces and ran down to the top of his nose. When a group of POWs rioted in the middle of the night, Marvin found himself in the middle of a knife match between a POW and Homer. If the POW didn't stop because he realized he was slicing a guard's face open rather than a dirty infick, Marvin could have easily died. After getting stitched up in the plantation's medical facility, Marvin hung the guilty POW by his feet and beat his entire body and face with a hammer until he took his last breath. To guarantee his corpse wouldn't untie itself and fight back, Marvin stabbed his still heart. He left him hanging near the field the POWs worked on until Marvin's colleagues could no longer stand the smell. The Organization valued his barbaric methods because they instilled order on the plantation.

Being in the presence of him made Heather's job of appearing frightened easy. Marvin's scar and how he checked her out gave her the chills, and she felt she was on the verge of pissing herself. Heather put an undeserving amount of trust in Ariana to eventually save her from living the rest of her life as a sex toy for LaVonte Jackson and his men.

"Damn, I like this one. I can't wait until she hits the open market," Marvin said.

"Don't bank on that happening too soon," Ariana said, hoping Heather would find that reassuring.

"Get in," she said to Heather, tossing her in the boat like she was a piece of equipment. "Make it quick, Marvin. We're on a time crunch."

"Yes ma'am. Damn you're fine!" he said to Heather. "I could definitely do things quick with you girl."

Hearing the misogyny embedded in her husband's Organization intensified the guilt she felt towards who she chose to live with the last seventeen years of her life.

"Don't even think about it, Marvin. You wait your fuckin' turn like everyone else. Right now, you get us back home safely. I've been through enough already. I don't want to have to shove your dick back in your pants."

"Damn girl! I'm just trying to have a little fun. It isn't like you and your man don't get your way with the ass back home."

Ashamed for Heather being privy to Ariana's role in it all, she slapped Marvin across the face. "Keep your fuckin' mouth shut and get us back."

Marvin's smile vanished as he stared coldly into her eyes.

"Careful, girl," he said.

"Careful who you're talking to."

Marvin untied the boat and programmed it for California before stooping down to the lower deck.

"Where did he just go?" Heather asked barely above a whisper.

"There's a room down below. Don't worry about him. He isn't high enough on the food chain to act that way. He just thinks he's hot shit because no other men are between him and a piece of ass. He usually gets the scraps," Ariana said. It sounded more reassuring in her head than aloud.

Talking that way astonished both Ariana and Heather. Mrs. Jackson's role in this operation had gone on for way too long.

Phil woke up out of his slumber in a poolside lounge chair, right where Richard left him. His mouth was as dry as the Sahara Desert, and his headache was so painful each time it throbbed he felt like someone was bouncing a bowling ball on top of it. He prayed a glass of water was on the table next to him but was heartbroken to only find an empty glass he slugged wodin out of the night before. He was so parched he briefly considered filling it up with pool water.

Phil rolled off the lounge chair, almost losing his balance in the process. He zig-zagged his way inside, holding onto his head. Collapsing and attempting to sleep it off was easier than forcing himself up, but water and his instant pain relief medicine he kept plenty of were in the kitchen. He was a wrecking ball, crashing into the corner of counters and sliding open all the drawers in hopes of finding his pain medicine. He was too disoriented to recall which drawer he kept it in. He finally found it and tossed back three, triple the amount he needed.

The bowling ball stopped coming down on his head within five seconds, but the emotions from the night before that made him feel miserable were still very much there. He filled up a glass of water again and downed it a consecutive time. After releasing a wodin-flavored belch, Phil turned around and saw three masked men standing in his kitchen. They had on fitted black pants and white, long sleeve shirts that hugged their entire upper body. Phil didn't know guns too well, but he could deduce the ones strapped across their chests classified as the big and scary kind.

"Who the fuck are you, and how the fuck did you get in my house?" He sounded tougher than he felt.

The three men said nothing in response.

Phil nervously took another sip.

"Well, what the fuck? Who are you people? How the fuck did you get in?" Just as Phil asked the last question, he remembered he disabled his security system before his lady friend came over to avoid the hassle of her passing all his clearances. After Richard left, he intended to turn it on, but the wodin got the best of him.

Realizing this wasn't going to be a fight, the man in the middle opted for his silenced pistol on his right hip and shot Phil in the heart. His dead body fell forward, head slamming on the counter in front of him before his entire corpse hit the ground.

Dillon pulled his mask off and strutted over to Phil's dead body.

"Good shot, little soldier," one of his new compatriots said.

"Time to bounce," the other said.

When Dillon turned around to face them, they both nodded in approval.

"Let's go finish this shit," the second one said.

A real sense of belonging came over Dillon for the first time in his life. Surrounding himself with like-minded people who genuinely gave a shit about him was an empowering feeling, one he could see himself getting used to.

CHAPTER

2089

The government was able to keep closer tabs on citizens after 2045 because of A.I.'s advancements, making it less likely for an aspiring mass murderer to execute his aspirations. People were also less inclined to attend large gatherings because of the fear-based sentiment towards new viruses. There were still opportunities to murder by the masses, but the deeply troubled had to get creative with how they unleashed their anger on undeserving, innocent people. Perpetrators became savvy hackers. Because so many people congregated on Internet platforms, they became easy targets.

In the early years of the sonoravirus pandemic, Daniel Wilmington's parents had a one-night stand that resulted in him being born nine months later. He was often reminded of the circumstances he was conceived under. His parents were working-class folks in Southern Oregon, a demographic hit hard by what the government shut down due to the pandemic. Making ends meet for themselves was a struggle, let alone providing for their unwanted responsibility. They occasionally performed odd jobs, depending on the willingness of others to expose themselves to unfamiliar workers, and were uncertain if they would be lucky enough to eat three meals each day. They could've moved in together to cut costs and improve their untraditional family's quality of life, but both his mother and father resented one another for producing their son. Daniel symbolized their shared hardship.

Throughout his childhood Daniel was emotionally and physically abused by his father Tom, his father's girlfriend Amber, and his mother Becca. His earliest memories of his mother were her bitchin' about how he ruined her youth and happiness. Becca claimed she would have gotten much further in life if she still had her prepartum body. Men would've still considered her desirable without the extra baggage that was her son. Maybe some big-time tech executive would've scooped her up and the pandemic wouldn't have depleted her bank account if it hadn't been for Daniel.

Fuckin' Daniel.

His father incessantly harped on how expensive he was to keep alive. Amber frequently complained he interfered with her role in Tom's life. They ridiculed him for costing his father so much of his hard-earned money and being useless during the hardest of times. As a child he wasn't big and strong enough to help his father with the odd, manual jobs he managed to pick up in order to scrape by. He needed them because what the government was issuing was not sufficient enough to support his girlfriend and son. The least Daniel could have done was go out and beg for some extra money, but he was too scared to try that again after getting beat up for a few bucks by a diswor-turned-beggar.

Fuckin' Daniel.

The worst year of his life was as a fifth grader, when he started to grasp how his parents' aversion to him was abnormal. This is also when they ramped up the physical and verbal abuse. A decade into his life, nearing the end of the pandemic, they expected his existence to alas prove it was worth something, but Daniel failed them when he didn't live up to their unrealistic expectations. That year stood out to him as the most tumultuous. In hindsight it was the turning point that unfolded the monster he grew up to be. His demons didn't want other fifth graders to experience happy childhoods if he never had that chance.

Daniel didn't realize he possessed the gift of a high IQ until he ran away from home at sixteen. Instinctively fighting for survival, he applied himself to learn the ins and outs of technology. He caught on quick, and a few agricultural software companies took a chance on him by hiring him for contract work. His work ethic proved tenacious, and Daniel regularly produced innovative solutions and increased their productivity. Despite accumulating accomplishments, he never received a satisfactory amount of acknowledgment from his employers. After facing constant criticism from his parents for being a worthless burden, Daniel sought affirmation he was finally making something of himself, contributing to society rather than being an expense weighing others down. But the tech world didn't fill this void. These companies reaped the benefits of his services without dishing out the appreciation Daniel felt he deserved. He worked tirelessly to earn the approval of others, but he couldn't make a notable enough impact to receive the recognition he longed for.

Utilizing his knack for software engineering, Daniel devised a discreet method of hacking virtual schools in 2052, kicking off an epidemic that threatened the lives of innocent children for decades to follow.

Daniel's first act was substituting a section of a fifth-grade boy's history book with what he called his, "Scripture" detailing how the rise of smartphones in the early 2000s was the first sign the government wanted to exterminate most of its people. In it he described how pointless their lives were, how their parents considered them nothing more than burdens to their own success, and that the afterlife was a more productive way to spend their time:

> *Unfortunately, your existence in this world, an artificial one, is not only pointless but also a mistake. A once great country now only wants a select amount of its citizens to succeed. If you are reading this, you are not one of those citizens. Your parents, along with the rest of the country, will be better off once you take your life. Nothing you do will amount to anything. You still being alive makes the world a worse place. The best thing you can do for everybody else is take your life. It is essential you know this sooner rather than later because waiting any longer to take your life will only make the process more difficult. Doing it now will help those you will leave behind and also allow you to live the best life after death you possibly can. What waits for you on the other side is happiness, self-worth, and appreciation. Do what is best for you and for your parents. Kill your pointless existence and join those with real purpose.*

Daniel's other excerpts contained gruesome stories from his own childhood with the intention of scaring them into following his "sermons". He even suggested ways to commit suicide. Out of the twelve students he targeted for suicide with his "Scripture", eleven killed themselves. The twelfth failed because her mother walked in just before she hung herself from the top of the staircase in her family's home.

Before finally being caught in his studio apartment in Granger, Washington, Daniel infiltrated dozens of classes across the country with his disturbing writings. Because he sought out children who were at impressionable ages, Daniel was able to manipulate them into very dark acts. If he wasn't brainwashing them to kill themselves, he was instructing them to strangle their pets, stab their siblings, inflict pain on themselves, and sexually harass their classmates. His version of justice for how his parents treated him was by ensuring others suffered from the same thoughts he did. He found it fulfilling, as the children who carried out the acts affirmed his work was making an impact. Daniel finally discovered his purpose.

Daniel's method of terror became more common amongst other disturbed young White males the more the media publicized it. Murdering the masses by this advanced form of cyberbullying became known as "The Wilmington Way", resulting in the suicide rates among children and adolescents in America to skyrocket to tragic levels. The statistical trends in the United States mirrored mass shootings before the pandemics, significantly higher than what other developed countries were dealing with.

Despite secretly looking up to Daniel, Dillon recognized he didn't possess enough intellect to hack educational curriculums to get his point across. He had a difficult time admitting it to the friends he made in the dark corners of the Internet, but he knew he didn't have the balls to inflict that severe of harm on innocent children because of his own problems. That's why Dillon elected on doing things the old-fashioned way.

At the core of his resentment, Dillon felt isolated. No one in his family truly cared about his well-being. Dillon didn't long for companionship with someone closer to his age. He had Moe for that. Dillon's void lay within his parents not caring enough to go out of their way to check in with him. Children and adolescents require a strong foundation in order to progress in life. That starts with a healthy at-home life. Something Dillon could never claim, despite all his family's fortune.

His mother's love for his father never appeared authentic to him. She lacked conviction, and at times he despised her for it. Heather not loving Richard wasn't what ate away at him inside; it was pretending to love him so she could maintain her lifestyle that bothered him so much. How someone, let alone his own mother, could inject that much energy towards faking love for someone baffled Dillon. She could have redirected it towards something worthwhile, like raising Dillon to be a happy kid. Aside from her new friend Ariana, all of her fake friends looked like what Heather was: a fraud. She disgusted him.

Then there was his father. Fuckin' Richard. The audacity his father had to unleash that level of rage and then address Dillon on his thoughts about their "family" was a joke. A few confrontational conversations did not undo the past. It did not make his upbringing acceptable or forgivable. It actually made it worse. It made it worse because Richard was apparently capable of being a decent parent the entire time, but he elected to be a deadbeat. He was reactive instead of proactive. A horrible trait. Dillon promised himself he would handle his father once and for all.

Life dealt Dillon a shitty hand. It was something he couldn't control or change. All he had power over was what he could do about it. The first step was finding a sense of belonging, affiliating himself with a group working towards a cause it believed in, part of something in which people worked together towards a common goal. There wasn't any camaraderie in his household, so he had to seek it out himself.

During his time away from school after the domestic violence incident, Dillon ramped up his preparation and research to become involved with a group that fit his bill. As long as it punished others, he wasn't too picky. The need to associate with people capable of working together trumped everything else.

The more he learned about foot growers the more he consumed himself with the idea of becoming one. Their shared purpose brought them together, enabling them to operate as a team. Most grew up in devastating situations and were victims of the system, which is what drove them to their success. Outsiders didn't predict they would make anything out of their lives, but they fought hard to defy those odds.

Dillon's biggest hurdle would be convincing them he belonged despite not sharing their roots. Traditionally, foot growers' families were victims to A.I. replacing them at work. Minorities who had never tasted prosperity. It was an uphill battle for the son of a billionaire to prove he was as angry and motivated as the rest were.

Persuading the Organization's foot growers in Morple to take him seriously was the hardest part. He had to demonstrate his commitment to their cause and would go to extreme lengths to be part of their crew. Dillon knew they didn't let just anyone in. Their people must denote loyalty, ruthlessness, and intelligence. Dillon sold them on his commitment and intelligence by telling them his story and who his family was and convinced them in due time he would demonstrate his ruthlessness once they were out in the field. For some reason the Organization's foot growers in Morple developed a fondness for the uber-wealthy eighteen-year-old. No one from his stature had ever approached them before. This in itself was a key indicator he could eventually evolve into a key contributor.

Dillon quickly acclimated to their operation. The veterans trained him on how to use firearms and how to abide by their protocols, created and enforced by his best friend's uncle.

Dillon's dedication to his newfound craft was evident straight out of the gate. He was fitting in nicely and valued the respect all the foot growers possessed for each other. His attitude not only reflected he knew he was going to have to earn his way up the rankings, but embraced it.

Dillon was impressing them, but no one could be certain as to how he would perform until it was showtime. Including him.

CHAPTER

2089

L aVonte was hologramming with a few politicians on his payroll
while he waited for his wife to arrive with Heather Lawrence. His
employees were lecturing him on how his business practices were
becoming careless and putting him on track to crash and burn sooner
rather than later. Subtleness was still a desirable trait in his line of work,
and LaVonte's puppets told him he was too connected with prominent
figures like themselves to have a problem like the one he currently had
in South America. If his predicament became exposed, it would be a PR
nightmare for him and could ultimately end the Organization's reign.

LaVonte smirked knowing if what they said was true the nightmare
would be theirs to share, and their reputation would take a much bigger hit
than his ever would. That was the beauty of his industry, people expected
him to lack morals. Politicians fucked up by disguising their true selves
to the masses.

LaVonte's relationships were an integral part of what allowed him to
accomplish what he had, and they would continue to elevate his business
to heights no kingpin had ever had before. Kingpins from the past, going
back to the days of Colombia's Pablo Escobar, had always fallen. None
adopted sustainable business models. The reason for that, according to
LaVonte, was because they didn't keep everyone in their networks happy

for long enough. If they were going to upset someone, at least order that person murdered to avoid complications that could disrupt the business further down the road. Just like any other industry, trafficking was all about relationships.

LaVonte pretended to comply with his government employees' requests. He could play a diplomatic businessman as well as he could play a ruthless kingpin. He concluded the call by informing them he had plenty of new girls to entertain them next time they visited, highlighting a special arrival who was due momentarily. LaVonte found this usually stopped their bitchin' and resulted in a soon thereafter visit to the Organization's plantation.

When he hung up one of his personal bodyguards entered his office and reported Ariana was back. The anticipation aroused him.

LaVonte instructed the guard to bring her to him as soon as possible. He wanted to appear calm, but on the inside, he was as excited as a little kid on Christmas morning.

Heather stumbled in with her hands cuffed behind her back. Ariana held them tightly in place before shoving her on the couch to go greet her husband. Ariana tossed her getaway bag on the floor before jumping in his arms. They exchanged a wet, tongue-laced kiss he had been craving since she departed. As if there wasn't a prisoner sitting on his office couch, LaVonte sat Ariana on his desk and buried his face in her neck, playfully biting and licking her in the process. His wife caressed his face and head and moaned softly, whispering indecipherable things in his ear that caused him to press into her harder.

Ariana grabbed LaVonte's ears and pushed him away from her and said, "I brought you something baby." She nodded towards the couch Heather sat on.

LaVonte released his hold on Ariana and crept over towards Heather, who maintained her downwards gaze, too frightened to look her staged-captor's husband in the eye. Even with Ariana on her side, at least she hoped, she could only remember being this frightened of someone one other time in her life. LaVonte's big frame towered over her, and she felt his cold eyes penetrate her soul. His demeanor was overpowering, and she began to lose confidence as to how Ariana and she would get out of this alive. Heather's trepidations led her to believe Ariana never intended to save her; maybe Ariana's breakdown earlier that day was part of the plan. The more she considered this possibility, the more she believed it to be true. Before LaVonte said a word, she was already picturing how miserable the remainder of her existence would be as a sex slave for a former business partner of her husband's. A husband she never even loved.

LaVonte's first words to Heather instructed her to stand up. Trembling, Heather obliged. Because of the cuffs, she had to roll over on her stomach and power up her legs to stand. Heather felt her face redden, embarrassed by how limiting the cuffs were. She hunched her shoulders and hung her neck over her chest to avoid looking LaVonte in the eyes. Based on Ariana's observations, she wasn't acting. Her apprehension was too authentic. Ariana fought the urge to confirm the knife leaned against her ankle was still concealed after LaVonte was frisky with her. Her husband was so enamored with Heather's feminine assets he probably wouldn't notice if she did, but she couldn't risk the fatal mistake of getting caught. At least not this early. She was already fortunate the knife didn't reveal itself after he set her on his desk.

"Mr. Lawrence must have some fuckin' style reeling you in," LaVonte said. He abruptly rubbed both her breasts simultaneously and squeezed them together before gripping both ass cheeks, spreading them apart, all with a sick smile on his face.

After he was through violating her, LaVonte took a step back and said, "Look up at me and relax."

Warily, Heather lifted her head and met his possessed gaze. She did not try to hide how alarmed she was by the sight of LaVonte, which he relished in.

"What's wrong? No wealthy niggas where you're from, huh?" LaVonte chuckled and lightly stroked her face. He turned to his wife and said, "My, my. She must be amazing, baby. I can't wait to get in that ass. Richard kept that shit tight as hell."

Somehow Heather managed to hold back tears but hearing him openly discuss raping her was numbing. She experienced that torture as a child and never planned on putting herself in that dire of a situation again, yet that is exactly what she did today. Each minute that passed Heather was losing confidence in Ariana remaining on her side partly because she could not fully trust her, and partly because Heather didn't think she had it in her to stand up to a man of LaVonte's stature and physical ability. But it was too late to back out now. Supporting Ariana to stop her husband's reign of terror and reunite the Karros family were two tasks that could be what ultimately killed her.

"Have you seen what all this is about yet, baby?" LaVonte asked.

His wife shook her head, feigning an enlivened facial expression. The thought of Ariana regularly engaging in this type of behavior with helpless women and her husband sent a shiver down Heather's spine.

"Man, your husband is a piece of work. All he had to do was honor our agreement, and he still would've been coming home to hit this every night. Why would anyone pass on that, huh?"

With his full strength on display, LaVonte ripped off her shirt and yelled for one of his guards to come unlock her cuffs. As if this day couldn't get any worse for Heather, she thought to herself *was it so much to ask the guard to take them off before ripping off my shirt*? But fortunately, he was well trained and didn't dare take a peek. The thought didn't even cross his mind.

"Relax, Mrs. Lawrence. There isn't anything to be scared of now. You're in good hands. We'll take good care of you here. I promise."

After unclasping her bra, LaVonte ran his hands all over her upper body, feeling every square inch of her bareness, pinching her nipples. He stood close enough to Heather for her to feel his erection rising towards her stomach, sending goosebumps throughout her entire body.

"Are you familiar with your husband's line of work, Heather?" LaVonte asked.

Exposed and petrified, Heather shook her head. Even if she wanted to say something, she was far too frightened to mutter so much as a single word.

"No, you don't know? Big-shot Richard Lawrence doesn't tell his wife about what he does?"

Heather's first mistake was assuming LaVonte asked rhetorical questions. After failing to acknowledge it, LaVonte lifted her chin up with a single finger and slapped her across the face. The sting lit her face on fire, but she began crying more out of fear than anything else.

"I asked you a question. Does big-shot Richard Lawrence not tell you about what he does at work?"

"No, uh, no, he—he doesn't."

"Oh, that's unfortunate. I always wanted to be friends with him. You know, come visit Morple and go out with him and our wives. We always knew he snatched up a fine wife, and we wanted to see for ourselves. You are a valuable asset he must not appreciate if he let you go this easily. But here you will be appreciated. My organization appreciates a fine woman like yourself Mrs. Lawrence. So much that we let them live with us here and take care of them. Really, you're in better hands with us now. As long as you cooperate, you'll see life here is actually really good. Beautiful women like yourself can get really far in a place like this."

The entire time he was addressing her, LaVonte's right hand rested on Heather's cheek, and his thumb softly rubbed the space under her right eye, wiping away the tears streaming down.

"Why are you crying, Mrs. Lawrence? I told you, you're in good hands now."

As she sobbed harder, LaVonte released his grip on her and struck her face again. Much harder than the first time, leading to her losing her balance and buckling to the ground. Ariana caught herself flinch but regained her composure before her husband noticed. Going along with his demented game, Ariana sneered at him in approval for his actions.

LaVonte reached down for Heather's arm and pulled her back up with ease. Her face was bright red where LaVonte slapped her, and her eyes began to swell.

"You're going to learn your new life here isn't so bad. You'll come to appreciate what my wife and I will do for you. Won't she, baby?"

"Yes, she will," Ariana said.

Disgusted with herself for all the times she had played the role of her husband's accomplice made Ariana want to throw up, but it would soon be over. She just needed to be patient for the perfect moment. She was only going to have one shot at this.

LaVonte pressed Heather's shoulders down so she was sitting on the couch. He now stood only inches away from her, so his midsection was level with her face. He grabbed her hair and compressed her face into his crotch and forcefully rubbed it before commanding her to take him by the mouth or allow herself to be "hunted by his wolves."

Heather hesitated to move in hopes her new ally would intervene. This earned her another slap across the face.

"You'll get along a lot easier if you do as I say." LaVonte clawed a bundle of her hair and pushed Heather back into him so hard it hurt his balls.

Heather's confidence in Ariana saving the day was entirely diminished now. She accepted she was in the early stages of her new reality and began to do what she was told. As she was unzipping his pants and preparing herself for the inevitable LaVonte stroked the side of her face and told her how he liked it. He explained what she should do with her tongue and how she should touch herself to demonstrate her enthusiasm towards having the privilege to please LaVonte Jackson.

His focus was so concentrated on his latest subject he quit looking Ariana's way, which allowed her time to remove the knife from against her ankle. Just as Heather was about to begin doing her duty, LaVonte said, "Come join the fun, ba—"

Ariana clasped her left hand over his mouth and stabbed the knife through the right side of his neck with the other. Blood spewed down his neck onto his shirt like a dam collapsing. The shock, pain, and area his wife stabbed him hindered his ability to say anything, but Ariana kept her hand over his mouth to lessen the possibility of one of his henchmen hearing him in distress. Even though the office was soundproof, she couldn't be careful enough. LaVonte remained standing straight up, so Ariana buried the entire blade in his neck to ensure she wouldn't botch what she came back home to do. His knees buckled and his masculine body and larger-than-life persona were useless in fighting back. When he collapsed to his knees, fighting to stay upright for as long as possible, Ariana removed the knife from his neck. LaVonte's eyes were now bulging out of their eye sockets, glassy and red, and his nose was perspiring uncontrollably. When Ariana determined death was inescapable even for her seemingly immortal husband, she released her grip over his mouth.

LaVonte audibly gasped and attempted to catch his breath, but it was leaving him too fast. He was losing too much blood too fast to muster up the energy to try and save himself. He came to terms with his fate, and before he went, he told his wife a notch above a whisper, "I love you."

LaVonte was staring straight ahead waiting for his wife to say something before he finally gave into his demise. He regretted this because the last thing he would ever hear was Ariana telling him, "Fuck you, too" before jamming the knife in his kidneys. After another audible inhale, his last, LaVonte's eyes locked open, and he crumbled to the floor, making a loud thump in the process that startled Heather.

Ariana crouched down and laid two fingers on his neck to confirm there was no pulse. Once she did, she got on her hands and knees and bent down to softly kiss his forehead, one of the few areas not lathered in blood.

Only hours apart from each other, Ariana murdered the two men responsible for imposing a stranglehold on her life up until this point. For the first time ever, it was finally hers.

Ariana stared down at her deceased husband and reflected on all the years they spent together. Some of the memories that ran through her head were pleasant ones, as their marriage was not entirely mired by the control LaVonte exercised on her. She would be lying to herself if she said she was never in love with him but killing him was the only way to escape the cycle she found herself in for the last four decades.

She was in such a deep trance she nearly forgot Heather was there. Ariana found her in the corner of the room with her face buried in her knees, doing her best to muffle her cries. All of her attention was on guaranteeing her husband didn't live through her murder attempt; Ariana did not even consider how traumatizing witnessing that could have been. Especially because he was on the brink of raping her seconds before it happened.

Ariana wanted Heather to focus on the next task and forget about what just transpired. She didn't think someone could just forget an event like that, but Ariana couldn't afford Heather to lose her composure at this point in their mission.

"Don't worry. This place is soundproof, but let's get the hell out of here before one of his men finds a reason to try and come in."

A few minutes ago, Ariana would have said "our men," but her change in allegiance was now official.

Heather hurriedly dressed herself after both women examined her for LaVonte's blood. They were relieved when they determined the clothes she came in would cover any up.

She hadn't said anything yet, but she was keeping pace with Ariana. Ariana realized her abruptness was insensitive, and that she should check in with Heather.

Ariana grabbed Heather's shoulder and asked, "Hey, are you alright? I'm sorry. That must have been awful, but you did great."

Heather exhaled a nervous laugh. "Yeah, I'm, uh, I'm okay. I expected it to be awful, but I—"

Her bottom lip quivered, and tears welled up again.

Ariana pressed her. "But what, hon?"

"I, for a second, I didn't think you were going to save me."

Heather barely confessed her trepidation before pressing the crown of her head into Ariana's chest. Ariana stroked her hair, careful to avoid bloodying her, as Heather wailed. Ariana shed a tear and promised her she never even thought about turning her back on her. Ariana kissed the top of her head and apologized for everything she put her through.

After both women shared this moment, Heather said, "Let's finish this, yeah?" She pulled away and grabbed Ariana's cheeks to wipe her tears away with her thumbs. Observing Ariana's adrenaline subsided and the severity of the situation was setting in, Heather planted a kiss on her forehead.

"You're right, okay," Ariana said. She took a deep inhale and collected herself for what was next.

Ariana swapped what she had on for some new garments that weren't as incriminating, and stored more blood-soaked clothes in her getaway bag. One that was beginning to look like a souvenir bag from various murder scenes.

She silently thanked herself for being so prepared by packings several outfits, and almost joked they were proving to be more important than the financial documents she had stowed way. Ariana decided, along with her phone, the documents would come with her in the crease of her waistline and the bag that would implicate her if anyone in the outside world found it could stay behind. It didn't matter if the Organization's men stumbled upon it; all the evidence they needed to know something went amiss was their boss' corpse.

The phone's digital files were identical to the ones on the computer, so breaking the latter by slamming it against one of the legs of LaVonte's desk was an easy decision.

Since the blood was still wet on her skin, it was easy to wipe clean, but she still had Heather examine her to be certain she didn't miss a spot. That would be her fatal mistake if she did.

Before confronting LaVonte's men on the other side of his door, Heather and Ariana needed to be certain they didn't have expressions on their faces that indicated they each played a role in murdering the most successful kingpin the world had ever seen. Heather had more wiggle room since she was a "captive", but Ariana needed her stone-cold look to return.

All the men who worked for LaVonte knew if an order came from Ariana, it was coming from their boss. This privilege allotted the women time to do what they needed to do before escaping the plantation. Eventually, not hearing from their controlling boss would raise his men's suspicions, but Ariana banked on her clout giving them just enough time to leave California unscathed. Ariana didn't even want to think about the consequences If it wasn't.

After removing LaVonte's body from the guards' line of sight, cleaning his blood off her, and erasing the shocked look on her face, Ariana cuffed Heather and they exited the office. Ariana locked it before they were immediately confronted by three guards. If she didn't move her husband's corpse, they could have easily caught a glimpse of it.

"He said to leave him alone for the next few hours. Some bullshit with his politician friends is going down. This one's coming with me," Ariana said.

Instructions more detailed than that would've aroused suspicions. Ariana hoped all they needed was a few hours to extract Bobby and get to Morple alive.

Kalin lingered in Bobby's quarters for hours without him saying as much as a word. She began to worry she did something wrong. Apparently, Bobby sensed it.

"What you can do for me is tell LaVonte I fucked your brains out. But really, I have no desire to sleep with you. Sorry, not because of the way you look or anything. It's just—"

Bobby stumbled over his words. Kalin was a very attractive woman, but he had a type. He felt obligated to convey this to her.

"Oh, okay. Did I do something wrong?" she asked.

"No, no. Not at all. This just isn't always my thing."

Relieved, Kalin relaxed and took him up on his offer to enjoy his amenities. As a valued Organization worker, Bobby had the nicest setup of any slave on the plantation. It was so pristine some of LaVonte's foot growers expressed their qualms about it. What they didn't understand was Bobby was just as miserable there as he would've been if he still slept in the warehouse.

Once Kalin was at ease and out of his hair, Bobby retreated to his room for some alone time. As he situated himself on his twin mattress, his front door flew open.

"Bobby!"

It sounded like Ariana.

"Bobby!"

Bobby jumped off his bed and ran out to the main room. Kalin looked petrified at the sight of Ariana and an unfamiliar woman barging in in a shared state of distress. The latter anxiously rubbed her wrists. Ariana had a determined look in her eyes he was familiar with.

"Uh, hi. Can I help you? Are you okay?" Bobby asked.

"Yes, I'm fine. We have to go," Ariana said.

Bobby lifted his arms up in surrender. He initially thought this was a trick to see if he'd leave without direct permission from LaVonte. Something he never anticipated, and something that now would never happen. But he didn't know that, yet.

"Let's go! We're wasting time, dammit," Ariana said. She stomped her foot down as if she was his angry mother.

"Ariana, what are you talking about? LaVonte told me I have the rest of the day off."

"LaVonte's de—"

She didn't want to tell Bobby LaVonte was dead in front of Kalin. She couldn't trust what she would do with the information and really didn't want to kill anyone else. But she was willing to if that's what got Bobby home to her sister.

Ariana scolded him. "Bobby, you mother fucker, come with me right fuckin' now."

Bobby had no choice but to comply. If he needed to plead his case to LaVonte, Kalin could vouch for him.

"Okay, okay. Fine. Do I need to bring anything?"

"Just the clothes on your back," Ariana said.

"What about Kalin?" Bobby asked.

"She can house sit for the time being. Fuck Bobby, let's go," Ariana said.

Ariana, Heather, and Bobby stormed out of his quarters and hopped in Ariana's car. She programmed it to drive them to a dock where she knew LaVonte kept a boat in case of an emergency. Until recently, she never thought they'd need it. She was half right.

Once they were in the car Bobby asked, "Now can you tell me where we're going? And who is this? Jesus, are you alright?"

Ariana glanced down at herself and saw patches of dried-up blood on her right hand. How none of her husband's men noticed the spots she missed was pure luck.

Ignoring his question, Ariana said, "This is Heather, one of Robin's friends."

Heather managed a little smile as Bobby studied her. For a second, he thought Ariana was making a bad joke.

"And she is one of the reasons you're going home right now," Ariana said.

"What do you mean going home?" he asked. Bobby spent too many years of his life slaving away for LaVonte Jackson to believe he would all of the sudden be set free.

"Home, Bobby. You're going back to your family," Ariana said.

Ariana instructed Bobby to conceal himself in the back of the car she had driven from the main house to her brother-in-law's quarters. Getting from point A to point B within the confines of the plantation was easy but leaving it without raising any red flags was the part Ariana felt least confident about. But she couldn't reveal this to either Heather or Bobby. They were plenty scared thinking Ariana had complete control over the situation.

To keep suspicions to a minimum, Ariana made certain the car wasn't operating at speeds that would pique the interest of her husband's henchmen. As they were making their way closer towards the plantation's exit, Ariana, for what she hoped was the last time in her life, took in the sights of the place she called home for close to half her life. There was the warehouse Bobby made a name for himself in, the facility that refined the Organization's product, diswors scattered all over the plantation slaving away in her deceased husband's fields, and dozens of oversized Black men strapped with Barrett REC7s to keep those diswors on task.

It wasn't long ago Ariana waltzed around this property feeling invincible, and even proud of what she assisted her then-husband in creating. Her involvement in the Organization's trafficking operations provided her with purpose, and it permitted her a perspective she had never possessed until meeting LaVonte: a position of power. It took Ariana reuniting with Robin and her family and spending time on her own to come to terms with the life she had on the plantation under LaVonte's rule was not making her happy. At a point in time, she believed this was what would fulfill her, but in reality, all it did was compound her inner demons. It was time to take control of her own life.

Ariana snapped out of her trance as the vehicle approached the edge of the plantation's property. There a guard stood pat to ensure everyone coming and going had authorization to do so, including the boss' wife.

"Mrs. Jackson," Jayceon said, slightly above a mumble.

Hidden in a storage compartment primarily used for weaponry under the backseat, Bobby shook when he heard Jayceon's voice. He was one of the most barbaric men on LaVonte's payroll. Just the other day Jayceon required Bobby and the rest of his team to watch him tie a noose around a POW's neck and shove him off a two-story distribution facility. Jayceon had tied the end of the rope to a secure fixture atop the building and left the POW hanging for twenty-four hours to send a message to the rest of the plantation's workforce.

"Hi Jayceon. Please open the gate." She hid her right hand beneath her right thigh.

"Didn't you just get back?" he asked. "And what is she doing leaving?"

Ariana departing the plantation with a new captive appeared dubious, but not as dubious as her leaving solo.

"We have some business to take care of, Jayceon. Now can you open the goddamn gate? I won't ask again."

Ignoring her, Jayceon radioed his buddies in the main house. He didn't get a response right away, which gave Ariana butterflies in her stomach. Heather wished all she felt were butterflies in her stomach.

Still waiting for an answer, Jayceon eyed her and said, "They would've told me if you were leaving."

Ariana raised her voice to remind him of their standing in the Organization. "Have you forgotten who the fuck you're talking to? Open the fuckin' gate."

She could tell she rattled him, but not enough for him to adhere to her command.

"Mrs. Jackson is trying to leave. Is she authorized to do so? Come in quickly," he said into his phone everyone on the plantation used to communicate.

Ariana threw her hands up and muttered some obscenities directly aimed at Jayceon. Then it occurred to her she may have just committed a costly mistake. She quickly returned her right hand to its hiding spot without him showing the faintest sign of recognition.

Ariana almost released a sigh of relief before she thought better of it.

Don't be so stupid for two fuckin' seconds.

"Sorry ma'am, but you know I am under orders."

"Yeah, and apparently you forgot who else you're supposed to take them from."

Jayceon ignored her snarky remark and awaited a response. A long minute later, it came through. "Can't disturb the boss right now, per Mrs. Jackson's orders. She's good to go. Let her out."

"Understood."

Ariana raised an eyebrow at Jayceon.

"Sorry, ma'am. Rules are rules."

"Yeah, yeah, whatever. Open the goddamn gate."

"Yes ma'am."

Once the gate opened just enough for her car to fit through, Ariana put the car in manual mode with her free hand and peeled out of the plantation, spraying pebbles and dust Jayceon's way.

Ariana disabled the vehicle's tracking system, which led back to a monitoring system inside LaVonte's locked office, just like the plantation's video surveillance. Now that she was comfortably cruising towards the coast and was a comfortable distance away from the plantation, Ariana confirmed Bobby was in the clear to come out of hiding.

"Holy mother fuck. That was close," he said.

Ariana ignored him and kept her attention on a statuesque Heather. "You alright?"

"Just get us the fuck out of here," Heather said, practically whispering.

"On it."

CHAPTER

2089

Ariana, Heather, and Bobby arrived at the Jackson's emergency boat in under an hour. No one was after them and no one attempted to contact her. Once LaVonte wasn't heard from and his men discovered his corpse Ariana would be on the run for the rest of her life. In fact, she already was. As long as she delivered Bobby back to Robin and their sons before her husband's loyalists found and killed her, she could die happy, no matter how gruesome her death would be. Up to this point, she accomplished minimal good in her life. She was working hard to fix that before it was too late.

Bobby and Heather situated themselves in while Ariana booted up the Whaler's autopilot system. On the ride over there hadn't been much conversation. Bobby bombarded Ariana with unending questions until she abruptly silenced him. "Can you please just shut the fuck up until we're out on the water? I have a lot of things on my mind, and answering your questions isn't one of them."

She didn't expect him to respect her now nonexistent authority for much longer, so she took advantage of it while she still could. As Ariana prepared the boat for Morple, Heather felt Bobby's curious stare. Being in the presence of someone who had recently been around his wife felt like progress to Bobby. He hadn't felt that in sixteen years. There were a million questions he could've asked her as well, but Heather appeared more uneasy with the situation than Ariana. Because she played a part in getting him out, he respected her space for the time being, but he could only wait so long.

Readying the boat took long enough to worry both Bobby and Heather. Doubt crept into Bobby's mind, and Heather feared they weren't going to flee in time. When the boat distanced them from the shore, they all took a deep breath out of relief for getting this far. The mission was far from over, but they were making significant strides.

Once she felt comfortable at sea Ariana addressed Bobby's questions. She confessed she murdered LaVonte in order to get him back to Morple. Even with blood on her hand and Heather vouching on her behalf, it took a while to convince Bobby Ariana had actually killed her husband. Bobby felt conflicted about it not because he cared for his brother-in-law but because he feared what the retaliation would be. Ariana assured him that was her concern and hers alone. She filled him in on how she inserted herself back in Robin's life, also explaining how Heather fit in the picture. Happiness came over Ariana for the first time since Heather and her started their day when she told him how much time she was spending with Moe and Jonathan. She described Moe's looks, maturity, and how he was playing man of the house quite nicely. Ariana assured Bobby his wife was in good hands. Her eyes watered when she talked about Jonathan. She described the outings she'd take him and Wallace on. Bobby's heart stopped when she mentioned Wallace. Realizing he didn't know who Wallace was, Ariana made it clear Wallace was his forever loyal dog and not Bobby's replacement. Jonathan's best friend being an abused Pitbull warmed Bobby's heart.

Bobby couldn't help but feel grateful for Ariana in this moment, for she had come a long way since the day they met. He knew enough about her past to understand she'd have her struggles as an adult. While he wished they weren't at his expense, she was doing her best to fix it. Better late than never, he thought.

Heather chimed in and praised the boys, assuring him Robin did an amazing job raising them. Richard and her valued Dillon's and Moe's friendship and believed their son was a better person for having Moe in his life. Heather praised Robin for being a second mother to Dillon.

Hiding his tears of joy was useless at this point. He covered his face and cried like a baby. Leaving the plantation didn't seem possible just over an hour ago, but now, he found himself on his way home to his beautiful wife and sons he'd been longing for for sixteen years.

CHAPTER

40

2089

Maurice and Damien Williams supervised Dillon during his first official task as a foot grower. Being twenty years-old, the twins were the obvious choice to take eighteen-year-old Dillon under their wing.

After their father's murder during a social justice protest when they were five years old, their mother, once an admirable, gentle woman, became a heavy orgacal user. Her drug use was moderate at first but escalated quickly, ultimately segueing to heroin. From before Maurice and Damien were born until her days as a widow, she had a stable job with a wealthy family as a nanny. They paid her handsomely and included a paid year-long maternity leave. Her income provided the Williams family some stability, especially since her husband struggled to hold a job when he was alive. Once the family discovered her drug habits shortly after her spouse's death, it sought out help for her, but she was not prepared to address her deep underlying issues that led her to addiction. Feeling helpless and nervous with her around their children, the family had no choice but to let her go.

The twins' mother became another hopeless drug addict who needed an opportunity in a world without any. The livelihood of the Williams family was dependent on measly universal income checks. As the boys got older, her addiction worsened, and the checks' amounts didn't correlate with their increased living expenses. As kind of a soul as she was, her boys needed somewhere to live and food to eat, two necessities their mother was not capable of providing.

At sixteen, Maurice and Damien Williams decided they had to fend for themselves. Orgacal was responsible for ruining their mother's life and their upbringings, so they decided to hold it accountable and ensure it paid them for their hardships. The Organization welcomed them and provided the proper training and tools to evolve into everything they once despised: ruthless mercenaries for a kingpin responsible for ruining the livelihoods of communities across the world.

Afterall, something had to pay their bills.

Maurice manned the getaway car with Dillon sitting in the passenger seat, and Damien was in the back to keep an eye on the newcomer in case he tried to pull a fast one.

"That shit wasn't bad, man," Damien said. "You didn't even hesitate like I thought you would, White boy."

"He was kind of nice with it," Maurice said.

Dillon flashed an embarrassed smile and fidgeted nervously. He had only completed one task for the Organization and was being showered with compliments. This type of assurance was what he had been seeking his entire life. He'd do anything for these guys. They were the brothers he never had and would take him to heights neither of his narcissistic parents ever could.

"Felt kind of good. Fuck him," Dillon said.

"Damn boy! Mother fucker only has one under his belt and he's already getting off to this shit," said Maurice.

"That was nice White boy, but you think you could kill someone's moms?" Damien asked.

"Phil was my dad's closest friend going back to their college days. I think I'll be straight."

"He'll be straight, damn!" Maurice said. He brought his fist up against his mouth as he dragged out "damn." This got a chuckle out of an all-of-the sudden confident Dillon Lawrence.

"Good to know, White boy. You're going to need that type of attitude," said Damien.

The brothers locked eyes through the rearview mirror.

Robin was still distraught hours after Marty's visit, having not even left the kitchen table. Hearing "fuck you" from Moe was enough to make her have a bad day, but learning her sister kidnapped her husband was downright heartbreaking.

She considered calling Ariana but then thought better of it. It would do no good. In her head Robin played out asking Ariana why she would kidnap Bobby and ruin her life, but ultimately determined she didn't have enough courage to confront her sister about such a serious matter. Even on the phone. Robin wouldn't be able to control her emotions and maintain a strong enough front to talk to Ariana. And if her younger sister was as ungodly as Marty claimed she might react in a way that would depress Robin even more. She didn't need an additional reason to hate her. Exercising her best judgement, Robin decided she was going to let the situation play out. If Marty and his team were able to track her down and lock her up Robin couldn't say for certain how she'd feel. Processing how much she loathed someone she loved so deeply was confusing.

Robin realized how selfish she was being. Moe witnessed his aunt abduct his father. If that wasn't traumatic enough, when he mustered up the courage to open up to his mother about it, Robin immediately disregarded him. Even if she didn't believe him right away there was no harm in asking him to sit down and explain how he came to that conclusion. Getting her to believe him would have been difficult, maybe impossible, but she could have at least heard him out. During that altercation Robin regressed to being someone she was working on leaving in the past.

Wallace's bark brought Robin out of her transfixed state. She knew he didn't bark unless he sensed a threat. She opened the front door and found Jonathan struggling to redirect Wallace towards their house. He was relentlessly pulling Jonathan down the street, but Robin didn't see anything out of the ordinary minus a couple seemingly empty cars. Jonathan was begging Wallace to quell. Robin ran out of the house and pinched Wallace's hips. This brought the barking to a halt and shifted his attention to her. He leaped on her and incessantly licked her face as if he just saved her from a near death experience.

"Wallace honey, please. Please calm down," Robin said, easing the stalky dog down to all fours. He was panting profusely. It was evident he was nervous and abnormally heedful.

"What was that about, sweetheart?" Robin asked Jonathan as they walked towards the house.

"Uh, uh, uh, I, I, I don't know. He does only that if something is dangerous. We didn't see anything, though," Jonathan said. On top of how emotional the day had already been, the consternation in his voice saddened Robin. It didn't happen often, but when Wallace exhibited stress, it increased Jonathan's anxiety. Robin collected herself to make sure her eldest was alright.

When they were finally in the house Wallace pounced on Jonathan like he did to Robin outside. His jump was so forceful Jonathan fell down. Wallace took advantage of this and pinned him down in order to lick his face. Once Robin realized Jonathan was laughing, she could finally breathe. She shamed herself for thinking, even for half a second, Wallace would ever turn on Jonathan, or any of them for that matter. He was their protector.

For a while Robin convinced herself Wallace was Bobby's way of coming back into their lives. The thought of this made her cry on multiple occasions, but it was actually a comforting feeling thinking her husband still had a presence in their home.

"Wallace! Wallace! I, I, I love you, too!" Jonathan managed to say between licks over his nose and mouth.

Wallace eventually calmed down and allowed Jonathan to stand up. His hair was now rumpled, face sticky with slobber, but he was grinning from ear to ear. Robin kissed Jonathan on the head to avoid kissing the slobber and scratched Wallace between his eyes.

"Uh, uh, uh Wallace is really excited."

"I can see that. I haven't seen him act like that in a long time," Robin said. "How was your morning?"

"Uh, uh, uh good, Momma."

He didn't seem like he was too inclined to elaborate, and after the morning Robin had, she would only be pretending to listen if he did.

"Good. I'll make you some lunch."

"Alright, White boy. I'll handle the dog, and you'll cap her and her son. He's the only one there right now, but when the other gets home you can have him," Damien said.

Dillon hadn't said much since the car parked on the Karros' street. He knew there were going to be two jobs but didn't know any details about the second one. The chances of Phil being a target were small enough, but the odds of knowing all of their targets were way too slim to be a reality.

Dillon felt naive, and his newfound coolness quickly dissipated.

"What's wrong wit you?" Maurice asked. "You're looking a lil' uneasy over there."

Maurice leaned over the middle console to stare deeper into Dillon's eyes. Maurice and Damien didn't reveal it, but their intel told them Dillon was friends with Moe. But none of that mattered anymore. He was now a foot grower for the Organization. Relationships from his past life were irrelevant. Orders from LaVonte Jackson were gospel.

"Nah, I'm good. I'm good. I'm just thinking, that's all," Dillon said. His voice was noticeably edgy; neither twin appeared satisfied with his answer.

Displaying weakness on the first day would not get him very far with his new friends. Dillon had to force himself to get his act together. Shit happens in life, and sometimes certain people have to get hurt. Even if those certain people are the ones you love the most.

"I'm fine. I'm just thinking about where the other son will be and what will happen if he happens to bring someone back with him," Dillon lied. He was doing his best to dehumanize his best friend. Mentally preparing to kill him.

"That someone would be in the wrong place at the wrong time," Maurice said. "Don't trip."

"Okay, works for me," Dillon lied again. "What did they do?" He couldn't suppress his curiosity.

"Pissed off LaVonte. That's all we need to know," Maurice said.

"Alright, enough of this bullshit. Let's roll, White boy," Damien said. Without another word, the three of them flipped their safeties off and pulled their masks over their faces.

As they walked up to the Karros' house Dillon's forehead leaked sweat. Damien and Maurice were in front of him and kept their gazes forward, disregarding the possibility of any neighbors witnessing them wearing masks and carrying Barrett REC7s and Sig Sauers on their hips in broad daylight. As subtle as possible, Dillon looked around in hopes of seeing Moe coming home. Moe was the type of guy who always knew the right thing to do. If Dillon saw him maybe he could do the right thing, too. To his disappointment, Moe was nowhere in sight.

CHAPTER

41

2089

Dillon's head was on a swivel as Maurice, Damien, and he neared the Karros' family home. The odds of Moe showing up and inspiring him to do the right thing were dwindling by the second.

Maurice and Damien leaned their ears against the front door. All three of them already saw Robin, Jonathan, and Wallace go inside, but they wanted to determine what they could expect upon breaking and entering. The twins heard some movement, indicating their targets would be there to greet their unexpected visitors. Maurice and Damien turned around and looked at Dillon whose mask felt drenched with sweat. He feared it was obvious, but neither twin said anything or gestured to indicate they noticed. Dillon consciously slowed his breath to disguise his fear.

"Ready, White boy?" Damien asked.

"Yeah, let's do this," Dillon said. He surprised himself by saying it with so much conviction.

Preparing to kill his best friend and his family was impossible. He concluded all he could do was go with the flow and whatever was going to happen was going to happen. Dillon inhaled deeply, shook out his arms, and tightened his grip on his Sig Sauer.

Maurice busted down the door with his shoulder. A menacing Wallace greeted the foot growers with a thunderous bark that caused Dillon to jump. The Karros' protector was running full speed at them until he collapsed after Damien fired a few rounds in his bulky chest.

"No! Wallace, no!" Jonathan cried out. He was unwinding on the couch with Wallace laying on his feet before his entire world came crashing down in an instant. His screams were deafening. Not even the sight of three masked men with heavy artillery could distract him from witnessing his best friend's murder.

Robin bolted from the kitchen and sprung on Jonathan to shield him with her body. She stroked his face and attempted to convince him everything was okay. Until she glanced over at Wallace's dead bloodied body sprawled out in their entry way.

"Get the fuck out of our house! Look what you've done" Robin shrieked. Two of the three men stood in front of her confidently, unperturbed by the distress they were causing. But the third one standing behind them didn't share their arrogant demeanor. Almost like he was second guessing what they were doing.

"Man, shut the fuck up," Damien said.

Maurice looked at his brother and released a troubling laugh from the bottom of his throat.

"Yeah, fuck you and your infick boys. Don't worry, y'all will meet up in the same place soon. With this bitch ass dog, too," Maurice said. He cocked his leg back and kicked Wallace's head, hard enough that his neck could be heard snapping into two. Robin and Jonathan both shuddered and gasped. Robin placed her hand over her son's eyes, but he already saw what they did to his companion.

"We haven't done anything to deserve this. Please, just get out. You've already caused us enough pain. Look at what you are doing to my son," she said. Her tone was more defensive now as the severity of the situation was really setting in. Why she didn't ask Marty for protection was a huge mistake, but she never would've thought in a million years Ariana would send her thugs to hurt her and her family. It was ignorant of her to believe that, given the fact Ariana was responsible for her boys growing up without a father and her living without her husband.

"Man, shut the fuck up!" Damien scolded her.

Damien pulled Robin and Jonathan apart without much trouble. Jonathan cried even harder until Maurice punched his stomach and knocked the wind out of him. He slumped to the ground and struggled to get his breath back. As he tumbled down Robin tried to check on him, but Damien shoved her back to where she was on the couch and threatened to slowly cut his head off in front of her. Robin complied.

Damien locked his eyes on Robin while Maurice pulled Jonathan up and pushed him back onto the couch about an arm's length away from his mother. The brothers stared at their victims, both uncontrollably shaking and sobbing with their heads facing down. Robin lived in fear for the first half of her life, but even during that time she had never experienced this type of horror. Her son in these killers' crosshairs was the most blood-curdling reality she ever endured. The thought of it escalating was spine-chilling.

"Too bad we gotta kill your fine ass," Maurice said.

Robin's gaze remained on the ground, but even through his mask she felt his invasive stare.

"All right, White boy. It's your go," Damien said.

The brothers parted separate ways so Dillon could step up and have clear shots at his best friend's mother and brother. He couldn't see Maurice's and Damien's facial expressions, but like Robin, he felt their intensity. Not having the balls to go through with this would probably cost him his life. He was only given four bullets at the beginning of the day. One was for Phil. The other three were for Robin, Jonathan, and Moe.

"Alright, cool," Dillon said. He leveled his Sig Sauer at Robin's chest. Both brothers relaxed their rifles and turned their gazes towards her so they could watch her die. Their fatal mistake.

"Fuck you niggers."

Dillon shot Damien in the head and pivoted to do the same to Maurice. Both of them were dead before they hit the floor.

Jonathan screamed and buried his face in his lap. He laid his hands over his head as if that would protect him from the next bullet. Robin's reaction was more shock than fear. She was silent and petrified by what unraveled in front of her eyes. Noticing she had a window of opportunity to get back to protecting Jonathan, she slid over and wrapped herself around him and began crying all over again. Robin was so grateful he was alive she almost forgot there was an active shooter in her family's home. Robin craned her neck up and saw Dillon Lawrence staring back at her. His mask was in one hand and Sig Sauer in the other. His lips were quivering, and his eyes were puffy and red from crying. All Robin could do was stare at him agape. The polite, humorous kid best friends with Moe was not the young man staring at her at this very moment. The Dillon that was in her family's home at that very instant was angry, troubled, and lost. A darkness she didn't know he had buried down deep inside of him was on full display, and she wasn't sure if their relationship was enough to put it at ease. Still speechless, Robin was rubbing Jonathan's head to keep it down so he didn't have to see who was seconds away from killing them. Before she could muster up anything to say Dillon inserted the pistol in his mouth and discharged the fourth bullet.

CHAPTER

42

2089

It was pure pandemonium in front of the Karros' home. Sirens from police cars and ambulances lit up the dusk sky, and their radio communication with their respective headquarters echoed throughout the entire neighborhood. Neighbors lined the street whispering to one another, presumably speculating about what occurred just hours before. Police and men in suits huddled near their vehicles and on the front porch. There was a steady flow of them walking in and out of the house. Numerous officials were frantically jotting down notes from their ongoing conversations into their tablets. Little drones floated around them snapping pictures of the residence and surrounding area. Paramedics loaded three stretchers into the back of an ambulance, causing the unlikely trio to assume the worst.

Ariana solemnly stared ahead. Heather was in shock. Bobby whimpered in the back.

"No, no. Please, no," he cried. This wasn't what he envisioned seeing when he returned home after sixteen years of slavery.

Ariana parked an Organization vehicle a safe distance away from the crime scene until they collectively decided how to proceed. If it was Robin, Jonathan, and Moe on those stretchers her life would serve no purpose. Taking Bobby home only to discover his family was dead would probably result in him assisting both the authorities and LaVonte's loyalists in tracking her down. Being on the run the rest of her life was something Ariana anticipated before devising her new plan, but it would still be nice to know her brother-in-law wasn't hunting her down, too. These were selfish thoughts, though. If she was unsuccessful in reuniting the Karros family, getting caught was probably the best outcome. It would put her out of her misery and give her life some finality.

Finally, Heather broke their silence. "Oh my God. There's Richard."

"What? Who's Richard?" Bobby asked.

"My husband."

Bobby leaned forward and stuck his head between the two front seats to have a closer look at the scene. They saw Richard hugging someone. From their vantage point it was impossible to see who it was until she pulled away to dry her eyes.

"Oh my God, Robin!" Bobby shrieked.

"Bobby, wait!" Ariana said. She reached back to grab him, but he bolted out of the car too fast for her to get a hand on him.

"Mother fucker!" Ariana yelled. She punched the car's dash out of frustration. Bringing Bobby back to his family was something she needed to do for him, Robin, and their sons, but with how everything transpired, she hoped to be there to explain herself. Witnessing the jubilation on their faces when they embraced one another would have been rewarding. *Not like I deserve that*, Ariana thought.

"Let him go, hon. This is what you set out to do. You wanted to put their family back together, and look, you did it," Heather said. She rubbed Ariana's arm, who started to cry.

"I just—I just wanted to be part of it is all."

Ariana buried her face in her hands and allowed herself a healthy cry. Heather scooched closer and extended her arms around Ariana's neck and kissed her head, rocking her from side to side like a mother would do to her wailing child.

"I'm so sorry, Heather. I'm so sorry," Ariana softly said into Heather's chest.

"You did everything you could. You made everything alright."

There was too much adrenaline pumping through Bobby's veins for him to absorb his old neighborhood. He was expecting to experience nostalgia, but given the circumstances, he didn't care about anything else besides having Robin in his arms. He forgot he still didn't know if their sons were still alive. The euphoria of seeing his soulmate overrode that uncertainty for the time being.

He yelled from half a block away. "Robin! Robin!"

Running towards a crime scene yelling at the top of his lungs the name of a woman who was nearly murdered wasn't the best way to reintroduce himself. Multiple armed officers ran towards him with their guns drawn.

"Sir, stop right there!"

"Put your fuckin' hands up!"

"Get on the fuckin' ground, now!"

Realizing his mistake, Bobby obeyed, dropping so hard to his knees they both tore open. He lifted his hands above his head to prove he was no threat. He had endured too much for his journey to end by being mistakenly shot by the police.

"I'm sorry, I'm sorry!" he said. "That's my wife, that's my wife! I swear. I swear she is."

"Who the fuck are you?" a policeman said.

"I swear I'm her husband. Please, just ask her."

One of the policemen cuffed Bobby's hands behind him and shoved him to the ground. He pressed his gun to the back of his head. "Stay down!"

Robin watched the alarming scene take place from her front porch. She assumed he was another lunatic Ariana deployed. In a sense, she was correct.

"Sir, please! She's my wife! Robin!"

Familiarity kicked in once she heard her name again. She began shuffling towards the man the police had in custody. As she got closer, she picked up the pace. By the time she was fifty feet away she was in a full sprint.

"Oh my God, oh my God! Please, get off him! Bobby!"

The policeman who held Bobby at gunpoint eased his weapon down and lifted him up to his feet. Still cuffed, he was regaining his balance when Robin ran into an embrace. The collision would have knocked Bobby over if the policeman behind him didn't break the fall. Robin squeezed him tight with the intention of never letting him go again.

"Holy shit, Patterson. Get the cuffs of him," an officer said to the policeman who had Bobby in his crosshairs just moments ago.

Right when Patterson removed them Bobby's arms came out from under him, and he hugged his wife.

"Oh Robin. I've missed you so, so much, baby. So much," Bobby cried.

His name was all Robin managed to say through her cries.

After close to ten minutes of crying, hugging, and kissing each other, Patterson apologized for mistaking Bobby as a threat. Bobby shook his head and said, "Please don't apologize. Seeing someone protect my wife's life like that was reassuring. I thank you for being so well-intended."

Oh, how Robin had missed her Bobby.

They walked back to their house with both of their arms wrapped around each other. Simply locking arms or holding hands wouldn't suffice. A cruel world drove them apart from one another for way too long. There was so much to say, so many questions to ask, but now the formerly estranged couple just wanted to bask in their counterpart's company.

Reuniting with Robin made Bobby forget about the scene in front of their family home. When he came back to the present moment, so did his fear.

"What's going on here?"

Knowing he was really asking if those bodies on the stretchers were Moe's and Jonathan's, Robin reassured him their sons were safe inside and would love to see their father.

Still in the front yard, Bobby pulled her in for an extended kiss in front of a plethora of paramedics, cops, and lawyers. When their lips unlatched, he kissed her forehead. Robin pressed her head hard into his chest as they rocked back and forth in each other's arms.

"I know there's a lot to discuss, but don't be mad at her. She brought me back home," he whispered in her ear.

Robin began sobbing again. The emotional rollercoaster Ariana took her on was never ending.

CHAPTER

2089

Marty Perlman allowed Bobby and Robin some privacy before he welcomed Bobby home. Marty usually succeeded in separating personal matters versus business ones, but he struggled to avoid bombarding Bobby with questions. An inkling told him Ariana had a role in his return. While Marty was happy she decided to do some good, it didn't absolve her of her crimes.

"Welcome home, my friend," Marty said. "I'm so happy you're back where you belong."

The lawyer and long-lost husband and father gave each other a big bear hug.

"Thank you for looking out for her, Marty. Thank you for everything," Bobby said.

Marty brushed off his gratitude and joked how Bobby resuming his role as the man in her life took a load off his own shoulders. Eager to extract information out of Bobby, Marty's legal team circled around him like a pack of wolves closing in on its prey.

"Oh, give him a break," Marty gestured for them to get away. "Let him see his family for crying out loud. We can handle all that later."

Discouraged, the lawyers lifted their masks back on and meandered away from the Karros' house.

Meanwhile, the police were pestering Richard about Dillon, demonstrating little to no empathy for what he was enduring.

"Were there any signs he would act out like this?"

"Describe his behavior as of late."

"Have there been any notable incidents that could have sparked this?"

"Has he demonstrated any destructive behavior in the past?"

"Has he ever expressed an interest in violence, in particular murder?"

"Have you or your wife picked up on an signs of suicide ideation?"

Not knowing his wife's whereabouts and losing his father, best friend, and only son was an unfathomable reality. He confessed to the police about cracking Dillon's head open. How the day's events escalated made their domestic violence incident quite relevant in their investigation. Later on, Richard would sit down with psychologists, lawyers, and other professionals to determine what drove Dillon's involvement with foot growers. The son of a billionaire from a prominent family running with those types wasn't common.

For now, the police needed their preliminary questions answered and wanted to gauge Richard's knowledge of, or lack thereof, his son's dark side. His genuine devastation indicated it blindsided him. Investigators collectively agreed it was too soon to tell him his son killed Phil in cold blood. Leaving that up to the higher-paid professionals freed them of that burden.

Seeing Richard endure intense questioning out of the corner of his eye, Bobby considered informing him his wife was alive and well but thought better of it. He realized he couldn't be certain of this now that she was alone with Ariana. Bobby knew Ariana's ruthless side had no limits. He also knew Heather's involvement in LaVonte's demise was more than enough reason for the deceased kingpin's men to murder her if she was unlucky enough to be found. Just killing them wouldn't satisfy that crew, though. Both Ariana and Heather would experience a grueling amount of torture, that both women would wish they were dead. But it wasn't the time to think about these things. Bobby wasn't going to permit the harsh realities of the dark world he spent the last sixteen years in pollute his thoughts. Robin, Jonathan, and Moe were what he was going to focus on. Afterall, he had a lot of catching up to do.

As the ambulance left with Dillon, Maurice, and Damien, the commotion simmered down, and Robin led Bobby inside their home.

Feeling her guide him every step of the way he said, "Darling, I remember how to get inside."

Embarrassed, Robin dropped her head onto his shoulder and laughed. "I'm sorry, baby. It's just been a while."

He kissed the top of her head and laughed with her.

Because of Jonathan's hysteria the authorities cleaned up Wallace's body and the insides that spilled out of it as efficiently as they could. The space where it happened would remain taped off in case the area required further examination. Robin observed Bobby staring down at it.

"They killed Wallace. He was trying to protect us, but they killed him," Robin said softly.

Bobby's eyes darted back and forth between the door and where the taped off area was, trying to imagine the traumatic scene that took place not long ago.

"Wallace was our d—" Robin started to say.

"I know who he was. Ariana told me all about it." Bobby muttered her name quietly. "I was looking so forward to meeting him."

Robin rubbed his arm. "You know I told myself he was you coming back to us as a dog. Saying it to you sounds so crazy, even stupid. But the way he cared for us and protected us, especially Jonathan, was so similar to how you were. He took on the role of being the man in our house. We loved him so, so much."

Bobby's wife keeping him alive in her memory as a protective, loving dog warmed his heart. "Oh, baby. I can only imagine how sad you guys are that he's gone."

It was so on brand for Bobby to empathize with the struggles of others even though he was the one who sustained the most suffering in each other's absence.

After they finished mourning Wallace some more Bobby's attention turned towards the kitchen table and saw two familiar faces he was once afraid he would never lay eyes on again. One of them was still bawling over Wallace's death and the other, even though he still had tears in his eyes, reminded his brother they still had each other.

Despite everything his family just lived through, witnessing Moe console his older brother was a pleasant sight. It nearly planted a smile on Bobby's face, but that would've been insensitive. Sensing her husband didn't know how to reintroduce himself to his sons, Robin spoke up.

"Boys," she said, treading carefully.

"Uh, uh, uh, yes Momma," Jonathan said. He attempted to control his cries and display a strong demeanor.

Moe's eyes widened when he saw who was standing next to their mother.

"Someone is here to see you. This is Bobby, your f—"

"Dad!" Moe exclaimed. He jumped up and sent his chair flying backwards towards the wall.

When Moe came to a halt in front of his father, he stared at him unsure of what to do. Bobby's eyes teared up again, petrified by the moment.

He finally managed to say, "Hi, Moe."

Moe hugged him tight and surrendered to his father's grasp. His day began with verbal warfare with his mother and ended in finding out his best friend committed suicide after being on the brink of killing his mother and brother. His father being there to tell him everything was going to be alright meant more than he ever could have imagined.

"Uh, uh, uh Momma? Is that Bobby?"

Robin pressed her hands flat together and laid them over her nose and mouth and nodded. Her family reuniting brought on an intense wave of bottled-up emotions, too many to formulate a verbal response. Jonathan remembering Bobby after all that time passed signified the impenetrable bond they formed when he was young. Jonathan gently nudged Moe so he could wrap his arms around Bobby, too.

Robin practically fell down on top of the group hug her boys formed and vowed she would never permit anything or anyone to tear them apart ever again.

The Lawrence family had turmoil, yes. In fact, it probably encompassed more issues than most families, but Richard never envisioned it unraveling like this. Every bit of information from officials he received sent shockwaves throughout his body. Heather lied about being at her sister's and was presumably kidnapped by Ariana. To add fuel to the fire, there was evidence Heather was present at his father's house when he was brutally murdered. And now she was missing. Richard thought the news of Dillon committing suicide would've brought her back if she was free to.

Law enforcement possessed indisputable evidence Dillon killed Phil. Phil got himself into the shitshow that was the human trafficking industry. Him being murdered didn't surprise Richard, especially after learning how careless he was. But why did it have to be Dillon who murdered him? The fact Richard was asking himself this made his stomach feel like it was turning itself inside out. He didn't think Heather and he were horrible enough parents to cause Dillon to resort to this type of violence. But apparently his mental health was too far gone, and Richard and Heather were too preoccupied with their own lives to intervene. Years of less than subpar parenting combined with extreme wealth created a killer. A killer who took someone close to his own father before ending his own life.

That has to be the most fucked up type.

Learning about his father's role in Robin's and Ariana's upbringings was disturbing, to say the least. Richard knew his father had an affinity for younger women, but he was unaware it was to the extent it was. Being told how he regularly raped innocent little girls was hard to digest, but what was more difficult to comprehend was how Richard himself was so oblivious to this. It made him feel like he didn't know his father at all and reflecting on how happy his father was during his own childhood caused him to reconsider everything he once thought of him.

Was it because you had your way with two innocent girls, Reginald?

A lawyer told Richard a detailed account of what happened the morning after Ariana knocked his father out. He begged her to stop telling him the story, but she didn't until Richard began bawling in the briefing room at the state government's headquarters. As he was mentally readying himself to leave and drink himself into oblivion at home the lawyer required him to sit down for one more piece of crucial information: Jonathan Karros was his half-brother, and their own father was responsible for his brain damage. The natural liking Richard always took to Jonathan now made sense; an unknown bond gravitated him towards his younger brother. Discovering he had a sibling should've been good news, but the circumstances didn't allow Richard to revel in this. It only saddened him more when he put together his father intentionally harmed his kid brother.

Over the next couple of days following Dillon's suicide Richard learned more about who Ariana really was, details of the lawsuit Robin won following Morvo, and how intertwined the Lawrences's, Karros's, and Jacksons's really were. Investigators interrogated him mercilessly but didn't waste time pursuing him as a suspect in any of the events that transpired. The police, lawyers, and other officials entangled in the case made it crystal clear Ariana would be a hard woman to find; therefore, discovering Heather's whereabouts would be challenging, too. At first, Richard was adamant on finding her until he accepted their relationship was a lost cause. Their sex hadn't been enjoyable for years, and her absence brought him to the conclusion the love she had for him was ingenuine. Richard acknowledged he used her to claim a trophy wife, and she used him to reap the benefits of a trophy wife. Richard didn't wish ill will on her, no, but he didn't want Heather reinserting herself back in his life. Her role entailed being a hot wife who fucked her husband right and a good mother who raised a respectable child. She failed at both, miserably.

When Richard mustered up the mental strength, he ordered his lawyer in charge of the Lawrence trust over. With Reginald dead, Richard had more to his name than ever before. Originally, his fortune was going to be left for Heather and Dillon in the incident something catastrophic happened to him. Dillon was dead so removing him was a seamless process, but since Heather's status of being alive or dead was unknown it could've been tricky if it weren't for a clause stating she didn't have to be present to object any changes to the trust within the family. So, he couldn't have left his riches to Robin without his wife's presence, but he could legally leave them to his half-brother. After all, it was his money, and he wanted to keep it in the family. Of course, his father already had to muster up a sizable chunk of his worth to Robin, but no amount would undo what he did to two innocent girls. To his lawyer's displeasure, he created the documentation for Richard to sign so he could leave everything the Lawrence's worked for to Jonathan. All eighty billion dollars of it.

The Lawrences tortured the Sorens, Karros, and a single Jackson for as long as Morple had been in existence. To ensure the cruelty would come to an end, Richard dove off the one hundred fifty-foot cliff next to Lawrence Drive headfirst. In midair he prayed for the water instead of the rocks, only to laugh when he realized it made no difference.

CHAPTER

2089

Authorities, including Marty, didn't stay away from Bobby very long. During his first week home he underwent nearly fifty hours' worth of interviews all relating to his time spent on the Organization's infamous plantation. They asked Bobby to walk them through the processes of getting there and back; he described the ins and outs of the plantation, including its day-to-day life and gang culture; he revealed loads of information pertaining to the women kidnapped and brainwashed into being sex slaves. To feel comfortable about divulging this information and not having to worry about his family's safety, authorities had to work extra hard to convince him the Organization was crumbling. But Bobby knew one of LaVonte's men would be there to pick up the pieces and pick up where the former boss left off. How loyal that individual was to LaVonte would dictate whether or not Bobby would be a target.

With support from Marty, Bobby demanded his family receive state-funded protection around the clock indefinitely. With Richard Lawrence's fortune combined with how much Robin accumulated over the years, the Karros's could've afforded security on their own, but they felt it was within their rights for the state to pick up the tab.

Bobby detailed Ariana's personal involvement in the entire Organization, but most of all in his particular situation; being abducted and being saved.

Bobby emphasized the lengths she went through to extract him from the plantation, further proving investigators' suspicion about her being the prime suspect in murdering LaVonte, in an attempt to showcase her heroism and get them off her tail. The chances were slim because evidence proving she played an intricate role in her deceased husband's operation was mounting against her, but he had to at least try. Bobby vouching for her surprised authorities, being she was the one who took him from his family in the first place. But at the end of the day, she was part of his family, and knowing what he did about her childhood, Bobby felt like she deserved some slack. If she was going to get it was out of his control.

The interrogation process was exhaustive. Investigators made it clear Bobby was not enduring their aggressive line of questioning under the premise of being a suspect for any wrongdoing, but based on how combative their questions were, he second-guessed this multiple times. Especially because he confessed he was a murderer, but apparently his circumstances excused this. They classified Bobby as a valuable witness to LaVonte's crime-riddled operation. Helping them learn more about the Organization's human and drug trafficking businesses should've felt good, but Bobby couldn't help feeling frustrated by it. They decided to step in when the head honcho was dead, his number two was gone, thousands were dead or taken away from their families, and Bobby was already home. During a grueling part of the interrogation, he lost control of his emotions and turned the tables on the investigators when he asked where the hell they were the time he was defending himself from being sodomized by White supremacists, and why they didn't intervene when he was being forced against his own will to grow drugs that destroyed communities across the globe. Their lack-of-substance answers told Bobby everything he needed to know: the good guys and bad guys were on the same team. He would do his best to let it go and concentrate on making up for years' worth of lost time with his family.

Bobby's insertion back in his sons' lives was more seamless than he envisioned it would be. The three of them gelled, and even though he knew they would eventually reach that point together, he never thought it would happen so naturally. Jonathan would always have his deficiencies but having a constant male figure in his life noticeably impacted his progress. Robin and Moe were both pleasantly shocked his stutter occurred less frequently. There was a certain confidence in his voice that didn't exist during the sixteen years Bobby was gone. Outside of their home Jonathan was more inclined to speak up and engage with strangers. Bobby didn't think anything of it, but Robin and Moe observed the drastic changes immediately. Bobby's place in Jonathan's life didn't quite fill the void Wallace's death left, but his presence definitely helped him cope with the loss. Bobby articulated to Jonathan how Wallace died doing his life's work: protecting Jonathan. There were more tears when they discussed Wallace's death, but Bobby's perspective provided Jonathan some much-needed closure. Once their home was no longer an ongoing crime scene, the family held a private ceremony for Wallace. The four of them circled around Wallace's ashes and a picture of Jonathan and him Robin enlarged in a beautiful frame. In the picture Jonathan was gazing out to the ocean petting the top of Wallace's head. The dog was sound asleep in his lap after a strenuous day on the water. Robin didn't realize it until they admired the photo as a family, but Ariana was the one who captured it.

Moe relished in having a man around the house who he could relate to. Bobby and Moe dedicated time to developing an authentic father-son bond. It was evident to Bobby he passed down his nurturing traits to his son. How he cared for Jonathan and his mother proved this. Moe and his father discussed how Dillon evolved from being his best friend to a monster. Moe's outlook on it displayed his maturity. He was transparent about how he experienced conflicting emotions about him knowing his former best friend once committed to killing his mother and brother but had a change of heart in the nick of time. Moe also expressed guilt about not recognizing Dillon was suicidal, referencing their conversation at the pier when the latter mentioned Daniel Wilmington. As someone who prided himself on being available to talk to, Moe beat himself up for not being able to prevent the tragedy.

Bobby digested Moe's thoughts. He was in awe of how honest his son was about his emotions, but also saddened by him having to endure this at such a young age. He had already been through so much pain. Hopefully for Moe and the rest of their family it was finally over. Especially being there were no more Lawrence's to worry about.

Bobby's and Robin's initial one-on-one communication didn't include much conversation, as their physical chemistry took up a majority of their time. Both were unable to suppress their urges. Every chance they had they made passionate love like it was the first time every time.

Robin's body pleasantly convulsing on top of him was captivating, causing him to finish multiple times without ever taking himself out of her. How he missed her perfect breasts and hips bounce as he gripped her. No other woman came even close to looking as desirable as she did in the heat of the moment. How beautifully she aged turned him on even more. It was like he was falling in love with her all over again.

At her age Robin didn't think her body would respond to sex like it was with Bobby. His orgasms shot themselves in her so strong they triggered sensations she didn't know were possible. Him throbbing in her was so powerful it was almost violent, if not for it being so prepossessing. Robin welcomed his eyes and the passion they had in them absorbing into every square inch of her naked body. It was empowering and caused her to feel a certain way she hadn't in at least sixteen years. Bobby remained handsome as ever and didn't forget his way around her.

Once they were finally able to suppress their lust, Bobby and Robin discussed serious matters regarding their family. Robin apologized countless times for the fight they had before Ariana kidnapped him, and after forgiving her countless times, Bobby detailed his life on the plantation. He was honest about his involvement with the women LaVonte's foot growers kidnapped, confessing he slept with ones who reminded him of Robin. Opening up to his wife amplified his guilt about his involvement with those innocent prisoners. In his early days on the plantation Bobby failed to recognize he was contributing to the problem. Robin consoled him and reiterated he was a victim, too. To work through the trauma that was Bobby's reality the last sixteen years, Bobby had intensive therapy to look forward to in his foreseeable future. But his wife promised she would be there for him every step of the way.

For the most part the Karros's being a family again was blithe, but Robin recently learning how close she was to Reginald Lawrence without knowing it sent a shiver down her spine. Of course, she had thought about the last name of her son's best friend-turned-killer, but she concluded it was relatively common and didn't necessarily mean there was a connection. Richard's suicide saddened her, but as much as she loathed admitting it,

Robin felt a sense of relieve there were no more Lawrence's to worry about. Plus, Jonathan's inheritance was a bright spot in all of it.

For a while Bobby and Robin sidestepped a topic they both knew they must address: Ariana.

"She took you away from our sons and me, Bobby. I'm not sure I can ever forgive her even if I had the chance. Yeah, people make mistakes, but there are some that are harder to forgive than others."

"You know, for the first few years on the plantation I hated her. She took me away from you and our boys, and I'd see her waltz around the plantation with her evil husband and all their henchmen like they were a god and goddess. Which in their own little world I guess they were, but after a certain amount of time passed, I forgave."

"How, Bobby? She is the reason we lost so much time together."

"Yes, she came here and took me away from my family, but I came to realize she was not the reason. Your sister was brainwashed into following orders from her deranged husband. You even said it, she gravitated towards LaVonte because it was a familiar situation. It reminded her of what you two grew up in, except this time she had a little bit of power that made it enticing. It isn't an excuse for her actions, but it makes sense.

"When it comes down to it, your sister is a very, very disturbed person. She has made horrible decisions in her life that have harmed others but remember not everyone can handle things as well as you did after everything the both of you went through. Her life has been a clusterfuck, yes, but we have to remember she is family. And one thing I know for certain is her love has never wavered for you. That I promise," Bobby said.

Robin's lip quivered and tears rolled down her cheeks. "I allowed her to get close to our boys, to develop relationships with them. I put them in harm's way just like I did to you. I'm so sorry Bobby, I'm so, so sorry for everything."

Bobby wrapped his arms around his wailing wife and kissed the center of her forehead, rocking her back and forth and tenderly shushing her cries.

He whispered against her head, "This isn't your fault, my love. None of it is, and we are all safe and back together now. And the now is what matters. Don't focus on anything else but what we have now. We are a family again, and I am going to make sure it stays that way until our dying day."

It was unlikely Bobby's sister-in-law would ever have a role in their lives again, and as much as he wanted to thank her for fixing what she broke, he was going to take his own advice and concentrate on what he had in front of him: a family he would never let go of.

EPILOGUE

2094

A riana hopped out of bed well before the sun was up and hastily walked to her bedroom window. She would have loved to sleep with it open so she could inhale the warm ocean breeze throughout the night, but she lost that privilege when she decided to spend the rest of her life on the run. Ariana cranked the window open and surveyed the deteriorating cobblestone streets beneath her flat. Before even peeing or brewing her coffee, Ariana diligently examined her surroundings for anything or anyone out-of-the-norm. On a few occasions, some hoodlums loitering near Ariana's building gave her a scare, but when she realized they were utilizing the area to continue the party from the night before she let her guard down. Anyone coming for her wouldn't be sloppy enough to attempt capturing the one formerly known as Mrs. Jackson under the influence.

This morning an unfamiliar car caught her eye. Because her neighborhood was primarily residential and cars were now rare in Mallorca, Spain, Ariana was familiar with which ones belonged to neighbors and which ones were worth worrying about. She reached for her phone and zoomed in on the car with her camera to obtain a better visual. From her vantage point the vehicle appeared empty, and nothing she could see in the backseat raised an additional red flag. She reiterated to herself she wasn't in the clear yet and to check on it after saying good morning to Enzo.

Ariana proceeded with her morning routine: use the bathroom, brew the coffee, and then wake up her boytoy. Enzo was freshly twenty-three and had no aspirations in life except for allowing his "Mamacita" to take care of him. Wearing nothing and still looking more tantalizing than women significantly younger than her, she quietly pushed his bedroom door open and slid in beside his naked body. Enzo slept without sheets, and Ariana immediately noticed he was already ready for her. She spit on her hand and grabbed what she wanted of his, stroking the tip softly to stir him awake. After a few times he tiredly moaned and wrapped his left arm around her, cupping her breast farthest from him. "Buenos dias, Mamacita."

"Buenos dias, mi amor." She mouthed his neck and hopped on top of him, seamlessly fitting him inside of her. Ariana switched off between moving her hips laterally and bouncing up and down and placed her hands on his chest so her biceps squeezed her breasts together towards his face. The hand that was just cupping her breasts now laid on her right ass cheek. Enzo would have preferred if he could touch her with both hands, but Ariana was adamant on tying his right one up at night for, according to her, security purposes.

Once she was through having her way with him, she gave him a wet kiss on the mouth and unlocked his single cuff. "I'll make you breakfast, amor."

After putting a workout onesie on, Ariana edged over to a window in her flat's kitchen that gave her a similar view to that of her bedroom window. She no longer saw the car that made her suspicious just moments ago. Whether or not that put her at ease or heightened her senses, she didn't know yet. Mallorca's streets were generally quiet at this early hour, but it wouldn't have been the first time someone other than herself was off to an early start.

As she was peering out the window, a pair of hands glided over the bottom of her stomach and circled the area between her legs. Ariana gasped and instinctively shook the person off.

"What's wrong, Mamacita?" Enzo asked. "I just want some more of you."

Ariana had one hand on her heaving chest and the other palmed her forehead. "I'm sorry, amor, I'm so sorry. You startled me. I'm okay."

She crept over and embraced Enzo to put him at ease. "Please, come sit, and I'll make you something to eat, amor."

Enzo nodded and accepted her invitation. Not like he had another choice.

As Ariana conjured up some *pinchos de tortillas*, she found herself wondering about Heather Lawrence for the first time in quite a while. The first six months after delivering Bobby back to Robin, Heather and Ariana traveled around Europe, changing countries at least twice a month. Both of them went into it with positive attitudes, but it soon became a strain on their fellowship. Ariana and Heather both lashed out at the other. Heather blamed Ariana for pressuring her into accompanying her, and Ariana ridiculed Heather for being a shitty mother and wife who blamed her problems on everyone else. On a couple occasions, when wodin and wine were flowing, it got physical between them. The first time Heather struck first, and then the next Ariana took a cheap shot on her.

Ariana was regretful because she knew Heather was dealing with complicated emotions after learning about her son's suicide all while trying to play it cool and keep a low profile. Less than a year into their lives on the run, they decided it was best to go their separate ways. Since Heather didn't have a dollar to her name, Ariana transferred her enough money to last her a couple of years. After that, she was on her own. Despite both of them committing to staying in touch, neither had the intention of doing so, which is why Ariana hadn't heard from or reached out to Heather in over four years.

Shortly after Ariana left the plantation for the very last time in 2089, Jayceon and his brethren went into crisis mode. The allotted amount of time Ariana said LaVonte needed to be left alone had passed yet no one had heard from him. After banging on his door a couple of times and failing to garner a single response, LaVonte's detail scaled the walls of his mansion and broke through one of his office windows. They quickly found out why they hadn't heard from him.

Since their reaction was so delayed, Ariana had plenty of time to disassemble the tracking equipment and cover up her tracks, leaving no indication as to where she initially took Bobby Karros, Heather, and herself, even though it was obvious. They deployed men in Morple, but they only found Bobby, whose home was under way too much government surveillance for them to risk recapturing one worker. There was no sign of Ariana anywhere, and they didn't bother investing their resources in finding Heather, even if her son was responsible for murdering two of their own kind. They had plenty of able-bodied women who could pick up the slack.

Jayceon and the rest of the men restructured the Organization's hierarchy and resumed thriving after their revenge efforts failed. The Organization didn't experience the type of year-over-year growth it did under LaVonte, but they were still making a living, to say the least. What they were able to accomplish that LaVonte never did was establishing a dominant presence in North Africa and Spain. Because of their proximity, the Organization could get creative with their distribution methods and be prevalent in regions of both respective continents. Jayceon and the rest of the team were aware the chances were slim, but that didn't stop them from putting out a BOLO on the highly sought-after Ariana Jackson to their European and African partners. A few years ago, most deemed finding her a lost cause, and some of the new kingpins even forgot about it, until recently.

During a congregation in Madrid, one of their partners in Spain flew in one of his street-level dealers from Mallorca to brief Jayceon and company about a new revelation he thought the Organization would appreciate learning about. Apparently, Javi, the street dealer, had a buddy who recently called it quits because he found a "Mamacita" who wanted to take care of him. Javi said his buddy Enzo once had to deal orgacal in order to make ends meet, but with the type of money his new woman was throwing around, his earnings from dealing were pennies in comparison. Enzo told his buddy his Mamacita prohibited him from divulging her real name to any of his friends. This piqued Jayceon and company's interest.

Jayceon asked Javi to describe the woman in detail.

"Oh man, she's fine as hell, man. Big bouncy tits and a big fuckin' ass with long, dark hair. Enzo said he hasn't fucked another woman like her."

"Eyes?"

"Brown and round, man. Sexy, man."

As Javi described mystery woman, Jayceon and his partners all exchanged similar expressions. The kind that said, "We got her."

It took him a week, but Jayceon finally hunted down Ariana. He was at a point in his career where he didn't need to be the guy on missions like this, but what Ariana did to him five years ago classified this as a personal vendetta. And he was going to make certain she paid for it. Jayceon kept an eye on her from a flat across the street from hers. Gathering she was paranoid, rightfully so, he observed her fixate on a random car parked on the end of the block upon waking up, but this random car didn't seem to alarm her too much, which was good for what he had planned.

From his view, Jayceon was able to monitor all of Ariana's movements in her bedroom. He even earned himself a nice angle of her breasts; ones he coveted seeing for so many years. Once he saw her walk out of her bedroom, he left his rented flat and headed across the street. After three days of spying on her, Jayceon was certain he'd have enough time to make his move and enter her building. To his pleasant surprise the building did not have added security. He assumed she chose this one because it allowed her to blend in, or blend in as much as someone who looked like Ariana Jackson could. His recent sightings of her confirmed Javi's description of her was accurate.

Ariana's unit was on the fifth floor, the very top, so Jayceon had ten flights of stairs to climb up. Feeling his adrenaline spike, he had to control his urge to run up the stairs. He wanted to reserve his energy for what he came here for.

Once on her floor he practically tip-toed to her front door, which he configured was the one by matching his count of the windows on the outside of the building to the doors on the inside. He ever so carefully pressed his ear against it and heard that familiar voice telling her lover what their day was looking like. It was clear the kid had no say in any of it, but Jayceon had to admit, this Enzo kid didn't have it so bad. He refocused and readied himself.

Jayceon could easily barge in the apartment by bulldozing the door with his big body and butt of his Barrett REC7 assault rifle, but he wanted to remain patient until the most opportune time. Quietly proctoring open the keyless lock and stealthily entering was the ideal scenario.

"Amor, I'm going to finish getting ready, and then we'll go," he heard Ariana say.

"Okay, me too," Enzo said in heavily accented English.

Once Jayceon felt confident they were out of the kitchen, the process began. He scanned the lock with a device that manipulated its algorithm, essentially tricking it into opening. It worked seamlessly, just like his team told him it would.

He carefully pushed the door open and paid attention to any movements. The last thing he needed was to get this far and have Ariana blindside him with a knife to the throat or a bullet to the brain. He found the main room and kitchen of the flat empty.

Jayceon's vantage point from across the street told him Ariana's bedroom was adjacent to the kitchen, which ran along the wall opposite of the front door. That meant the bedroom he saw to his right was Enzo's. Drawers were opening and a low hum was coming from it, the latter indicating the morning was status quo, so far.

Because his frame was abnormally large, Jayceon paid attention to his steps, making sure they weren't too heavy to signal his arrival. As he inched closer to Enzo's bedroom, his humming became more enthusiastic and morphed into singing a tune in his native tongue, Castellano. It was just loud enough to divert Enzo's attention from his soon-to-be killer.

Taking a few big strides, Jayceon was now directly behind him. Moving briskly, Jayceon clamped his right hand over Enzo's mouth and pulled him back against his own chest. Enzo attempted to yell for his Mamacita, but Jayceon's paw muffled anything Enzo attempted to cry out.

"Shut the fuck up, and you'll live. Understood?"

Eyes wide and his heartbeat through the roof, Enzo exaggerated a nod to demonstrate he was at the intruder's mercy.

"Good. I'm going to remove my hand, and you aren't going to say shit, right?"

Enzo nodded again.

"Promise?"

Another nod.

Jayceon released his hold over his mouth, slid that hand down to Enzo's chin, placed the other atop his head, and snapped his neck in under three seconds.

So his collapse wouldn't echo throughout the entire flat, Jayceon broke his fall and eased him down carefully. He shifted his focus so fast he didn't even notice if Enzo died with his eyes open or closed.

Jayceon exited the room more briskly than he entered it with. He knew it was only him and Ariana left, but he had to remind himself to exercise more caution. He didn't know how prepared Ariana was for an attack like this.

The door to her bedroom was nearly closed all the way. Jayceon closely approached it and didn't hear a thing. He allotted about thirty seconds to pass before deciding to make his presence known.

As he drew his rifle and readied his leg to kick it open, a sharp pain submerged into his left kidney and exploded throughout his entire body. He gasped for air when he felt the dagger corkscrew further into him, and when he felt blood begin to soak his pants his knees buckled from underneath him. Once Jayceon was on his knees, he lost the necessary strength to hold his rifle, and couldn't help but let it fall to the floor.

Moments after she unarmed him Ariana slowly released the dagger from Jayceon's back. Until that point, he had done a decent enough job masking the incomprehensible amount of pain he was in, but there was only so much a man could take.

Ariana crouched down so her mouth was next to his ear. With a grin on her face she said, *"Nos vemos en el infierno, hijo de puta."*

Ariana speared his right carotid artery and watched Jayceon's oversized body slam onto the floor in a pool of his own blood.

Going to have to try harder than that, Ariana thought to herself.

ACKNOWLEDGEMENTS

S till in the early stages of my career as an author, I have overcome several obstacles to get to this point, which is just a preview of what's to come as I continue along this path. I was able to write and publish *The Abandoned* in part because of how hard I worked, yes, but receiving the support from others along the way empowered me to stay the course, no matter how much doubt started to creep in.

My parents, siblings, girlfriend, extended family members, friends from all phases of life, and current and old coworkers have all expressed their support, and even admiration, for what I'm pursuing. Without them, I'm unsure if I would have remained confident enough to see this project through, so thank you.

I love you all.

While the aforementioned groups of people supported my morale from start to finish, Keidi Keating enabled me to release a readable book. Without her identifying inconsistencies in the plot, providing me an invaluable perspective and putting up with my endless questions, you wouldn't be reading this right now. I couldn't have asked for a better person to lead me through this process, and I can't wait until we get to work on the sequel.

Last but certainly not least, thank you to everyone who read *The Abandoned*. On top of striving to provide you entertainment, I hope this world I created provoked some new thoughts. Maybe you found yourself resonating with a certain character's struggles, or one reminds you of someone you're close to. Maybe you will find yourself rethinking your perception of others.

Whatever the case may be, my wish is it made you feel something. Hopefully I did enough in *The Abandoned* to make you stick around for what else is to come.

Sincerely,

Jake Cavanah

THE ABANDONED SEQUEL

Ariana manages to escape from government authorities and her deceased husband's loyal henchmen with the help of a new group of outlaws she has sworn allegiance to.

Robin and Bobby are happily married and now grandparents. They moved Costa Mor, adopted a new dog, and spend their days enjoying each other's company.

But when Robin's troubled sister grabs the attention of a couple determined federal agents, they are forced to face a dark part of their past.

Their sisterhood was once empowering, but now, Robin must protect her family from it.

No matter how removed they appear to be from each other, fate has brought Robin and Ariana back together.

And this time, only one will make it out.

Heather created a new life for herself on the other side of the world, vowing to never return to Morple or anywhere else in the United States, but hard habits are difficult to break.

She eventually discovers she can't get out of her own way, and, consequently, finds herself dealing with the same problems she thought belonged in her past life.

Subscribe to my weekly newsletter for updates on *The Abandoned Sequel*, free content, exclusive promos, and more.